"ARE YOU SAYING YOU WILL MARRY ME?"

Paul's ebony eyes penetrated hers as he spoke. Shannon felt as if he were looking into her very soul.

She hesitated before answering.
"People shouldn't marry without love."

"Love, whatever that is...a word that means... nothing!"

It means everything to me, thought Shannon as her heart plunged into despair.

Suddenly, Paul reached for her, enfolding her in a powerful embrace. "I'll show you how much you want me...."

He crushed her lips with his mouth, forcing them open to admit his thrusting tongue. Shannon's eyes stung at the betrayal of her body. In spite of the momentum of her aching need, she knew this was all wrong, and she feared Paul would never understand why....

RACHEL PALMER
is also the author of
SUPERROMANCE #4
LOVE BEYOND DESIRE

Robin Hamilton's archaeological job on a
Mexican hacienda promised to be an
exciting venture. But she soon found herself
drawn into the midst of a dark devastating
turmoil.

She should never have let herself fall in love
with her employer, the proud and fiery
Ernesto Lopez. He fully intended to marry
the highborn beauty Ynez as family tradition
dictated, all in order to gain a precious jade
legacy.

Robin had no choice—she must fight her
hopeless love. For a future as Ernesto's
mistress was no future at all....

NO
RACHEL PALMER
SWEETER
SONG

A SUPERROMANCE FROM

WORLDWIDE

TORONTO · NEW YORK · LOS ANGELES · LONDON

Published April 1983

First printing February 1983

ISBN 0-373-70058-X

TO THE READER

JUAN GOMEZ, Portuguese sailor-turned-pirate, was born in Madeira in 1778 and died in July, 1900, at Panther Key off Florida's gulf coast. His long life embraced three centuries and such rare adventures as being kidnapped and then employed by the legendary pirate José Gaspar (Gasparilla), being inducted into service in the Black Dragoons of Spain, where he met Napoleon Bonaparte, fighting in the Cuban revolution and serving with Zachary Scott in the Seminole Wars. He was also a blockade runner during the Civil War.

Captain Walter Collier, an island-hopping trader, met Gómez in 1870, when the old pirate was ninety-two. Collier wrote that his friend was still husky and strong. Fourteen years later Gómez returned from one of his many mysterious voyages with a charming English bride of seventy-eight. She never would tell Collier much about her past. The Gómez couple seemed to have plenty of money until the final years of their lives.

Captain Collier and his son, William, recorded the tales that Gómez loved to tell...of casks of doubloons and chests of jewels still hidden in the bayous and islands along the coast. For a fee he often sketched crude maps for gullible visitors. Exactly what was fact and what fiction in his intriguing narratives has never been ascertained. It is true that Gómez was in St. Augustine in 1831, and legend has it that Gaspar did hide treasure on Anastasia Island.

The treasure in the novel is fictitious. Gómez's descendants, the Websters—and specifically Shannon Webster—exist only within the pages of this book. As far as the author knows, the treasure of Gasparilla and his pirate band is still buried exactly where it has been since the early 1800s on Anastasia Island.

CHAPTER ONE

SHANNON WEBSTER SAT at the grand piano in the practice studio, her long fingers flying through the intricate runs of Haydn's "Gypsy Rondo." In her junior year at the University of Illinois, she was practicing for her spring recital. When for the second time she missed an F sharp, she sighed with exasperation.

"It's the day," she muttered, glancing at the window, coated now with chilly rain. "Something had better happen pretty soon that is *nice*."

The morning mail had brought a note from the dress-shop owner for whom Shannon had worked during the past three summers. The shop had been sold, and Shannon's job had evaporated. With the end of the semester less than a month away, Shannon was worried. Without summer income, she might not be able to return to school in the fall.

She ran her fingers through her long dark hair, still damp and straight from her dash through the rain. She did want to look sophisticated for her concert date tonight, and Jack Fenton was only part of the reason. The other part was Paul Cypress, the performer. Not that she had a crush on the handsome and famous singer, as most of the girls in the music department did. Quite the contrary.

Jack Fenton was a senior piano major. The music department was to host a gala reception for the famous baritone after the concert, and Jack was chairman of the event. He and Shannon had been dating for some time, and although he was becoming more serious than Shannon liked, she enjoyed his company.

Shannon hadn't told Jack that she had known Paul Cypress long ago in what seemed like another lifetime. She had been ten when Paul worked for her father, helping Edmund Webster hunt for lost pirate treasure on Anastasia Island in exchange for vocal lessons and assistance with his newly begun musical career.

She had often hidden behind the studio draperies to listen to him sing. Paul's golden voice had thrilled her, and his darkly handsome features were still indelibly etched upon her mind. She had adored him.

And then Edmund had died, his boat dashed to pieces on the reef by the storm. Paul had come back alone, and in her grief, Shannon had blamed him for letting her father drown. How often had she rubbed her forehead in perplexity, wondering exactly what had happened? She had tried so hard to remember, even though deep inside, something had said, *forget*.

She could remember overhearing an argument between her father and Paul. Edmund had said, "Someday you'll have it all!" And she had watched it happen. Paul had used her father's death as a spur to his own career. He had filled out Edmund's concert commitments; immediately he was in the spotlight, the protégé who was willing to stand in for his mentor. If he hadn't been good he wouldn't have lasted, Shannon had to admit; but he did have it all, just as Edmund had predicted. Fame, fortune and finally even the Webster estate at Pirate's Cove.

It was more than resentment that Shannon felt. A nagging suspicion that Paul could have saved Edmund had crouched at the back of her consciousness. She had been so sure that Paul had staggered ashore with her father in his arms. She had run down the rocky path to see, to help. And she had fallen, striking her head. She had known nothing more after the concussion and the pneumonia until much later. She had been mistaken. Paul had come in from the sea alone.

Shannon had turned away from Paul. It was she who had sent him after her father. Why had he come back without him? Why should he survive?

It was a childish reaction, and as Shannon matured, the sharp edges of her resentment wore away. Out of curiosity she bought Paul's records and found that she was deeply moved by the richly varied tones of his magical baritone. Sometimes it had a rollicking quality that made her feel lighthearted; or it could be full and tender enough to bring tears. She began to follow the reviews of his performances. The range of his musical talent as well as his dramatic ability made him a sensational artist.

A recent album cover showed a darkly handsome

Paul Cypress with a shock of crisp black hair and brooding brown eyes above prominent cheekbones. The brow was broad and intelligent, the skin a light russet tone that hinted at his Indian ancestry. Because he was known to cherish his privacy, little had been published about his background except that he was part Seminole.

Paul's ex-wife, Merlene Madden, had co-starred with him in *South Pacific*. Shannon wondered whether they had been able to spend much time at Pirate's Cove and whether they had loved it as it deserved to be loved. Surely no one could ever love the coquina-block house by the sea as much as she did.

Bonita Webster, Shannon's mother, had sold the cove to Paul and taken her daughter to Chicago, where she found work as an actress. Shannon had grieved about the move, scarcely comprehending their loss, not only of Edmund but also of the fortune that made the move necessary. Edmund had been careless about money, too trusting here, too generous there, always banking on finding that elusive treasure.

SHANNON BEGAN TO PLAY Verdi's "Miserere"; it matched her mood. It, too, would be part of her recital. Unlike the Haydn, "Miserere" caused her no trouble, and she felt better for having played it through perfectly.

Shannon let her fingers make the transition to a brighter selection. Chopin's "Minute Waltz" always brought dancing lights to her eyes. Small and almost delicate in appearance, Shannon had a quick eagerness of smile and movement that told of her keen interest in everyone and everything around her. Her tawny amber eyes were spaced wide apart in an oval face whose clear olive complexion hinted at Mediterranean ancestors.

Idly she began "The Impossible Dream" from *Man of La Mancha*. It was the song with which Paul usually closed his performances. Would he do so tonight? Shannon wished she could put Paul out of her mind. Why did he have to be here anyway? She would have liked to skip the concert, but with the whole music department coming out to honor him, she could hardly not attend. If only she didn't have this nagging resentment, this feeling that Paul could have saved her father. That he just. . .didn't.

To obliterate her thoughts, she changed keys, improvising, making the bass notes progress like the footsteps of the multitudes who search for the ideals of which dreams are made.

"Wonderful!"

Shannon turned, startled. Paul Cypress stood in the doorway. She felt the blood rush to her face, and her heart began the once familiar staccato beat that had always marked her confusion and delight at Paul's appearance.

Paul dropped his wet trench coat on a chair. "Play it again," he commanded softly, "and follow me."

Shannon didn't move. It was as though Paul had stepped out of a dream. An impossible dream. She had been willing him out of her thoughts, and now he was here in the flesh.

Paul began to sing, motioning to her to accompany him. Numbly she raised her hands to the keys; and as Paul's sensitive voice sang the vibrant desires of the heart, she found herself entering his mood, supporting and enriching his interpretation, culminating in the triumph of stars attained in spite of all obstacles and pain.

"Wonderful!" he exclaimed again, leaning into the curve of the piano, his dark eyes aglow with appreciation. "You have talent." His eyes roved slowly from her cascade of black hair to her small face and then over her trim figure, pausing frankly at the soft fullness beneath her knitted shirt before moving to the slim waist and the slender hands resting on the keyboard. "I can use you."

Shannon turned away. He was too boldly appraising. She felt like a piece of merchandise, and she resented that.

She was about to collect her music and leave when he said, "Wait, please." He opened a leather portfolio and took out a sheaf of sheet music. "Tonight's program," he said briskly, setting it on the rack before her. "Play in your own style. And follow me."

"But I...."

"You what?" he demanded impatiently. "I want you to play for me. Come now, play."

Piqued by his imperious manner and moved by a stubborn desire to show him that her talent was not limited to one familiar selection, she fanned out the music. She knew the titles. "All right," she said tersely. "I have time for one." And she began "Di Provenza il mar" from *La Traviata*.

Paul sang it softly, yearningly. Against her closed eyelids Shannon could picture Paul's face. The picture on the album cover had not done him justice.

"You hardly used the score," Paul said.

Shannon stiffened. "You told me to use my own style."

"I wasn't criticizing," he said gently. "Whom do you usually accompany?"

"Rarely anyone. I'm a soloist," she said proudly.

"Well, you must accompany me tonight."

Shannon stared. Surely she had misunderstood.

"My pianist is in the hospital. Appendicitis. It happened just a short while ago. I was looking for Professor Moore to see whether she could find someone else for me tonight, but now that I've heard you play, I want you."

Shannon collected her music and rose. "Dr. Moore's office is just down the hall. I'm sure she can find someone for you."

Paul's hand pressed her shoulder, willing her to stay. She pulled away from the electric shock of his touch, but he blocked her way. "Why not you?" Frowning, he went on, "When you played, you were warm and sensitive. But now...what is it? Why are you ready to run away?"

She felt his gaze slide over her face again, summoning up an unwelcome blush. "I can't play for you."

"Of course you can. Surely you have performed."

"Recitals, yes, but—"

"Do you belong to the union?"

"Yes, but—"

"Don't you think I know when I have a good pianist?"

"Well, but—"

"But! But! But!" he said impatiently. "Do you always argue and waste time like this?"

"Do you always interrupt and stop people from saying what they want to say?" she retorted. Even as she spoke, she was aware of the tremendous force of Paul's will. She felt the old desire to please him, to bring a smile to his lips and eyes, to make him happy. Dismayed at this sign of weakness in her armor, she hurried on. "There's no time to rehearse."

"A couple of hours. I'll work with you."

"But you mustn't sing just before a performance."

"I said I'd work, not sing. I'll go over the scores with you. You can mark your copies."

"I might make mistakes. I could spoil your whole concert."

"If *I* don't doubt your ability, why should *you*?" he reasoned with a winning smile. "We have rapport. Surely you feel it, too. Even before I sang with you, I knew that you felt 'The Impossible Dream' exactly as I did, and it's been that way with all the music."

It was true. The musical bond was there, and Shannon felt herself wanting to work with Paul, wanting to show him what she could do. She felt the challenge and wanted to rise to meet it. And yet the old antagonism and doubt were there, warning her to turn away.

"I was about your age when I performed for the first time," Paul said, "and I'm sure you'll do better than I did. You'll see, once you and I and the audience are lost in the music, everything will go smoothly."

Was it possible that some force beyond their control had thrust them together, Shannon wondered. Could she trust him? Rely on his confidence in her? Was she really good enough to accompany the famous baritone after only a few hours' practice?

She stared at Paul. He was more ruggedly handsome than any recent picture had shown him to be. The jaw was more stubborn, the crisp hair more unruly, the skin swarthier. He looked athletically fit, a strong man apparently used to getting his own way. Reluctant admiration pushed at the resentment she had nurtured through the years. Nevertheless, she fought the persuasion she found in his eyes.

"You don't even know my name," she said, her eyes holding his. "I'm Shannon Webster."

Paul tilted his head and lifted shaggy black eyebrows. "Not...Edmund Webster's daughter?" he demanded.

She nodded soberly.

"You've been a small ghost at Pirate's Cove for years," he accused, frowning. "You left your marks all over the place. Even on the piano."

Shannon grimaced. "I shouldn't have marred the Steinway."

"You were the shy child who hid behind the curtains when I took my lessons. After I bought the cove, I wanted to paddle you for your vandalism. But later," he added thoughtfully, "I understood. You must have hated to leave it all. The beach, the piano...and your little valley beside the orange grove."

"That's still mine!" Shannon said defiantly. Paul had *almost* everything now, but not the small shallow valley half-hidden on the far side of the grove. And not the old orange trees sheltering the shaded hollow. Her mother had not sold that acre, the last bit of the Webster heritage. Although Bonita had no desire ever to return to Pirate's Cove, she knew how much it meant to her daughter; and on Shannon's eighteenth birthday, she had deeded the grove and the little dell beside it to Shannon.

"Yes," he said, "I know." He studied her quietly for a moment. "You are a fine musician, Shannon Webster. Edmund would have been proud. Now, then, you will play for me tonight, won't you." It was hardly a question. He was sure that she would agree.

Instead she stood up and tucked her music under her arm. "Sorry."

Once more his fingers gripped her shoulder. "I need you. Don't you understand that? I want *you*, no one else." His eyes narrowed. "Why are you so... hostile?"

Shannon stared significantly at his hand until he removed it. "I have no feeling about you at all." She walked quickly toward the door, but Paul blocked her way.

"Not true," he said, his eyes smoldering. "At least be honest. Do you still resent me because I survived?"

The air between them was electric.

"Yes!" It was torn from her. The old resentments she had thought buried in the past sprang suddenly to life. "And for taking what was my father's—his home and his life and his fame! You're the last man on earth I'd play for!" Tears streaked her face as she ducked beneath Paul's arm and fled.

A HALF HOUR LATER she was called to her dorm phone. "Dr. Moore, Shannon. I'd like you to accompany Paul Cypress tonight, dear. He tells me that you and he have already rehearsed a bit, and he won't hear of anyone else. We are both confident that you can handle it, so please don't hesitate."

"But Dr. Moore, I just can't. . . ."

"Paul is an old friend of mine, and I do hope you'll do this for me, Shannon. Please. He says he'll have to cancel if you don't come through."

Allison Moore had encouraged and helped Shannon numerous times. How could Shannon disappoint her now? "All right. . . if you think I can do it."

Shannon called Jack with her apologies. He was proud that Shannon had the opportunity to accompany the great star and didn't object that she would not be able to sit with him at the performance. "It's a real plum for you, honey," he pointed out. "Put it in your vita. But watch out," he teased. "Paul Cypress is known for his collection of beautiful women!"

"No problem," she retorted. "Paul Cypress is the last man on earth, as far as I'm concerned."

Thankful that she had just bought a lovely gold-and-white chiffon gown for the coming recital, Shannon dressed carefully. She accented her cheeks and eyelids with color, knowing that the harsh stage lights could make a performer look ghostly. She brushed her hair until the buoyancy and shine were restored, fastening it at the nape of her neck with a gold barrette to keep it firmly in place. The barrette was an antique, intricate in design. She had found it on Pirate's Cove the last summer she had spent there, and it would always have a special significance for her. For luck she wore the antique gold chain her father had thought was a part of the lost treasure. It had been her tenth and last birthday gift from him.

THE RAIN HAD STOPPED when Shannon hurried to the auditorium. Paul, immaculate in his black tuxedo, was pacing backstage. "Where the hell have you been?" he growled. Tension, she noted, had made him slightly hoarse.

Paul almost shoved her into a small studio, where he instructed her as they went over several difficult passages together. As she followed him effortlessly, he relaxed and the hoarseness disappeared.

"Okay," he said at last, "just watch the timing and follow me."

Once Paul began to sing onstage, Shannon lost

herself completely in the magic of his voice. With her eyes upon him she was able to sense every mood, every nuance of expression that he poured into his songs. And when the university crowd burst into riotous applause before the intermission, Paul went to her and extended his hand, sharing the acclaim with her.

As they left the stage together, Paul said, "You're a gifted pianist, Shannon Webster." The quiet, personal praise sent the blood to her cheeks and wild excitement to her heart. She shook her head, mutely discounting the tribute, knowing instinctively that she could never accompany anyone else the way she had Paul.

When he insisted that she go with him to the reception at the University Club, she shook her head again. "I already have a date."

"Break it," he ordered. "I must talk to you."

His arrogance made her stubborn. "No. I won't break it. I had to desert Jack for the concert, but I intend to go to the reception with him."

Paul's eyebrows shot up. She knew he was surprised, perhaps even amused, that she had turned him down. She stuck out her chin.

"All right," Paul said with a shrug of his broad shoulders. "But I'll take you back to the dorm. We need to talk, and I leave early in the morning."

Shannon thought she knew what was on his mind. She shouldn't have lashed out at him the way she did. Nevertheless, he had asked her to be honest, and she couldn't apologize for what she still felt, even though it distressed her as much as it must have Paul.

The stage manager interrupted. "Miss Webster, you're on."

"What?"

"The audience is awaiting your special number."

"My what?" She whirled to face Paul.

"My pianist always performs a solo during the first minutes of the intermission," Paul explained. "I guess I forgot to tell you."

"You can't expect me to just go out there cold!" she sputtered.

"Isn't there something you can do from memory? Something from your recital maybe?"

"No!" His amused smile infuriated her.

"All right. I'll have the manager announce that you are not prepared to assume that part of the program."

"Not prepared!" Shannon was seething. "I could do it, but I see no reason why I should jump every time you tell me to do something!" When Paul turned to speak to the manager, Shannon grasped his arm. "Wait a minute!" she stormed. "How could you forget such a thing? Or were you afraid I'd have to take precious time from rehearsing with you to go over my own number?"

"I really did forget," he told her calmly, still with that antagonizing quirk at the corner of his mouth. "You'd better forget it, too. Take an aspirin or something, hmm?"

"Oh!" She turned away and marched onto the stage. To the spattered applause she bowed briefly and then arched her long fingers into the first thunderous octaves of Rachmaninoff's "Prelude in C Sharp Minor." The succeeding gentler chords and demanding runs disciplined her turbulent emotions, and gradually the tension ebbed away in the slumberous conclusion.

Lost in the music, she was startled by the volume of the applause. Paul was waiting in the wings, smiling his approval. "Be ready in fifteen minutes," he said as he pressed something into her hand.

Shannon stared after his retreating figure.

In the powder room she looked at the crumpled scrap of paper. She smoothed it out on the dressing table and discovered two aspirin tablets.

"Coming," she called later in answer to a knock at the door. She thought it was the signal to return to the wings, but instead it was a messenger with a florist's box. Shannon took out the corsage of yellow rosebuds and baby's breath, and a card fluttered to the floor. "Something else I forgot," was penned in a hasty scrawl. She pinned the flowers to the narrow strap of her gown with trembling fingers. What an exasperating, surprising man Paul Cypress was.

At the concert's end the audience came to its feet. Paul's finale, "The Impossible Dream," drew almost endless applause. Paul took Shannon's hand for bow after bow.

Finally he drew a folded sheet of music paper from his pocket and handed it to Shannon. "I have begun to collect and record the songs of my people," he told the now hushed audience. "They are very old folk tunes of the Seminoles, rarely heard by others.

Tonight I'd like to share one of them with you. Miss Webster, will you please play this lullaby through once before we try it together?"

Shannon scanned the sheet of single notes, handwritten without the harmony or accompaniment. Her smile was disarming, but her eyes shot sparks as she whispered tersely, "What other surprises do you have for me?"

Smoothing the music against the rack, she studied the melody: it was simple and slow and in a minor key. Paul's notations were precise, with the lyrics spaced correctly below. Shannon played it through carefully. But when Paul began to croon it softly, as though to a sleepy child, she began to improvise, lending a background of night sounds as images to the soothing lullaby. As the last note faded, Paul bade the audience a husky good-night and strode offstage.

JACK DROVE SHANNON to the University Club. She had expected to remain in the background, helping Jack with the details of keeping the refreshments ready and the guests circulating. Instead, she found that she was the darling of the music department as well as of the university and local press corps.

At midnight the fans surrounding Paul began to tap their glasses as Paul mounted a small podium. "Thank you for your kindness," Shannon heard him say. "You must forgive me for an early departure. I have to catch a plane in the morning." He turned toward Shannon and Jack halfway across the room.

"I'm sure the young man with my talented accompanist won't mind letting me have the pleasure of taking her back to her dorm this one time?" Paul's raised brows challenged Jack, who was obviously surprised and a bit dazed at suddenly being the focus of attention. Jack self-consciously nodded his consent.

Threading his way toward Shannon, Paul tucked her hand into the crook of his arm and led her firmly to the elevator. "We have unfinished business," he said tersely to her murmured protest.

In the cab Shannon snapped, "Of all the high-handed nervy tricks! Jack must think I knew you were going to do this!"

"I told you I had to talk to you. Shannon, your interpretation of the Seminole lullaby was perfect. I sang the melody," he mused softly, "but you gave it the moonlight."

"Thanks." She refused to let Paul overcome her displeasure at having been abducted this way. "Say whatever it is you have to say; because no matter where *you* intend to go, I intend to take this cab back to the club. I want to help Jack clean up."

Streetlights touched Paul's angular face for brief moments as the cab slid through the business district. Shannon knew that Paul was studying her, and the thought that he found her annoyance amusing made her press her full lips into a tight disapproving line.

"I'm having surgery tomorrow," Paul told her lightly. Shannon gasped. Another surprise. "Nothing serious," he went on. "A thyroid tumor. However, the vocal cords are involved, and I'll have to return to full voice gradually. I plan to recuperate at Pirate's Cove. I'll need a pianist. Are you interested?''

Again she gasped, her eyes wide as she tried to read his features. Was he serious?

''I'd want you at the cove by mid-June, and I would expect you to stay until Labor Day. There would be some light secretarial work for you, too.''

Shannon's tawny eyes reflected the sparkles of light that invaded the cab. Summer at Pirate's Cove! She could scarcely believe that it was possible. To walk again on the warm white sand beside the foamy surf, to become a part of the sunny gold Florida days and cool blue nights, to go home again . . .

Jack's warning flashed across her mind: ''He's known for his collection of beautiful women.'' It must be true, for she herself could feel Paul's devastating magnetism. Even when he antagonized her the most, he caused a quickening of her pulse, an alarming heightening of her senses. Danger signals. Though Shannon understood how it could easily happen, she was determined never to become one of his ''trophies.''

''Well?'' he prodded. She shook her head slightly, but in the darkness, he seemed not to notice. ''Do you have summer employment?''

''No.''

''Good. Then it's agreed. You'll come. I'll arrange for . . . .''

''I don't think so,'' she said in a small uncertain voice. It cost her a great deal to refuse.

"Why on earth not?" Paul was obviously astonished. "Oh, the salary. I forgot to mention it, but I'm sure you'll find it adequate." He named a generous figure.

"It's not the money," she managed, even though she silently admitted that the idea sounded more and more appealing.

"Then what? Don't you see that this is an opportunity for you?" Paul leaned forward, trapping Shannon in the corner of the cab and blocking the light that had flickered between them. She wanted to push him away, needing space to think clearly; but instinctively she clasped her hands tightly together. If she touched him, she would yield.

His voice became gentle and coaxing. "Talk to me, Shannon. Tell me what you're thinking." When he was gentle like this, he was harder to resist. The cove, work she loved to do...Paul....

"It...it just wouldn't work," She tried to twist away, but he pinned her shoulders with strong hands.

"Use your head, Shannon. At the end of the summer my praise and recommendation will help you into graduate school or into whatever job you choose. Doesn't that mean anything to you?"

Despite his logic, Shannon could not allow it... and his closeness...to sway her. "I don't want to work with you!" she blurted tensely. "Is that so hard to understand? Maybe the rest of the world jumps when you snap your fingers, but you can just consider me the exception. *I do not want to work with you!*"

Unable to see his face, she felt her own tension seep into the space between them and wrap tentacles around him. The cab had halted at the curb in front of the dorm, and for a moment the silence was breathless. Then Paul sighed, and Shannon could feel his soft breath against her cheek. "But you must come, Shannon."

With a quick twist she tried to wrench free. In pulling away, her face brushed Paul's, and suddenly his arms were around her and his mouth was against hers.

Before she could protest, he let her go. The kiss had been gentle, tender, a surprise to both of them. "That's in memory of the little girl who used to like me well enough," Paul said huskily. He opened the cab door for Shannon but did not go with her the few steps to the dormitory. She stood on the sidewalk, dazed.

When the cab had gone, the unbelievable night seemed as though it had never been. Later in the darkness she relived everything, even her tingling response to Paul's brief kiss and the rising warmth of an emotion that swept her deeper into his arms for the length of a heartbeat.

She pressed her fingertips against her heated cheeks, angry because of her body's betrayal. She could never trust Paul Cypress. He shouldn't have kissed her. He shouldn't have tried to bully her into taking the job at the cove. He had no right.

Why did that job have to be there? Why did she have to know about it? Oh, she had been tempted to take it. The pay was good, and the location...oh, how she loved the island cove! But Paul Cypress... how could she cope with him? Arrogant Paul. Paul, the womanizer. The man who had kissed her with such tenderness was also the man she had sent to help her father in the storm; he had returned with empty arms. No, she could never work with him, resenting him as she did. He had almost everything that had once been Edmund Webster's, but he was most certainly not going to have her, too! Not as a pianist or as anything else!

Shannon stared ruefully into the darkness. All he wanted was a pianist-secretary. One impulsive kiss didn't mean anything else. Nevertheless, Shannon felt a telltale spread of warmth over her body at the memory. No, the summer job at the cove was not for her. Her reaction to Paul was too strong and unpredictable.

She would find another job in Chicago where she could live at home and save most of her earnings. She had made the right decision. She would put Paul Cypress right out of her mind...where he had been for the past ten years...more or less.

CHAPTER TWO

AFTER TWO WEEKS as a counter girl in a fast-food chain, Shannon was ready to admit to herself that she had made a mistake. Early June temperatures had broken records, and she arrived home each day after a long crowded bus ride too exhausted for anything but rest. She dreamed of the cool Florida surf. And of a man with a golden voice who bent to touch her lips.

So what if Paul was a known womanizer? She could handle him. And if he were responsible for her father's death...well, she had no proof, nor was she likely ever to have. It was just a feeling that she had, one that she might as well forget. She had forgotten almost everything about that terrible night. After she had slipped on the wet path and hit her head on that rock, she had blacked out, remembering only the figure of Paul striding out of the sea and the fog, a burden in his arms. Why couldn't she forget that picture, too? Why couldn't she accept what Paul had said...that he hadn't even seen Edmund's body?

Bored and irritable, Shannon began to lose weight. Her mother suggested that she call some of her old friends, but Shannon knew that the ones she cared most about had left the city's heat on vacation.

Paul's note arrived on the tenth of June. It read:

> I am about ready to begin voice therapy. Please recommend a pianist—your young man, perhaps. Send someone who is both competent and good-tempered, for God's sake.
>
> Paul Cypress

Shannon drew a long breath to calm the quickening of her heart. She'd send him someone! Herself!

Bonita agreed to let her take the Chevette but shook her head in bewilderment. "I thought you didn't like Paul, dear."

"I don't. But I love the cove and the Steinway and *not* working at the counter anymore," she rejoined happily.

"Shouldn't you call and talk with him?" Bonita wondered. "Since the two of you didn't get along very well, maybe he really does want someone else."

Shannon grinned impishly. "He'll just have to hire me if there is no one else."

TWO LONG DAYS LATER Shannon sped along Interstate-95 to St. Augustine. She was going home, home to the broad windswept beach that stretched like a ribbon beside the blue green sea. Home to the great coquina stone house on a shelf of the low dune. Home to the fragrant old orange groves that her great-grandfather had planted when he came from England to America.

How she had missed Anastasia Island! How long it had taken her to come home!

She wondered fleetingly how Paul Cypress would react to her appearance, unannounced as it was. Well, she would think about him later. For now, she would not let anything interfere with her high, happy spirits.

The warm June breeze teased wisps of Shannon's long dark hair into tendrils that captured golden flecks of the Florida sunshine.

Amber eyes sparkling, cheeks pink with excitement, she looped off the interstate, passing the old stone city gates and the Castillo de San Marcos into the nation's oldest city, St. Augustine. She didn't remember that there used to be such crowds. There were tourists everywhere, especially on restored St. George Street with its charming shops and historic houses abutting the cobblestone thoroughfare.

Parking just off St. George, Shannon looked about for a quiet café. She needed time to think about all that going back to Pirate's Cove meant to her, and now, most of all, she needed time to prepare for the confrontation with Paul Cypress on the island.

She chose a quaint little inn whose shingle proclaimed it The Monk's Vineyard. Clusters of grapes hung from the rafters, and dusty wine bottles protruded from niches along the walls. A brown-robed friar introduced himself as Brother James and led her to a hand-hewn table and bench, where he poured sweet sangría into a goblet for her.

She settled into the dim corner of the refectory and told herself once more that she was glad to be in Florida. She wanted this job, and she would soon have it. She should never have let pride and unfounded doubts stand in the way of accepting it gladly and at once. The opportunity to play for such a famous artist should have been incentive enough. The added joy of being able to work at Pirate's Cove...what could she have been thinking of!

Paul would probably be hard to work for. Demanding, impatient...a perfectionist. A womanizer. At this, Shannon felt a flush of anger, and her long fingers twisted in her lap. Well, she'd let him know firmly and from the beginning that she was off limits. She would manage to get along with him. Lots of people didn't like their bosses. Or their employees. They would just have to respect each other's talent and ability. And she would enjoy the cove and the work that she loved best in the world. Shannon began to relax. She would stop brooding once and for all about whatever Paul's role had been in the ten-year-old tragedy.

Brother James served the thick vegetable soup in an earthenware bowl. He also brought her a selection of fresh fruit and a platter of thickly sliced monk's bread. She thanked him and found the hearty soup delicious.

But her hand trembled slightly as she raised the spoon. Self-doubt crept into her thoughts; Bonita could be right. Paul might send her away. Her outburst had been harsh and uncompromising, and they had parted as though neither wanted nor expected to see the other again. She would have to convince Paul that she could be businesslike and amiable as well as competent.

She bit into a buttered wedge of dark bread. "More wine perhaps?" the young monk suggested.

"No, thanks." For Shannon, even one glass often relaxed her to the point of sleepiness.

Brother James's eyes rested thoughtfully on her face. "May I get you something else?"

"No, I've dawdled too long already," she told him with a smile.

"Then I'll hope to serve you again soon," he murmured.

"Yes, I'll come back," she promised. "I enjoyed the meal very much."

His blue eyes looked puzzled. "Do I know you?" he asked hesitantly. "You look familiar. . . ."

"I doubt it," she returned quickly, rising.

Brother James seemed about to say something else when a diner across the aisle motioned to him. He handed Shannon her check with a hurried "Please wait a moment," before he went to the customer.

Shannon paid the bill and left. As she passed the macrame-draped window, she noted Brother James watching her. She was used to admiring glances, but she had no intention of becoming involved.

SHANNON DROVE SLOWLY over the Bridge of Lions, nodding to the great stone creatures for whom it was named, just as she had done as a child. Passing the island's barber-pole lighthouse, she turned south on Anastasia's A1A. New hotels and shops lined the highway; then a few miles beyond the rambling old inn was the gleaming pearl-white beach of the cove that she remembered and loved so well.

She was eager to see the Pratts...Thelma, who had been the Websters' housekeeper, and her husband, Leo, driver and handyman. When the house had been sold, they had stayed to work for Paul. They always wrote at Christmas. Shannon had sent them her picture last year.

The gentle rise of the dune to her right hid the stone mansion and the orange trees beyond it. Even so, the feeling of *home* brought tears to her eyes. She stopped the car at the foot of the lane and stepped onto the familiar sand.

She looked hungrily at the tide rising and curling toward the shore, reaching across the beach with wet fingers that picked at the road skirting Pirate's Cove. She listened to the roar and chuckle of the surf as it broke into rough caresses on the sand.

Turning, she followed the curving lane upward toward the house. She wanted to let it grow into her vision and into her heart bit by bit. She stepped onto the flagstone path that angled up to the terrace, and as she crested the shoulder of the hill she caught her breath. Nestled on a shelf of the dune was the old gray-stone house, its thick solid walls hewn from the ancient coquina quarries of the island.

The broad terrace, spread like an apron before the house, held wicker chairs and lounges and little tables, just as she remembered. A wrought-iron balcony bordered the second story, its graceful stairway curved like a protecting arm about the south end of the terrace. Sheer draperies were drawn across the long windows and glass doors.

Shannon stood irresolutely before the carved Spanish portal. It didn't seem right for her to knock when she still thought of this as her own home. She went around to the kitchen at the back. The woman who was lifting a steaming pie from the oven heard her step and turned.

"Shanny Webster! Welcome home, girlie!" Thelma Pratt almost dropped the pie in her excitement. She hurriedly set it on the butcher block and flung her arms around Shannon. "Why, you're even prettier than your picture, darlin'! My bones must have told me you were comin' today, for it's a blueberry pie that I've made. You still do favor it?"

"Blueberry and you, Thelma. I favor both," Shannon assured her warmly. "Oh, it's good to be home!" She looked around the familiar kitchen and then back at the old housekeeper. "You haven't changed, and neither has your kitchen."

"This is home to Leo and me. We were happy and grateful that Mr. Paul wanted us to stay on." She drew Shannon to a chair and plugged in the coffeepot. "Now tell me what brings you back, child."

Shannon explained briefly that she had met Paul in Illinois and that he had spoken to her about summer work.

Thelma looked puzzled. "I knew he was expectin'

a piano player one day soon. But he never said 'twould be you, though he must've known we'd be so happy...."

"He didn't know that I'd be the one to come," Shannon said. "I said no at first, and then I changed my mind." Though Thelma still looked perplexed, Shannon decided to drop the subject of Paul and went on to tell about her work at the university and about her mother's role in summer stock. Then she asked for news of Thelma's family.

The housekeeper spoke proudly of her only son, Leonard, who had moved to Texas at about the same time that Shannon and her mother had gone to Chicago. "We don't see them often," she finished wistfully.

"What about Jimmy?" Shannon warmly remembered the Pratts' grandson and the fun they'd had as children during the long lazy days of summer when he visited his grandparents at the cove. Though four years older, Jimmy had enjoyed Shannon's companionship as they dug clams and made sand castles and swam and pretended they were pirates.

"Hadn't seen Jimmy in years," Thelma said. "Even Leonard and Jane didn't know where he was." Her lined face broke into a smile. "But he's here now, Shanny. Turned up at Christmastime, when Leo and me were on a month's vacation an' Mr. Paul was here alone. Jimmy got a job in town, an' we're hopin' he'll stay a while. He's livin' in the old cabin below the groves, 'cause rents are so high in town. Mr. Paul says that's still your property, and we didn't think you'd mind.''

''Of course I don't mind. I just hope it's weather-proof. Even when we were kids, it was pretty run-down.''

Thelma held up her hands. ''Let Jimmy worry about that. He's twenty-four years old, an' that's old enough to take care of hisself. Guess he's been doin' it for some time, though I don't know how good.''

''I'm eager to see him again,'' Shannon said, ris-ing. ''But now I suppose it's time for me to speak to Mr. Cypress about that job. Do you think he's in the studio?''

''Either there or in his suite.'' Thelma rose stiffly. ''I'll just call him on the intercom and tell him you're here, honey.''

Shannon touched Thelma's arm. ''I'd rather sur-prise him.'' She wanted a chance to present her case in person; she did not want to run the risk of being dismissed without a hearing. ''How has he been since the surgery? Has he been singing?''

Thelma pursed her lips. ''Moody, restless. No, he hasn't sung a note. Seems to feel all right, but. . . .'' She spread her hands, letting one come to rest on Shannon's arm. ''Don't let him gruff you. Some-times he's like a bear with a bee sting, but he don't mean it so bad. You just have to stand your ground.''

That was something Shannon already surmised. Paul would not be an easy man to please. Or to know. ''I will,'' she promised.

She crossed the foyer and mounted the wide blue-carpeted stairs, her footsteps soundless in the deep pile. At the studio door she paused, peering into the beloved room where she had first touched the magic keys that had made such lovely sounds.

A single lamp glowed near the Steinway, leaving most of the enormous room in shadows. Before Shannon had a chance to adjust her eyes, she was greeted by an unmistakable baritone. "What the devil are you doing here?" Paul's long frame unfolded from a wing chair in a dim corner.

Her carefully rehearsed speech was forgotten; the quick reminder of her qualifications and of Paul's job offer stuck in her throat.

Paul walked slowly toward Shannon, his eyes black smudges in a face whose pallor mocked the bronze look of health that she remembered. A brown scarf was tucked into the open neck of his knitted beige shirt, hiding the scar she knew was there.

"I asked what you're doing here." Paul's voice was tense, ragged.

"I came to...to play for you," she managed, annoyed at the tremor in her voice. "I'd like that job." She searched the dark depths of his eyes for a glimmer of encouragement, but her heart sank when she found none.

"I asked you to *send* someone," he rasped. "I expected your Jack What's-his-name."

"Jack is in summer school."

Paul ignored that. "Someone competent and good-tempered."

"That's what you've got," she said with a lift of the chin. "I am competent. You said you were pleased with—"

"With your playing," he interrupted, "not with your behavior. I can't work with someone who is temperamental and unreasonable."

"I'm not!" she flared. With an effort she forced herself to speak calmly. "Really, I don't have trouble getting along with people." She tried a tentative smile.

"Only with me? Well, then that's the problem, isn't it? You told me quite plainly that you did not want to work with me. The whole world might jump when I spoke, you said, but you were the exception. Well, I'm ready for someone from that whole world to come and work with me, and what do I get? The exception, you!" He ran his fingers through his luxuriant hair in exasperation.

"Please, Mr. Cypress, I've come all this way—"

"Without an invitation," he finished stonily.

Shannon bit her lip, but it was no use. The angry words were going to spill out. What did it matter? She was not going to get the job. That her bitter disappointment was her own fault didn't for the moment quell her resentment of Paul's power to offer and then retract the job and the joy of a summer at the cove.

"Good luck then," she snapped. "I'm sure you'll have no trouble finding another accompanist. There must be dozens ready to fall all over one another for the job." She glanced about the room once more, memorizing its dim details through misty eyes. She had come so close to coming home that leaving now seemed almost unbearable. And all because of this arrogant man!

As she turned to stalk away, a viselike grip spun her around. "What now?" Paul demanded. "Do you think I'll let you reject my offer a second time?"

Shannon stared at him, confused.

He gave her a little shake. "Why in hell did you come almost a thousand miles if you aren't going to stay and work?"

"But I thought . . . you said you couldn't work . . . ."

"With someone who is temperamental and unreasonable, which you say you are not. So what is your reason for wishing me luck in finding someone else?"

His voice and grip were harsh, the corners of his mouth drawn down in a suggestion of displeasure. Was he serious? Teasing? "I don't understand," she murmured.

"Obviously." Paul led Shannon to a leather chair and sat down opposite her. "So you'd better get some things straight. In the mornings you will answer my mail, keep my records straight, that sort of thing. Time spent on music will increase as my voice becomes stronger."

"You mean . . . I have the job?"

"I'm stuck with you, wouldn't you say?" he countered dryly. "You probably guessed that I had checked out what few pianists are in St. Augustine for the summer. I want to begin therapy at once, so . . . what choice do I have?"

Shannon lowered her gaze. That was exactly what she had figured. Practical Paul. It had nothing to do with her.

"But I'll stand for no more nonsense. No more balking at orders, no arguments, no childish tantrums. Understood?"

"Yes," she agreed.

"Your hours may often be scattered; you're to be available whenever I need you, depending upon the condition of my voice and sometimes simply upon my mood. Usually you'll know your work hours for the day at breakfast time."

"Breakfast? Here?"

"Well, of course. You'll be living here."

"Oh!" It was a sigh of delight. She wouldn't have to hunt for a room in town. She could save almost all of her salary. Best of all, the cove would truly be her home for the summer. "Thank you, Paul." His name had slipped out unintentionally.

"Glad to see you've finally remembered my name," he growled. "Incidentally, my son will arrive soon to spend the summer at the cove. Part of your duty will be to keep an eye on him. He's nine, sometimes a handful."

Shannon leaned forward, searching for the softness in Paul's face that she heard in his voice when he spoke of the boy. She liked children. "He must love the cove," she offered, breaking into the long pause.

Paul stirred from his quiet thoughts. "His name is Jason. He hasn't been here much. I wish—" the dark eyes rested on Shannon "—I wish he could grow up here. As you did."

Shannon sensed that Paul was troubled about Jason, and she felt a stirring of sympathy. In the still twilight she wondered what was happening to her. Paul's magnetism, his charisma was powerful. Were her resentments and doubts already tottering? How could she so quickly overlook his rude sarcasm? His reputed womanizing? She gave her shoulders a slight shake and stood up. "I'll get my things. I left my car down the lane."

Paul rose and held out his hand. "Give me the keys, and I'll have Leo get your car while you freshen up."

Across the hall they both paused before the door of the room that had been hers for the first ten years of her life. Paul took her hand and guided her fingertips across a rough patch in the panel. "My name," she murmured. "I carved it there the day we moved."

"So who else could possibly stay here?"

"I might have sent Jack."

For the first time a trace of a smile touched Paul's mouth, and Shannon surprised a twinkle in his eyes. "Dinner is at seven," he said huskily, turning to leave her.

IN HER ROOM, Shannon felt as though she had stepped into the past. The yellow flowered wallpaper had faded a little, but the ruffled gold draperies and spread were fresh. Her maple desk and dresser were polished to a mirror finish. In a starched pinafore a forgotten doll sat propped in the rocking chair, smiling patiently as she had for a decade. When Shannon and her mother had moved, it had seemed a sacrilege to take what so naturally belonged here. Besides, there was too little room in the tiny Chicago apartment.

From the French balcony doors Shannon could see the stone path that angled down to the road and the beach. To the south was the bluff on which the neglected orange grove stood, and beyond that was Shannon's secret valley and the patch of rocks at the end of the coquina quarries. Even farther, the island narrowed to a mere breakwater between the ocean and the Matanzas River.

The fruit trees had been brought by Shannon's great-grandfather as saplings from the famous groves of Spain almost a century ago. After the disastrous frosts of the 1890s, Joseph Webster had turned to other enterprises, and the grove had been only sporadically tended by succeeding Websters. But the springtime fragrance of its blossoms persisted, though the fruit that followed was disappointingly small.

After a warm shower, Shannon found her luggage just inside the door. She shook out a sleeveless sheath of gold linen. After a vigorous brushing, her dark hair fell in soft resilient waves down her back and across her shoulders. She caught it loosely under a narrow yellow ribbon. The antique gold chain nestled in the folds of the draped linen neckline. She touched her lips with color and her wrists and earlobes with jasmine.

Paul, waiting in the candlelit dining room, had changed into a light blue silk sport shirt and navy slacks. Tucked into the neck of his shirt was a navy scarf that hid his scar. His eyes flicked over Shannon's face and hair, her trim figure in the snug sheath and her shapely legs and small sandaled feet. Then they traveled lazily back to rest upon the gold necklace. "Your birthday gift, wasn't it?"

"Yes. Dad thought it might be part of the lost treasure." Aware of Paul's quiet appraisal, Shannon knew that she was blushing. Annoyed at her telltale reaction, she buried her face in an arrangement of scarlet anthuria for a moment. Then, "I read in *Variety* that you are to sing Don Quixote in *Man of La Mancha* this fall in Europe."

Paul's laugh was short and humorless. "There are always rumors about performers. I suppose you also read that Merlene Madden, my ex-wife, will be singing Dulcinea?" When Shannon nodded, he continued, "And that she and I are about to patch things up?"

"Well. . . ." That had been the gist of the article, but Shannon hadn't meant to pry. Nor to put that bitter note in Paul's voice.

"How can anyone tell when my voice will be ready again when I myself have no idea? You can hear how it is now. There's no range, no volume, even for speaking." He drummed his fingers on the mantel. "As for Merlene. . .I've no intention of complicating my life with her. Or with any other woman. Of course we sang together last year after the divorce. We had contracts to fulfill. As for the future...." He paused to fill two glasses with white wine. "Let's drink to the future, Shannon."

DURING DINNER, which Shannon scarcely touched because of her hearty meal at The Vineyard, Paul entertained her with stories about his tours to all parts of the world. But when she commented on the fun and excitement his travels must bring, Paul said wryly that she shouldn't forget the endless rehearsals and identical hotel rooms, the early flights and late receptions. Shannon wondered whether a performer became jaded after a while, weary of the never ending demands of an adoring public.

He spoke of Jason, too. "Our separation has troubled him," he admitted. "The headmaster has asked that we find another school for him next fall. His behavior hasn't been good." Paul eyed Shannon moodily through long straight black lashes. "If I could bring him up here.... He needs a home full-time. He hates boarding school." Then abruptly, "I want full custody, and I intend to get it."

Shannon remembered how lonely she had been at boarding school one year when her mother had gone on tour with her father. "If you do, then are you planning to keep him with you and hire a tutor for him?"

"Not *if*," he corrected. "*When* I gain custody, Shannon. I have some plans." His eyes narrowed. "I think they'll work out. Yes, I'm sure they will."

Apparently he didn't intend to elaborate, though his steady and compelling gaze remained on Shannon. She felt as though he were trying to communicate something to her, and the slow unwelcome flush crept above her neckline once more.

This time she forced her eyes to meet Paul's. The electric current of his gaze shocked her. It was as though they had physically touched and the searing point of contact had spun threads of fire in every direction through her body. She was aware of him as she had never been aware of any man in her entire life...of his strength and power, of his will and drive and of his ability to change the course of her life.

Moments before, he had spoken of plans. In Paul's dark gaze Shannon thought she had read that she was a part of those plans. She shook her head slightly, dismissing the fancy. She had a job. She would not permit the slightest personal involvement to complicate it.

CHAPTER THREE

LATER THAT NIGHT Shannon changed into a comfortable multicolored caftan and wrote a long letter to her mother. Tired but not relaxed enough yet to sleep, she finished unpacking and putting away her clothing.

She stepped out on the balcony, where the mellow breezes teased her to go down to the starlit beach for a reacquaintance with the capricious sea. She could not resist. An hour beside the whispering waters would soothe away the strain of the unsettling day.

She remembered every flagstone of the path that curved down from the edge of the terrace. The full moon hung in the east, spilling a rippling gold banner across the ocean. Enchanted, Shannon dropped to her knees, reveling in the beauty of the Florida night and the feeling of belonging to the seascape.

"Shannon?"

Startled by the intrusive voice, she whirled. The man who looked down at her wore a long brown robe with the hood pushed back so that the moonlight touched his blond curls with gold. He dropped down beside her. "Shannon Webster," he said softly and quickly pulled her close for his kiss.

Hastily Shannon pushed him away and got to her feet. "What do you think you're doing?"

"Shanny, it's me, Jimmy Pratt. Today in the restaurant I wasn't sure. You left, and I didn't get a chance to ask. I could hardly wait to get off work tonight. Gee, you're all grown up," he said appreciatively, taking in her slim figure outlined in the wind-blown caftan. "No wonder I didn't connect you with the freckle-faced kid who used to hunt treasure with me. Gran showed me your picture a few months ago. That's how it finally dawned on me who you were."

"Jimmy!" She let him take her hand and draw her down beside him. "You are Brother James! Thelma didn't tell me you had taken orders. I'm...surprised."

Jim chuckled. "If I had, it would surprise me, too. No wonder you were shocked when I kissed you. No, I'm not a religious. This is the uniform waiters at The Vineyard wear. I was so anxious to get here, to find out if the gorgeous girl I served today could really be you, that I didn't stop to change." He laughed again. "Now let's start over."

This time when Jim kissed her Shannon didn't pull away. "It's good to see you," she told him earnestly. "Good to be back at Pirate's Cove. How did you know where to find me?"

Jim smiled. "Where else would you go? Fate seems to have brought us both home at the same time, Shanny. Maybe that's significant."

"Maybe," she agreed lightly. Jim's gaze was intense and Shannon stirred uneasily. She hardly knew

Jim after the separation of years, and yet he seemed to want to call forth a deep and immediate response from her, a response that she did not feel. Not yet.

"How about a moonlight swim, Shanny?"

"We're hardly dressed for it," she reminded him.

Jim's low laughter was close. "That never used to stop us." Shannon felt a flush creep over her neck and face. She remembered the spontaneous skinny-dipping of their early childhood. Sensing her embarrassment, Jim added, "You're right. We're not kids anymore. We could change and come back," he finished hopefully.

"I'm pretty tired tonight," Shannon said. "I've had a long drive."

"Is Bonita here, too? Where are you staying and for how long?"

Shannon explained the circumstances of her arrival and that she was actually staying here at the cove. Jim listened thoughtfully. When she asked how he had spent the years since she had last seen him, he shrugged. "My fortunes have been up and down."

"I'd like to hear, Jim."

After a pause, "Okay. How about tomorrow? I don't go to work till noon. Let's have an early swim, and I'll fix breakfast at the cabin afterward."

It was Shannon's turn to laugh. "I'm a working girl, Jim. I'll have to check with Paul about my hours."

"I'll be swimming at eight. Do come, Shannon. We'll breakfast on the beach and have a good talk."

"You're hard to resist."

"I'm glad to hear it." He would have kissed her again, but Shannon quickly rose and with a wave ran across the sand and the road to the path up the hill. When she reached the terrace, she turned and found Jim still standing on the moon-clear beach.

IN THE MORNING Shannon awoke with joy. She was at Pirate's Cove on Anastasia Island, the place she loved best in the world, and she had a job that was bound to be a challenge and a pleasure. And Jim was here. It would be fun to spend time with him. It always had been. They could explore the island and St. Augustine during their free time. They could share their thoughts and plans and dreams, just as they used to.

Shannon tiptoed down to the kitchen in her robe and slippers to ask Thelma when Paul was usually up and ready to work. The housekeeper held up her hands. "Nobody sees Mr. Paul till about ten, and I'm not a-blamin' him a bit, for he's still gettin' over that operation. He's often up late, and he's got to sleep sometime."

"Good. Then I'll go for a swim, but I'll be back before ten."

"Goin' with Jimmy?"

"How did you guess?"

Thelma grinned. "He swims every mornin' early. And I saw the two of you down on the beach last night kinda late."

"Spying!" Shannon teased affectionately. "Yes,

I'm to meet Jim. And I'd better hurry or I'll be late."

She put on a white bikini and draped a beach towel over her shoulder. Selecting a length of orange yarn from a many-colored bundle, she tied her hair in a high ponytail.

Jim came out of the surf to meet her, looking like a Norse god with his broad tan shoulders, slim waist and hips and muscular, well-shaped legs and arms. The monk's robe had hidden his strong youthful build completely, and Shannon caught herself staring and smiling approvingly.

Jim's low whistle was a compliment. "Say, you've really improved with age, Shanny. You could be a model."

"I'd rather make music."

"Play your cards right, and I'll bet Paul Cypress will see that you get top billing in a hurry."

Her unexpected shove sent Jim sprawling, and she splashed into deep water to escape retribution. They frolicked for an hour in the clear cool Atlantic, riding the gentle swells of the morning surf and finally scuffing into the warming sand.

Towel dried, they strolled south along the beach. "Gramps helped me put on a new roof and make the old shack snug. It suits me. Wouldn't mind staying for a year or so."

"You may if you like. Mother sold Pirate's Cove, but not the orange groves. That part of the property is mine now, so I give you permission to live there as long as you like."

Jim's blue eyes shone. "Really? I'll pay rent."

"No need for that. It was empty, and I'm sure you've had to make improvements."

"You're still very good to me, Shanny. Very good *for* me," he corrected soberly. "Thanks."

As they came in sight of the little cabin, Shannon stopped in surprise. The once tumbledown one-room shack now had new shake shingles, and the once broken shutters, repaired and painted, were open to reveal sparkling windows. The steps, which she remembered as almost buried in drifted sand, had been swept clean, and a wooden bench waited invitingly on the tiny porch. A few feet from the bottom step a tripod straddled a stone-lined firepit in which embers glowed beneath gray ash. A tattered but clean blanket was spread nearby.

"This can't be the wreck we used to play in!" Shannon exclaimed.

"It is. Come inside."

The inside walls had been whitewashed, and there were blue-and-white checked curtains at the two miniature windows. Shannon recognized the table as a repaired three-legged ruin from the storeroom back of the big house. A similarly discarded chair had also been mended and painted. On new shelves there were dishes, cans and canisters of food as well as some pans and books. Hanging from wall pegs were Jim's jacket, the monk's habit and some shirts and jeans. On the wooden bunk Jim's fine Goya guitar lay on his unrolled sleeping bag.

"There's no electricity," Jim told Shannon, indicating the oil lamp on the table, "but I've got running water." There was a single-tap sink with a Styrofoam ice chest tucked beneath it.

Shannon pointed to a small kerosene heater. "Do you cook on that?"

"It's fine for a pot of coffee or a pan of soup, but you can't have both at the same time," he said with a grin. "Anyway, I get most of my meals at The Vineyard."

"Even on your day off?"

Jim shrugged. "Don't pity me. This is great. Gran's always good for a dish of leftovers if I need something, and I love any excuse to cook out on the beach. Like now. Just watch." He took a pail with a bail handle from the shelf and filled it half-full of corn oil. "Hang this on the tripod out there, Shanny, and I'll be with you in a jiffy. Take the cups, too, and help yourself to coffee."

Shannon went out and sat down on the blanket to watch the little bucket of oil to be sure that it stayed securely suspended over the embers. She poured a cup of coffee from the enamel pot that was warming near the fire's edge.

Hugging her knees, she watched a curious gull waddle toward her. He examined her first with one bright eye, then the other. "Stay awhile," she invited, but when Jim came out, it fled.

With a chipped bowl in one hand and paper towels in the other, Jim announced, "Doughnuts. But I don't have a cutter, so I guess we'll have dough balls." He scooped up spoonfuls of batter and dropped them into the hot oil.

Shannon knelt to watch the sizzling globes bob to the surface, swelling as they browned. "Jim, I'd never have guessed that you'd like to cook."

"There's a great deal that you'd never guess about me," he admitted soberly.

Shannon sat back on her heels and pulled the sodden bit of yarn from her ponytail, shaking her hair free to let it dry. "You promised to tell me about yourself this morning."

Jim laid several thicknesses of paper down and lifted out the first batch of dough balls with two peeled sticks. "You first while I fry these masterpieces, honey. Tell me about you."

Shannon talked about her home in Chicago and Bonita's work and about her own work at the university and her plans to become a concert pianist.

"Sounds like this summer job with Cypress is a lucky break for you, Shanny. Let him help you up the ladder."

Frowning, she said, "It's a job, Jim, and a darned good one. I'm not sure what you're implying, but I didn't accept the work so that I could use Paul."

"If you want something, you use whatever can help. If I get the story straight, Paul Cypress started using you five minutes after he met you."

"Don't you like Paul?" Shannon asked shortly.

"Maybe I don't trust him because he's rich and famous. Guys like that think only about themselves and how they can profit the most. They don't give a damn about anything or anyone else."

"You're generalizing." Was his remark a reflection on his own wealthy parents as well as on Paul? She hadn't known Leonard and Jane Pratt very well; they had deposited Jimmy with his grandparents at the end of the school year and picked him up on Labor Day. "There are exceptions, you know," she said sharply, disappointed in his cynicism.

"Hey, let's have no frowns on that beautiful face," Jim said. "We've just found each other after all this time, so let's forget about Paul and just be happy."

"Okay," Shannon agreed, a rueful smile softening her generous mouth. Jim still had that boyish charm that could banish their differences in a twinkling. She bit into a hot tender dough ball. "Delicious! Let me know whenever these are on your breakfast menu, Jim."

"Anytime you'll come," he promised.

Shannon reminded Jim of his promise to tell her where he had been the past ten years. "Start with Texas," she suggested.

Jim nodded. "The folks are still in Borger. Dad's a big oil man, and mom's big on society stuff. I've always been a disappointment to them." Shannon shook her head, but Jim went on. "I wasn't ready for college at seventeen. I didn't give a damn for football. Didn't make the team. Didn't make much in grades, either. So after a while I just . . . disappeared."

Shannon eyed his powerful legs and great shoulders and guessed that he could be any kind of athlete he wanted to be. But that was the key . . . wanting to be.

"I played football in high school, but I didn't care about it too much. I loved music, you know. When we were kids, I used to pretend that I was part of your family, Shanny, where music was everything.''

She touched his arm sympathetically. ''Maybe your folks didn't know how important it was to you, Jim.''

''Anyway, I quit the university. Closed out my checking account by buying the Goya. I just drifted for a while.'' He sat quietly, reliving memories.

''Didn't you contact your folks?''

He shook his head. ''I didn't want to be found.''

''You must have had a hard time of it.''

''Sometimes,'' he admitted. ''I worked on an oil rig in the gulf for a while. Then I went to Brownsville, on the border. That was . . . rough. Eventually I got away, though. Lived on Padre Island. It's beautiful there, Shanny. There's a wilderness, natural and wild and free. And healing,'' he added softly.

''But you've come back.''

''Yeah.'' With a sigh he said, ''A man has to eat. And I guess a man can live alone only so long. You know, I'd like to study classical guitar someday. With someone like Segovia or Montoya—'' he laughed apologetically ''—but it's probably just a foolish dream.''

''Why should it be?'' she challenged. ''Jim, I always thought you could do whatever you made up your mind to do. I still think so.''

Jim reached for Shannon's hand. ''Now that we're together, I wish I had finished college.''

''I don't think less of you because you didn't,'' she assured him.

''I'm touchy about education . . . or my lack of it,''

he admitted. "I want you to care about me and look up to me the way you used to. I've thought about you often, Shanny."

"In between a dozen other girls," Shannon said roguishly, wanting to steer the talk into less serious channels. She stood up and brushed the crumbs from her legs.

Jim's hands on her shoulders made her straighten, and then she was in his arms. "We're home, Shannon," he said, "and we're together again." His voice was deep and vibrant.

As his lips touched hers, she put her hands against his chest, resisting. But he held her locked against him, his mouth working a sensual magic that made her aware of the warmth of his body, the strength and pressure of his arms and legs, the vibrant yearning of his caress.

"I wonder if you could spare a few hours to earn your first day's salary," Paul rasped behind her.

With a gasp Shannon wrenched away. Her back had been toward the cove, and she hadn't seen Paul's approach. But Jim must have. She glared at him. His brows were slightly raised above suspiciously innocent blue eyes.

Paul stood like a statue cut from the island's coquina. In tight gray slacks and a lighter gray turtleneck sweater of summer-weight knit, hands thrust into his pockets, his face was chiseled in sardonic, disapproving lines.

"I'm sorry if I'm late, Paul. I told Thelma I'd be back—"

"Before ten." Paul scowled down at his watch. "It is quarter **past**, and you are hardly ready for work." His eyes raked over her slender body in the brief white suit.

"My fault," Jim said coolly. "We were talking."

"What you were doing doesn't concern me," Paul said pointedly. "Our work does," He turned to Shannon. "I'll wait while you dress."

She felt the hated color mount to the roots of her hair. "I didn't undress here!" She stalked past Paul and began the climb up the hill without another word.

"See you soon, Shannon," Jim called after her, but she was too upset and angry to acknowledge the promise. She knew he was intentionally adding fuel to the fire. Jim had kissed her knowing that Paul was approaching. She resented that.

BY TEN TO ELEVEN Shannon was ready to work. In tailored tan slacks and a beige-and-tangerine print blouse, she looked neatly efficient, her damp hair held smoothly in place by the intricately wrought gold barrette. She sat down at the piano.

"We will not begin this late again," Paul fumed, pacing.

Shannon nodded. "Sorry."

"Mornings you'll get the correspondence out of the way." He indicated a stack of unopened mail on his desk. "Letters have piled up recently. You'd better get at them."

"Don't you want to sing first?" she asked, surprised.

"Do I sound as if I could now?" he rasped in irritation. "Beginning this late hasn't improved my voice. Or my temper."

"I said I was sorry," Shannon snapped. She bit her lip. In spite of her intentions, she was starting out her new job badly.

To her dismay, Paul left abruptly. Because she felt uncomfortably responsible for his angry mood, she decided that she would make amends by clearing up the backlog of mail. She found a silver stiletto in the desk and methodically slit each envelope and stapled it to its letter. There were some bills, which she put in one pile, but most were fan letters. What now? Was she supposed to answer them?

She rubbed her forehead, recalling her father's custom. During that summer ten years ago, Paul had been Edmund's secretary. Sometimes Paul had shown her the letters of praise. And he had let her hand him the photos and form letters to stuff the envelopes he addressed. Remembering, she knew exactly what to do.

In the downstairs study she found a box of photographs of Paul and form letters in the wall cabinet, exactly where Edmund used to keep his own fan material. She typed the necessary envelopes and inserted Paul's pictures and notes, finishing just as the hall clock struck twelve.

She freshened her lipstick and freed a lazy curl on each side of her face before going into the dining room.

"Well, you're on time for lunch," Paul commented from the window.

"Always," she said cheerfully. She would not let him rile her.

He came closer. "I stopped at the studio, but you weren't there. I thought you might have run off again."

"Hardly," she said, forcing a smile. "One scolding is enough for today."

A bit grudgingly, Paul agreed. "Right. After lunch I'll show you what to do with the mail, and then we'll try some scales."

"The fan mail is taken care of," she told him, "and if you'll trust me with your checkbook, I'll do the bills and have the checks ready for your signature in half an hour."

One black eyebrow rose. "Just how did you take care of the fan mail?"

"The way you used to do dad's mail."

There was a glint of pleasure in his eyes. "You haven't forgotten."

Thelma came in with a steaming casserole, and the intimate moment of a memory shared was gone.

After lunch, Paul didn't vocalize long. Shannon could see that the limitations of his voice were a source of frustration and irritation to him, and she was glad when he said that he would rest during the hot part of the day.

THE DAYS BEGAN to take on a pattern. Paul's previous custom of appearing at ten o'clock changed; he was ready for breakfast at eight and for dictation by nine. At some point in the busy morning he would stop abruptly, saying he would practice arpeggios and runs. They would go to the studio, where Paul's annoyance and impatience with his impaired voice would increase as the hour progressed.

"Damn it!" he exploded one day. "I don't have any range or power! It will be months before I can sing in public!"

"Paul, you've got to be patient. You've only been singing since last week."

"Maybe I'm all through," he muttered savagely.

"Of course not!"

"How could you possibly know?" he demanded.

"Well, it can't help to strain. Try to relax," she coaxed.

Paul left the curve of the Steinway and sat down in the big Morocco chair. "All right, I'm relaxed. Get on with the therapy, Dr. Webster."

At the frank mockery, Shannon looked down at her hands. "You're trying to fight your way back, but with music you have to sort of *grow* back." She caught her full lower lip between her teeth for a moment. "Once I sprained my wrist on the ice. I tried to make myself play all the difficult things too soon. Then Dr. Moore said I should treat my hand like a patient that was just learning to function again. She was right, you know."

Paul regarded her intently. "Maybe." He didn't sound convinced. "I suppose we could do some work on those Seminole songs for a week or so. They're simple in range. These damned ten-note stretches are what tear me apart. Maybe I am pushing too hard," he admitted grudgingly. "I've got to be ready by October."

"*Man of La Mancha?* Where? New York?"

He shook his head, growling, "That's not for publication yet," and her interested smile faded. Sometimes he made her feel overly inquisitive, though she hadn't meant to pry. "It's not fully worked out yet. About the folk songs—I have written down the melody notations and the lyrics. Do you think you could write in the harmony and work out some kind of accompaniment? I could sing them for you. . . ."

"Oh, yes," Shannon responded eagerly, "I'd like to try."

And when Paul sang the love songs and lullaby tunes of the Seminoles, his tension and huskiness were forgotten, for he was not preparing them for critics and sophisticates. He sang them because he loved them and wanted them to be recorded and remembered. He forgot himself and his voice problems as he crooned the minor-keyed songs softly, so that Shannon would know how they should *feel*. So that she would find the right blend of the piano keys for them.

SHANNON KNEW WHEN his voice began to heal itself, but she said nothing. It was enough that the tension was gone. Enough that they could work together on the long road back. Another week sped by, and Paul began again to work on arpeggios and double octaves, and although Shannon sometimes surprised a look of despair and resignation in Paul's dark eyes, he kept his frustrated outbursts under control and persisted in vocalizing regularly, doggedly. For her part, Shannon tried to make the sessions as pleasant as she knew they used to be for Paul. She refused to be offended when he shifted the blame to her for a badly executed passage, knowing that it was something he had to do in self-protection. He had to believe that he could make the come back, that he was already well on his way.

Once, after an attempt at "The Impossible Dream" with its difficult sustentation of strong high notes, Paul ran his fingers through his thick mop of blue black hair, his eyes snapping angrily as he leaned over the corner of the piano rack.

"Wait! Don't scold!" Shannon said, reaching out to touch him briefly. "That's a devilish song, but if you had to try it, I should have had sense enough to come on with a stronger support. I can improvise, like this...." And she ran her fingers nimbly over the keyboard.

Suddenly her hands were lifted from the ivory keys as Paul sat down beside her on the bench. When he didn't release them, she looked at him questioningly. "You really are good-tempered after all," he said tiredly. "Peppery as you are by nature, it must be quite a struggle sometimes. I know I'm not the easiest person to get along with."

Shannon didn't know what to say. It was uncharacteristic of him to be apologetic.

"You're good for me, Shannon." He turned her

hands over, studying the narrow palms and tapered fingers. "I need you. Badly. I'd never have guessed how much."

"Thank you, Paul." The huskiness in her voice almost matched his. Deep inside her, something began to sing. She felt the old delight that had always spread through her when Paul was pleased with her. She wasn't just any good pianist to him; he thought her special.

Idly his thumbs moved over her palms, and her fingers curled over them. When he raised his eyes to hers, they were dark and penetrating, stabbing into hers with a new awareness that disturbed her with an electric shock. Self-consciously she drew her hands away.

CHAPTER FOUR

SOMETIMES SHANNON MET Jim for a late-evening swim, accepting his jolly camaraderie and frank admiration and enjoying the light easy companionship they had enjoyed as children. That Jim might hope for something more in the future did not trouble her. The future would take care of itself. For the present they were good friends, and that was enough.

She took Jim to task about the kiss at the point of Paul's arrival on the beach the day after she had come to Pirate's Cove. "You must have seen him coming," she accused.

Jim's smoothly handsome face wore an impish grin as he eyed her through long gold lashes. "Sure, I saw him. And I let him know that you're not about to fall into his arms." He sobered. "You know his reputation with women, Shanny. If he gives you any trouble, I'll take care of him."

"Thanks," she said wryly. "That won't be necessary."

Jim's eyes narrowed. "No passes yet? That's hard to believe."

Shannon felt the unwelcome blush creep over her

chin and cheeks as she recalled Paul's sudden kiss in the cab last spring.

"You're a beautiful lady, honey, and if it hasn't happened yet, it will. Bank on it."

She changed the subject. "Remember the fun we used to have hunting for buried treasure? When Paul's son, Jason, comes, we can tell him all about Juan Gómez and the pirates."

"I'll bet the kid knows the story. The old records are still at the house, aren't they?"

Shannon nodded. She had found them stored in the small guest room next to hers. "I don't think the Cypresses spent much time at the cove, though. I wonder if Paul ever thinks about the old treasure legends."

"Maybe that's why he bought this place," Jim guessed, "so he could go on with the search that he started with your dad."

She doubted that. Paul had never seemed to have the burning conviction that had plagued Edmund's last years—that the treasure was still on the island, waiting to be discovered.

"Hey, Shanny, some of my friends are having a party in town Friday night. How about it? Want to go?"

"I may have to work," she said hesitatingly.

"At night?"

Shannon explained that sometimes she had the morning or afternoon off, which extended her work hours into the evening.

"I can't go till I'm through work anyway," Jim

said. "Do you have to be on duty after about nine-thirty?"

Recognizing Jim's malicious implication, she smiled wickedly. "Not so far. See you Friday. Probably."

THE REST OF THE WEEK was busy, and Shannon forgot about the party until late Friday afternoon as she was stamping the last letter. Although her schedule was flexible and largely regulated by herself now, on this particular day her duties had been light. Paul could rightfully claim some work hours after dinner if he chose. She didn't expect any objections to her evening plans, but she felt that she should at least make Paul aware of them.

When she didn't find Paul inside the house, Shannon stepped onto the terrace, shading her eyes to scan the beach. Thelma was scrubbing the wicker furniture. "Lookin' for the boss?" she asked. "He'll be gettin' a nice tan this afternoon for sure."

"Is he on the beach? I don't see him."

"He's one for likin' his privacy, Shanny. Remember that secret place of yours beyond the groves? You used to hide there from Jimmy when you were mad at him. Mr. Paul often goes there to catch a bit of sun."

Shannon started for the path. "I'll find him."

"If he's in a mood, he won't like you to surprise him," Thelma cautioned. "He doesn't like bein' gone after."

"Does he sun in the buff?" Shannon asked with a laugh.

"Well, no, but he's touchy about folks seein' that scar of his. Leo says it ain't that bad, but—"

At the ringing of the phone, Thelma hurried inside, and Shannon headed for the shortcut to the valley through the groves. The hill back of the house was covered with scrub pine, palmetto and tangles of underbrush, and she wished that she had changed from shorts to jeans. Ragged sun-dried saw grass scratched her bare legs; she hoped that there were no snakes.

Gaining the old orchard, she paused to catch her breath in the shade of the wind-twisted trees. She dropped down upon an old log and ran her fingers through the spongy punk and dead leaves and blossoms. *Someday I'll make this grove come alive again,* she promised herself. The scent of orange blooms would cover the dunes and waft out to sea. And so would the music from the conservatory she would build in the hollow beyond the grove.

She walked carefully across the weed-overgrown paths until she came to the south edge of the orchard. A jumble of rocks formed a natural retaining wall for the slope of the dune; the dell below was small, with great gray boulders jutting all around it. It was part of what once had been a coquina quarry. Other larger stone quarries stretched down the length of Anastasia Island.

The gigantic fort of San Marcos, as well as much of the early village, had been built of the pale com-

pressed shell rock. The exterior of Pirate's Cove
house, too, was constructed of coquina, except for
the original shelter, a cavelike room in the dune back
of what was now the kitchen. It had been Juan
Gómez's first home at the cove.

Gómez had filed title to the land in 1845, when
Florida became a state. His estranged wife, Elizabeth, had deeded it to her grandson, Joseph. It was
Joseph Webster who planted the orange groves. But
because Joseph was embarrassed to have had a pirate
ancestor and because he rarely spoke of Gómez, facts
and fiction about the infamous band and the legendary treasure had been all but lost until Edmund began
to collect and study them.

Edmund had found a few silver coins in the sand
with a metal detector, and he had found the gold
chain that he had given Shannon on her tenth birthday. Shannon herself had discovered the gold barrette near the entrance to the shallow cavern in
her secret valley. Sure that these were carelessly
dropped bits of the fabled treasure, Edmund had
extended his search to the reefs that once had
been part of the coastline. This had cost him his
life.

Shannon scrambled over the stones and dropped
down to a rock shelf. The bowl-shaped valley was
much the same as she had left it, a sanctuary hidden
away from the rest of the world. Bent wind-
fashioned palms stood like sentinels along the south
and west, providing a rim of cool shade. On the east
lip that overlooked the Atlantic, one could bask in

the sun and listen to the voices of the sea and the gulls and the wind.

Clad in white swim trunks, Paul lay on a towel in the sun. His back and legs were deeply tanned, his head pillowed on his arms. He was asleep. Shannon came close and quietly knelt beside him. The broad shoulders and tapering ribs moved rhythmically with his even breathing. Her eyes followed the outline of his body to the narrow waist and firm hips and down the muscular thighs and legs with their dusting of wiry black hairs. Always—and increasingly—aware of his magnetism, she felt a strong desire to touch him.

Paul stirred. Had he, too, sensed the electric current between them? Lazily he turned onto his back, opening his eyes to rest on her face. His velvet-brown gaze was warm with surprise and pleasure.

He sat up slowly, and his eyes became somber as he followed Shannon's glance to the scar across his throat and the vague purple blotches that spread down to hide in his mass of curly chest hairs. "Do they repulse you?" He reached for the white scarf lying beyond Shannon, but she picked it up and held it away from him. "Ugly things, scars."

She twisted the square of silk. "They'll heal. They don't trouble me, Paul. You don't need to hide them on my account."

He swung his gaze away from her. "Okay. You may be big enough to overlook appearances. But what if I never sing again professionally?"

"You *are* singing. You *will* be as good as ever. Why, every day your range gets better, Paul."

"But not my vocal strength," he insisted moodily. "The cords are damaged. By this time we both know it."

"You'll heal; I know you will!" She couldn't let him doubt it. "So what if it takes more time than you thought? We'll work together and be patient, and it will happen. You'll see!"

The lines of Paul's mouth softened and he took Shannon's hand. "You really believe that, don't you?"

"I believe in you." This time it was Shannon who looked away. She didn't want him to see the strange blind adoration that he was able to summon from her. It had been born ten years ago; and although in one tragic harsh night of fog and death it had almost been blotted out, the feeling was still there, ready to be nourished into a maturity she didn't want and wouldn't allow.

What had become of her doubts? Her fears? Had they all been imagined and groundless? She needed them now to wear as a cloak, a protection against vulnerability.

"You know," Paul mused, "many singers make the mistake of singing longer than they should. We should stop at the height of our abilities. What's left for me? Ten years? Fifteen at most? Less if the damage to my voice is serious." He sighed. "It's not unthinkable that I may quit the stage pretty soon." At Shannon's look of astonishment, he went on with a crooked smile. "I have other plans, equally challenging and maybe better for me."

"What are you saying?" It was a shocked whisper.

"What I'd really like to do is establish a school here on the island where musicians of all kinds can train."

He waited for Shannon's reaction. Finally she managed, "Dad's dream." Was everything of Edmund's to be taken up by Paul? Even his dream? Edmund had predicted that it would be so. The old doubts crept back into Shannon's heart.

"Yes," Paul admitted with a frown, "Edmund was counting on the treasure to finance that dream." He gave Shannon's hand a little shake. "What do you think? Does the treasure really exist?"

Shannon drew her hand away and hugged her knees, feeling chilled. "Is that why you bought Pirate's Cove—just for the treasure?"

Paul studied Shannon's pinched face. "Didn't Bonita tell you anything?"

Nothing, Shannon answered silently. Talking about Paul Cypress had been too painful, and Shannon hadn't asked about him. She had believed that all her warm affection had turned to fear and suspicion and that there was no turning back. Now she wasn't sure.... Perhaps the old feelings weren't dead, but only sleeping, waiting to be awakened and reassured.... She shook her head against her knees. Such thoughts were best sorted out alone, away from the magnetism of Paul's brown eyes and husky voice.

"I told you that I fell in love with the cove. Isn't that reason enough?" His voice was harsh, and when she raised her head, she saw that his eyes were cold, remote. "As for the treasure, Gómez probably moved it to Panther Key in the gulf, where he spent his last years. Edmund needed something to absorb his energies when his voice began to fail. Hunting for treasure was good therapy."

"What are you talking about? Dad was only a few years older than you when he died, and his voice was still excellent. He had a lifetime of singing ahead of him!"

"You must admit that you're somewhat biased."

"Oh!" She could feel the flush and the anger rising together, but she didn't care. "You're obsessed with the notion that *your* voice is done for! And you can't accept that anyone else—especially dad—could have a career years longer! Damn it, Paul, I have tapes of dad's voice. I've always thought you sound a lot like him. That's why I bought all your records and tapes—" She stopped.

Paul's crooked smile teased her. "So you have my collection?"

"We're talking about dad's voice," she snapped. "You implied that his voice was failing. You're dead wrong."

"And if I'm right, would you have cared less for him?" The smile gone, he turned away. "A performer is almost worshiped for his talent. When that's gone, there's nothing left."

She hesitated. Sometimes that was true. Not always. "I loved my father so much. It wouldn't have mattered." Remembered sadness washed away the anger.

"Maybe Edmund was luckier than most of us." Paul got to his feet and held out a hand to help Shannon. "He had his little treasure right there with him all the time."

Standing so close to him, Shannon sensed the irony in his tone. It was like a barrier between them. She again felt the intense desire to reach across it, to touch and comfort, to brush aside the cynicism.

With her hand still in his clasp, Paul slowly drew her closer; his body was a magnet that she hadn't the will to resist. She read in his eyes a desire, a question that made her tremble, and she knew that the imagined barrier between them had been breached.

When Paul lowered his head, Shannon closed her eyes, waiting. Her lips parted under the brush of his kiss, and her free hand found his waist. He pulled her close against his chest, and she felt the tautness in his long legs measured against her own and in the muscular arms that bound her to him. One hand, trapped against his chest, felt the thud of his quickened heartbeat.

When she felt the stir and rise of his passion, Shannon gasped against Paul's mouth. Involuntarily her hands pushed against him. But Paul's tongue had found its opening, and his arms were immovable bonds. With a little moan of longing, Shannon pressed closer and tipped her head back to allow the invasive delight of Paul's mouth.

The ten years of nagging questions and doubts dropped away; all the old adoration and trust surfaced, mature now and demanding.

Paul made a rasping sound as he lifted his mouth and pressed Shannon's head against his chest. She reached up to rest her fingertips against his cheekbone, her palm cupping the rough texture of his jaw. She had been surprised at the happiness she found in working with Paul; but she was astonished at the surge of delirious passion that swept her in response to Paul's demanding caress. She had never known such depth of emotion was hidden inside her.

"Shannon?" The question that had lurked in his eyes was spoken now, demanding an answer. She lifted her face as she slid her hand to the back of Paul's head, pressing it down to meet her lips once more. She was hungry for him, famished, as though her whole life had been starved for the taste of him.

His hands moved over her back and sides, molding her, pressing her willing body against him. Her own long fingers explored the skin across Paul's straining shoulders and the bones of his spine and ribs, urging him closer.

He reached for her breast, and she knew that even through the cloth of the halter, he could feel the turgid, aroused nipple. He knew his answer, but she had to say it. "Yes! Yes!"

For a moment they stood motionless, seeming to drink in the intensity of what was happening to them.

Tawny amber eyes and midnight black eyes burned into each other, only a whisper apart. The tiny hidden valley was casting its spell; it was a miniature world where nothing outside mattered, a sanctuary for impossible dreams.

Shannon felt Paul's body stiffen, and she saw his gaze shift beyond her. She knew that they were no longer alone. There was an intruder in her valley.

The voice was a throaty contralto. "A new one, isn't she, Paul?"

A tall, slender but curvaceous woman stood silhouetted against the sky between the rocks that bordered the path from the beach. A snug black satin sheath accentuated her tiny waist and full bosom. She drew closer, sensuous scarlet lips parted and blue eyes wide with studied surprise. The pale gold of her hair was swept sleekly back into a chignon. Merlene Madden.

Paul kept his arm around Shannon. "I thought you were to arrive Sunday night."

"Yes," she said, "I guess you did."

"Shannon, this is Jason's mother, Merlene Madden." The increased huskiness in his voice told of his agitation. "Merlene, Shannon is my pianist for the summer."

Shannon struggled to calm her still-rapid breathing as she acknowledged Merlene's nod.

"We'll go back to the house," Paul said. "I'm sure you're anxious to get Jason settled and be on your way."

Merlene's laugh was musical. "Oh, no, darling. I

read about your surgery in *Music World*, so I gave up my summer role and my apartment at once. You never were any good at taking care of yourself. We're still friends, aren't we? Why shouldn't a good friend come and help?'' Her cool blue gaze slid suggestively over Shannon. ''In fact, I may stay all summer.''

Paul's annoyance exploded into the quiet valley. ''You've brought Jason. There's no reason for you to stay.''

''Your health, darling. Your recovery.''

''As you can see, I'm just fine. I don't need you, Merlene.''

''Well, you won't deny me a little time to be here with Jason, will you?'' she pleaded. ''He's been in school all year, and I haven't been able to see him very much. I'm sure he'd like us all to be together just for a little while.'' Shannon wondered how much of the pathos was sincere, how much merely an act.

Paul's arm had relaxed, and she stepped away from him, ashamed of her instinctive dislike of Paul's ex-wife. She had no right to judge her.

''If you're staying,'' Paul said tersely, ''I'll phone for a room at the Island Inn.''

''No vacancy,'' Merlene replied. ''I checked on the way in. Paul, surely you'll soon know whether we have the *Man of La Mancha* contract. Couldn't I stay a few days until we get the news?'' When he didn't answer, she hurried on, ''I did give up my work and my apartment—''

"I didn't ask you to." It was almost the same retort he had hurled at Shannon when she appeared at the cove.

"Please, Paul, just a few days, till we hear something. And to spend with Jason," she added.

Paul growled, "Come on then," and strode toward the confusion of rocks that banked the orange grove. Merlene held out her hand appealingly, but he ignored it.

She turned back to take the easier beach route, picking her way carefully, her ankles turning with the thin spikes of her pumps. "It will be easier if you take off your shoes," Shannon offered.

"I don't need your advice," Merlene snapped. "I know this place better than you ever will."

Shannon caught her lip between her teeth. Paul hadn't mentioned her last name, and Merlene hadn't recognized her. Of course not; Shannon looked nothing like the child who had lived here ten years ago. For that matter, it was hard to recognize Merlene Madden as the Marie Cypress she had been. Hair color and clothes did make a difference. "Right," she said cheerfully. "See you later then." And she swung past the older woman without another glance.

As Shannon neared the house, she saw the boy, Jason, come slowly from the terrace to meet his father. Paul put his arm around him, and together they went inside.

A sleek silver Jaguar stood in the driveway. Leo was staggering away from it with a variety of luggage. Shannon ran forward to help. "Aw, I can manage, Shanny," he protested, but he sighed tiredly. "Guess I'm not as young as I used to be. That woman never did travel light."

Shannon followed Leo upstairs to the northwest guest room, a large bedroom done in yellow, orange and brown. It opened onto the sun deck over the garage. An opposite door led into a yellow-and-white bathroom.

"Thelma said to chuck Miss Merlene's things in here and to put the laddie in the little room near yours," Leo said.

"I don't think Merlene will be staying long," Shannon murmured.

The old man wagged his grizzled head. "With all this stuff, I'd bet on at least a month. An' she usually gets her way."

Merlene's and Paul's voices preceded them, Merlene's sultry and coaxing, Paul's muttered. "We do have to talk, Paul. And I won't be in your way. We can start practicing our roles for *La Mancha*, and then when we hear that it's all set—"

"I'm not ready for that kind of rehearsing, and nothing is definite yet."

"I know, but. . . ."

Leo motioned to Shannon, and they escaped onto the balcony. Leo went on, but Shannon paused beside the boy sitting on the top iron step, his chin cupped in his hand. "Hi. You must be Jason."

"'Course." He didn't look up.

"I'm Shannon. I'm your dad's pianist and secretary this summer." No answer. "If you'd like to come into my room, I'll show you some pictures of Pirate's Cove when I lived here as a child."

He squinted at her. "You lived here?"

She nodded. "I wasn't much older than you are when your dad bought the cove from my mother."

"How come? Did your mom and dad split up, too?"

At least she had his interest. "My father was killed in a boating accident, and we couldn't afford to keep up this big place. We moved to Chicago so my mother could find work."

"Did you hate to move?" he asked with a trace of sympathy.

"Sure did," she murmured, remembering. He went with her to look at her snapshots, and when he heard Leo thud his suitcase down in the adjoining room, he looked up in surprise.

Shannon nodded. "You'll be in there. Want to take a look?"

Jason loped ahead of her. Hands in pockets, he stood in the middle of the blue shag carpet, a small figure trying to find a place for himself. He looked around slowly, his gaze touching the wide bed with the tufted blue cover, the sheer blue curtain at the double window that framed the view of the rocky hillside, the floor-to-ceiling shelves with the books and shells and sea treasures on them and above them the picture of the *Bonnyshan*, the ketch that Edmund Webster had loved and that had taken him to his death.

"It'll do," he decided. "I always used to have the yellow room across from mom's and dad's suite." The one Merlene now had, of course. "Do I have to share the bathroom with you?"

"I'm afraid so."

"Gee," he said disgustedly.

Shannon laughed. "We'll work it out."

Jason bounced on the edge of the bed. "What time's dinner?"

"Dinner? Oh, gosh! I forgot. Jason, please excuse me for a few minutes. I have to speak to your father." She hadn't told Paul about the party! With all the confusion of Merlene's sudden arrival, he might want Shannon to help out tonight, in which case she'd have to talk to Jim right away.

As she stepped into the hall she almost bumped into Paul.

"I've been looking for you," he said frowning. "Merlene and I have some things to straighten out. I thought perhaps you'd take Jason into town for an hour or two after dinner."

Shannon drew in her breath. She did owe Paul some work time today; and if there was to be a scene, it would be better for Jason to be away from the cove.

"What's the matter?" Paul asked sharply. "Did you have other plans?"

Jason had sidled close to listen, and Paul absently tousled his son's hair. "Well, yes, I did," Shannon admitted.

"Please change them."

Shannon glanced at Jason, a small replica of his father. "All right," she said hesitantly. "I meant to talk with you earlier, but...."

"But you didn't." For a second his eyes gleamed with the shared knowledge of why her plans had been swept away. He drew out his wallet. "Jason might like a movie."

Shannon quickly pushed the money away. "Let it be my treat tonight."

Paul studied her for a long moment before he said brusquely, "If you wish."

She watched Jason's face relax into a smile of anticipation. What a handsome boy he was, with even white teeth in a deeply tanned face and dark eyes twinkling below his mop of straight black hair. All the sullen moodiness that had clung to him earlier was gone.

"I'd better get ready for dinner," Shannon said, going through the bathroom to her own room. If she hurried, she'd just have time to run down to Jim's cabin to tell him she couldn't keep their date. Jim would probably be annoyed, but it couldn't be helped.

She slipped out to the balcony and ran down the stairs and across the dune. Breathlessly she tapped on Jim's door. There was no answer. "Not home from work," she muttered. "Darn! Why didn't I bring paper and pencil?" She tried the door and found it unlocked.

She found a pencil stub and a scrap of paper and left an apologetic note propped against the oil lamp Then she ran back to the house.

After a quick shower, Shannon chose a pale blue gown. The shirred scoop neckline made a low oval frame for a dainty sapphire pendant and chain. Matching earrings and bracelet made the set that had belonged to her grandmother. A smudge of blue on the eyelids, a touch of pink on cheekbones and mouth, a whisper of orange blossom on the wrists, and she was ready. Almost. Impatiently she buckled the blue ankle straps of her shoes.

She knocked on Jason's door, pushing it open. "Ready?"

He sat in the middle of the big bed, a game of solitaire spread in front of him. He looked clean and sturdy in a white shirt and blue pants, his hair damply brushed off his forehead. Sweeping the cards into an uneven stack, he slid off the bed. "Yup. Let's go."

Merlene was alone in the dining room. Her clinging strapless gown was exactly the shade of champagne as her smoothly coiffed hair. A clasp of diamonds gathered the bodice so that the shadowed cleavage was revealed. There were diamonds at her earlobes, and on her index finger she wore a square-cut sapphire. "I was beginning to think I was to dine alone," she said petulantly. "What can be keeping Paul?"

"Nothing," Paul said as he entered from the kitchen. "I've asked Thelma to begin serving."

When Thelma set Shannon's salad on her place, she said in a low tone, "Jimmy said to tell you nine o'clock, honey. He called while you were away."

"Who's Jimmy?" Jason wanted to know.

"Who cares?" Merlene snapped. "Really, Paul, your employees ought to have their private conversations some time other than the family dinner hour."

Paul ignored her, his dark gaze fastened on Shannon. Now he knew that her evening plans had involved Jim. She wished she knew what he was thinking.

The roast beef was rare and moist in its own juices, and Thelma's special wheat rolls were hot and tender. Jason ate quietly but enthusiastically, while Merlene addressed all her remarks and charm to Paul. She was a very beautiful woman, Shannon thought. Talented and sophisticated, too. Every movement was studied and graceful, her head tilted at just the angle to make the most of her classic profile. Was it possible that she was still in love with Paul, that she wanted him back? And Paul. . . what was he thinking?

It was Paul who suggested that he and Merlene take their coffee into the den. "Meanwhile you and Jason can make your plans for the evening," he said curtly to Shannon.

Jason scooped up the last of his chocolate-cake crumbs. As he leaned back with a satisfied sigh, Thelma came in from the kitchen. "Jimmy's here," she announced.

"Who's Jimmy?" Jason demanded for the second time.

"I'll introduce you," Shannon promised, leading the way to the kitchen.

Jim lounged against the outer door, scowling. "How come you have to work this late?" he wanted to know. "You ought to stand up to the man. He has no right to—"

"Jim, please!" Shannon stopped him with a glance at the boy beside her. "This is Paul's son, Jason. He and his mother arrived late this afternoon."

"I see." Jim's lips were pressed together disapprovingly. "Gran, couldn't you stay with the boy? My friends are anxious to meet Shannon tonight."

"Why, sure," Thelma agreed. "I got the dishes to do, but Leo can play you a game of checkers, Jason. Would you like that?"

"No!" His eyes were stormy. "Go on and do what you were gonna do before I came. I don't need a baby-sitter!"

"Jason—"

"Go on! I don't need you. I don't need anyone!" He whirled away from them, and they heard him thunder up the stairs.

Shannon started after him, but Jim caught her arm. "Tell me about it," he said quietly. "You owe me that."

Shannon had to agree. Briefly she explained the events of the afternoon. "Paul thought they weren't coming till Sunday."

Thelma added, "Jason's a good boy, but he's had a bad time of it. I didn't know Mr. Paul wanted him busy tonight or I'd've offered to take care of the lad right off."

"That's okay, Gran. Shannon, we'll talk to Jason together," Jim said. "I know what it's like to feel in the way. Bring him down here, will you?"

Relieved, Shannon hurried upstairs. She tapped on the door, but there was only silence. "Jason?" She went in and found the room empty. The window was wide open.

CHAPTER FIVE

THEY FOUND JASON at the base of the dune, near the entrance to the old storage cave. A huddled bundle of anger and resentment, he refused to talk at first. Finally Jim lowered himself to the ground beside the boy. "Well," he drawled, "you've got a choice. Shanny and me, we're going to have a beach party tonight, and we'd like you to join us. Or you can stay with Thelma and Leo. Maybe you'd rather do that, eh?"

"You don't want me tagging along," Jason pouted.

"Sure we do. I've got soda pop in my cooler, and I can hike over to the store by the campground for some hot dogs and potato chips while you change into your swim stuff."

"You were going to some other party," he accused. "You were sore because Shannon had to stay with me."

"I didn't have to, Jason," Shannon pointed out. "I could have told your father that I had other plans and that I wanted to keep them. I was sorry that I couldn't let Jim know earlier, but you can see that he understands now."

Jason turned this over in his mind. "Look," Jim said, "it's your first night at the cove, and that makes it special. If you want me to get lost so you and Shanny can go to the movies, okay. But I think the three of us could have a really good time. We could swim and roast hot dogs on my beach. And Shanny, remember those old pirate songs your dad taught us? We could teach Jason—"

"Jim! Your grandparents and my mother were shocked at those chanteys! We can't teach them to Jason!"

Jason stopped sniffling. "What's wrong with them?"

"They're wicked," Jim said solemnly. "I guess you wouldn't like them at all."

"I might."

Jim took that as acceptance. "I'll tell Gramps and Gran we're going to my cabin. I'll meet you two there in half an hour."

"Take my car," Shannon called after him. "Leo has a spare key."

Jason went with Shannon quietly. They took the outside stairs and went inside through Shannon's French doors. "You gonna tell dad I ran away?"

"No," Shannon said. "You didn't go far, and I don't believe you intended to be gone long."

"Maybe I did." He stood at the door to the connecting bathroom, twisting the knob back and forth.

"You'd have missed all the fun. Now get into your trunks, Jason. And take a T-shirt for when it gets cool. Knock when you're ready."

Shannon got into her white bikini and tied on a snug white terry robe. She found two beach towels in the linen closet. Jason knocked and came in carefully carrying a plate with three large slices of fudge cake, Thelma's contribution to the picnic.

The moon had risen round and yellow, lighting the narrow twist of a path and turning the sand to pale gold. They walked down to Jim's cabin hand in hand across the moonlit sand. After putting the cake on Jim's table, Shannon and Jason hunted for driftwood and downed branches at the base of the dune. By the time Jim joined them, they had a generous pile beside his firepit.

Shannon stepped out of her terry robe and made a dash for the water. "Last one in has to walk the plank!" It was a challenge she and Jim had used years ago. In moments all three were splashing one another, the droplets and spray turning to amethyst crystals in the moonlight. Jason proved to be a good swimmer. For the first time that day, he looked happy.

They played tag and rode the breakers and let the incoming tide nudge them toward the shore. Eventually they splashed onto the beach. Jason slyly pulled off Shannon's yarn tieback, and her long hair hung straight and black around her face. Jason ran ahead to find his shirt, for the sea wind proved to be chilly on wet skin.

Jim stopped Shannon at the water's edge and gently brushed her hair back of her ears. "Lord, you're beautiful, honey," he said wistfully.

"Like a drowned rat!" she bantered.

"No. Like a dream turned to flesh and blood." He let his hand caress the side of her face as his eyes slid over her glistening body. "You really turn me on, Shanny."

"Jason's waiting for those hot dogs you promised," she said. "And this flesh and blood is getting cold."

He gave a little laugh that ended in a sigh. "Okay, I can wait." He took her hand and together they ran to the cabin.

Inside, Jason was thrumming the strings of Jim's guitar. "You play, Jim?"

"Yep. How else could I keep Shannon on pitch when we sing those old sea chanteys?"

"Could you teach me?"

"Sure," Jim said. "I'll show you a couple of chords tonight after we've eaten. I don't go to work till noon most days, so you can come down mornings and practice if you like."

"Really? Dad says I've got a good voice."

"We'll find out after a while. For now, you and Shannon can open up the mustard and ketchup jars and the pop bottles. I'll start the fire."

The moon was high and small in the velvet dome of the sky when they settled down on Jim's old beach blanket with the last of the potato chips. A million stars twinkled like polished gemstones; Shannon recalled that she and Jim used to imagine the stars were the reflections of Juan Gómez's treasure.

"We were always hunting for that lost loot,

weren't we, Shanny? Why, we dug up half the beach and part of the orchard, too."

"What treasure?" Jason asked curiously.

Jim strummed a minor chord. "Settle back, boy. Shanny's about to tell you a tale."

Shannon laughed. "You were as greedy for the treasure as I was, Jim."

"What treasure?" Jason repeated.

"Well, my great-great-great-grandfather, Juan Gómez, a Portuguese sailor, was about twenty when the ship he was on was captured, looted and burned by the famous pirate, José Gaspar, or Gasparilla, as he was called, because he was a small man. Gasparilla admired Juan for his courage and daring, so he spared his life, and Juan became a member of the pirate band. I don't know how Juan felt about this, but he was smart enough to know he had no choice."

"I wish there were pirates now," Jason said. "I'd join up."

With a loud twang from his guitar, Jim said, "This is a lad after me own heart."

"Anyway," Shannon went on, "Juan Gómez was Gasparilla's right-hand man for many years. The pirate camp was on a couple of islands off the west coast of Florida. When Juan was in his forties, he fell in love with one of the young girls the band had captured, and I think Elizabeth loved him, too. They had a child, but that was after they were separated."

Jason sighed. "Them, too, huh?"

"Well, they didn't want to be separated. You see, the days of piracy were about over. American warships were chasing and sinking the pirate galleons one after another and either taking the sea robbers to prison or killing them.

"Gasparilla and his men were almost ready to leave their hideaway to settle in scattered places where they were unknown. The flagship was loaded with treasure, and most of the men and all of their women were aboard. Only Juan and a couple of helpers had stayed ashore to finish the cleanup; they had a yawl, loaded with the last of the chests, concealed in an inlet and waiting to take them out to the galleon.

"Suddenly Gasparilla—he was on the pirate ship, waiting for the last of his men and treasure—saw what he thought was a rich-looking merchant ship, and he couldn't resist having one last triumph. Juan saw his captain angle toward the oncoming ship, and he remarked to his companions that Gasparilla's galleon was likely to sink under the weight of any more treasure and prisoners.

"Then Juan was horrified to see the 'merchant ship' drop its camouflage and reveal that it was a U.S. warship. Gasparilla's galleon took a cannon broadside and began to sink. With a roar of anger that echoed to the island, Gasparilla wound the anchor chain around himself and threw it—and himself—overboard.

"Heartbroken because his Elizabeth was aboard the doomed pirate vessel, Juan raced toward the hidden yawl, hoping to save her; but he was strong-armed to helpless silence by his two companions,

who knew they were too far away to help. Revealing
their presence could mean death for themselves.

"Juan saw a longboat lowered from the warship,
but he didn't know whether Elizabeth was among
those saved when the pirate ship went down. He
spent most of the rest of his life looking for Elizabeth."

Jason gaped at the exciting story. "How do you
know all that? And what about the treasure?"

"Some things are on record," Shannon explained.
"We know that Juan escaped because later he fought
in the Cuban revolution. He was on the losing side
and had to flee in a small boat. He was almost dead
of thirst and sunstroke when a ship picked him up
and brought him here to St. Augustine."

"Did he have any of the treasure with him?"

"Not then. He must have hidden it earlier. Elizabeth kept a journal, and she mentioned St. Augustine
as the place she and Juan planned to make their
home. But then they were separated, and after a time
she must have thought he was either in prison or
dead. She moved to England. I don't think she ever
saw Juan's treasure. Juan did live here for a while.
He built a little room in front of the cave, and that
was his house."

"Maybe the government confiscated the treasure," Jim guessed.

"Dad didn't think so," Shannon said. "There
were a couple of traders, Walter Collier and his son,
Bill, friends of Juan's the last years of his life. Juan
told them about casks of doubloons and pieces of

eight, jewels, gold bars and church ornaments hidden in several places. Captain Collier wrote about Juan Gómez, saying he was in good health, even though he was very old, and that he apparently had plenty of money until almost the end of his life.

"Collier said Juan was tall, dark, well built, heavily bearded, a man who shinnied up coconut trees to get the fruit he credited with keeping him in excellent condition. Gómez died in 1900 at the age of one hundred twenty-two."

"Aw, you're kidding!" Jason scoffed.

"Not only that, but after one of his mysterious disappearances from Panther Key, he brought back a wife. He was one hundred six, and the lady was seventy-eight. Collier said she was well educated and well preserved, though she never talked about her background. They lived happily together fourteen years. Her name was Beta."

"And nobody ever found the treasure?" Jason persisted.

Shannon shook her head. "Your dad and mine hunted for it, but except for a few coins and my chain and barrette, they found nothing. I think that if there really is a treasure, it has to be either here or on Panther Key."

"Dad never told me about all this," Jason said doubtfully.

"He probably doesn't think there is a treasure," Jim guessed.

Shannon suddenly shivered and pulled her short robe closer around herself. It might be that Paul just never wanted to talk about the treasure or the tragedy that put an end to all their searching.

"We had a theory, Shanny, remember?" Jim went on. "We thought that when Juan—and later Beta, too—sailed off on those mysterious trips, they came back here to get some of the treasure to trade for supplies."

"But," Shannon added, "Collier said that toward the end of their lives they were poor. So we thought maybe she was sick and Juan wouldn't leave her all by herself on Panther Key, and that's why they ran out of supplies and out of the means to get any more. In which case there could be some treasure still hidden here."

"That's what we wanted to believe anyway," Jim said with a grin. "The truth may be that he really did use it all up."

"Or that it never was hidden here," she said.

"Or that there never was any," Jim finished.

"Aw," Jason said, "I bet it's still around. I'm going to read all that stuff in my room about it, and I bet I find it, too. You just wait and see."

Jim strummed a triumphant chord. "That's the spirit! Treasure hunting is fun. I've got two coins I found on Padre Island off the Texas coast. Always carry them for luck. When we go up to the cabin, I'll show you, Jason. What do you say, Shanny—shall we go back to our old hobby and help the boy find the Gómez treasure?"

She hesitated a fraction of a second. "All right." Why not? It would keep Jason interested and happy.

Ten years was time enough to forget the terrible things that could happen if a treasure hunter were not careful, if he became so obsessed with the search that he thought of nothing else, not even his own safety. A frown creased Shannon's forehead, and the voices of the other two faded. *Dad was an excellent swimmer. And Paul was there to help him. But the two men had quarreled. Oh, why can't I remember more about that night?*

"Shanny?" Jim turned her chin with his fingertip. "Where'd you go, honey?"

"Out to the reef," she nodded toward the water, "but I'm glad to be back."

Jim drew his fingers lightly across her cheek and lips in a gesture of understanding. The *Bonnyshan* had been wrecked on that reef. "Time for a wicked sea chantey," he said softly, plucking the strings of the Goya and launching into a song.

"As I was a-walkin' down Paradise Street
  Weigh! Hey! Blow the man down!
  A pretty young damsel I chanced for to meet,
  Give me some time to blow the man down!

  Says she to me, 'Mister, will you stand a treat?'
  Weigh! Hey! Blow the man down!
  'Delighted,' says I, 'for a charmer so sweet.'
  Give me some time to blow the man down."

"That's not wicked," Jason complained. "Sing a bad one."

"Wait, there's more," Jim said mischievously. "You see, this girl was working Paradise Street, and—"

"Jim!" Shannon warned sharply.

"Oh," Jason drawled, looking intrigued, "a hooker, huh?"

IT WAS AFTER ELEVEN when Shannon tucked a tired but contented Jason into bed.

"I had a good time, Shanny," he said sleepily, and she smiled at his use of Jim's nickname for her.

"Me, too."

"You aren't mad that you didn't get to go to that party?"

"I never was. Neither is Jim."

With a yawn he turned over, and Shannon turned off the light.

After showering away the sea salt, she put on a short sheer beige nightie and matching peignoir and sat down to do her nails. She had some thinking to do. Her thoughts had been in turmoil, but there had been no time to sort them out since the arrival of Merlene and Jason.

She and Paul had been so close, trembling together at the very edge of the well of passion, ready to drink to fulfillment. Had they averted disaster? Or joy?

Shannon groaned, remembering the ache of wanting Paul. She had felt nothing like it for any other man, not even for Jack, whom she had thought she cared for a great deal. But Paul had said he had no intention of complicating his life with involvement with any woman. And Shannon knew herself well enough that when she gave herself to a man, it would be because she loved him. Because she was totally committed to him.

But I don't love Paul, she told herself vehemently. *I can't.* Yes, she had felt an overwhelming desire for the complex, virile, wonderful man who was Paul Cypress. She had never realized that there were powerful passions within herself lying dormant. She had always thought of herself as cool, reasonable, controlled. What had happened—or almost happened—in her valley made a mockery of those assumptions.

She capped the little bottle of coral polish and spread her fingers on her bare knees to dry. Aroused once, she and Paul could be aroused again. *Would* be, for she had not given Paul any reason to think she would resist. She'd have to make him understand that she was not easy, that she would not be just another one of his conquests.

She closed her eyes and relived Paul's kiss, the closeness of his arms, her own awakening. Oh, it would be easy to fall in love with him. Was it possible, even remotely, that Paul could learn to care for her? That somehow she could break through the hard shell of the man and get through to the tender vulnerable core? She wondered what hurtful blows life had dealt him to make him build up that shell of self-protection. What would it take to break through?

She shook herself and got up to stand at the window. Hugging the flimsy peignoir around her, she stared down at the phosphorescent surf licking the shore. The sea tides were faithful, predictable; not so the tides of human passion. What was the use of indulging in an impossible dream? She knew that she wasn't anything like the sophisticated kind of women Paul's name was often linked with. She had seen their pictures, all sought after in their own right by the press. And Merlene, the woman he must have loved once. Maybe he still did. Maybe the divorce wasn't his idea at all. Maybe that was why he hadn't objected to her staying at the cove for a while.

Will I become like Merlene someday, she wondered. Would success harden her, make her cherish her wealth and independence more than love? More than a husband and maybe children? *No, I won't let that happen.*

Her own home had been happy, full of love. Although Shannon wanted a career as a concert pianist, she didn't see that as interfering with her desire to have a home and family, too. Once her career was established, she would limit her appearances; and home base would be a lovely place... like Pirate's Cove.

But Paul would not be the man in her life. He didn't want any sort of commitment; he had been honest in saying so. Surely not with Shannon, naive and unproven as she was.

And she could never share him. She knew that when she gave herself to a man with love, she would do so faithfully and completely. If he failed to return that love in the same manner, her heart would break.

Even now, thinking of Paul holding someone else.... *No,* she protested.

At a small sound behind her, she turned. "Jason?"

Paul stood in the bathroom door. He pulled it shut quietly. "I looked in on Jason. Looks as if he's been asleep a long time." He kept his husky voice low. Only the small dresser light was on, and she couldn't see his face very clearly. "You just came in?" he asked, the light slanting across his eyes that were glinting in a way Shannon had not seen before.

"It's pretty late," she began, conscious that he was eyeing her scantily clad figure. "I was just going to bed."

He came closer, and Shannon caught her breath. "I thought we could finish what we started earlier on the beach. Come here, Shannon."

"No, Paul." She moved back a step, her heart beginning to beat uncontrollably.

"What do you mean?" The huskiness became rasping. His eyes held hers, and Shannon felt herself responding to the powerful promise of passion she saw there. His voice was intense when he continued. "Change your mind? May I ask why?"

"Please, Paul," Shannon said breathlessly. "You shouldn't be here. Jason might wake up and—"

"Then you'd better be quiet." He reached for her. Shannon's dodge was useless as Paul's strong fingers gripped her bare shoulders. She could smell that he had been drinking.

He gathered her in his arms as a deep moan

escaped him. Shannon felt her body molding to his, despite her frantic efforts to pull away.

"I want you, Shannon," Paul said in a voice heavy with emotion. "And you did want me." He buried his face in her neck and murmured, "Oh, my lovely Shannon...what happened?"

She put her trembling hands against his chest to push him away, though her heart was hammering in answer to the passion that threatened to overwhelm them both, and her legs felt as if they could no longer support the weight of her slight frame. "Nothing happened," Shannon said, fighting for control. "You're my employer, Paul. We mustn't...." Her voice trailed off, and tears of confusion began to well into her eyes.

Paul pulled her even closer, the heat of his body fanning new fires of passion within Shannon. "I'm a man first. And you're a woman. Don't play childish games with me, Shannon." His arms banded her against him.

Shannon struggled, but she knew that Paul would not let her go. And her wish to turn away from this raging tide was lessening. Together they were drowning...drowning in the churning waters of desire.

"You were honest this afternoon, Shannon, and so was I. We wanted each other. You wanted me, I know you did." He lowered his head, and Shannon gasped as his breath caressed and inflamed her ear. His tongue flicked over the lobe, causing Shannon to moan with a pleasure she had never known. "I'll make you want me again. Now."

He crushed her lips with his mouth, forcing them open to admit his thrusting tongue. Her struggles were no more effective than a bird's against its cage bars. Her mind began to reel, plunging her into a world of spinning lights. She could taste the liquor that erased the sweetness of his earlier kisses, and she choked back a sob. *Oh, Paul,* she thought, *oh, my darling! I want you so much. But please, not like this...never like this!* Shannon renewed her struggles urging Paul to release her, but this only seemed to inflame him more as he traced a path across her sensitive throat with his lips, searing her and stirring her to awakening delight.

One of Paul's hands kneaded her shoulder, and Shannon felt her flesh ignite under his sensuous touch. He pushed away the filmy fabric of her gown to explore and mold the fevered length of her against his passion-taut body. She felt the heat of desire explode within her. There was no escape. Not for her flesh, and not for her feelings. Gradually her struggles ceased as Shannon surrendered herself to the mists of ecstasy that enveloped and transported her to the brink of wild abandon.

Her eyes stung with tears at the betrayal of her body, for in spite of the momentum of her aching need, she knew that something was wrong. But it was too late for reason to interfere. There was only the throbbing desire. Close as she was, Shannon wanted to be closer, to be a part of Paul, to hold and absorb him and to be taken by him in a union that would carry them together to a new world of love. Her hands went up to touch the pulse in his neck as she thrust her straining breasts against him.

Sensing her body's yielding, Paul's arm relaxed its crushing hold. His hand trailed a velvet touch over her collarbone, blazing a trail to her sensitive breast. Shannon moaned as he stroked and fondled her.

Slowly he raised his head. "I want you, Shannon," he murmured, his eyes glittering. "In the valley you said yes. I'm holding you to that." As he spoke, he circled the vertex of her nipple with his fingers, and Shannon leaned closer against his primed body. Paul pressed his lips first on one temple and then the other. "Yes, little Shannon...yes?"

"Yes." But there was a sob hidden in the word, and Shannon's eyes were downcast, the lashes wet.

"Tears?" he said gently, and he bent to kiss away the salty wetness on her cheeks. He tilted her head so that she had to meet his gaze. "Why, Shannon?"

The deep and forbidding sadness that had dueled with Shannon's rising ecstasy had finally won. "Because I want you, too," she whispered, "and I don't want to want you." She buried her face against his chest...felt it rise on a sharp intake of breath as his body stiffened.

"Why not?"

Oh, Paul...Paul. Don't leave me now, Shannon pleaded silently. She touched his cheek. She had to make him understand. Her voice was gentle, tinged with regret. "Not like this, Paul. You've been drinking...."

A harsh sound came from his throat. "What did

you expect?'' he growled, pulling away. Shannon tightened her arms around his neck. She couldn't let him go now. She couldn't let it end like this. Paul looked down, the tenderness draining from his face, replaced by a grimness that chilled her. ''I'm only human, you know.'' He didn't wait for her to respond. ''It was tough with Merlene. The one thought that kept me going was that you'd be in early...that you'd be waiting for me. Instead I find that you went with Jim after all.''

Shannon shook her head, but Paul's increasing fury made him plunge on. ''What did you do with my son while you were with Jim?'' The implied accusation etched itself into her heart like acid. Biting, hurting. ''Or did you bring Jason in and then go back to the cabin?''

Shannon put her hand over Paul's mouth to stop the flow of angry words. ''It wasn't like that, Paul...believe me.''

He jerked his head away as if her touch, which had inspired him to passion only moments ago, now repulsed him. Shannon swayed, devastated, but Paul did not stop.

''Did you react to him as you do to me? More? Less? Tell me!'' He shook her roughly, unmindful of his strength, and her shiny moist hair cascaded around her face. Finally her frightened exclamations broke through, and Paul stopped abruptly. There was an electric pause.

Suddenly he pushed her backward onto the bed. ''I saw your swimsuit hanging in the bathroom. My

God! You might as well be naked!'' He began to pace, fueling his jealous rage. "I'll bet he couldn't take his hands off you, could he?'' He turned sharply, impaling Shannon with steely eyes, demanding an answer.

"Stop it! Just stop it! You don't know what you're saying!''

"Keep your voice down!'' he commanded, his own voice straining, low and tense. "I know what I'm saying, all right.'' Shannon heard his breath rattle and catch. "You drive a man crazy!'' His glance blazed over her, scorching wherever it touched.

She sat up against the pillows. She was exhausted but no longer frightened. If Paul wanted a fight, she would damn well give it to him. "I didn't dress for company,'' she hissed, angry now. "And if you saw my suit in the bathroom, you must have seen Jason's. He was with us....''

Folding his arms across his chest, Paul stopped pacing. He stood with feet apart, the muscles of his thighs bulging with suppressed tension. "There's just yours. What the hell do you want with Jim anyway? He's a drifter. A bum.''

Shannon scrambled to her knees, incensed. "And what are you?'' she snapped. "You're cruel, and you're drunk. All you want is a quick lay, and you're not going to get it! Not from me!''

Paul didn't make a sound as he lunged for her. Shannon rolled away a fraction of a second too late, for he caught the hem of her flimsy nightie, and it tore as she bounded off the other side of the bed.

Stunned and shaking, Shannon crouched there, staring first at Paul's contorted white face and then at her own nakedness. Her breath came out in a long agonized sigh as she buried her face in her hands against the spread.

For an eternity the only sounds were the distant swish and boom of the sea and their breaths slicing the air with ragged edges. Then, a whisper. "Shannon?"

She shook her head, not answering. She shut her eyes tightly, trying to control the shattering images that were forming just behind them. She needed to be alone now. She needed time to think. Her mind was in great turmoil. She hated this madman who accused her falsely and was ready to believe the worst of her. But even so, a small inner voice was pleading that she loved Paul Cypress!

It couldn't be true. Paul had wanted to use her. He had just demonstrated how little he cared for her. Surely the madness of the last moments had nothing to do with love. Paul Cypress was not capable of love. She knew that now. She wished he would leave her. His presence was too painful to bear.

She sobbed brokenly against the side of the bed, clutching the spread for comfort. She wept because she was angry, and she wept because she was sad. She wept because there was nothing left to do.

The hands that tried to raise her were gentle, but she shrank from them. "Don't touch me," she whispered savagely.

The hands were gone then, but she heard the voice,

Paul's voice, choked with what might have been tears. Could it be possible? His voice was so low that she thought he was talking to himself; maybe she was not meant to hear.

"I didn't mean it to be like this. I wanted it to be so good. What have I done?" He sounded bewildered, the pain in his voice matching the pain in Shannon's heart. But she would not look at him, for she knew that if she did, she would be lost.

None of what happened was her fault, she reasoned. But that didn't matter. What mattered was that his desire, his need for her was devoid of any real caring or concern. Shannon knew she must hold fast to that knowledge. It was the only thing that could save her from the blinding love she felt for Paul.

His voice penetrated her thoughts. He sounded far away, as if speaking to her from the edge of a dream. "Shannon... please."

"Get out," she managed, exhausted and utterly drained. "Leave me alone."

"All right." Shannon heard the weary misery in Paul's tone. "I've done a terrible thing, Shannon. Perhaps Jim is better for you after all. Perhaps he'll treat you better."

The long pause begged to be filled with words of comfort, but Shannon could not find them. They were not in her.

"Forgive me, Shannon." The plea was so low and fragile that she wasn't sure that it had even existed. Footsteps receded toward the door, and Shannon wept quietly for the impossible dream that had died.

At last, spent and shivering, she got up to find another gown. She glanced toward the bed that might have cradled and nurtured their love. The torn nightie and peignoir lay there, reminders of the passions that had been wasted in anger. She gathered them up and threw them in the wastebasket as she went into the bathroom to shower away the memory of Paul's touch.

She had to move the hanger with the two tiny parts of her bikini. Jason, however, had not hung up his trunks. They lay in a small heap behind the shower door, where he had carelessly tossed them.

Paul couldn't have seen them.

CHAPTER SIX

SHANNON ROSE EARLY to begin her packing. She had decided, during a sleepless tormented night, that under the circumstances she had no choice but to leave Pirate's Cove. She could not resume her work with Paul Cypress.

She skipped breakfast in order to avoid Paul and was not surprised that he didn't hunt her up for their usual midmorning practice. By noon she was ready to leave.

"Shanny, it's lunchtime," Jason said, poking his head into her room. "Coming?" His eyes rounded with surprise. "Where are you going?"

"I have to go back to Chicago, Jason." At his look of disappointment, she added, "I'm sorry. Truly I am."

"How come? I thought we were going to hunt for treasure."

"You can do that with Jim. Something has come up, and I...I just have to go home."

"Aww!" It was a genuine expression of regret. "Dad said we could get a metal detector. When we were having breakfast I told him all about our picnic last night, and he gave me a couple of books and a map of the island. They used to be your dad's. Wait, I'll show you.'' He darted back to his own room.

Shannon looked around the room with a sigh. It would hurt to leave this place. She had been happy here, especially living in the fantasy that Paul might learn to care for her. She wouldn't go down to lunch with Jason. She would leave Pirate's Cove—and Paul Cypress—quickly and finally; she would ask Thelma to pack a small lunch while Leo went up for her things. Then she and the Chevette would take to the highway north. She stepped onto the balcony for a last look at the ocean. She took a deep breath to capture and store up the smell of what to her would always mean home.

She heard the inner door open. ''I'm out here, Jason.''

''You can't leave me now,'' Paul said quietly.

She looked up at him briefly, stepping back. ''You never knock, do you?''

''Last night I imagined that I was expected. Today I was pretty sure you wouldn't let me in. Shannon, we need to talk. After lunch—''

''I'll be gone by then. Now if you'll excuse me, Jason has something to show me before I leave.'' She tried to pass Paul, but he placed a restraining hand on her arm.

''I sent him downstairs. I told him you and I would come down in a few minutes. Look at me, Shannon. Listen to me.''

''There's nothing to say, Paul.'' Moving past him she brushed his hand from her arm and went on downstairs. She hesitated by the dining room door. She would have liked to speak to Jason again, but maybe it was better this way. A clean break.

The Pratts were astonished at her sudden decision to return to Chicago. "Does Jimmy know?" Thelma asked. "Lordy, he's at work now, and he'll be that upset! What is it, Shanny? Nothin's wrong with your ma, is there?"

Shannon shook her head and asked Leo to go up after her bags. "Is it Mr. Paul?" he asked wisely.

"Oh, Shanny, I told you not to let him gruff you. He's been so much better with you here, honest. Maybe with Merlene underfoot again he's been soundin' cross, but—"

"It's just that the job isn't working out," Shannon interrupted. "I really want to get going, so if you'll bring down the rest of my things, Leo, I'll get started." She kissed them both. "It's been wonderful being here with you."

As Thelma prepared and packed a sandwich for Shannon, she fretted, "Whatever will Mr. Paul do for a piano player now? He was comin' along real good, too. Oh, yes, I like to listen to the two of you. Now what'll he do?"

"I don't care what he does!" Shannon's hurt made her words snap out, and as they did, Paul's big frame filled the doorway. Shannon snatched up the sandwich bag, and with a final hurried goodbye for Thelma she disappeared through the door into the garage.

To her astonishment, her Chevette was not there. She looked out on the driveway, thinking Leo might have taken it out for washing. It wasn't there.

She turned around and stormed back into the kitchen. Paul was leaning casually against the door frame, his face a mask.

"Paul, what have you done with my car?"

A corner of his mouth was pulled down before he answered. "I had Leo take it into St. Augustine for a tune-up, lube job—the works—right after breakfast. After all, you had driven it all the way from Chicago to come to work for me. It was the least I could do to get it back in top-notch condition."

"Leo didn't say anything about it to me," she fumed.

"I was just goin' to," Leo said, coming into the kitchen empty-handed. "I was so upset by your leavin' that it went clean out o' my head till I got upstairs and remembered there was nuthin' to pack your bags into."

Shannon noted that Merlene and Jason had entered the room, but she could not hide her mounting irritation. Furiously she turned on Paul. "You did this on purpose!"

"Hey, when's lunch?" Jason squeezed past his father's legs. "Isn't anybody else hungry around here?"

"Sure," Paul said, "and I think we're ready now." The quirk beside his mouth deepened as he looked at Shannon, addressing only her. "Then we'll talk."

Shannon clamped her jaws angrily. "I'm not hungry."

"Well, come and sit with us," Jason coaxed. "I brought down your dad's old pirate map for you to look at before you go, Shanny." Jason grabbed Shannon's hand, leading her eagerly into the dining room. Merlene and Paul followed.

"Shanny?" Paul questioned.

Jason giggled. "Jim calls her that."

Sensing the need to change the subject, Shannon redirected the conversation, "How long before my car will be ready?"

"Mmm, two days. Maybe three," Paul supposed.

"Two days!" Shannon sputtered, dismayed. "That long?"

Paul nodded. "I'm having it gone over thoroughly. The garage was rather busy, so they couldn't do it all in one day, of course."

"Of course!" He was making her a prisoner. Well, she would show him. She turned to Merlene, whose eyes had darted from one to the other of them curiously. "If you're going back today, I'd appreciate a ride into town. I'd like to check on my car."

Merlene took a dainty bite of her salad. "No," she said coolly, "I'm not leaving for several days. But if you are leaving, I'll be glad to take you into town."

Abruptly Paul pushed himself away from the table. "First we have some things to settle." He stood behind Shannon's chair. "Come with me, Shannon."

Stubbornly she remained seated. She reached for the platter of hot crepes. "I haven't eaten yet."

"I believe you mentioned that you weren't hungry. I require your company. Now." He moved her chair out from the table, and Shannon had no choice but to rise and follow him unless she wanted to risk a scene before Jason and Merlene. In the hallway Paul directed her, "In the den." He held the door for her. "Sit down." Leaning against the closed door, he indicated a tweed reclining chair before the fireplace.

"I'll stand, thank you. I'm sure this won't take long."

He shrugged. "As you wish." He plunged right in. "At breakfast Jason told me all about last night. My own conclusions were hasty and wrong. I apologize."

How could an apology manage to sound so utterly arrogant, she wondered. "I'm glad you can at least believe Jason," she commented. The atmosphere in the room was tense.

"I admit to having a bias against Jim. I don't approve of anything about him, and I don't see what you see in him."

"Of course you don't. They're qualities you wouldn't understand."

He ran his fingers through his thick black hair, a gesture characteristic of his agitation. "I'm trying to make some sense out of what happened last night, Shannon," he said sharply. "Please let me get on with it." Pausing, he came to stand in front of her, motioning again to the chair. Reluctantly she sat down, and Paul took the chair opposite her.

"Merlene and I had several drinks. Too many, I guess. We had a lot to thrash out. As I told you, it wasn't pleasant." *Nothing about the late evening was,* she thought. "I waited for you. I wanted to talk to you, see what you thought about my plans."

"Whatever plans you and Merlene have are no concern of mine," she heard herself say.

Paul's eyes glittered, and she saw the little muscle in his jaw tighten.

"Finally Thelma told me you had gone out with Jim after all. I understood then why you didn't take my theater money. You knew you wouldn't need it, didn't you?"

"I don't expect you to believe that I didn't know I wouldn't be needing it. After all, you seem to have trouble believing anything I say."

"Damn it, Shannon! Don't be that way!" He added desperately, "We ought to get away from here, somewhere where we can be alone, get to understand each other."

"It's too late, Paul."

He leaned forward, reaching for her hands, but she pulled them back. "All right," he said, his eyes burning into hers. "I suppose I understand how you feel now. But I don't want you to leave." She opened her mouth to speak, but he hurried on. "Don't say anything for a minute. Shannon, I need you. I need your playing and your encouragement. I've admitted that. And now my son needs you, too. It's been a year since I've seen him so enthusiastic and...alive, the way he was at breakfast this morning. He had fun last night. The old pirate stories gave him something interesting to think about and plan for. You did that for him.''

"Jim, too.''

They exchanged glances, and Paul finally acknowledged her defense of Jim with a sigh. "Jim, too. But Shannon, you have a good job here with me. Don't throw it all away now. You say you love the cove. Then why do you want to go back to Chicago and have to start looking for a job all over again?''

"You know exactly why!''

"All right! If it's an apology you want, you already have it! I won't repeat such behavior. I've never taken a woman against her will; and if you are honest you'll admit that I wouldn't have been doing so last night!'' Noting her quickly clenched fists, he hurried on. "We misunderstood each other last night, Shannon. Let's put it out of our minds and go on with our work together.''

Shannon relaxed her hands, hesitating with a final decision. She thought she had already made it, but the car was gone. And Paul had apologized, after a fashion.

He was quick to push his advantage. "I promised that I would help you with recommendations next year. I can't do that if you leave now, Shannon. I don't have to tell you my word carries some weight. I can even arrange to have my agent help you if you decide to go on tour. Or if you want to go to graduate school or study in Europe, I can arrange that, too. That should be worth something to you; think about it."

She looked at him as she weighed what he said. His knitted yellow shirt was open at the throat; he had not replaced the scarf she had taken from him in the valley. She held her eyes closed for a moment, the valley memories crowding in on her. When she opened them, his fingers were laced beneath his chin, his long legs crossed, his whole attitude one of waiting.

How persuasive he was. He knew she wanted to stay. Did he know, too, that she was afraid to stay? Afraid of her own weakness where he was concerned?

"Merlene will be staying a few days, maybe a week or so." His lips began a tentative smile. "Even she will need you. She wants to start rehearsing the Dulcinea role. She's quite confident that she'll get it."

"Oh." The rumors were true then. They would be doing *Man of La Mancha* together in the fall.

"I'll double your salary for the week she is here."

"No, don't do that. You pay me quite enough."

"You may change your mind when you try to work with her," he said dryly. Then the smile broadened. "Who knows? We may even find the treasure. You'll want to be in on that, won't you?" When she refused an answering smile, he became stern. "I believe it's illegal to quit without two weeks' notice. I may test that in court."

Shannon gasped. "You wouldn't!"

The wayward eyebrow shot up as he gave a slight nod. "Try me."

As the flush of anger spread over her face, Shannon knew that, at least for the present, she was defeated. But beneath the anger there was a faint hum of joy. She could stay at the cove for two more weeks.

Paul got up and went to the padded-leather bar to pour two glasses of sherry. "Truce?"

"Just for two weeks," she said stiffly.

"And then?"

"Then I'm going home."

"No matter what?"

"No matter what."

"So you want to punish us both for what didn't even happen," he mused softly. "What a child you are."

The angry flush waved over her again, stronger than before. Paul was laughing at her, making her feel like a prude. "One minute you call me a woman, the next a child. Can't you make up your mind?" she snapped.

Paul took a long sip of sherry, watching her over the rim of his glass. "Oh, yes, my mind is made up." His gaze roved over her throat and breasts, and she knew he was seeing her after he had inadvertently torn the nightie away.

"Two weeks. Business only," she said.

She had the satisfaction of seeing the dull red mount over his cheeks and disappear into his dark hairline. He liked to make the rules himself. "Business only," he growled, "unless you decide otherwise."

Shannon went up to unpack. They had at least cleared the air. She could handle two more weeks. Two months would be too long to try to hold her distance from Paul; an affair, waning by Labor Day, could only mean a bittersweet heartbreaking memory for Shannon and an interval soon forgotten by Paul. "No, thanks," she muttered to herself. "I have another year of hard work, and I can't spend it pining away for Paul."

FOR MORE THAN A WEEK Shannon accompanied both Paul and Merlene. Tensions were taut and tempers lay just beneath the surface. Increasingly annoyed because his voice showed such slow improvement, Paul snapped at everyone.

For relaxation Shannon spent time with Jason on the beach. They dug for treasure at the foot of the cliff and explored the island for likely hiding places. Together they read Edmund's collection of information about Gasparilla, the pirate leader, and Juan Gómez. When Jim had some time off work, he joined them.

Paul, too, became caught up in his son's interest in the treasure, and on Sunday, when Jason urged, "Come with us, dad, we're going to dig in the grove," Paul agreed. They found nothing, but Paul seemed more relaxed after that.

But Merlene was restive. "Why haven't we heard

about the Dulcinea role?'' she fretted. ''Call your agent, Paul.''

Paul clenched his jaw, a sign of rising impatience, and Shannon was surprised when he answered calmly. ''Merlene, I told you not to count too heavily on the Dulcinea role.''

''I'm counting on you to work it out for me,'' she returned sweetly. ''After all, we have an agreement.''

''I can only do so much. I've done all I can.'' With a curt nod, he signaled Shannon to play the haunting ''Dulcinea.'' Paul sang the words that endowed the tavern girl with the qualities of nobility and loveliness that only Don Quixote could see.

Merlene broke into the musical reverie with her derisive aria, insisting that she was Aldonza, the barmaid who enjoys men and gold more than honor; Don Quixote continues to call her his Lady Dulcinea until his belief and love actually transform her. Then together Paul and Merlene sang ''The Impossible Dream.''

Until the high notes at the very end, Paul was performing better than usual. Perhaps Merlene's badgering was good for him after all. Was it possible that beneath his ex-wife's metallic exterior Paul, like Don Quixote, saw something warm and beautiful that brought out the best in him?

At the conclusion, Shannon turned with a smile to tell Paul that he was improving but that he still shouldn't attempt such a wide range. Merlene's blue eyes widened. ''Are you coaching as well as accompanying?'' she asked innocently.

Shannon shrugged. "Not really."

"Good. Because what we really need is more support on the piano in such difficult places. Paul wouldn't have any trouble if your playing were stronger."

Shannon's eyes glittered. One more week of this. She glanced at Paul, but his face was expressionless.

"Try not to be quite so wooden, Shannon," Merlene suggested.

"Wooden!" Shannon bounced up from the bench. "I am not wooden!"

Merlene smiled and Shannon knew that she was pleased at her reaction. "Well, maybe just a bit stiff. We all need to relax. I have an idea. Let's do the trio with Sancho Panza. You can be Sancho, Shannon. After all, that doesn't require much talent, so you'll do nicely." Shannon simply stared at Merlene. "You're a music major, so you must be able to sing a little," Merlene coaxed.

Shannon let her hands hit the keys in a discordant crash. "Go to hell, Merlene!"

She heard Merlene gasp, and a choking sound came from Paul behind her.

"You can't talk to me like that! Paul...." Merlene turned to him.

"I've had it with your snide remarks and criticisms, Merlene Madden. I'm through playing for you. Get yourself another pianist!"

"But I'm a guest here. We're practicing together, Paul and I," Merlene sputtered. "You *have* to play for Paul."

"But not for you, and that's final." She glanced at Paul and caught him straightening out the quirk beside his mouth. "Let me know when you want to practice alone," she advised him as she left.

Shannon paced back and forth in her room. Enough was enough. If Paul wanted to fire her a week before her time was up, that was fine with her. Glancing out the window, she saw that rain clouds hung low over the ocean, threatening showers. A good storm would match her mood, she thought.

She needed to cool off and had hoped she'd have time for a swim. What she didn't need was to be cooped up with her boiling temper. The day's correspondence was finished, and she had no intention of going back into the music room. No more confrontations with Merlene.

She decided to get into old clothes and go for a hike on the beach after the storm to see what the waves had washed in. She peeled off her blouse and slacks and rummaged in the drawer for her faded cutoffs and the old halter that tied in the front above her midriff.

After two sharp taps on the door, it opened to admit Paul. Shannon sucked in her breath as he eyed the white lace that barely covered her small firm breasts and the matching brief panties. The cutoffs and halter were still in her hand. "Don't you *ever* knock?" she demanded.

"I did. I was sure I heard you say, 'Come in.' "

She turned her back, recognizing the lie, and

stepped into the old shorts. "What do you want? I was going out."

"In the rain?" The first patters spattered on the balcony, and Paul shut the window.

She whirled around, annoyed at the interrogation. "Maybe. Are you just going to stand there and watch me dress?"

"Okay. Thanks for asking."

"Oh!" She threw the halter at him. Wearing it required the removal of her bra, and she had no intention of going through with that performance. She went to the closet to find another blouse.

"Let me," Paul said behind her. "I'll find something nice for our holiday."

"What holiday?" When she turned, he was so close that she instinctively backed into the closet.

"The one you and I deserve for trying to work with Merlene all week," he said with a grin. "Come on, we'll get lost in the tourist crowd for a while, and then we'll have dinner in town." He put his hands on her shoulders to remove her from the closet, but she twisted free, alarmed at her instant reaction to his touch.

"No, I-I was going down to the beach," she stammered, finding and shrugging into a robe.

Paul immediately dropped his hands, and his eyes hardened as they raked over her figure suggestively. "Jim again? Is he off work early today?

Maybe it was better—safer—to let Paul think that Jim did claim all her attention. She didn't answer.

"Well, I'm off work, too, and you still owe me

some paid time. Call it work, if you like, but we're going into town." He looked through the clothes and drew out a pale peach sun dress, the brown-and-gold trim of the bodice twisted into a braid that tied at the back of the neck, leaving the wearer's back cool and bare. "This will do." Noting the tags still attached, he added. "Never been worn? Please... wear it for me." When she hesitated, he said, "Come on, Shannon, let's get out of here for a while. Jason is helping Leo in the storeroom, and Merlene's off pouting somewhere."

"Why do you put up with her?" The question seemed to spring from her.

The grim strained look recaptured Paul's face. "There's a reason. It shouldn't be too much longer."

The agreement? About what? Merlene was beautiful, seductive, and Paul had needs. Somehow the custody of Jason figured in the agreement, too.

Paul seemed to read her thoughts. "She has agreed to give me custody of Jason if I see that she gets the long-running role of Dulcinea in *Man of La Mancha*."

"Opposite your Don Quixote," Shannon finished, a sinking feeling in the pit of her stomach. They would be together for months. A family. The way the fans wanted them to be. "Will the judge agree?"

"If he is convinced that I can provide a more stable home for the boy. And especially if Jason prefers to stay with me." Paul went to the window to watch the gray clouds spill the slanting slashes of rain on the beach. He looked gloomy, like the day. "Merlene's career has lagged this past year. She thinks that if we remarry, we'll help each other's careers.''

''Yours doesn't need help!'' It was out before she could prevent it.

Paul's glance flicked to her beneath raised brows. ''Thanks.'' Then he turned back to the rain-blurred window. ''I'm gambling that when—or if—things work out, she'll get what she really wants.''

''You mean you'd remarry her?''

''Hardly,'' he said sardonically. ''I told you that was out of the question.''

Her lover then? After all, they'd be together, sharing their career, Jason, life. They could let the world think they had remarried while they lived without the complications. But how would that benefit Paul, except in personal gratification? Is that all he wanted from any woman? And would just any woman do? And if they just lived together, there would be no need for a custody change. Shannon rubbed the frown line between her eyebrows, puzzled.

''In a few days we'll know whether my plans have worked,'' Paul said. ''Now are you going to put this dress on, or shall I help you?''

''Wear my new dress in the rain?'' she stalled. ''I haven't said I'd go with you.''

Paul sighed and turned away from the window. ''It's clearing. Storm's over. Inside and out. Now get dressed and meet me at the car in ten minutes. I want to talk to you. And don't worry, this is business, not pleasure.'' He closed the door as he left her.

Shannon opened the French doors. Paul was right;

the sudden summer storm was over. The ocean still churned restlessly after the rough assault of the rain, but the soft summer wind was working to soothe and retame it.

Although the sweep of long ebony hair hid the golden tan of her back, the peach sun dress set off Shannon's smooth shapely arms and legs and her oval face to advantage. She brushed her eyelids and lips with color and her wrists with perfume, then fastened the thin thongs of her wedge-heeled sandals.

PAUL WAS WAITING in the garage, wearing a fresh blue shirt and white slacks. The familiar white silk scarf was once again tucked into the open neck of his shirt, hiding his scar. As he helped Shannon into the Lincoln, his hand rested lightly a moment on her back, sending little thrilling flames into her body. Why did she have such a strong reaction to Paul? It was as though electric currents were generated from his hands, sending imperative messages through her skin. Messages she didn't want to receive.

They skimmed down the island and crossed the Bridge of Lions into St. Augustine. Paul's manner remained polite and impersonal. She could find no fault with it.

"Have you thought about selling your orange groves to me?" Paul asked offhandedly.

"Oh, no. I'd never sell." So that was what the "business" was all about.

"But if you leave your job next week, you'll need money to finish at the university, won't you?"

"Oh, I'll find another job in Chicago," she said airily.

"A six-week job? You'll be lucky if you find one. Sure you won't stay and work for me? I've been a model of good behavior."

He was right. But remembering his touch and the smoldering desire she surprised sometimes in his eyes, she knew it couldn't last. Not six weeks. Not for either of them. She let the silence answer for her.

"I'd like to put the music school on the dune." He didn't argue about her staying; proof, she thought, that he didn't really care whether she left or not. "I've drawn some plans," he went on. "Would you like to see them?"

"I might. I might be interested in a share of the school. A business venture. I think sometime in the future, I could help you...financially, I mean," she said thoughtfully, "and I would like to have a part of dad's dream."

Paul smiled. "Think about it. I'm in no hurry. It will take lots more money than I have now to get under way." He looked at her speculatively. "I think we could be a good team."

"How could you manage the school as well as your concert tours?"

"I'd live here nine months of the year, while Jason is in school. I'd do weekend concerts and schedule tours during the summers. It would be enough. And Jason would have a home. Roots."

"I thought touring the world would be fun. Glamorous," Shannon said thoughtfully. "Do you get tired of it?"

"Yes. Oh, I wouldn't give it up entirely. But I'd really like to carry out Edmund's plans for a music school where talented students could come whether or not they had tuition."

"That would be wonderful," she said slowly, "but I couldn't give up my grove."

As they pulled into the parking lot, Paul eyed Shannon with a look that made her heart beat faster. It was one of those electrical messages that she didn't quite understand.

"You wouldn't have to if you worked there with me, Shannon."

She put her hand to her throat. What an idea! To live and work at Pirate's Cove! To make it a home base, a haven to come to when tours and concerts were finished! Her eyes sparkled, for suddenly they were sharing a dream.

Paul parked the car and rested his arm carelessly on the seat back. "You have plenty of time to think about it. Probably even to get in several years of concert work, too. It will take money, Shannon. Lots of it. That's why Edmund was so obsessed with finding the treasure. It would have financed the school nicely." He got out and came around to the passenger side to help Shannon. "Enough of that. Let's be carefree tourists. I haven't explored the historical sights of St. Augustine for years."

Paul hired a carriage, and they threaded their way down the narrow historic streets, past the sixteenth-century marketplace where slaves were once auctioned, and past the great city gate that used to lock the colonists in at night, safe against enemy attack. They stopped for a cool sip of water at the famed Fountain of Youth before the horse clopped into a cobblestone side street. Paul had the driver stop before a small shop with the sign Jack the Treasure Man. Jack proved to be a gray-bearded ex-diver who had assisted in treasure retrieval all over the world. On shelves around the shop there were ancient Chinese coins, gambling markers and opium pipes from Colorado mining sites; a twenty-five pound nugget from California; doubloons found just under the surface of Florida beaches; muskets and iron kettles from the Great Lakes; silver bars from sunken ships.

Paul selected a beat-frequency metal-locator kit as a surprise for Jason. "That'll find metal objects up to a yard down," Jack said. "Don't forget to test caves, even small ones. They could have drifted over through the years."

Shannon shared Paul's satisfaction with the purchase. "You and Jason will have a great time putting it together and using it," she said. "It's a wonderful present. He'll love it."

Paul touched her elbow, guiding her across the busy street to the imposing Castillo de San Marcos. As always when he touched her, Shannon's skin tingled, and she became vibrantly conscious of his strong body so close to hers.

He kept his hand under her arm as they joined the

crowd to watch the artillery demonstrations. The guide explained that the fort was really impregnable; the sixteen-foot-thick coquina walls were porous enough to absorb enemy cannonballs. Sometimes the fort soldiers had pried out the balls at night and shot them back at the attackers the next day.

They were led through windowless storage rooms and prisons, and Shannon shivered. "Have you had enough?" Paul murmured, checking his watch. "I think our dinner should be ready by this time."

"Did you make reservations somewhere?" she asked in surprise.

"In a way, yes." They crossed the drawbridge over the moat. "It's not far, a couple of blocks. Shall we walk?"

He was already propelling her down the walk at a brisk pace, and Shannon laughed. As usual, Paul had already made up his mind, and his question didn't require a reply. She didn't mind. It had been a lovely afternoon, free of tensions and frustrating rehearsals.

She tried to match her stride to his, but it was no use. Paul's long legs required that her shorter ones do a double skip now and then to keep up. "You must be hungry," she teased.

They came to the municipal marina, and Paul led her onto the long pier. At the end of it a beautiful white forty-foot yacht was moored, its deck and cabin ablaze with lights. "A restaurant on the water?" Shannon exclaimed with delight. *The Impossible Dream* was painted at the stern.

Paul chuckled. "Wait and see."

He helped her board the craft, and when she stood hesitantly on the afterdeck, he put his hands on her shoulders and steered her down the few steps to the lounge. A white-coated waiter was arranging delicious-smelling covered dishes on a linen-draped table laid with gleaming silver and china. "Good evening, Mr. Cypress. Shall I stay to serve you, sir?"

"No, Anton, we'll manage. And you will have someone drive my car back to Pirate's Cove, won't you?"

"Yes, sir, I'll see to it myself." He lit two tall white tapers and arranged the ice bucket and champagne on a small table next to the captain's chair. "Shall I mix drinks for you, sir?" he asked, flicking off the lights.

"Shannon?"

"Nothing, thanks. Not now." Her eyes shining, she was enjoying the beauty of the trim craft, its lovely appointments and thick carpeting, the wraparound windows that framed the twinkling lights of other boats in the harbor.

When the waiter had left, Shannon said, "Whose boat is this? It's. . .it's perfect!"

"It's mine."

Her eyes widened. "But you never mentioned it! Don't you use it?"

"There was some trouble with the engines. My mechanic thinks he has it fixed now. We'll give it a trial run after dinner."

Shannon sobered. This was far from a business dinner. "Where are we going?"

"Back to the cove," Paul said abruptly. "You heard me ask Anton to see that my car was driven back."

In her excitement, Shannon had forgotten. "Oh, I just thought...."

"I can imagine what you thought," Paul said. "Relax, Shannon. I told you that nothing would happen that you didn't want to happen."

The trouble was that Paul knew the strength of her desires. And how to arouse them. Even his touch on her arm could awaken a thrill of longing.

"You can freshen up in the guest head," Paul told her, leading her through the compact galley to a small V-shaped forward cabin with its tiny bath. "Anton brought the food from the hotel, so don't be long. It won't stay hot forever." Her suspicious question about their destination had brought a scowl to Paul's brow. Shannon regretted asking it. Paul had shown her a wonderful holiday, and the surprise of dining aboard his yacht was a fitting climax to the day. In the few days that were left, she had no wish to quarrel.

The dinner was excellent, its character Spanish: *arroz con pollo*, *chiles relleños*, hot buttered rolls with a green salad and *biscochitos* with Spanish cream for dessert. Shannon shook her head to a second glass of champagne. "I don't manage drinking very well," she demurred. "I get sleepy right away."

"Interesting," Paul murmured. "Do have some more."

Believing that he was teasing, Shannon laughed. "Not a chance." She got up and started to clear the table.

"Leave it," Paul said. "Anton will send someone soon to pack everything back to the hotel." He smiled crookedly. "I do have dishes and silver aboard, but it was easier this time to let Anton do everything. Come up to the helm with me."

There was a comfortable vinyl-covered lounge behind the helm, and they sat there watching the stars brighten in the night sky. Shannon waited for him to tell her whatever it was he wanted to say, but he was silent a long time. He sat with his arm over the back of the lounge, but he didn't touch her.

"All right," he said suddenly. "I'll make you a business proposition, Shannon. If you'll stay with me until the end of the summer, I'll underwrite the rest of your education."

Shannon's jaw dropped. She must have misunderstood him.

"I need your help. I don't want another pianist. I want you to play for me until Labor Day, as you originally planned. In return, I'll take care of your tuition and dorm expenses next year."

"It means that much to you?" she asked incredulously.

"I'm used to you, don't you understand that? It isn't easy for a singer to switch accompanists, especially when there's a voice problem." He leaned toward her, and the hand that had been close to her arm raked through his hair. "Shannon, I've been asked to sing at the amphitheater here in August. I'll never be ready if you leave me."

"So soon!" *He might not be ready in any case,* she thought, steeling herself. He didn't have to accept the St. Augustine engagement.

"I'd like to do it. I can if you help me."

"You shouldn't attempt a program that soon, not if you expect to be ready for *Man of La Mancha* in October. Paul, you've been out of surgery only a few weeks."

"We could take the yacht and cruise the coast. We'd be so relaxed. I know it would work."

Shannon stood up and leaned against the rail. "This is impossible. In the first place I would never let you pay for my education. Don't even think about it. And the cruise. . . that's out, too."

Paul stood, but still he didn't touch her. "Why? Don't you trust me? Surely you remember our agreement. Business only, unless you decide otherwise."

She hesitated a second before saying frankly, "I don't want an affair, Paul. Maybe I'm afraid of being hurt. I have lots of hard work ahead of me, and I just don't want to be emotionally involved with anyone. Besides," she added with a rueful smile, "you don't need *me* specifically. Someone else—"

"Jason needs you, too," Paul said. "It's not just me. Surely you can see that. He's fine with you and me. . . better adjusted. He's finally accepting the divorce. But Merlene won't give up custody without a fight.''

''You said there was an agreement.''

He ran his hands through his hair once more. ''If my plan works, she'll get the Dulcinea contract, but there are things about it she's not going to like, and she'll be fighting mad.''

''But how could my being here help?''

''If the custody goes before the judge again, I'm sure he'll decide in favor of the one who can provide the most stable home for Jason.'' He looked out over the star-reflecting water and for a moment seemed to have forgotten Shannon. ''If I had the school... if we could be at Pirate's Cove most of the time, there'd be no question. But I'll have to work hard for years to get that kind of money.'' He sighed raggedly.

Other voices pattered across the harbor, and an outboard started up nearby. Shannon felt as though Paul had slipped away. His profile was outlined with moonlight, the prominent cheekbones tapering to the strong cleft chin, the hairline full over the broad brow. Arms leaning on the rail, his able brown hands were clasped as though in supplication.

That Paul admitted his need for her touched Shannon, though she recognized that it concerned only her music and her special relationship and ability with Jason. Paul was such a proud, reticent man; it must have cost him a great deal to spell out his need for her. Fleetingly she questioned her resolve. With her heart and soul she yearned to help him. She wanted to meet his needs. So what if they drifted into an affair? Couldn't she, like Paul, keep it light and recover reasonably easily? No, she decided. Love was not to be treated lightly. That was not the answer.

Disturbed at her thoughts, Shannon stirred. "Paul, I'm only your pianist. I don't see how my presence would help your custody case, no matter how close Jason and I are."

"It would help a great deal," he said, turning to her at last, "if you were my wife."

CHAPTER SEVEN

SHANNON GASPED, her eyes wide. She took a step away from Paul, but he quickly imprisoned her with his arms clasping the rail on either side of her.

"Hear me out, Shannon. Merlene will know about her role this week, and after that we'll petition for a review of the custody. By Saturday we can take off on our cruise. Give it a chance, Shannon. I promise, you won't be sorry."

Suddenly the wind strengthened, churning in from the sea. The gusts picked up strands of Shannon's hair and blew them like shreds of black silk across Paul's face. Shannon shuddered as the familiar electric current ripped through her. Even without her willing it, a part of her had reached out to Paul, establishing contact, vibrating into life that surge of passionate longing that was possible only with him.

"No." Her voice was scarcely audible. Perhaps Paul didn't hear.

"I'll have a piano put aboard at Daytona Beach. We'll just relax...you and Jason and I. He'll love it—"

"No!" A sob carried the word. "You...you want

a wife...just so the judge will give you Jason?'' She shook her head, for she knew the answer.

The moonlight touched his eyes with silver specks as he leaned closer. "I've never denied that I want *you*, Shannon."

She turned away, knowing that tears were close. She knew now why she couldn't allow herself to agree to Paul's plan. Before, she had suspected that it might devastate her, and instinctively she had thought of flight. She hadn't allowed herself to examine her feelings too carefully; she had convinced herself this was the only way she could still be free.

But now Paul had acknowledged his needs and desires and was ready to use her to fulfill them. And as she understood fully that she was to be a means to an end for Paul, it made her aware of how much more she wanted to be to him. She was in love with him. It was already too late to avoid the hurt.

Paul tucked a strand of hair behind Shannon's ear and drew her close. He let his hand cradle her face and then firmly tilted her chin so that he could look into her eyes. "Don't cry," he said softly. "It will be all right. You want me, too. I know you do."

The tears spilled over. He would have kissed them away, but she turned aside, and because he wouldn't let her go, the tears ran unchecked.

"I can't marry you, Paul. It would be a big mistake for both of us."

She felt him stiffen "Isn't marriage what you want?"

"You don't want to marry again. I've heard you say so."

She heard the little growl of exasperation deep in his throat. "I've been honest. I thought that I would never marry again. But right now it seems the most practical way to keep us together, Shannon. Marriage can work for us."

Shannon raised her head so that she could look into Paul's eyes. She wished that she could stop the flow of tears, that she could speak coolly and logically enough to convince Paul that he should let her go. "I know what you want—a pianist, a mother figure for Jason and someone to share your bed. You can find someone, Paul. It doesn't have to be me."

"You weren't listening. I want *you*, not someone else. You suit me fine, Shannon. We're good together." When she shook her head, his voice took on a sharp edge. "I want the truth. What stands between us? Why can't we be close? There is a wall, a shield between us that you won't talk about. In Illinois it was there when you said you wouldn't work with me. Still, you came when I needed you. And in your little valley the other day we were close, and then you pulled away. What is it, Shannon? Why can't I find you? You want to be with me, but something stops you. I can't fight it unless I know what it is."

A dark figure at the bow called out, "All clear to cast off, Mr. Cypress!"

Paul's arms relaxed as he said under his breath, "Hell! What timing!" then called, "All clear!" in response to the dock man. "We've got to finish this later,'' he said to Shannon as he turned to start the engines.

She needed a little time alone, time to formulate her answers to Paul's questions, time to deal with the knowledge that she was in love with Paul. She went down the companionway to the aft deck. Dully she noted as she passed the salon door that the remains of the dinner had been cleared away and that the candles were burning low. Strange, the things one noted under stress. She blew out the candles before she crossed to the aft rail. The boat's wake was silver in the moonlight as *The Impossible Dream* sliced a path through the water.

Her love for Paul throbbed inside her. It was the source of an ache almost too great to bear, since it was not returned and could therefore never ripen and grow into joy. Paul desired her, but he didn't love her.

Anger toward Merlene washed over Shannon; because of her, Paul was so disillusioned and cynical that he had encased his heart in a shell. Now, at last, Shannon knew how vulnerable, how open to pain a person in love was. Before she became hopelessly entangled—with or without marriage—she had to escape.

The shaft of knowledge that had stabbed through her when her hair had whipped across Paul's face was as raw as a wound. There was no way to avoid the hurt. Flight, she thought, would hasten the healing process. But Paul would demand an explanation.

The engines quieted and the speed lessened as they

neared the cove dock. The pier light was a tiny pin-point of welcome to the island, and Shannon thought how ironic it was that in the past weeks she had begun to think of the cove as home once more. Now she was banishing herself. Forever. She had to.

The Impossible Dream bumped gently against the tires at dockside, and Leo loped out of the darkness to help with the mooring. "How's that port engine, Mr. Paul?"

"Not good." As the line was secured, she heard Paul's step behind her. "We'll be in after a while, Leo. We're not quite ready." He put his hand on Shannon's arm to keep her from going ashore.

"Okay, I'll go on in then." The old man approached the afterdeck. "I was tellin' my grandson about your engine trouble. Maybe you ought to let him take a look. He worked for a boat service on Padre Island, an' I've an idea he's good. Always did like motors."

"If I have any more trouble..." Paul said non-committally as Leo drifted away.

"I want to go ashore, Paul," Shannon said.

"Not until you explain your negative—and unreasonable—reaction to my proposal."

"You mean your proposition, don't you?" Her chin came up defiantly.

"No, I don't! I need you for a number of reasons, and you need me, too!" His hands were on her shoulders, gripping angrily. "We both have physical needs, Shannon, and you're neither honest nor very bright if you deny that."

"You're hurting me!"

"I've told you why I need you. For Jason. To help me get back my vocal strength. Weren't you listening?"

"Yes, I heard!" The power in his fingers reminded Shannon how easy it would be for Paul to impose his will.

"I've told you I'd help you through the university, and then you can study in Europe or begin your concert career. You can be a part of the conservatory when it's built. You can travel with me, perform with me. God, girl, what more do you want?"

"If you let me go, I'll tell you!" He released her, looking down at his hands as though he hadn't realized their strength. Shannon rubbed her tender flesh as she caught her breath. "For one thing," she began, "I will never marry a man who doesn't love me."

"Ah!" It was a long sigh. "So you want all the declarations of undying love that wear thin and snap like old rubber bands in no time." Again he sighed. "That's only in romantic operas and musical comedies. Why kid ourselves? If we're realistic, I think we can make it work, Shannon. Marriage, I mean."

Shannon fought to retain her poise. "A second point," she murmured. "I get the distinct impression that you don't have much regard for lasting love and commitment. Well, I feel differently, Paul, and I can't accept that. When I marry—if I marry—it will be because I believe that the man I choose and I will continue to love each other always."

Paul regarded her silently. Then, "You really mean that, don't you?"

"Yes," she said quietly.

"Shannon, I...I like you so much. More than any woman I have ever known." She could barely see his rueful smile in the moonlight. "I respect your faith and sincerely hope that you're never disillusioned. In fact—" he stopped, searching for words "—I want to protect you from that kind of hurt. I don't want someone else to win your love and then.... Damn it, Shannon, I want you with me. I offered to make you my wife. I thought that would make it seem right for you."

"You don't want a wife—"

"You're damn right I don't! But I don't want you running away. I want you to stay with me." His mouth came down, hard and insistent.

Shannon felt the familiar but unwelcome ache of desire spring to life deep inside her. She struggled. She had to make Paul understand that she meant what she said. She did not want an affair, not even the beginning of one. She tugged at the back of his belt and shirt, but he leaned closer, pressing her between himself and the rail. The cold metal creased her back, and she gasped.

Paul lifted his head, tangling his hand in her hair and tipping her face so that he could read it. "Shannon?" he whispered huskily.

She didn't answer, and he kissed her face, tasting the salt of the tears she had tried to deny. "Don't cry. I had to show you that you want me and just how much I want you!"

"I know," she whispered. "You didn't have to show me. And that's why I can't stay, Paul. We both know where we're heading, and I can't go there with you. I wish you could understand." She slipped her hand under his loosened shirt and felt his muscles quiver in response.

When she tried to move away, he held her head against the hollow of his shoulder for a moment before he let her go. "We've just begun to learn how to get along with each other," he said. "We need some time, Shannon. Don't leave me."

"It's better to make the break now, Paul."

"There is one question you've avoided," Paul said soberly. "I asked you about the barrier I've sensed between us. What is it, Shannon?"

"I don't know what you mean."

"I think you do."

She felt the hammering heartbeat and the sickening fear that always accompanied questions into the past, into that dark forgotten specter in the back room of her mind. She shook her head, not wanting to open the door.

"Shall we talk about that night, Shannon? Will that help?" He searched her eyes for confirmation before he continued. "When Edmund died, I had to leave right away. I know you must have had questions."

"No," she said quickly.

"Remember, we are going to be honest," he reminded her gently.

Now that she loved Paul, she wanted desperately to believe that Edmund's death had in no way been his fault, and yet...she had been so sure that it was. When she was a child, she had been sure.

"Trust me, Shannon. Talk to me."

She raised eyes plagued by old doubts. "I do...I want to trust you." The words trembled low into the stillness. "You couldn't have...hurt him. But... couldn't you have brought him back?" And suddenly the old grief was heavy again. "Why didn't you bring him in?" Her voice became more demanding. "I thought you had dad in your arms. What happened to him?"

Paul reached for her once more. "Poor Shannon. Poor little girl. I never dreamed that you thought I could mean to let Edmund drown." He rocked her as though she were still the child waiting on the shore. "You must know that I tried to save him. I couldn't find him. He was gone." His own voice broke huskily.

"I was so sure you had him." The words were muffled against Paul's shirt. "I saw you. I saw you with him."

"No. No. You saw what you wanted to see. I couldn't find him. Oh, Shannon, what a burden you've carried about me. I could never have hurt your father. He had done so much for me, you know."

"But I heard you quarrel."

"You and I quarrel, too, but we could never hurt each other."

Shannon pushed away and looked up at Paul, a sad expression on her face. No, Paul would never mean to hurt her. But it could happen. He would not have meant to hurt Edmund, either, but that, too, could have happened. For the first time Shannon considered the possibility that Paul had not deliberately left Edmund to drown that night. If only she could remember everything that had happened, everything she had seen. . . .

As though he read her thoughts, Paul said, "Someday you will remember. And we'll talk again."

She put her fingers over his lips. "No more now. Let's go home."

Paul smiled and kissed her forehead. "I like hearing you call the cove 'home,' Shannon. Now then, about the cruise; say you'll come."

There was a little catch in Shannon's laugh. "Didn't you hear a word I said? I'm going back to Chicago."

"Suppose we don't get married. Just work for me."

"I'll help you find a pianist. I have some school friends who may not have jobs."

"Suppose I promise to be a respectful boss. Nothing more."

"A promise neither of us might want to keep? Paul, *The Dream* would keep us in a small space. With Jason. Think of him."

"I do. He adores you, Shannon. Maybe he and I together could get you to stay with us a long time. And, you know, I like what you said about us in a small space. And about neither of us wanting to keep foolish promises."

"They're not foolish, Paul. Maybe impossible, though."

"Then you won't stay? You won't change your mind?"

"No, Paul, I won't." She saw the grim line of his mouth. *Don't be bitter with me,* she said with her eyes. Aloud she said, "I have to do what is right for me. I have to be free."

"You don't know what's right for you...for both of us!"

"And you do?" she asked gently.

"Yes! Shannon, you're not making any sense. We'll do it any way you like. Just come with me."

"No." She made the step onto the pier.

"I don't understand you."

LATER SHANNON SANK onto her bed. Her life at the cove was almost over. How bleak it would be without Paul. And Jason and the Pratts, too. But most of all without Paul.

She tiptoed through the bathroom into Jason's room. She touched the thatch of black hair, so like his father's. If only Paul loved her, she would be happy to spend her life with him and Jason. She thought of the fun they had shared, talking about the treasure, studying the books Edmund had collected, digging on the beach and the dunes. She thought of the music they both loved and of the work they had done on writing down the Seminole folk tunes.

She thought about Paul's dream of building the conservatory, too. Edmund's dream. And her own.

Yes, it would be ideal to do concert tours during the summers, when Florida was hot, and to live in residence at Pirate's Cove, working at the school the rest of the year.

Oh, Paul, you said it could work. Could it, even though you don't love me? Could it?

Pressing her fingers to her lips to still the anguished answer, she left the boy's room. She couldn't forget what Jim had said. And before him, Jack Fenton. Paul was a womanizer. He liked to have a collection of beautiful women. She had known long ago that she could not share a man she loved. Now, loving Paul, it was clearer than ever that she could not emerge whole if he left her for someone else. And he would. His needs were physical and material. That was all.

She took a long, warm shower, hoping to wash away her longing and to soak up some relaxation. She would not think about the end of the week. Saturday. The day of parting.

CHAPTER EIGHT

IN THE MORNING Shannon went directly to the study to do the correspondence. The face that had looked back at her from the mirror had been gaunt, the eyes shadowed. She had spent much of the night examining her decision, trying to see Paul's point of view and returning again to her own. She skipped breakfast in order to avoid Thelma's kind concern. And maybe Paul's.

With touches of makeup, she camouflaged some of the signs of the sleepless night. She donned orange shorts and a brightly striped T-shirt to suggest a gaiety she didn't feel.

She had stepped into the study when she saw that Paul was sitting in the big wing chair. He was talking on the phone. She would have left, but he motioned her to stay. "That's good news," she heard him say. "Then everything is all set on both counts?" And after a pause, "Good work, Sylvia; I'll make it up to you, darling, I swear."

Who was Sylvia? How easily 'darling' slipped from his lips. Did it mean anything? Or everything?

"Okay, I'll wait for your call. Don't be long." Paul sounded elated as he finished his conversation.

He turned to Shannon. "I'm going to show Jason how to put that metal detector together this morning, and then I'd like you to take him along the beach. Show him how to work it."

"All right."

He came to stand close to her. "Troubled?" he asked gently.

She lifted hooded eyes. "Do I look that bad?"

He laughed. "Not a bit. But I do work at trying to understand what you're thinking."

"Last night you said you couldn't understand."

"I said I try. Sometimes I don't succeed. Shall we talk some more?"

Shannon shook her head. "Nothing has changed. If you will make a list of the things you'd especially like to have me do before Saturday, I'll do my best to get them done," she said tonelessly.

"Cut it out, Shannon," he bit out tersely. He put his hands on her shoulders. "You're retreating again, and I won't let you do that anymore." His voice softened. "We did get a step closer last night. We talked out our viewpoints and reasons. Both of us. That's something."

She nodded. "I'm just tired, Paul. I can't think straight."

"I know where you could have restful nights and lazy days without telephones or letters or very much work. Good companions, too."

She slanted a look of mock disgust at Paul. "You never give up, do you?"

"No, I don't." She was surprised at the intense seriousness of the three words.

"Use your head, Paul. An affair with me won't do your custody suit any good. You mustn't lose Jason. Just leave me out of the plans."

The telephone jangled, and Shannon reached for it. "Let it ring," Paul said. "Thelma will get it." But he went to the door and looked down the hall. Indistinct voices wafted from the dining room, and Paul seemed to be listening.

"Let's not argue," Shannon said, turning to her work. "Let me just enjoy these last few days. Please."

"All right."

She looked up in surprise. Her plea had been an earnest one, and she had not expected the offhand impatient agreement it had received. His agile mind was coping with a dozen problems at once. He was difficult to understand, impossible to predict.

At the sound of heeled slippers approaching, Paul came back into the den and leaned casually against the desk. Shannon had to peer around him when the footsteps halted. Framed in the doorway, Merlene's tall near-perfect figure was outlined seductively in the sheer purple-and-gold tunic that clung to her. Her corn-silk hair was for once loose and soft about her regal head, giving her a Delilah look, all but impossible for a man to resist, no matter how strong he might be.

The china-blue eyes were wide, the pink lips slightly parted in a triumphant smile. "I've got it," she said throatily.

"You've got what?" Paul asked mildly. But Shannon sensed a controlled tension that he chose not to show.

"The Dulcinea role." She went quickly to Paul and wound her arms around his neck. "Darling, you did it! You did it for me. You won't be sorry, I promise." Her eyes glittered with satisfaction. "We'll be together, and I'll make you proud. We'll be wonderful together!"

"The role is made for you, Merlene." Paul's congratulatory kiss was meant for her cheek, but she turned her face so that their lips met. She melted against Paul, moving her hands against the fabric of his shirt.

"Will you call your lawyer right away?" Paul asked coolly. "You remember your promise." He put his hands on her arms, but Merlene was not ready to let him go.

"What's the hurry, darling?" she said, pouting. "Let's at least take today—and tonight—to celebrate."

Paul's voice was silky but firm. "I expect you to keep your part of our bargain, Merlene. And you know how anxious I am to get things settled."

She pushed him away then. "Why do you always think of Jason first? Why can't you just be glad for *me* for once?"

"The agreement was that if you got the part, I'd get Jason. This show is going to have a long run. Be sensible, my dear. You can't drag the boy all over Europe and Africa. And he flatly refuses to go to boarding school."

"Africa?" Merlene's eyes searched Paul's. "Did you say Africa? I thought we had two months in Europe. Is the tour extended?"

"Excuse me," Shannon said, collecting the letters. "I'll go...."

"We'll be through in a minute," Paul said, "so just stay."

She felt like an eavesdropper, but she stayed, trying to concentrate on her work. The "bargain" Paul had hinted at was taking shape, but it didn't concern her.

"Well," Merlene went on, "Europe, Africa—what does it matter? You'll be there, too, and you can always handle Jason better than anyone. We'll get a tutor for him. And really, darling, if we're together again, there's no hurry about the custody business—"

"No stalling," Paul said sharply. "You've got what you want. After this tour you'll be able to command good roles anywhere in the world. But you've got to understand that I'm not going to sing the Don Quixote role. Don English will be your co-star."

"What?" Merlene's face registered shock. "What?"

"I'll never be ready for such a strenuous tour by then."

"You tricked me!" For once her controlled, studied gestures and diction were totally gone. "I believed you and I would do *La Mancha* together! That's why I agreed to let you have Jason. I thought we'd be together. What a rotten trick! Well, the deal is off. Forget it."

Paul grasped her arm before she could run away. "Oh, no! You know Treva Scott wants that role as badly as you do. It was a toss-up, and I swung the decision your way. I can change things yet."

"I've been offered the part."

"You don't have the contract, though." Paul's mouth was a grim line. He could be ruthless when the stakes were high. "You won't get it till I call the producer with a final okay. You see, I'm the main financial backer of the show. They'll listen to me."

Merlene's eyes had become cold steel. "You're not the only one with something to say, Paul Cypress. If you ruin that contract for me, I'll go to the press and tell them all about it. And there's a lot more that I can tell your adoring public. Ever since I've known you, you've manipulated things. People, too. I could rock your little tin throne, so don't you threaten me!"

"We made a bargain. I expect you to keep it. It's as simple as that." Paul, too, was a figure of cold steel. Shannon shivered, wishing she could slip away unnoticed. "Think of your options, Merlene. Keep Jason and start job hunting. Or become the star of *Man of La Mancha* and let me have him."

"Damn you!" she said between her perfect teeth. "You know I can't have a kid with me when I'm touring two continents!" Her eyes glistened behind tears. "I told Jason we'd all be together," she said plaintively. "I need time to think."

"The role must be filled at once, you know that. It's already late for casting. I guess you know

now why the decision has been so long in coming.''

"Because of your manipulations," Merlene said bitterly. Shannon understood the struggle that must be raging within Merlene. The role of Dulcinea was everything that she had ever wanted. But giving up Jason meant giving up her hold on Paul, a man Shannon was sure Merlene still wanted. With him as her co-star, ally and lover—possibly husband—her fortunes were assured. Without him, she would be on her own. She had been without him the past year for the most part, and obviously she had not fared well. She was frightened. Yet, to star as Dulcinea was an opportunity that might not come again. Paul had helped her to win the role, but if she did not live up to her end of the bargain, she could never expect his help again.

"You win, damn you," she muttered. "Let's get the custody settled."

Shannon almost felt sorry for Merlene as she preceded Paul into the hall. They continued to talk in low tones, but Shannon went on with her work, glad that they had left.

IT WAS ALMOST NOON when she finished. With the sheaf of letters and checks needing his signature, Shannon went to locate Paul. Not finding him downstairs, she went to her room to freshen up. She'd catch him at lunch.

She heard their voices on the balcony, Merlene's persuasive and wheedling now, Paul's low, indistinct. "...doesn't have to be this way, darling. We were good together. We can be again." Merlene was coaxing.

Shannon was unable to move away. She couldn't understand Paul's answer, but Merlene went on, "Give me another chance, Paul. You know you still want me."

Paul's low, soothing tones reached her. "You'll be gone, perhaps for a year. We can't predict what will happen."

"You give me hope, Paul," Merlene said. There was a long silence, and Shannon was tortured by the mental image of Merlene in Paul's arms, her exquisitely seductive body pressed against his. "I can make you love me again."

Shannon crushed back a groan. She leaned against the wall, unable to see the two on the balcony. She could hear; that was enough. Too much. "We won't fight about Jason, darling," Merlene said more briskly. "You'll see that he has a good school, won't you?"

"Of course I will. And you'll petition for the custody change?"

The petulance crept back into Merlene's voice. "Yes, I suppose I must."

The voices faded as the speakers moved away. They must have gone into the studio.

Shannon clenched her fists and looked at the wrinkled corners of the letters with dismay. She'd have to do some of them over...and all because Paul sounded so...so accommodating. He collected beautiful women, Jim had said. It didn't seem to matter whether he'd once been married to them or not.

She went downstairs and dropped off the letters in the den. She would have to do something about the damaged ones. She took the checks and slowly approached the dining room. The phone rang, and this time she answered it. A young feminine voice asked for Paul.

"Whom shall I say is calling?" Shannon asked, curious.

There was a slight pause. "I called to be sure that he was at home. I need to talk to him. I can come right over." The voice sounded hurried. "I'll be there in ten minutes." There was a click before the familiar buzz.

Paul and Merlene sauntered in. "Who was that?" Paul wanted to know.

"I don't know. She didn't give her name, but she's coming to see you shortly." Shannon handed him the checks.

Paul frowned and shrugged before he left them. "I'll wash up. Jason and I finally got that detector together."

Merlene poured herself a drink. As she raised her glass, the full sleeves of her purple-and-yellow tunic gave her a butterfly appearance. "To *Man of La Mancha*," she said gaily. She fluttered her lashes at Shannon. "I suppose you think that leaves you a clear field."

"I don't know what you mean." Surely Paul hadn't told her about last night.

"Of course you do. I've seen how you look at

Paul.'' Her throaty laugh was sardonic. "You can't wait for me to be gone. But I'll tell you something, my dear. Paul will break your heart. He won't be faithful, you know. And he won't hide his affairs, because he's a fanatic about truth. Take my advice and get out of here while there's still time.''

"Save your breath. None of this concerns me," Shannon said coldly. "And don't speak to me as though I were a child. Shannon Webster has grown up in ten years.''

Merlene gaped, her poise shattered. "Sh-Shannon Webster? Edmund's daughter?'' Merlene's face was pale, her pupils dilated. She set her drink down on the buffet, her shaking hand spilling the liquid, and blindly left the room.

"What's the matter with her?" Paul said, entering the room. "She passed me as though she didn't see me.''

"How could Merlene not have known my name? It's not a common one. She seemed stunned when I told her who I am.''

"So that's it," he mused. "Merlene doesn't really pay attention to other women, you know. I don't suppose she ever used your name, now or ten years ago. She was here then, you know.''

Oh, yes, Shannon knew. At ten, she had been heartbroken when her idol had produced a wife. Merlene—she was Marie then—had changed since those far-off days.

"She came just before the accident. A week or so.'' Paul was watching Shannon closely.

"Why was she so surprised just now?" Shannon's brows knitted together in her effort to remember. What was buried far back in her memory, locked away as a result of her fall that night?

"Forget it," Paul advised, and the words were an echo of what she had heard long ago. "She'll be gone soon. Just remember the good things about Pirate's Cove." His voice took on a deeper quality, and she knew what he meant.

Paul went to pour two glasses of Crème d'Or. Accepting a glass, Shannon sat down near the window. She saw the young woman coming across the terrace and knew at once that this was the girl who had called. "She's here," she said.

"Who?" He turned as he said it, stiffening as though cast in bronze.

She was beautiful, a tiny girl with dark eyes and short black hair like a shining cap framing her piquant face. She wore a yellow linen suit, crisply feminine, its white lace collar and cuffs setting off the burnished tan of her skin.

"Jeanie!" Paul reached her in long strides and drew her inside.

"I must talk to you, Paul." It was the beautifully modulated voice that Shannon had heard on the phone.

"I'll have Thelma delay lunch," Shannon murmured. Paul seemed not to hear her nor notice her leaving. At the door Shannon turned in time to see Paul hold out his arms. The girl responded, her eyes luminous and her smile tremulous. Paul gathered her to his chest for a second before he kissed her.

"Jeanie, it has been so long. Too long," Shannon heard.

Shannon fled to the kitchen. Were they all coming back? All the old loves? Merlene, Jeanie and who was that other caller? Sylvia? Shannon swallowed the lump in her throat. To have considered, even briefly, being able to find a meaningful place in Paul's life when there were always others.... It had never been more than an impossible dream.

"Ah, there you are, Shanny," Thelma said. "Are you wantin' the lunch served now?"

"Paul has a visitor," Shannon muttered.

"Shall I be settin' another place then?" Thelma asked.

"Who knows!" she said sharply.

Shannon heard the intake of the housekeeper's breath. "I'm sorry," she said to the woman contritely. "It's been a bad morning."

Thelma nodded understandingly. "Music folks are apt to get knotted up," she observed. "Nothin' a good lunch won't untangle." She began to take the cold cuts and salads from the refrigerator. "I'll set up the buffet right now. Mr. Paul can just invite his company, if he likes."

"Wait," Shannon cautioned. "I don't think you should disturb him now."

The old woman's eyebrows shot up questioningly. "Well, it is a trifle early at that. We'll give him ten minutes." She arranged generous squares of frosted spice cake on a glass platter.

"Mmm, that looks good!" Jason said, coming in from the garage, grimy from his struggles with his new detector. He darted a finger over the frosting, managing to scoop off a tiny bit.

"Go up and wash!" Thelma ordered sternly, and he giggled.

"Just wait till you see my detector. And wait till you see the treasure I'm going to find with it! And, Shanny, did you see our yacht at the dock? We're going on a cruise! Isn't that something?"

"Up and wash!" Thelma repeated, giving him an affectionate shove. Then she looked at Shannon curiously. "You all right, honey? You've said not a word hardly. Somethin' wrong?"

"No." Her denial didn't fool her old friend.

"You're sad to be leavin' us so soon, is that it?" she said kindly. "Well, we're sad that you're goin', but I suppose with Mr. Paul an' the boy goin' away, it's got to be. Jimmy feels bad about it, too. He'll be over to talk with you about an idea he's got."

"What is it?" Shannon asked.

"It's about him goin' back to school. He'll be tellin' you. I guess his mind's really set on it. Jimmy was over last night while you were out, but Leo says you came in late. Jimmy was goin' to wait on the beach, but I guess you didn't see him, eh?"

"No, I didn't." She wondered whether Jim had waited, had seen her with Paul on the afterdeck. It was strange that if Jim wanted to talk with her, he hadn't come over this morning.

"Come on now, lunch will brighten things a whole

lot,'' Thelma promised. "You bring the ice tea, Shanny.'' And she elbowed her way through the door with a platter in each hand. "Nobody here but hisself now,'' she said over her shoulder.

Paul stood at the sliding doors, watching the trim yellow-clad figure walk down the driveway to where she had parked a low white car. When Jeanie waved, Paul's face lit up.

IF IT HADN'T BEEN for Jason's excited chatter about buried treasure, *The Impossible Dream* and the coming cruise, lunchtime would have passed in unusual silence. The adults were each immersed in their own thoughts, although Shannon did her best to give Jason her attention.

"Can we go to the beach right after lunch, Shanny?'' Jason wanted to know as he collected the last crumbs of his cake.

"I have a few letters to do,'' she said. "Paul, are you planning to sing?''

"What? Oh, no. I have some things to do in town. Perhaps we'll work tonight,'' he said absently.

"Aw, I thought maybe you'd come with us,'' Jason said, disappointed.

"Not today, son.'' He turned to Merlene. "Are you ready? We'll take *The Dream*. I want to give that engine a thorough workout this week.''

"Yes, I'm ready.'' She had changed into a white sheath with narrow black edging around the V-neck and sleeves. Her hair was swept back severely behind a black satin band that framed her face. She looked subdued and untheatrical for once. Although Shannon thought the change an improvement, she was at a loss to understand it. Was Merlene trying a new tactic on Paul? Or did it have something to do with her surprise at Shannon's identity? Again she felt a stirring in that corner of her mind that had been blank for so long, and automatically her eyes rested on Paul. Their eyes met and held.

"I'll find a way to work things out," he said softly. Shannon couldn't guess what he meant; he was looking directly at her, but he must have been speaking to Merlene. He was talking about Jason's custody, of course. As far as Shannon was concerned, there was nothing to work out.

Paul excused himself and went upstairs. Jason soon followed, pausing at Shannon's chair to say, "I'll get that map of the cove that your dad marked. We'll need that."

Merlene stopped him before he could pass her. "A little kiss for luck, darling," she said, giving him a peck on the cheek that left a pinkish smudge.

Jason looked surprised as he muttered, "Thanks," and sped away.

Merlene pushed aside her untouched cake. "I just didn't recognize you," she murmured to Shannon.

"Neither of us looks the same," Shannon remarked shortly.

"Do you remember me from that summer?" The question was hesitant, her eyes carefully avoiding Shannon's.

Shannon shrugged. "Some."

Merlene's long sigh seemed to express relief. Still, she waited for Shannon to elaborate. When she didn't, she stood up. "Nothing important, I guess. Well, I'll be going."

"When are you leaving?"

Merlene spun around. "Not as soon as you wish, I'll bet. I meant that I'll be going to town with Paul. I have a million things to do before I can leave Florida. Like arranging that transfer of custody. Who knows how long that will take! But don't worry, I'm as anxious to leave as you are to get rid of me!"

Merlene's switch back to her usual nature was so sudden and unexpected that Shannon drew back. "Really, you'd save yourself a lot of worry if you'd open your eyes. There is nothing between Paul and me."

"Oh, sure! Well, I told you what he's like. And he'll come back to me one day. You'll see. We've been apart before, but we always come back to each other."

But they were divorced this time. And if Paul had Jason...would all that glamour and sex appeal still call him back? "I will probably leave Florida before you do," Shannon said dully.

"What?"

"I'm going home Saturday morning."

"Home?" Merlene blinked uncomprehendingly. "You mean you're not going with Paul and Jason?"

"That's right."

"I don't believe it." Once more Merlene was too surprised to assume a role. "Paul said—"

"It doesn't matter what he said or what you believe." Shannon had had enough. She rose and walked out of the room.

"Shannon, wait!"

She didn't. She hurried to repair the damage to the the wrinkled letters and then went to her room to change into her old faded cutoffs and a sleeveless shirt. Tying her hair into a ponytail because the day had become extremely hot, she went through the bathroom to Jason's room.

"Thought you'd never get done with those old letters," Jason complained. He, too, wore cutoffs. He had cut the sleeves off a torn T-shirt and looked rather ragged, but cool.

"Hey! Anybody in there want to swim with me?" Jim stood on the hill outside the window.

"Jim!" Jason raced to the open casement. "Hop across!"

Jim entered through the window. His cutoffs were ragged and threadbare, with colorful patches stitched haphazardly over most of the holes. He wore no shirt at all.

"You gonna swim in your jeans?" Jason asked interestedly. "Shanny, can I, too?"

"Beats taking time to change," Jim reasoned. "The salt will wash out."

"Why not?" Shannon was glad that Jim had come, glad that there would be no time for brooding this afternoon.

"Good girl!"

Shannon got the towels while Jason told Jim about

his new detector and invited him to help in the treasure hunt. She draped a towel over each of them. "No work today, Jim?"

"Just a half-day. I worked this morning. Business is slack. Tourists don't come to Florida in midsummer." He sounded worried. "I wouldn't be surprised if I got laid off."

"Then maybe you could go on the cruise with us," Jason suggested. "There's lots of room."

Jim chuckled. "I don't think so, though I'd sure like to take a look at that craft. Gramps says your dad is having trouble with one of the engines. I'm good with motors."

"Okay, I'll tell dad you can fix it," Jason said cheerfully. Then he made a dash for the window. "Last one in the water has to walk the plank!" he challenged as he disappeared.

Jim helped Shannon make the leap to the sandy slope and kept her hand in his. "That boy is something else," he said soberly.

"He thinks the world of you, Jim."

A faint smile crinkled the corners of his eyes. "What about you, honey? Do you care about me?"

"Of course I do."

"I mean...do you think you could learn to love me?" He pulled her to a stop at the base of the dune, and she knew that this time she would have to answer. They were alone, with only Jim's yearning for her shimmering around them like the sunshine itself.

"I want to go back to school, Shanny. I'll make you proud of me, I swear I will. I'll borrow whatever

I can, and I'll work. I want to study classical guitar. With you in my corner, I can really be good. I know it. And I'll never stand in the way of your career, honey." His blue eyes were pleading, loving.

"Oh, Jimmy," she said softly, "I'll always be in your corner, but—"

Suddenly his mouth was on hers, and she was swept against his hard young body, his heart pounding against her hand. She almost hoped to feel the stirring inside her that was the forerunner of the abandon she had felt with Paul's arms around her. It would mean that she could love again, that she was not hopelessly committed to a man who didn't love her. But it didn't happen. She reached up to touch Jim's cheek and saw his blue eyes cloud with the knowledge that he had evoked only tenderness in her.

"Don't say anything," he said. "Just give me some time, honey. I'll prove myself to you."

"You don't have to, Jimmy." She wasn't aware that she had used his childhood name.

"Paul told you about me, didn't he?" he said bitterly.

"No, Paul hasn't told me anything," she said, surprised.

Jim's eyes narrowed on Shannon. Then he turned to stare at the yacht, which was still at the end of the dock. Suddenly its engines roared to life, then quieted down, and *The Impossible Dream* chugged deftly away from the pier and the cove. Paul and Merlene must have gone aboard before Shannon, Jim and Jason came down to the beach. Why had they waited until now to leave the cove? Had Paul been watching?

"I thought he'd told you," Jim was saying. He looked at her with bleak eyes. "I've got a record, Shanny. Drugs. Oh, I was a mess. But I'm clean now, I swear it."

Shock made her face pale under the tan. "I believe you, Jim. I know you're strong. But how did Paul know? The Pratts wouldn't have told him. Would they?"

"They don't even know. They were gone over the holidays. Paul was here alone when I turned up. I'd tried to cure myself before...." He dropped their towels on the sand and motioned with his head toward the shore, where Jason was impatiently beckoning. "Anyway, Paul hauled me in. Practically locked me up and *made* me get off the stuff. He was hard as nails! I hated him."

"But don't you see? He helped you, Jim!"

"Yeah! Mr. Perfect! After ten years I came to the cove stoned and broke. And there *he* was, rich and famous and owning the place! Oh, I hated him, all right!" Just before Jason came to get them, he added, "Paul Cypress hasn't got a heart."

CHAPTER NINE

JASON HAD BROUGHT the metal detector down earlier, and after they had played in the surf for a while, they splashed ashore to experiment with it. Jim adjusted the controls so that a loose low rattle indicated the absence of anything significant. The speed and tone of the vibrations intensified in the presence of metal objects.

"Better always carry a spare battery," Jim advised. "This is a loudspeaker model, and the battery runs down after about seventy hours. Keep track. And if you haven't used your metal detector for a while, check it out. A leak will short-circuit the wiring. Always handle it with respect, and who knows what luck it'll bring?"

Jim buried a dime and a quarter at ten inches. The dime brought a flutter of sound, but the quarter caused a strong signal. "The larger and flatter the object, the better the signal," Jim said.

Jim had brought a small bundle of tools he had used to hunt treasure on Padre Island: an army trenching shovel with a folding handle, a garden trowel and a screwdriver. They took turns playing the detector over a wider range. When Jason heard a definite buzz, he dug excitedly, sure he had found Gómez's treasure. He unearthed three dirt-crusted bottle caps, a rusty nail and a bent and corroded spoon. "You can learn something even from this stuff," Jim said before Jason could throw his find away. "Rusted, broken or bent things have been lost a long time. Nobody has disturbed that layer of sand. We're the first."

"So maybe the treasure is farther down?" Jason guessed eagerly.

"I doubt it. Shanny and I and your dad and Edmund turned over this beach pretty thoroughly, but that was ten years ago, probably before somebody dropped those bottle caps and the spoon and nail. But the beach is a good place to practice."

They spread out Edmund's old map and studied the marks on it. "I guess your dad knows what they all mean," Shannon said. "You can see that they used it a lot." She traced the worn creases with a fingertip.

"We'll get him to come with us tomorrow," Jason planned.

With another hot hour of toil, they discovered three pennies, a watch—minus its band, crystal and hands—and half a pair of scissors. Smudging his brow with sweaty hands, Jason suggested a swim.

Refreshed, they lay on their towels and talked about the treasure. By this time Jason knew almost as much as anyone did about Juan Gómez, but he loved to talk and dream about the old pirate.

"I thought he might hide the chest in the cave

where he lived. . .you know, the storage cave. But I looked all over. That's the first place I took the metal detector after dad and I got it together this morning.''

''If there were any secret places in there, the fellow who built the house and paneled the cave would have found them,'' Jim guessed.

''That would be my great-grandfather, Joseph Webster. He was Juan's grandson, the one who came from England with his bride to claim this property.''

It was Jason's suggestion that they act out the old pirate stories about Juan Gómez and his captain, Gasparilla. ''I'll be Gasparilla,'' he volunteered. ''You said he was a little guy.''

''Okay,'' Jim agreed. ''I'll be Gómez and you're my woman.'' He leered playfully at Shannon.

''Elizabeth,'' Jason said. He knew that Elizabeth had been the Louisiana girl captured from a ship that was to take her to school in England. Juan had bargained with Gasparilla for her life. Elizabeth had kept a journal. Shannon supposed it had been in the family all along. She and Edmund had found it in a strange hiding place.

''Where could it be now?'' Jason wondered for the hundredth time.

''Edmund usually kept it locked in his desk, but sometimes he forgot,'' Jim recalled. ''So once when he forgot to put it away, we 'borrowed' it. Remember, Shanny? We spent the afternoon reading it.''

''Did you get a whipping when your dad found out?''

The slap and crash of the surf was loud in Shannon's ears. She watched a little crab scuttle sideways past her feet. Finally Jim said, "We weren't whipped, Jason. Later we just forgot about the journal. We never did finish it all, but we did read about Elizabeth's voyage and about her capture by the pirates. She said Juan was kind to her and that they could understand each other, because she could speak Spanish. There was more, but we had to go in, because it was getting dark."

"In? Where were you?"

"In the secret valley over there." Shannon motioned to the rocky wall of the dell beside the groves. "We went back to the house to have supper. And then that storm came up."

"Which one of us had the journal?" Jim wondered. "You or me? If I did, I can't remember where I put it. Afterward, I looked in my room, but it wasn't there. So I thought you must have taken it to Chicago with you."

"Funny you can't remember," Jason said with a frown. "Maybe it could tell us something."

"That was the night of the accident when Shannon's father died," Jim said quietly, "and none of us thought about anything else for a while. Then I went back to my folks in Ocala, and Shannon and her mother moved to Chicago."

Jason tried to coax them back to the drama of lost treasure by assuming the tough stance of Gasparilla, and for a while they invoked the magic of pretense. When the sun sank behind the dune and cooling

shadows crept over the beach, Jason announced that
he was hungry. As they slowly collected their towels
and treasure things, they heard the high-pitched hum
of heavy motors change to a lower key and rhythm;
The Impossible Dream was nosing toward shore.
Jason ran to the pier.

"There's a problem—maybe the fuel line," Jim
muttered. Then he grinned. "His problem, not
mine." He drew Shannon close for a quick kiss. "I'll
make you some doughnuts on the beach tonight," he
tempted.

"Have to work," she told him, pulling away,
"since I've played all afternoon."

"Damn," he said, "I want to see you as much as I
can these last days that you're here." He hesitated.
"Say the word, honey, and I'll chuck my job and
drive you north. I'll find work, and—"

She laid her hand on his arm. "No, Jim. It's hard
finding work in the city these days. Here you have a
job and a place to live; even if you are laid off for a
while, you know things will pick up as soon as the
weather cools. You can see about starting at Flagler
College here in St. Augustine in September."

Jim looked away toward the pier, where Jason was
trying to help his father secure the line. "You're trying to tell me something, Shanny. It's Paul, isn't it?"
She, too, looked toward the dock. She wanted to be
safely away from the beach before the three came
along. When she didn't answer, Jim finished heavily,
"I don't blame you. Ten years ago we both liked him
a lot. Now I'm jealous as hell. To him I'm just a

bum, but someday I'll show him!'' He squared his shoulders. ''Someday I'll have it all, too.''

The words jogged her memory. She had heard her father say, ''Someday you'll have it all,'' to Paul during that last quarrel. What had happened then? Edmund had left the room...hurried down to the dock....

Paul and Merlene and Jason were coming. It was too late to make an escape. Merlene called out, ''Come up to the house for a drink to celebrate my good fortune, you two!''

Jim looked questioningly at Merlene, and she explained about the Dulcinea role. Jim started to make an excuse, but Merlene said, ''Oh, I insist!'' She eyed his brown torso appreciatively. ''You're both fine the way you are. We'll have it on the terrace. Come, now. It isn't every day a girl wins a year's tour with a role like Dulcinea. Indulge me.''

Paul had said nothing. Jim's eyes narrowed on him for a moment before he shrugged and, taking Shannon's hand, said, ''Why not?''

Jason had been dancing excitedly between his parents. ''Is that what you told me about?'' he demanded of his mother.

''Yes, it is.''

''The show dad's going to be in, too? We're going to be together a whole year?''

Too late she realized that she hadn't prepared Jason for the truth...that the togetherness she had promised him was not going to happen after all. ''Well, darling, I'll tell you all about it later. Now run along and ask Thelma to fix something cool for us.''

''But—''

''Please, Jason.'' He recognized the tone that meant trouble if he didn't obey. But he moved away reluctantly. Shannon saw him stoop to examine something at the rocky foot of the trail. He reached for a stick and poked at it.

Suddenly Jim darted forward, scooping up a stone as he rushed toward Jason. He pushed the boy violently aside as he aimed the stone at a brightly banded snake. The creature was too quick for him, slithering aside to be partially hidden by a bush. Unblinking eyes in its coal-black head stared at Jim as it boldly curved its yard of red, yellow and black bands forward to challenge him. The coral snake was ready to punish.

Paul and Shannon reached for the shaking Jason at the same instant. Distracted by their sudden movement, the snake's attention was diverted long enough for Jim to retrieve the rock and crush the snake's head. ''Extremely poisonous,'' Jim said. ''Corals don't coil and strike, but their bite is deadly.''

''My God!'' Merlene managed, almost paralyzed with shock.

''I—I didn't know there were any bad ones around,'' Jason said. ''It was so pretty.'' He couldn't stop shaking.

Jim grinned at him. ''You can help me preserve the skin, and you can keep it. I'll get a book out of the library about snakes so we'll both know which ones are friendly and which ones aren't. I just happened to know about this fellow from past experience.''

Paul held out his hand to Jim. "You saved my son's life. You might have been bitten yourself." A new respect shone in his eyes.

Jim took Paul's offered hand. "Some of my past experience comes in handy once in a while." Jim's smile looked innocent, but Shannon knew that he was scoring a point. And Paul, one arm tightly around Jason, the other shaking hands with Jim, also smiled. Not sardonically this time, but with agreement and gratitude.

"Let's go up and have that drink," Merlene said breathlessly. "I know I can use one!"

THELMA DIDN'T LIKE the idea of delaying dinner, but when she learned that Jim had been invited, she was mollified. After a quick martini, Jim went back to the cabin to dress, while Thelma did her best to keep the food perfect and her comments about being kept informed to a minimum.

Shannon knew that Merlene would wear something exotic as usual, and although she didn't really think it important or even necessary to try to dress comparably, she decided tonight to wear a strapless blue gown with a delicate diagonal of hand-embroidered valley lilies across the bodice. The slit skirt revealed her slim shapely legs and gold ankle-strap shoes. Without time to wash and blow dry her sea-salty hair, she brushed it thoroughly and twisted it into a French loop low at the back of her head.

When she entered the dining room, Paul was leaning against the mantel. She caught her breath at the handsome and masculine picture he presented in navy slacks and matching turtleneck shirt. Faust could not have looked more intriguing and compelling. His husky voice reached out to her. "You look especially beautiful. For my benefit? Or someone else's?" Lazily he pushed himself away from the fireplace and came to her, his eyes scanning the shape of her body and the loveliness of her dress.

"I thought this was a celebration," she said, "and that we were dressing. I see that I was wrong." She regretted her sharp criticism as soon as it was said. Paul, although dressed very casually, had never looked better. The style suited him perfectly. He merely grinned as he turned to Merlene and Jim.

Merlene had tucked Jim's arm through hers, his hand a captive. She was stunning in a figure-hugging gown of gold cloth, her hair completely hidden in a turban of the same material. She wore a broad band of gold above her elbow and loops of gold in her ears. She looked dramatic, exotic.

In new jeans and a spotless white shirt, Jim grinned, refusing to be embarrassed. The brown shoes were part of his monk's costume, and his yellow curls, wetly slicked back, were already impishly springing out of place.

Thelma bustled in with steaming bowls of vegetables and a platter of ham and prime rib. Jason trailed her, proudly carrying a basket of biscuits.

"Smells great, Gran," Jim said.

Merlene dropped his hand as though it had suddenly become red-hot. "'Gran'? Of course. The Pratts are your grandparents, aren't they? So you were here, too?" She searched his face as though she had never seen Jim before.

Thelma eyed the still untouched salads as she looked reproachfully to Paul. "I thought you'd be ready for the hot things, Mr. Paul. I did have the divil's own time keepin' the meat from gettin' too done."

Paul led them to the table, and although Merlene said no more about her discovery that she had known Jim and Shannon as children, her blue eyes had a brooding expression when they rested on the two. Shannon wondered what could be bothering her.

After dinner Paul suggested that Jim might like to take a look at *The Impossible Dream*. Jim didn't try to hide his eagerness. Merlene challenged her son to a game of checkers before his bedtime. Shannon was about to go up to her room when Thelma beckoned her into the kitchen. She wanted to talk about Jim's plans for college. "I know it's expensive," she worried. "I wanted him to write to his folks, but he won't hear of it. Wants to do it all hisself. D'you think he can, Shanny?"

"I think so," Shannon reassured her. "This time he's doing what he wants to do, and he's made his own goals. He'll be all right."

Leo joined them and they chatted for some time. After a while Shannon went up to the studio, expecting Paul to return for a singing session at any minute. When she heard *The Dream*'s engines, she stepped out on the balcony and was surprised to see the yacht's running lights coming back to the cove dock.

Clouds intermittently veiled the moon, and she couldn't see the two clearly, but she could hear the voices. They sounded easy. Friendly. If saving Jason from the snake's venom had made Jim seem more of a person in Paul's eyes, she was glad.

She sat at the piano, ready. Paul stopped at Jason's door, then came into the studio, asking Shannon abruptly, "Has Merlene explained to Jason that he will be with me and that she will be away for a year or so?"

"I don't know, Paul. They were together in the game room before he went to bed."

He scowled, rumpling his hair with his fingers and folding his long frame into a leather chair. "He's asleep now," he muttered. "I want to talk to Jason myself, but I suppose it can wait till morning?" There was a slight inflection at the end, as though he wanted her opinion.

She nodded. "Then you got custody?"

"What? Oh, not so fast. The judge set the review for the end of August. But Merlene did come through with the petition. I don't see that there'll be a hitch. But I'm not going to take any chances."

"What do you mean?"

Paul eyed her with a lazy smile as he let his head rest against the high back of the chair. She had the feeling that he was teasing her, but she didn't know why. "I told you I usually get what I want." His thick eyebrows went up. "How? Careful plans."

Was he talking about Jason's custody? Or something else? "Are you ready to sing, Paul?"

He sighed tiredly. "No. It's been a long day, and we'll skip that."

"All right." It was the first day that he had not practiced, and Shannon was worried. From the balcony she had noted wisps of fog; the night dampness seemed to have given Paul's voice added huskiness. Would he begin to neglect his work on the cruise? What if he didn't find a suitable pianist? "I'll call Dr. Moore first thing tomorrow about a pianist."

"I don't want to talk about that now," he snapped. Shannon got up. "Don't go yet," he said more kindly. "Stay with me awhile."

"You're tired," she began.

"Come for a walk," he said, ignoring her protest.

"No, I—"

"A little walk, a little conversation, maybe a nightcap on *The Dream*?" His wicked grin made him look more like Faust than ever. "Don't you want to hear what Jim and I talked about?"

"I imagine he'll tell me himself," she drawled.

"Damn it, Shannon, there you are looking as though you ought to be—as though you *want* to be— held in the moonlight. You knew I'd come to you tonight. Where is the warmth we had such a short time ago?"

Instead of answering, she smiled. "Tell me about

Jim." The electric current between them was operative; she wanted to be with Paul.

He went to the double-glass door to the balcony and rolled it open. Holding out his hand he said, "On the beach. You owe me some work time today, so call it work if you like. I want to be with you, talk to you, and I want us to be relaxed. The sound of the sea helps, Shannon. It washes away all the unimportant worries. Come with me."

He sounded authoritative, and she couldn't resist teasing just a little. She had always resisted being "bossed." She put her hands behind her back, but her smile was still warm and playful.

"Still afraid to trust me?" he taunted softly. "Shall I promise, scout's honor, not to touch you?" He dropped his inviting hand. "I told you I wouldn't try to make love to you unless you wanted me to."

"Must you remind me of feelings I'm trying to discipline?"

"Are you saying that you're afraid to trust yourself as well as me?"

"I won't admit to being afraid, Paul. Okay, a half hour on the beach, and then I'll have to come in to pack. Tomorrow will be so busy...."

"True, tomorrow will be full because I've promised Jason that you and I will hunt treasure with him. And then I'm taking you out to dinner. So if you're planning to leave early Saturday morning, you'd better pack tonight."

She frowned. Paul was giving his share of orders tonight. "You should take Jason out alone tomorrow. You said that you need to talk with him about living with you.''

But Paul was firm. ''I can always fit my son into my schedule, and so can you. We'll all treasure hunt together tomorrow. You seem to forget that Jason adores you. He is counting on both of us on this great hunt of his, the last one before cruise time. I'll join you two when I get back from town. You and I will have dinner later.''

''Dinner? I may have too many last-minute things to do.''

''Better not. Everything is arranged. I want you to have dinner with me.''

''I don't like to be told,'' she said firmly. ''I like to be asked.''

''I did. Just now.''

''That's asking?''

He shrugged, unrepentant. It was hard to see him in the darkness with his navy clothing and black hair, but she heard a faint chuckle. ''Remember when you first came and you insisted that you were good-tempered and easy to get along with? What happened?''

''Oh!'' He knew what had happened. They had battled about many things, and she had had to stand her ground. She refused to be led, cajoled or badgered into following Paul's pattern when she felt it was wrong for her. She loved him, but self-preservation was strong motivation, too.

With her first step on the sand, Shannon's heels sank their full four inches, and the grains crept under the straps to irritate her tender skin. "I should have worn sneakers," she muttered.

Again Paul chuckled, and Shannon thought how lovely it was that the tensions had eased and that they could laugh together. He knelt to unfasten the ankle straps, and her hand hovered uncertainly over his head. Suddenly she knew why Paul had worn slacks and a sweater to dinner. He had known that Jim wouldn't have dress clothing; and with his new awareness of Jim, he had wanted him to feel at ease.

"You were good to Jim tonight," she murmured.

"He saved my son's life," he said, straightening.

"And you saved his once. Now you're even."

"Jim told you?" Paul carried her shoes by their joined straps as he led her toward the shoreline. She nodded. "All of it?"

"Enough."

"You know about his police record? About all the attempts at rehabilitation that didn't work? I guess he came here as a last resort."

"And you helped him, Paul. He's clean now."

"Not because I wanted to," he said gruffly. "I'm not due for sainthood yet. He was the Pratts' grandson, so I had to do something. They were in Texas over the holidays, and I was here alone when Jim turned up. It was my first Christmas without Jason, and I was...well, anyway, I was having some voice trouble, and I was ordered to rest, so I was here."

They stopped where the sand was firm from the ebb tide. A lopsided moon sailed out from behind a dark cloud, illuminating the spiderwebs of fog that fluttered here and there. Shannon shivered.

"Should have brought you a wrap," Paul said, "but—" he shook his head and traced the line of her collarbone with his finger "—it's good this way." He put his hands on her shoulders. "Let me warm you."

He already had, the warmth of his hands stirring fires on her skin. "No," she begged, "you said you wouldn't."

"Unless you want me to. Tell me what you want, Shannon." He pressed nearer and the moon dipped into a cloud again.

"I want. . .to hear about Jim. You said you would tell me about Jim," she said. "Did he tell you he knows all about motors? Maybe he can. . . ."

He dropped his arms. "What is it with you and Jim, Shannon? You kissed him on the beach today. And that first day, too. What's the story? I think I have a right to know."

"I don't think you do," she said spiritedly.

"I sure as hell do! I've proposed. Why shouldn't I know what the problem—or the competition—is? Besides, I thought we were going to be honest with each other? Why be reticent? Unless there is something—"

Shannon interrupted. "I told you I think a lot of Jim. I always have."

"Enough to go to bed with him?"

The slap she aimed at Paul's cheek was intercepted as he grasped her wrist and pulled her close. "I thought we were going to talk, not fight," she said grimly.

"He's not good enough for you!"

Shannon started to laugh, but the sound was more like a strangled sob. That was exactly what Jim had said about Paul. "You still hate him, don't you?" she cried, trying to escape.

"No, Shannon, I don't," he ground out. His other hand held her waist, immobilizing her so that she had to listen as the words poured out. "Today I learned to respect him, but he's still not good enough for you. In the past he was weak, and I believe he still has a lot of growing up to do. Have you ever seen a man cry, seen him grovel and beg for coke or heroin or anything that will put him out of his misery? Did you know he wanted to die when I refused to give in to him? That he wanted to kill me and get away? Sure I hated him then! He was everything I despised. A good boy grown to manhood and wasting his life. A stupid junkie. Trouble for me and heartbreak for Leo and Thelma."

"Did they know?" She wasn't struggling anymore.

"Of course they knew. Oh, I had them extend their vacation, told them I wanted to be alone for a while. But when they came back—worried about *me*, about my being alone so long, mind you—Jim was there. He was over the worst of it, but he was sick and miserable. And weak. I didn't have to tell them what was wrong. We didn't let him out of our sight for a minute, because I knew it wouldn't have been hard for him to find a supplier."

"Oh, Paul, you probably saved his life," she whispered. "Thank you."

"Don't thank me," he said roughly, "I didn't do it for you. I did it for Thelma and Leo. They didn't deserve what he was going to inflict on them. When he finally got a job and went to live at the cabin, I wondered...."

"He's clean, Paul."

"I know. We talked on the boat tonight. He's got plans and dreams, but they're pretty long-range. If they don't work...Shannon, you could get hurt."

"He'll make it. I know he will."

He let her go so suddenly that she stumbled in the darkness. "So you're going to gamble on Jim," he said grimly. "Well, what's to keep you from working for me the rest of the summer then?"

"I just can't."

"You just won't, you mean." He sounded thoroughly exasperated. "Your decisions are certainly beyond me. If you ask me, you need somebody to look after you."

"I didn't ask, but I suppose you mean you?" She kept her voice soft, not wanting to spoil their hard-won ability to talk things out.

"Yes, me. Or someone with some sense. Oh, Shannon, Shannon. You need me." He said it sadly as he held out his arms. "Really you do."

She let him hold her. The fog crept closer, and she was glad to be sheltered from it. Even his sadness was communicated to her along with his yearning desire. She knew that if the moment were prolonged, it would grow into passion, for there was so little time left.

"We should go back," she murmured. "The fog . . . it's coming in."

He felt her tremble. "It's all right," he said. "It's all right." She moved to release herself, but he didn't let her go. "Come on, I'll take you home." She felt the pressure of his mouth on her hair.

They walked slowly together, Paul's arm pressing her against him. She tried to match his long stride, and thought ruefully that everything about the two of them required adjustment.

They had made a second step. They had learned to talk. But there was only one more day.

CHAPTER TEN

SHANNON AROSE EARLY and went on with the packing that had kept her busy late last night until she had fallen asleep from sheer exhaustion. She snapped shut one suitcase, leaving the other open to put in all the things that she would need until it was time to leave the next morning. The open case was depressing, giving the cozy room a suggestion of flight. She lifted it from the bed and shoved it underneath; the other one she put in the closet and shut the door.

She decided to skip breakfast and go for a swim. Maybe she'd find Jim. He could always cheer her.

She met him at the base of the path. "Shanny, I was coming to find you. I knew you'd be at work soon, and I had to tell you the news!"

By his exuberance she knew that the news was good. "Nobody's getting laid off at The Vineyard," she guessed.

"Oh, I'll be laid off all right, probably next week," he told her cheerfully. They waded into the water together. "But it looks as if I've got a better job."

"Great! Where?"

"Right here. For Paul Cypress. You know, last

night I offered to fix that port engine—*and* the leak in the master head—and he was really interested. We never really talked before. Did you know he has been thinking of hiring an assistant for gramps?''

Shannon shook her head. ''Leo *is* getting a bit old for all the heavy work,'' she admitted thoughtfully.

''I know I can save Paul a bundle by taking care of the boat and the cars myself. I'm good at that.''

They let the surf wash them in and sat close on the warm sand. ''You know, Paul is encouraging me to go to Flagler College in town this fall. I could get the basics there and maybe study classical guitar later.''

Shannon gave him a quick, happy hug. ''I'm so glad for you, Jim! You see—''

''Don't say it,'' he said with a grin. ''You were right—Paul's not so bad after all. Hard to get to know, though. Tough as nails when he has to be. Guess I didn't really want to like him, especially after you came along. I knew I could never compete with him, and—''

She touched his mouth, leaving a smudge of wet sand. ''Jim, you'll meet a wonderful girl who will love you the way you deserve to be loved.''

''But as for you, honey, it's Paul Cypress, isn't it?''

She looked away. ''I didn't want it that way.''

Jim touched her chin and swiveled her face to face. ''I was on the beach when you and Paul came in two nights ago. Oh, Shanny, I just don't want you to be hurt.''

"That's why I'm going away. He doesn't love me, Jim."

"How could he not love you!"

Shannon smiled at Jim's loyal devotion. "Let's not talk about my leaving. Tell me about Flagler and your plans."

"Well, Paul thought I might have trouble swinging a loan for this fall, so he's going to lend me the tuition himself. Said someone helped him out that way long ago. He was going to talk to the registrar today to see if there's room for me in September. I just can't believe he's doing all this for someone like me."

"Don't you put yourself down, Jim! Do you think for one minute Paul would encourage you and hire you if he didn't see exactly what you're made of?"

"Which is?" he coaxed, grinning.

"Talent, ambition, perseverance... *sweetness*," she said with an answering grin.

"No wonder I'm crazy about you," he said with a laugh. "You understand me perfectly."

"I forgot modesty," she added.

Shannon refused a cup of coffee at the cabin, as it was time to get to work. "Are you free tonight after ten?" Jim asked wistfully.

"I don't know," she said hesitantly, remembering Paul's invitation. "I have a long list of last-minute things to do, and I ought to turn in early. I'll have a long drive tomorrow. I'm not good at goodbyes anyway, Jim."

SHANNON FINISHED ANSWERING the mail early. She decided to save the final packing till after dinner, positive that Paul would say no more about taking her out for a farewell meal. The farewell between them had been quite final last night. She wandered into the kitchen.

Jason was delighted to learn that Jim would be working for his father. So were Thelma and Leo.

While Jason watched Thelma fix a picnic lunch, an idea popped into his head. "Maybe dad will let me stay at the cove while he's on tour this year. I'd be awfully good, Thelma, honest. I'll bet dad thinks I'd be bad for you and Leo, but if Jim's here, he'd always catch me and make me mind, I know he would. Ask him, Shanny, please?"

"Jason, I don't know...."

"I won't go to boarding school! I hate it! I'll be good if I can just stay here and go to school."

"I'll speak to him," Shannon promised. "I know he wants you to be happy. But I can't promise anything."

The telephone rang and Shannon went to answer it. "Is Paul there?" Shannon recognized Jeanie's voice.

"No, I'm sorry. He's in St. Augustine."

"This is Jeanie. Am I speaking to Shannon?"

"Yes," she managed faintly.

"Paul has told me about you." How friendly she sounded. "Could you give him a message, Shannon? Just tell him that his father is to be released from the hospital tomorrow. I'll take good care of him, and

I'm sure he will be strong enough to see him soon. Tell him not to worry. He is doing the right thing.'' Her voice trembled when she added, ''We love him.''

Shannon replaced the receiver, a puzzled frown on her face. Somehow Jeanie didn't sound like a lover. A nurse for his father?

She knew so little about his family. Apparently his father had been seriously ill; is that what Jeanie had come to tell Paul? He had embraced her. Could she be a family member? But she had said ''his'' father, not ''our'' father or ''dad.'' A cousin maybe?

It was Merlene who interrupted her reverie. ''Did I hear the phone? Was it for me?''

''For Paul,'' Shannon said shortly.

Merlene continued to stand before Shannon, studying her. Finally she said, ''I'll get him back, you know. I'm no good alone. We'll be together again. You can bet on it.''

''I told you—''

''I know what you told me, and I don't believe you.'' She paused again. ''I told Paul that he can have Jason this year. I'm going to tell the judge that I want my son after this year's tour.''

So she was not going to live up to her bargain after all. Jason could still be shuttled back and forth after this year.

''You'll be making a big mistake if you marry Paul just to make a home for Jason,'' Merlene said.

''What? You're talking nonsense!''

''Oh, he'll ask you, if he hasn't already,'' Merlene went on, a twisted smile on her lips, ''because which-

ever one of us marries and provides a complete set of
parents and a home for Jason will win custody."

Shannon stood up. "You're worrying for nothing.
Let me pass."

"Oh, I'm not really worried," Merlene shot back
without moving, "because I'm pretty much in control. You might remind Paul that I could go to the
press with a certain story. I hope I won't have to,
but .. .." She let the veiled threat drift between them.

Shannon brushed past her. Whatever damaging
story she had as a hold over Paul—probably about a
woman—was nothing Shannon intended to worry
about. As for the possibility of a proposal from Paul,
it had already become reality. Shannon had no desire
to discuss it with Merlene.

SHE FOUND HER OLD cutoffs and shirt. Her digging
clothes. Again she tied her hair in a ponytail to keep
it off her neck and out of the way. Before going to
collect Jason and their equipment and lunch, she
quickly dialed Dr. Moore at the University of Illinois. To her chagrin she learned that her department head was on vacation. The secretary didn't
know offhand of a music student who could take a
job for a few weeks in Florida, but she would in-
vestigate.

Shannon knew that Jack was studying in New
York. His letters had been full of the excitement of
his summer in the city. No use calling him. She dialed
her mother's apartment and was surprised to find her
at home.

"Mom, I'm starting for home tomorrow," she began bluntly.

Bonita was astonished. She had understood that Shannon loved her job and the cove. "I thought you had even come to like Paul, dear."

Shannon cut her short, promising to explain everything when she came home. "Paul will need a replacement. Do you know of any decent pianist who needs a job? On a cruiser?"

"Not right off," Bonita said slowly. "A cruiser? You're giving up the job *and* a cruise? I don't understand you at all, Shannon. Sounds too good to give up. If I knew how to play, I'd come down myself."

"You've got a job," Shannon said shortly.

"Well, not right now. The play folded with Wednesday's matinee." At the little sound of sympathy from Shannon, she added cheerfully, "But something else will come along soon, I'm sure. Darling, have you been able to save enough to get through this last year at school? Jobs are so scarce up here now; you may not be able to find one for the rest of the summer."

"I'll find something," Shannon said with more conviction than she really felt.

There was a hesitation. "I don't like to pry, dear, but it must be Paul, right? Too many passes?"

Another pause. "Something like that." Anxious to put an end to questions, Shannon said, "If you think of anyone who can work till Labor Day, call back, mother. Someone will be here to take your call. And just tell the person coming to be here by Saturday morning if he can, though I suppose Paul would wait if he can't make it by then."

"I'll see what I can do."

ON THE BEACH Jason and Shannon ate Thelma's hearty lunch of thick ham-and-cheese sandwiches, sugared tomatoes, potato chips, ripe peaches and pears, gumdrop cookies and a big thermos of lemonade. When they had packed the leftovers in the basket, Jason spread out the worn map Edmund had drawn. He pointed with a sticky finger to the penciled circles. "Dad says the ones not crossed through are the ones they never got around to trying."

Shannon bent over the sketch. "There's one up there beside the orange groves. That must be in my valley. And there's a circle at the bottom of the dune, too."

They had no luck below the hill and were soon exhausted from scouting around and digging in the hot sun. They scuffed barefooted in the surf to cool themselves. "Too bad we didn't try my valley first," Shannon said. "It's shady up there."

"We still can," Jason said, refreshed from the brief splash. He picked up the heavy metal detector and started up the trail with it. Shannon followed more slowly. The trail back of Jim's cabin was steep, but Jason was like a mountain goat. He stood grinning at the lip of the valley entrance.

"Listen, Shanny!" The metal detector was emitting sharp signals near a rocky crevice. "Something's down there."

"What do you have?" They turned to see Paul coming across the valley. He had come through the grove and was already within hearing distance of the detector's excited beeps. Shannon was surprised that he had decided to join them. Well, he had promised Jason.

He ignored Shannon. "It'll be hard to find whatever it is," Paul cautioned Jason. "Those rocks have been wedged together for ages."

Jason dropped to his knees and tried to peer into the fissure. "Maybe Juan Gómez piled them up to hide the treasure."

A trio of rocks, one a great boulder and two others too large to move by hand, were wedged together over the signal site. There was a small opening into which Jason was about to put his hand. "Hold it, son," Paul warned. "That may be the home of some animal."

"Another snake?" Jason jerked his hand back. "What can we do?"

Paul climbed up the bank to the edge of the grove and returned with a stout branch. They managed to push it into the hole and pry the two smaller rocks apart. The detector's signal became stronger.

The cairn was almost filled with dead leaves and debris. With sticks as tongs, they carefully removed the rubbish. "Look!" Jason exclaimed.

Forgetting his father's warning, Jason reached down to retrieve something. Shannon hadn't seen it, for it was the color of the stone and debris. Paul whipped out his penknife and handed it to his son.

"Scratch the surface carefully. You may have something."

It was roughly the size of a silver dollar, but not as perfectly round. Where it was scratched, it shone like gold, and Paul wondered whether it might be a doubloon.

"We'll take it home and clean it," Paul said. "I don't know the value of old coins the way Edmund did, but I know someone who does. We'll see him on our cruise, Jason."

"Do you think it's valuable?" Shannon asked.

"Could be," Paul said shortly. "Turn the detector back on, son. Let's see if there's anything else down there."

The signal was merely a dull rattle now. Paul handed Jason a plastic bag for his coin. "I'll show you how to clean it on the boat," he promised.

"On the boat?" Jason was surprised. "Why not tonight?"

"I'm going back now, son. I'm going to help Leo load *The Dream*, and I'm expecting an important call, too."

Mention of the call reminded Shannon of Jeanie's message. "Okay, thanks," he said expressionlessly when she had told him.

"I called mother about an accompanist for you, too," she hurried on nervously.

"If nothing comes of your efforts, I'm sure I can find someone in Daytona," he said when she had finished, "if I decide that I need someone."

She wanted to protest that he must go on practicing. They had worked so hard together to bring his voice this far. It would be a shame to let it slip back. But Paul didn't want to be told what to do. Neither did Shannon.

Paul took them to the center of the valley, suggesting that they work outward toward the rim of the little dell. "I have to go back to town," he said, "but I'll come back as soon as I can." To Shannon he said with a crooked smile, "After we tuck away all the loot we find, we'll have that special dinner. It's all arranged."

"You're still assuming that I've kept the date open," she said sweetly.

"You bet I am," he growled before he swung away into the groves.

"Are we all going out to dinner?" Jason asked interestedly. Shannon knew that he must be puzzled about the relationships of the adults in his life.

"I guess your dad is taking me out for a farewell dinner since I'm going home tomorrow," she said.

"Oh. That's okay. Mom said she'd play games with me tonight. She's going away, too, you know," he added wistfully.

"I know." All partings hurt.

"I'm all packed," Jason said. "Gee, Shanny, I wish you were coming with us. Dad said it was okay for me to coax you."

That must have been a while back, she thought. "You don't mind too much that your mother is going away?"

"No," he said slowly. "I knew she'd have to go to

New York to rehearse for the tour. But I didn't know I wouldn't see her for a whole year." That much was sad, but then he cheered up. "I'll like being at the cove, 'specially with Jim here. And dad says he'll be back before Christmas. Did you ask him whether I can stay with the Pratts and go to school here, Shanny?"

"Not yet, but I will tonight."

They found a few things: a pocketknife blade, a nickel, a metal button...and one item that stirred their excitement because of its apparent age. It was a crucifix, dirt crusted and green. Under a loop at the top was the barely readable INRI. The two arms and the base were fashioned in the shape of a three-petaled flower. Shannon's trowel struck it at a depth of four inches. She brushed the sand and soil from it and handed it to Jason.

"Gosh, Shanny! Do you think it belonged to Juan Gómez?"

"I don't know if pirates carried crucifixes," she said. "I think it must be silver. See how green it is? The copper alloy in silver turns green from the moisture in the air. But see where I've brushed the dirt away? See how it shines?"

"Sure looks like silver! It's got to be a part of the treasure. Come on, Shanny, let's look some more."

Shannon stuffed the plastic bag with the cross and the coin into her pocket. Although they plied the detector carefully over the rest of the valley floor, the signal remained low and sluggish.

"Let's rest here in the shade," Shannon suggested

when they had climbed to the small ledge with its small cave. "Wish we had brought the lemonade."

Jason reluctantly turned off the detector. They leaned against the stones, mopping their sweaty faces. "The book says Juan drew a map for his wife, Shanny. I wonder what happened to it?"

"There was a sketch of some kind in that journal of Elizabeth's, Jason. It wasn't really a map, though. Jim and I couldn't figure it out, so we just left it in the diary." She rubbed her finger across her puckered brow, leaving a smudge. "I wish I knew where that journal could be. If only I could remember."

"We've looked all over the house," he said tiredly.

"Yes," Shannon acknowledged, "but I have a feeling that I had it outdoors. Of course, it would be ruined if I left it just anywhere. And I've looked in the cave and under the rocky shelf."

Jason reached for the detector and idly polished the handle with his shirttail. He accidentally activated the amplifier, and the signal was immediately high and strong. Jason jumped up and began to scan. "Right here," he said in front of the cave. Cautiously he moved the detector inside, and the sound quickened. He withdrew it and turned off the switch. "I'm going in, Shanny."

"Better just let me go first, Jason. I've been in there once before when I was looking for Elizabeth's journal. I didn't find anything but spiderwebs. We ought to go back for a flashlight, though."

Jason eyed Shannon and then the small opening. "You'll get stuck, but I can squeeze in. I've got this." From his pocket he withdrew a small penlight. "I'll be careful. I can't go far in such a little cave. Please, Shanny?"

She knew it would be hard to dissuade him. "Look inside first, then."

"Nothing here." His voice was muffled, trapped in front of his body. Soon she could see only the soles of his feet and the bottom of his soiled cutoffs above the brown legs, but she could hear the steady chunk and scrape of his trowel.

When the sounds stopped, Shannon called, "Found something, Jason?"

"Naw. Ground's too hard." He started to back out, and she could see an outline of light around his body as he moved his flashlight around the cairn once more. "Wait a minute!"

"What is it?"

Jason backed out quickly. "Look! An old book with a metal clasp. That's what made the detector buzz!"

"That's it, Jason! That's Elizabeth's journal!" Her excitement matched his. "I must have missed it when I looked before."

"It was 'way on the left, Shanny. I almost missed it."

The leather cover and the edges of the pages were a bit mildewed, and the book smelled musty. But the writing was still mostly legible. Jason and Shannon sat down and leafed through it. A single sheet fell out.

"The map, the one Juan made for her," Jason said. They opened it and spread it on a patch of smooth rock, anchoring the corners with small stones. Shannon had remembered correctly: it was more of a sketch than a map.

The drawing resembled a goblet. There was an odd bulge in its stem, and that was the base of the handle. The foot of the chalice—if that was what it was—was small and uneven. The outline was done in a curious curlicue scrawl rather than with straight lines.

They puzzled over the sketch, their heads bent over the creased and faded document. Jason traced the strange shape with his fingertip. "What is it, Shanny? Can you read the words?"

"I took Spanish in school," she said uncertainly. "*Mar* means 'ocean,' and *playa* means 'beach.'" She touched a blurred word scrawled across the bowl of the goblet. "*Palangana* means 'washbasin,' I think."

"Why would he draw a washbasin?"

Shannon sat back on her heels. "Maybe this isn't a guide to where the treasure is at all. Maybe it's a description of something that was part of the treasure. And those words under the picture, Jason... some are blurred, but I think they're the traditional Spanish greeting, *mi casa es su casa*...'my house is your house.'"

Jason turned the sheet over but found it blank. "That's no help," he said disgustedly.

"Anyway, her diary is in English. Maybe we'll find a clue there." She examined the sketch again. "Strange shape," she mused. "Look at that mark right in the middle of the bulge in the stem. It looks like a Chinese letter."

"Maybe it's a decoration," Jason guessed, "or a faucet."

Shannon hid a smile. "Look here at the bottom. The marks are different. Sticks instead of loops."

"And there's a broken place on the handle. Some treasure! Let's look at the journal, Shanny."

The first page said simply in flowing schoolgirl script:

> Elizabeth Stafford, age 15
> her journal of voyage
> to England from
> New Orleans
> begun April 10, 1821.

And the following page recorded that she and two other girls were to go to a fashionable finishing school in Southampton. They were accompanied by Sister Martha, who had been assigned to a position there. The page ended in a badly scrawled, "Seasick."

On April 16 she wrote the single word, "Pirates," and a week later:

> On an island. They killed everyone but me. The one they call Gómez kept me for himself, but if he comes near me I will die.

Shannon and Jason talked about what they had read in Collier's book about Gómez. Juan Gómez had told Captain Collier that Elizabeth had shown such bravery and spirit that he had thought she should be allowed to live, and he had asked Gasparilla to let him have her. He was delighted to find that the girl could speak Spanish as well as English. Gómez was Portuguese, but all the pirates spoke Spanish together.

"I guess she was pretty brave," Jason said.

At first Elizabeth huddled in a dusky corner of Juan's thatched hut, refusing to eat and afraid to sleep. Juan was kind and patient, and gradually she learned that she could trust him. Apparently she lost count of the days, for notations after that were not dated.

"Poor child," Shannon murmured at one entry: "He took me. It hurt."

Jason didn't question the words as he eagerly turned the page. Elizabeth said that only Gasparilla, Gómez and one other man lived on her island, but across a channel the rest of the band lived and caroused. On still another island, which the pirates called Captiva, they kept a house of women, some for their pleasure and some to exchange for ransom. Juan kept Elizabeth with him, protecting her, and after a while she wrote:

It doesn't hurt anymore. Juan is good to me. I don't think about leaving him anymore. He says he loves me.

"So they got married and lived happily ever after," Jason said with a snicker.

"Not quite. The United States Navy really got after all the coastal pirates, and Gasparilla's ship was captured. Gómez wasn't on it, and he escaped. The navy returned Elizabeth to her parents, and since Gómez was a hunted man, they were separated from that time on. Let's see what she says about that time."

The log read:

Juan drew a map of a place where he has hidden a casket of treasure. He is staying behind to clear the island and will come in the longboat. Juan says if we are separated, he will register that place in his name, and I am to meet him there, or if he dies, I am to take the treasure. If he dies, I shall want to die, too.

"Aw, I bet she came back and got it herself," Jason said.

"Unless she couldn't figure out the sketch any better than we can," Shannon amended. "Also, we know that Juan lived a long time after that, so it is just as likely that he came back for it himself. Gasparilla, you remember, killed himself rather than be captured by the navy, so we know *he* didn't get it."

Jason wanted to believe that the treasure was still somewhere on Anastasia Island. "We did find a gold coin, Shanny."

The final entries were filled with a sad despair. Elizabeth wrote of waiting at her parents' home for news of Juan, but it never came. Finally she had to tell her parents that she was pregnant. They were horrified, for they had no desire nor intention of rearing a pirate's child. They refused to believe that their daughter had come to love her captor and that she wanted to have his child.

When her mother made an appointment with a *bruja*, a Creole herb woman, Elizabeth rebelled. She ran away.

"Why?" Jason wondered. "Was the herb woman going to steal the baby?"

"She could make it die before it was born."

"How? With poison herbs?"

"I'm not sure how she was going to do it," Shannon said, and hurriedly read on aloud. Elizabeth had put on her father's clothes to make her look like a boy. She had gone to the docks and was hired as a cabin boy on a frigate bound for Southampton. Ironically, she was again headed for the place where she was originally supposed to go.

The crew discovered that Elizabeth was a girl, but the captain was kind to her. He helped her find her aunt, who lived in Southampton, and she lived with "Aunt Beatrice" for many years.

By the time Jenny was born, Elizabeth believed that Juan was dead. She had written to him at St. Augustine, near the island where they were to meet, and she had written her parents, begging them to tell Juan where she was if he came for her.

When Jenny was a year old, Elizabeth's father came to England to ask her to come home. But Elizabeth had found work as a seamstress, and Aunt Beatrice adored little Jenny and wanted her and Elizabeth to stay in England; so they did. Jenny grew up and married William Webster, and they had a son, Joseph. He and his bride were the ones who came to Anastasia Island and planted the orange groves.

Elizabeth's entries were always terse and unelaborated. Even such major events as Jenny's christening and later her wedding rated only a line or two. Sometimes whole years were uncharacterized. Thus, she compressed a lifetime between the pages of one volume. She concluded with two lines referring to the coming marriage of her grandson, Joseph Webster, to Lady Sally Kent-Willerton.

I have given them Anastasia as a wedding gift. Joseph has asked me not to tell the Kent-Willertons that his grandfather was a pirate.

"Was he ashamed?" Jason asked.

"My dad said he was," Shannon told him. "Joseph was dad's grandfather, but he never spoke about the old pirate until he was a very old man. Maybe he forgot about his embarrassment by that time, because dad said he was very forgetful. He told dad that Elizabeth had given him her journal when he and Sally decided to live in America, but he had hidden it so that his bride wouldn't find it and read about Gómez; and he couldn't remember where he had hidden it."

Jason closed the book and fastened the heavy

metal clasp. "Where did your dad find it, Shanny?"

Shannon remembered that day. She had awakened in the morning to the sound of dripping water. It was raining, and in the early gray light she could see that there was a leak at the corner of her room. Steady drips were bouncing off the Boston rocker while a patch of brown was widening on the white ceiling.

Edmund had found loose tiles on the roof. He crawled into the attic to see what damage had been done, and to his surprise he had discovered a box firmly nailed to the floor. He called to Shannon to bring him a screwdriver and hammer. From the top of the ladder she watched him pry up the box and force the lid. Inside was the journal. For years no one had happened to find it.

"Joseph had told dad stories about the old pirate and his treasure, but I don't think dad believed in them until he found this journal. He was so sure it was important and valuable that he kept it under lock and key."

"But you and Jim swiped it," Jason said admiringly.

Shannon wrinkled her nose. She had asked if she and Jimmy could look at it, and her dad had said he wanted to study it and that only he and possibly Paul might touch it. Shannon had been angry. After all, if she hadn't discovered the leak, Edmund wouldn't have gone up to the attic. She had brought him the tools, and she had even helped pry open the box. She reasoned that she had as much right as anybody to see what her great-great-great-grandmother had written.

And so one day when Edmund forgot to put the journal away in the drawer, Jimmy and Shannon "borrowed" it. They scanned it so hurriedly and nervously that it was a wonder they made any sense out of it.

During Paul's lesson, they planned to put it back in the den, which was just below the studio. Shannon was to stand on the studio balcony, hidden by the draperies; she would signal Jimmy when Edmund and Paul began the lesson so that he could slip into the den with the book. If anything happened—if Edmund left the studio, for instance—she would signal Jim to take the journal and run.

But there was no lesson that day. Paul and Edmund had argued. She could never remember afterward what it was about, but she did remember feeling abjectly miserable. She couldn't bear for the two men she adored to be angry with each other. And she did remember her father's words: "Someday you'll have it all. Everything."

The vague nightmare quarrel had come to haunt her often in the early years following the accident, blessedly less often as time passed. If only the two had been able to settle their differences. But Edmund had taken *The Bonnyshan* out, and the storm had taken his life.

"Why did he take the boat out that time?" Jason wanted to know.

Shannon explained that there was an old wreck lying submerged at the base of a coral reef not far offshore. Edmund and Paul had been diving to see what they could find. She didn't know why he had gone out alone, for they always worked together. He might have been going to take pictures of the reef, which at low tide was above the surface of the sea.

Frowning, Shannon rubbed lines from her forehead with slow fingers. Why were there so many facts she couldn't remember about that day? Some things were clear, but some were hidden behind a thick gray veil. Or behind mists.

"So Jim had the journal?" Jason prompted.

She shook her head. "I gave the signal, and he ran with it up here, to my valley. He had to help Leo soon, so he left it with me. I remember that now. And I must have hidden it here in the cave. Maybe I even sat down and read some more of it." Her brow puckered again. "I remember that it started to get dark, and I worried about a storm and dad out alone in the boat. I watched for *The Bonnyshan* to come in. . . . That's all I remember."

"Anyway we've got the book now. Wait till dad hears!"

"Wait till dad hears what?" Paul stood on the rock ledge above them.

Jason jumped up and waved the journal. "Look! Elizabeth's book!"

Paul jumped down lightly and reached for the leather-covered volume. "Tell me about it."

Shannon watched Paul as Jason related their afternoon adventure. Paul seemed to be in excellent humor, his expressive brown eyes reflecting excitement and pleasure as he listened keenly to his son's narrative.

Paul took the sketch and smoothed it over his knee. "We think that must be a basin from the treasure," Jason said. "Shannon says that word means 'washbasin.' "

"And that—" Paul's finger touched the odd little mark in the middle of the bulge "—is a pirate mark meaning 'treasure.' " His voice was husky, as it always was when he was tense. "Let me study this drawing a minute."

Shannon and Jason leaned closer to examine the sheet of paper with him. It was beginning to get dark, and Shannon rubbed her eyes. "I think I see something," she said hesitantly. "There, beside that opening into the stem—don't those curlicues spell out something?"

"You're right," Paul agreed. "*Las . . . las piedras*. 'The stones.' Possibly all those curlicues are stones or rocks."

"A basin made of stones?" Jason scoffed.

"*Palangana . . .* 'basin,' " Paul muttered. "Maybe a basin of land. A valley surrounded by stones."

"This valley?" Shannon asked breathlessly.

CHAPTER ELEVEN

PAUL POINTED TO THE BREAK Jason had noticed on the handle. "If those are rocks, this opening could be an entrance into a passageway. And here—" he indicated a thin place at the top "—this could be the entry to the valley. And the little crossed sticks could be the lean-to Juan built in front of his cave house."

Shannon eagerly followed his logic. "There's the sea and the beach," she said, touching the Spanish words. "Everything fits."

"But where's our cave?" Jason wanted to know. "The one where I found Elizabeth's book?"

Shannon's and Paul's hands touched as they both pointed to the open spot at the bottom of the basin. Shannon drew back, feeling the familiar shock. Paul flicked a quick glance at her, the corner of his mouth pulled down mockingly.

"Can't be," Jason protested. "Ours is little. I could hardly squeeze in. That one goes on down to the bulge." And he pointed to the sketch.

"And beyond that to Juan's cave house, if I'm right," Paul finished for him.

"You mean the treasure might be down there?" Jason squealed. "In the bulge?"

"It could be another blind alley, of course," Paul said, "another false sketch Juan made to fool someone. He made sketches for lots of people when he was an old man, but nobody found anything. I think he enjoyed his little jokes. Even if this map is a true one, maybe there is no treasure anyway. Juan may have taken it away. Or Shannon's great-grandfather Joseph may have found it and hidden the map in the book to throw people off."

"Well, let's find out!" Jason shouted, crawling toward the cavern.

Paul's eyes rested speculatively on Shannon. "It's late, son, and I've made plans for this evening. We may have to move rocks that are blocking the back of this little cave."

Jason didn't want to be sidetracked. "Can't we go in from the laundry room then?"

Paul tousled the boy's hair. "That room was lined with cement blocks and then paneled. Nobody can get through without dynamite."

"Let me just take a quick look," Jason begged. Without waiting for agreement, he worked his head and shoulders into the opening. They could hear muffled words as his toes dug into the sand to give him leverage.

"I have reservations at Pirate Jim's on Vilano Beach," Paul said quietly. "You'll come?"

"We don't have to. . . ."

"But let's anyway." There was none of the tension or anger of the previous night. Just a quiet reminder of the plans Paul had made. Before Shannon could

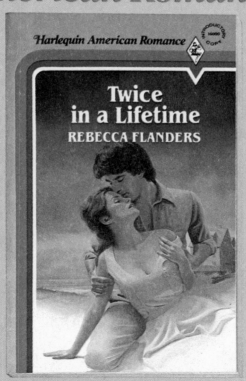

Enter a uniquely American world of romance with Harlequin's new

American Romances.

American Romances are the first romances to explore today's new love relationships. These compelling romance novels reach into the hearts and minds of women across North America...probing into the most intimate moments of romance, love and desire.

You'll follow romantic heroines and irresistible men as they boldly face confusing choices. Career first, love later? Love without marriage? Long-distance relationships? All the experiences that make love real are captured in the tender, loving pages of Harlequin's new *American Romances.*

What makes American women so different when it comes to love? Find out with Harlequin's new *American Romances!*

Send for your introductory free book now.

Get this book FREE!

Harlequin American Romance

Twice in a Lifetime
REBECCA FLANDERS

MAIL TO:
Harlequin Reader Service
649 Ontario Street
Stratford. Ontario N5A 6W2

YES! I want to be one of the first to discover
Harlequin's **new** *American Romances*. Send me FREE and
without obligation, "Twice in a Lifetime." If you do not
hear from me after I have examined my FREE book,
please send me the 4 new *American Romances* each
month as soon as they come off the presses. I understand that I will be billed only $2.25 per book (total
$9.00). There are no shipping or handling charges. There
is no minimum number of books that I have to purchase.
In fact, I may cancel this arrangement at any time. "Twice
in a Lifetime" is mine to keep as a FREE gift, even if I do
not buy any additional books.

354–CIA–2AAB

Name	(please print)	

Address		Apt. No.

City	State/Prov.	Zip/Postal Code

Signature (If under 18, parent or guardian must sign.)

Introducing Harlequin's new *American Romances...*
with this special introductory FREE book offer.

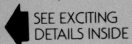

SEE EXCITING DETAILS INSIDE

Send no money. Mail this card and receive this new, full-length Harlequin **American Romance** novel absolutely FREE.

say anything else, Jason began to wriggle backward. He was grimy and scratched, but his eyes were bright with discovery.

"There's a rock at the back, dad, but I couldn't move it. I think it's just a slab, but it's tight. I couldn't get my fingers in to move it."

None of them could resist the challenge of the moment. By the time they had enlarged the small cave by digging out the sand and stones, the shadows were thick in the fading light. Shannon made a hasty run to the house for Paul's high-beam flashlight and a rope, while Paul and Jason worked at the slab, finally succeeding in prying it out.

The valley sand had drifted across the dell and into the cave through the years, but it was loose and not hard to dig away. But it took time and was hot work. Paul peeled off his shirt and Jason followed his example. Shannon rested on the extra small shovel she had brought back with her. She held the flashlight for the other two and was unable to keep her gaze from lingering on Paul's back, where the muscles rippled rhythmically as he worked. *Beautiful,* she thought. Later tonight his muscles would ache; she longed to be able to touch them, to massage them into comfort. But tonight meant goodbye. Tomorrow she would leave him forever.

Paul straightened and looked at her as though to stop her thoughts. "That's enough. Are you sure you don't mind having a very late supper?"

"We could skip it," she suggested. She repeated what she had told Jim. "I'm not good at goodbyes."

"Come on," Jason urged impatiently.

"We won't say them then," Paul said. "We'll just have the late dinner." He dropped to his knees and crawled inside the enlarged opening. They heard him grunt with effort, and then a muffled, "Hand me the trowel and my shirt." There was the chink of metal on stone. When he emerged, he eased another thin flat stone barricade to the sand. "It does look as though Juan—or someone—wanted the back of the cave sealed up."

"Did you see the treasure?" Jason demanded eagerly.

Paul grinned. "It's pitch-dark back there. Couldn't see a thing."

Jason thrust the strong flashlight into his hands. "You go first, dad. Me and Shanny will be right behind you."

Paul hesitated. "We've got the place open now. Whatever is down there can wait till daylight."

"But tomorrow we're going away! We've got to find the treasure now! While we're all to-gether!"

By this time Shannon's excitement and curiosity matched Jason's. "Let's vote. I'm with Jason. It won't be any lighter inside the cave in daylight any-way."

Paul shrugged. "It's on your property, of course. I suppose you ought to take a look while you're here. Unless you could stay longer at the cove."

"No, I couldn't. . . ."

"You'll want to protect your interests then, so I

guess we'd better go ahead,'' he said with elaborate and ironic courtesy.

Shannon clenched her teeth, determined to ignore the gibe. "I'll go last."

With the rope coiled over his shoulder, Paul entered the cave once more. There was just room for him to half turn back. "There's a passageway that bears to the right slightly and seems to descend. You won't be able to see very well because I'll have the light, so be careful."

"I've got my penlight," Jason said.

"Good. If there is any danger, we'll retreat. We may not have room to turn around, but if I give the word, back up. Understood?"

"Understood," Shannon and Jason echoed.

"One more thing," he said inching forward. "The cave, if we find one farther on, has been closed up for a long time. The air may be foul or even poisonous. I have matches and a candle in my pocket. I'll stop and light it from time to time. That should tell us whether there is enough oxygen."

Jason pushed in after Paul, and then it was Shannon's turn. She hadn't entered the cave since she was ten, and she took a moment to run her hands over its stony sides. On the left she found the rough ledge where she had once hastily hidden the journal. The cave had been just big enough for a small girl to admit her slim body. But she had never noticed that the stone at the back was smooth and straight and had apparently been *put* there.

Shannon moved on, following the glow of the

lights ahead of her. Paul's voice floated hollowly back. "Give me your hand, Jason. There's a sharp drop." Jason's light jerked downward. Then Paul's brighter flash shone briefly in her eyes. She couldn't see beyond the beam, but she felt that she was on a ledge. "There's enough room to stand up down here," Paul said. "Come on, Shannon. I'll catch you."

She dangled her legs over the edge and dropped. She felt Paul's arms around her, easing her to the floor while Jason held the two lights. Paul's arms lingered, his body warm in the suddenly chilly cave. He seemed to let her go reluctantly.

He lit a candle stub, and the flame burned clearly, bending slightly toward the back opening. "Must be fresh air from somewhere ahead of us," Paul muttered. He blew out the candle and took his flashlight from Jason.

The corridor ahead was narrow, and because of jutting rocks, they had to edge along sideways. But the rocks were dry, and the air continued to feel fresh.

Paul suddenly stopped. "Hey!" Jason cried as he bumped into his father. "What's the matter?"

Paul gave a sharp exclamation. "Looks as if this is the end, son. Come and look."

The passageway was wider here, and Jason and Shannon pressed close to Paul. "Gosh!" Jason exclaimed. "A room!"

"The bulge in the stem of the basin," Paul said. They were on another ledge, and eight feet below them was a natural chamber, roughly round in shape and about eight feet in diameter. There were several old candle stubs on the floor. Against the curve of the left wall was a large wooden chest with a hump lid. It was reinforced with metal bands and hinged fastenings. The locks lay useless on the floor, the hasps open.

"Gosh!" Jason said again. "Let's go down!"

The obstacle was a great mound of rocks. Whether part of the ceiling had caved in or whether Juan—or someone else—had laboriously hauled stones in and piled them up to hide the room was a mystery.

The three had been so eager to see what lay beyond the darkness that they had not realized they had climbed up the pile of rocks and now lay sprawled against the slope, peering down through a twelve-inch space that separated it from the stone ceiling. "It will take hours of work to remove all this," Paul said.

"But we've just got to see what's down there," Jason pleaded. "You could lower me. . . ."

"And have you break a leg if the stones shift?"

"I'll be careful. Put the rope around me, dad. Then you can pull me up later."

"I don't want you down there alone. We'll wait."

"I'm pretty light. I'll go with him," Shannon volunteered.

"I don't like it," Paul muttered.

"As you once said," Shannon said sweetly, "it's my property. According to the sketch, we're right under the orange groves. I agree with Jason that we ought to finish what we've started. Tonight is our only chance to do it together.''

Paul lay next to her, and she was very conscious of his thigh pressed against hers. He moved his arm with the flashlight, and his shoulder nudged hers. Involuntarily she shifted away to avoid the electric surge that his touch was generating, and he dropped the flashlight. It bumped down the stones to the floor near the chest, but it did not go out.

"Oh, dear," Shannon said, not very apologetically. "That was my fault. I'd better go after it." She couldn't tell whether the sound Paul made was one of disgust or laughter.

"All right," he said gruffly. "Jason first." There was nothing to anchor the rope to but himself. The other end he fastened around Jason's waist. "Untie yourself when you hit bottom, and I'll send Shannon down."

Jason was already trying to lift the heavy lid of the chest when Shannon joined him. "Let me help." How hollow their voices sounded. Even their breathing seemed to echo. The air continued to seem fresh and cool. With a quick glance around the room, Shannon noted that a dark corridor led away. It must be the passageway to the cave Juan had used as a shelter. The laundry room. But fresh air couldn't come from there, for that had been blocked up long ago. From where then?

Adding her strength to Jason's, Shannon felt the lid begin to give. Slowly it moved upward, fell back once, then finally rested against the stone wall behind it. Shannon reached for the flashlight and let the beam play inside the old chest.

"What's in it...in it...in it?" Paul's echoes demanded from above.

"Not much," Jason reported disappointedly. "Some metal chunks and a lot of dust. The trunk's almost empty."

"I think those are coins, Jason," Shannon said, rubbing one of them. "Pieces of eight. And there's a knife blade and an earring."

"There's something else, Shanny. A ring." Jason coughed. "Gee, there's so much dust. Maybe there's more stuff underneath."

They sifted through the dirt and rotted remnants of cloth that might once have been treasure sacks. They filled their jeans pockets with the odd-shaped silver coins, a pair of small cubes, the tiny earring, a gold ring and the knife blade. There were also three rods, each about a foot long and an inch in diameter.

"Candles?" Jason wondered, picking up one of the rods. His eyes widened. "Feel this, Shanny. It's heavy. I'll take one up for dad to see." As he turned to Shannon with the bar, he dropped it, and it clattered and rolled away over the sloping floor.

"Can you find where the fresh air is coming from?" Paul called down to them, and Shannon pointed the flashlight to the passageway she had noticed.

It was only about four feet high, but she crouched into it for a short distance. "I don't think this is it," she called, coming back into the cave room.

"Maybe here," Jason exclaimed. He was kneeling in the shadow to one side of the chest. "I found a hole. There's some junk in it."

Shannon knelt beside him and could feel at once the incoming shaft of fresh air. The opening was small, less than a foot wide. "This must lead in the direction of the old coquina quarry," Shannon guessed.

Jason got up and stuffed something in his pocket. Shannon asked if he had found something, but he only shrugged. "Just some old papers," he said. "We can look later. Maybe they're clues to more treasure, but I guess they'd be in Spanish."

"Don't forget the rod," Shannon said, pointing to where it had rolled near the newly discovered hole.

Jason carried the bar in both hands while he was hauled steadily up the rock pile. In the few minutes when she stood alone in the room as Jason disappeared above, Shannon had the strange feeling that the ghosts of old buccaneers were watching her from the dark corners of the cavern.

She welcomed the returning beam of light and the rope. She quickly fastened the cord around her waist and began her climb back to the world of the living. Paul took several moments to examine their finds, and his voice took on a note of suppressed excitement. "I think we've found something important!" he confided. "You say there are more bars like this in the chest? I'm pretty sure they're silver and probably worth a small fortune."

"Really?" Jason and Shannon said together.

"We'll try some of Thelma's silver cleaner on

them," Paul said. "I believe these are the kind of bars from which pieces of eight were chiseled in the early days. If I'm right—" he paused thoughtfully, but his eyes sparkled in the yellow light "—we shouldn't leave them down there."

"They've been there for ages undisturbed," Shannon reminded him.

"But now we've dug out the cave and left the diggings all around the entrance for anybody to wonder about. Shannon, Jason, I think we ought to haul them up and put them in the safe in the den until we know what we—what *you*—have." He was looking directly at Shannon.

"Me? We're all in this together!"

"It's your property, remember?"

"We don't know that for sure. Anyway, if there's so much, there will be plenty to share."

"Nobody just gives away a fortune," Paul scoffed. "But I still think it's smart to take out what we can now. I wish I could go down myself. Maybe if we move some of the rocks here...."

Shannon laughed. "There's no place to move them to. I'll go." Jason insisted on going with her, and in a short time they had carefully tied the remaining two bars to the rope to be hauled up.

At last they crept out of the mouth of the cave. Paul shouldered the shovels and metal detector and a precious bar while Shannon carried another one and Jason still another. They followed the beach; they didn't stop to pick up the abandoned picnic basket in the darkness.

THELMA GASPED WHEN she opened the door for the three dirty, disheveled and weary people. "Where have you been? Did you forget your supper? Ach, I'll be fixin' you somethin' while you take your baths."

Paul put down the rods. "We found something this time. All Shannon's, found on her property."

"Don't spoil the excitement and fun!" she said sharply as he disappeared into the garage with the spades. "Whatever it is, we'll share!"

Paul was back almost immediately, a teasing smile on his smudged face. "All yours." Then he turned to Thelma. "You remember that I'm taking Shannon out for dinner, don't you, Thelma?"

"Though it's so late?" she asked with a frown. "Well, then I'll be hearin' all about what you've been doin' from Jason while he has his supper," she said as she put a small casserole in the microwave oven.

Shannon lingered after Paul had taken Jason upstairs to share the master bathroom so that Shannon could use her own. "Tomorrow will be so hurried," Shannon fretted, "and I wanted to tell you that I'll miss you." She gave Thelma a hug, which Thelma returned, not minding Shannon's griminess.

"And I you, darlin' girl. Mr. Paul and young Jason will, too. Now you must scoot upstairs and get ready. There's a surprise for you up there."

Curiosity hastened Shannon's steps. On her bed lay an exquisite dress of soft mauve chiffon. Shannon caught her breath and touched the sheer fabric. A gift from Leo and Thelma. It looked expensive, and they shouldn't have done it. Yet she knew that they would be hurt if she didn't accept the gift. Her eyes misted as she held the delicate material of the skirt against her cheek. How very dear they were. How she would miss them.

In the bathroom she found Jason's dust-thickened jeans and shirt rolled into a ball. She picked them up and put them with her own dirty digging clothes. She would hand wash them when she came in. Thelma might not notice how terribly soiled Jason's things were, and if she put them with a wash load as they were, they might ruin the entire load.

She showered quickly and donned white lacy panties that scarcely masked the pale skin that was always hidden from the burning sun. Then she slipped into the lined strapless dress. The high-heeled burgundy metallic strappy sandles would be just right, she decided. They were already packed, so she got the suitcase out of the closet, put it on the bed and rummaged for the plastic bag that held the shoes. She didn't take the time to put the case away.

Hastily she brushed on lavender eye shadow and hunted for her plum lipstick. Luckily it was in her purse, the big utilitarian leather bag that would hold a variety of travel necessities. At the light tap on the door, she decided that there wasn't time to hunt for her small evening bag; she wouldn't carry one.

"Ready," she said, going to the door, but it was already swinging open. Paul lounged against the frame, his evening jacket of burgundy velvet a perfect complement to her dress. White slacks and shirt set off to advantage his dark complexion and blue black hair. His eyes gleamed as they roved over her in complete appraisal.

"I knew you would be beautiful in the dress," he said huskily.

"Y-you bought the dress?" she said on an intake of breath.

His white teeth flashed in a smile as his eyes came back to the smooth expanse of her shoulders and the rounded curves that began just above the softly gathered bodice. "Consider it a gesture of good-will."

"Paul, you shouldn't have done this," she said, dismayed.

He straightened and walked lazily toward her. "I was getting some things for the cruise, and when I saw this, I thought you would like it," he said. "Do you?"

"Yes, but—"

He quickly held up his hand. "No 'buts' this time. If you like it, keep it."

Sighing, she said, "I thought it was from Thelma and Leo. You shouldn't give me a present, Paul. You've paid me well."

He brushed this aside with an impatient gesture. "Forget money. I'd pay you more if you'd stay till September." As though the idea appealed to him, he raised his hand to touch her arm, then let it drop. "Will you?"

Shannon shook her head. "I can't."

His lips curled slightly. "The one woman without a price, eh?" He glanced around the room. "You've been packing. Good. Leo can load your car tonight while we're gone."

"I still have a little to do in the morning," she told him.

"Leo will be busy loading the yacht in the morning. It would help if you could at least get that ready right now. We're late anyway. A few more minutes won't matter."

She looked at Paul closely, sensitive to the deepening huskiness in his throat. Was her departure affecting him more than she had thought? Or had he guessed the reasons for her flight? Was it mockery that tensed his voice?

"I'll finish as soon as we've had dinner and come home," she said.

"You still call this home." It was a statement. Shannon had no light retort. Still touched by Paul's thoughtful gift, she didn't want him to see that his words, his eyes—all of him—touched her more, even when there was no contact. She picked up the bundle of soiled clothes she had discarded, rolled them up and stuffed them into the laundry bag. She put it in the suitcase and closed the lid, though she didn't zip it shut.

She picked up the gold neck chain from the dresser and was about to fasten it when Paul took it from her. "I'll do it."

She stood perfectly still, trying vainly to control the tingling delight that his fingers aroused. The mirror reflected a picture of the two of them, a study in harmony of color . . . and contour, she added achingly to herself; for in the flat, two-dimensional double portrait, they seemed closer than they really were, pressed together, Shannon's body molded closely against Paul's. She closed her eyes, blotting out the illusion as Paul smoothed the heavy links around her throat.

His hands went to her shoulders, and he turned her to face him. With a finger under her chin, he tilted her face. "Look at me, Shannon." His words were soft, sensuous. "You're young and sensitive. I haven't meant to hurt you. I haven't wanted that kind of power over you." He seemed to be searching for the right words, and there was a note of some new emotion...was it sadness? "Maybe I'll hurt you more before...you are free of me. I don't know how else to make you listen to me. Promise to try to understand?"

"What do you mean?" she faltered. "Tomorrow—"

His fingers quickly came over her mouth to stop the words. "Tomorrow is not to be thought of until tomorrow," he directed cryptically. "Let tomorrow take care of itself. Now, promise to try to understand?"

"I always try," she said with a little smile, "but it isn't always easy." What had he meant about hurting her before she was free of him? Did he intend to see her after his tour? Wasn't this to be the end after all?

"It's been a long and exciting day, Shannon. Let's relax and enjoy the evening."

In the kitchen Jason sat at the table, chin in hand,

his eyes drooping with fatigue. "You look nice," he said through a yawn.

"Elegant," Thelma amended. "Now don't you two be thinkin' about a thing but havin' a good time tonight."

SHANNON RELAXED AGAINST the luxurious softness of the Continental as it glided down Highway A1A into town and then across the May Street Bridge to Vilano Beach. Paul parked the car, and they walked quietly along the sandy boardwalk to Pirate Jim's.

"An appropriate place to end the day," Shannon approved. The nautical decor, the costumed waiters, the hideaway booths with souvenir "gold" pieces at each place brought an appreciative smile to her face.

Remembering her promise to Jason, Shannon said, "Paul, I promised Jason that I'd speak to you about letting him stay at home with the Pratts this fall while you're on tour. You know they'll take good care of him, and he hates the thought of having to go to boarding school so very much."

Paul's eyebrow rose. "Your idea?"

"No," she denied, "Jason thought of it himself. Personally, I think it's a good idea. He could begin and continue his school term right here. He'd be with his own class and teacher; and since it's his own idea, he'd have no reason to be rebellious."

Paul looked thoughtful for some time. Finally he laughed. "You're even beautiful when your brow is all puckered with worry that a decision won't go your way. You're right about Jason, of course. He might be a handful for Leo and Thelma, but with Jim around, I'm sure he'll be good. All right, we'll keep him at the cove.''

Shannon laughed, too. ''You can be quite nice when you put your mind to it.''

''The longer you know me, the nicer I get, too.''

But that was the extent of the banter. Shannon tried her best to stimulate a give-and-take conversation, but his answers were monosyllabic. She couldn't fathom his mood. He seemed as taut as a wound spring, though at times he tried to appear at ease...times that were quite unsuccessful.

''Paul, have I done something? Said something?'' Shannon finally asked.

''No. I'm sorry. I said we'd enjoy the evening together, but I'm not doing my part, am I?''

''Are you worried about something?''

He hesitated a second. ''Not enough to let it spoil this very special evening.'' He motioned for the waiter and ordered tropical rum drinks served in orange-shaped containers.

Shannon sipped slowly, hoping that the drink would relax Paul. ''I don't manage alcohol very well,'' she reminded him. ''I get sleepy.''

''Maybe dancing will counteract the effect.'' Paul rose and held out his arms, and Shannon went into them. She closed her eyes and let Paul guide her to the slow melodic rhythm. She would not think about tomorrow. Tonight was a little treasure box of time, something beautiful to cherish and remember.

The dance was over too quickly. Fresh drinks

awaited them at their sea-chest table. Shannon shook her head, but Paul said, "A second one may wake you up."

"Really?" She took a small swallow, enjoying the cool coconut-and-fruit flavor. She certainly didn't want Paul to remember her as sleepy and bored on their last night together. Paul watched her soberly. "You're sure you're not upset about something I've done?" she asked.

"Nothing you've done," he growled. "It's what you plan to do tomorrow that bothers me."

"I thought we weren't going to talk about that."

"It's not fair, you know. You agreed to stay, and I do still need you." He stopped, obviously making an effort to control his temper. "Forget it, Shannon. You learned weeks ago that I like things to go my way." He extended his open hand on the table. "Friends?"

"Friends," she agreed, laying her hand in his. When he stroked the back of her fingers with his thumb, she tried to withdraw, but he stood up and pulled her to her feet.

"Ready to go?"

She leaned against the table to steady the room. "Go? Oh, all right." She was vaguely disappointed that there would be no more dancing. No arms to hold and steady her. She was feeling alarmingly dizzy. She hoped the night air would clear her head.

When she stumbled on the single step down to the boardwalk, Paul caught her. "My feet don't want to go home yet," she told him.

"You don't want the night to end any more than I do," he corrected gruffly as he led her to the car.

She rubbed her forehead. "I'm just tired. It was crowded and smoky in there. I still don't seem able to see very well." Lights of the oncoming cars seemed blurred. "But the dancing was nice," she heard herself add.

"We could go to a place where it's not so crowded."

"Where?"

"I can guarantee no crowds, no smoke."

"But music for dancing?"

"Soft music, soft lights and dancing."

"All right. I don't think I'd better drink any more, though." She rubbed her eyes. They were driving across the May Street Bridge. "Is it just me, or is there a mist on the water?" she wondered.

"It's a little foggy. Probably thicker at the cove. It may be a good idea to get back there."

"Oh." She said with a sigh. "No more dancing. Too bad." Then she added, "I think I'm talking too much."

Paul chuckled. "I was thinking we could have that dance on my yacht."

Shannon peered up at him, blinking to clear her vision. "I don't think that's such a good idea, Paul. I ought to go home and finish packing."

In the dim light from the dash, she couldn't read his face. "Don't worry about it," he said tersely. They drove in silence through St. Augustine, then turned to cross the Bridge of Lions.

It's over, she thought unhappily. *All over. Unless.* . .and suddenly she wanted that last dance with Paul as she had never wanted anything in her life. She fingered the fabric of the dress he had bought for her. She had worn it no more than two hours. "It's not long enough," she whispered. "Don't make it end."

"What did you say, Shannon?"

"The night. . .it shouldn't end yet," she pleaded softly.

"Right. I'll make us some coffee."

"And we'll dance?"

"Sure."

"On the yacht?"

"Of course on the yacht."

Why did he sound so remote? So tense? The fog was getting thick along the coast road, but inside the car they were close, just the two of them. Or they were supposed to be.

Paul parked the car at the foot of the cove drive, but when he opened her door, she hesitated. "We could dance in the kitchen and have coffee," she suggested.

"Afraid?"

"No, but. . . ."

"Come on, Shannon. Have I suggested anything you haven't liked tonight?"

"No," she had to admit. Why did she have a vague feeling of regret and loss? What were those two drinks doing to her? Or had there been three?

"Come and see how snug *The Dream* is with everything stowed aboard."

"No funny business?"

Even his laugh was tense. "No funny business. One dance, one cup of coffee—which you need—a little talk, and that will be it."

She sighed. "I'll have to take my shoes off again."

Paul carried them for her. She wished he would carry her instead, but he didn't touch her. She was tired, and walking on the sand made her legs feel like lead.

In the salon she sank onto the deep sofa and reached for her shoes. "Don't bother," Paul said, dropping them beside her. "Just lie back and be comfortable while I fix the coffee. We've had quite a day." He puffed up a pillow and swung her feet up. Then he turned on the stereo softly and went down into the galley.

She could hear him moving around, humming with the music. "Cruising Down the River." A happy song, a waltz. After the coffee, they would dance.

She heard the music stop and shift to "Everything Is Beautiful." Beautiful and restful, yes. Tomorrow would be heartbreaking, but tonight everything was beautiful. She almost wished that Paul had been curt and aggressive so that she could be glad to leave him.

Although her eyes were closed, she knew when Paul stood quietly beside her with a steaming cup of fragrant coffee.

"Shannon? Asleep?" Her lips curved in a smile. His voice seemed to come from a distance. She was glad that they had come aboard. *The Impossible Dream* was a wonderful place, a place for loving.

"No!" She sat up quickly. The dream mustn't become real.

Paul quickly set the cup down on the end table. "Don't be startled. I'm offering coffee. Nothing else."

She blushed, feeling foolish. She reached for the cup, but her hand was shaking. "I was almost asleep. I told you I'd get sleepy," she said petulantly. "I shouldn't have had those drinks."

"So drink your coffee. I made it strong." He poured a cup for himself.

"I don't like it strong. Or black," she grumbled and was at once ashamed of herself. What was the matter with her?

"Mr. Paul? Are you aboard?" The voice came from the dock.

Shannon stood up, spilling the brown liquid into the saucer and onto the mauve skirt. "It's Leo," she said setting down the cup with a rattle. "He'll wonder why I'm here." Her cheeks were colored with guilt.

"Sit down, Shannon," Paul said firmly. "He's just bringing some last-minute luggage aboard. I'll take it from him."

But while he was gone, she paced the salon. Leo must have seen the boat lights. Maybe he had heard them talking and wondered why they were aboard. She pressed her hands to her burning cheeks. *Why am I acting this way? Leo doesn't care whether I'm with Paul on* The Dream. She felt a moistness on her face. *What about me? Why am I here tonight? Do I want to make love with Paul?*

Angrily she brushed the tears away. It wasn't true. And she shouldn't be here. *One drink too many and you relax to the point of stupidity,* she told herself.

She sat down to slip on her shoes. When she stood once more, she again felt light-headed and somewhat disoriented. She looked with distaste at the coffee and decided she could do without it.

She stumbled up the companionway to the afterdeck. The mist was swirling over the dock and the water, making a tiny island out of *The Impossible Dream.* She clung to the rail to get her bearings. She didn't see Paul, but she could hear him talking to Leo. She waited, hoping Leo would soon go back to the house. She would tell Paul that she had changed her mind, that she wanted to go home. Not home. Just *in.*

She shrank away from the running lights into the misty shadows, her breath coming in short gasps as she was shaken with an unreasonable anxiety. She remembered waiting in the fog once before, worried and fearful, depending on Paul to make things right. But this was *now,* she told herself. This was *The Impossible Dream,* not *The Bonnyshan.* No, she had waited in the valley, by the cave. She had waited for Paul to bring her father back from *The Bonnyshan.*

She heard Leo call good-night to Paul, and his heavy footsteps sounded hollow on the planks of the pier as he went away. She crossed the deck, reaching out to feel the rail. Missing it, she stumbled into the support, hitting her forehead. She cried out at the sudden pain, and Paul answered. "Shannon? I told you to stay inside."

Holding her forehead, she concentrated on finding Paul. In a moment he would emerge from the fog. She trembled uncontrollably, sensing what she would see.

When she saw him, she remembered everything. Paul was struggling through the mist with something—*someone*—in his arms. Edmund was alive... oh, God, he had to be alive! Shannon heard the soft strangled cry, knew that she had made it herself. All the agony and sorrow, all the anger and bitter disappointment came flooding back.

She reached out blindly, wondering dully why she couldn't run or speak. *You promised you'd bring him back! And you brought* her*! You let him die! I hate you, Paul!* Once more the words screamed through her brain, awakening that silent corridor of forbidden memory; but only Shannon heard them, for her jaws and mouth were clamped tightly, and the only sounds were the soft lapping of the waves against *The Dream* and the footsteps of the man swinging from the pier to the yacht.

When Shannon saw Paul coming close, she let go of the pain and let the blackness claim her.

CHAPTER TWELVE

WHEN SHANNON REGAINED consciousness, she was lying on a strange bed and Paul was bathing her aching forehead. For a moment she was dazed, and then the memory flooded back. She tried to roll away, but Paul put his arm over her body. Sitting up, she began to strike him until he held her close, immobilizing her.

"Stop it, Shannon." It was more of a plea than a command. "I hoped you'd never remember. We have to talk."

So some of the confusing memories she had spoken of had been real. Enough so that Paul knew she remembered. The quarrel, the storm, the *rescue*...all of it.

Pinned against Paul's body, she kept her eyes tightly shut and her face buried so that she wouldn't have to look at him. She heard the sound of the wet washcloth as it hit the floor, and his free hand began to stroke her hair. She shrank, not trusting the comfort he offered.

Dry sobs tore from her throat, making her ill from the very force of them. "You hit your head, Shannon. It brought back your memory."

"No. It was you coming out of the fog. Carrying *her*."

"Not her, Shannon. Just some extra blankets that Thelma thought we'd need."

"I saw her," Shannon insisted, pushing at Paul's stomach, freeing her head so that she could look at him with stony accusing eyes. "You told me to forget what I saw. It was none of my business!"

"That was ten years ago. Let me tell you why—"

"You quarreled with dad!" Near hysteria now, her voice was rising. "You let him drown! You saved *her*! Oh, how could you do it, Paul?"

His arms around her tightened, stilling her, and she felt his face in her hair as he begged hoarsely, "Don't, Shannon. Don't. Don't."

Rocking her, he let the words and the tears and the misery flow out of her until she was washed dry of emotion. The front of his shirt was soaked with her weeping, but neither of them cared.

When she had quieted, Paul relaxed his hold. With his handkerchief he wiped her ravaged face, and she didn't protest. "I didn't know Marie...Merlene... was with him," he told her. "*The Bonnyshan* had struck the reef. It was going down when I got there, and Merlene was in the water, screaming. I got her in the boat—"

"I want to go home now. To the house, I mean." Shannon tried to get up, but he held her.

"Listen to me, Shannon!" he said, shaking her. "All right, maybe I should have talked to you ten years ago. But you were sick, delirious. And I had to get Merlene away. I thought she was pregnant. I even thought, after what happened that day . . . ."

Shannon stared up at Paul. "What?"

"I even thought—" the muscle in his jaw was working "—the child might be Edmund's."

She flattened her shoulders on his knee so that she could look away. "No. That wasn't true."

"I know. Merlene wasn't even pregnant then. She told me she was so that I would marry her. We had been living together in New York to save expenses while we were hunting for jobs. Then Edmund asked me to come to the cove, and after a short time she wanted to be with me. She came down, and when she told me she was pregnant, I married her."

Shannon felt only indifference. She didn't want to hear any more about Merlene. But she was too tired to struggle. She would rest a little before she took that long walk across the sand and the fog.

"Shannon," Paul said gently, "you said you heard our quarrel. Did you understand what it was about?"

"Yes. You didn't believe dad. He told you the truth, that there was nothing between him and Merlene," she said tiredly. "I saw her. She threw herself at dad. He was surprised. Everything was her fault, but it's over. I don't want to talk about it anymore."

Paul sat quietly, his breathing irregular. She stole a quick glance at him and for the first time was able to see that Paul, too, was suffering. She looked away. She didn't want to deal with his pain. She had enough within herself.

"They were kissing," Paul said.

He should know that a man could kiss and not love. "They weren't having an affair," she said tonelessly. When she tried to get up this time, he laid her back against the pillows. He continued to sit beside her, but he didn't touch her.

"I thought they were," he said bleakly. "All these years she let me think...."

"So you did let him drown. You lied to me."

"No! Shannon, how could you possibly think I wanted Edmund to die? I kept diving, listening for his voice, a splash...anything! But I couldn't find him! I tried! How I tried!"

Shannon's heart wanted to believe him. It had to be true. With tears beginning again, she whispered, "He was so angry when he told you that you should leave him alone, that you would soon have it all."

Paul stood up and paced the small V-shaped space between the angled berths of the yacht's guest cabin, his hand at the scar on his throat. "Edmund had throat cancer, Shannon."

"No!" She sat up and rocked onto her knees. "I don't believe you!"

Paul ignored the outburst. "He had had an annoying hoarseness, and he hadn't seen a doctor for too long a time. That's why he wanted the treasure so badly. It was to take care of you and Bonita."

"His voice was always beautiful," she said, still not believing.

"We talked about Edmund's voice not long after you came here," he reminded her, "and I realized that you didn't know. But Bonita did."

Shannon buried her face in her hands. "Poor daddy."

"I've felt guilty every day of my life since then," Paul said, sitting down at the foot of the berth. "We had planned to take the boat out together, but then I had got after Edmund again about having surgery. Yes, he had finally seen a doctor, but the cancer was pretty well established, and Edmund resisted the idea of an operation. Sure I nagged him. Bonita begged me to keep after him.

"I don't know, maybe he didn't want to take time from treasure hunting. He was sure we were going to find it soon. Or maybe he was really afraid of the surgery. Anyway, he got very angry that day and told me to leave. That wasn't long before my afternoon lesson. When I went back in I found him with Merlene."

Paul ran his fingers through his hair. "That's what he meant about my having it all someday, Shannon. I guess he thought of me as a son, in a way. Someone to carry on for him. He wanted me to be a great singer, a star. He taught me how. If I've got it all, it's because he showed me how to get it."

"That's what he meant...about your having it all? Dad...wanted that for you?" she asked slowly.

His hand went to his throat again. "Edmund had the energy and drive of ten men, Shannon. He didn't allow himself time for rest. It was as though he knew he wouldn't have as much time as he'd hoped for. But it was too hard on his voice. I thought it was happening to me, too, this spring. The pattern was the same."

That's why Paul had been afraid, why he had been unreasonable and irascible. Her own heart contracted. "But you're all right?"

He nodded. "Yes," he said ironically, "I'm all right."

"Why did you go away so soon? Why couldn't you have stayed with us a little while?" she asked bitterly. "We needed you." She pressed back against the pillows and looked up at the translucent hatch through which the running lights shone. "Why did you tell me to forget what I saw?"

"I had to try to protect Edmund's reputation. He was dead, and I didn't want the world to know that he and my wife...it could only hurt his memory. And you and Bonita, too. I took Merlene away the next day. She wasn't badly hurt, but I admitted her to a private hospital. When they said it was all right for her to travel, we went on to visit my people, where I thought she could recover fully. I was worried about the child." He laughed bitterly. "No wonder she didn't want me to talk with the doctor."

Heavy lethargy was gripping Shannon. Emotionally drained, she was fighting to keep her mind clear. The small corner of it that wanted her to believe in Paul had to be disciplined into silence. He shouldn't have doubted Edmund's word. He should never have let Edmund take the boat out alone. He should have gone out after him as soon as the sky darkened and the mist thickened. He should have ignored Merlene's cries.... "God in Heaven, what am I think-

ing!'' she muttered through a groan as she flung her
arm over her eyes.

''If it's that I'll never be free of the guilt I
feel, you're right.'' Paul began to pace in an effort
to keep up with his runaway emotions. Three long
treads to the door, three back. Like a heavy pendu-
lum, swinging against the berth as he turned, nudg-
ing her to listen to the tortured voice. ''I've paid in
every way I could. The debt. . . the burden. . . I don't
suppose I'll ever be free of it.'' Her eyes widened, but
he didn't notice. ''He was like another father to me.
But then I thought he had hurt me, too. Through
Merlene.''

The lethargy was gone. What she interpreted as
self-pity stung her to fury. Shannon got to her feet
just as Paul's long step brought him within inches of
her. ''You paid? How? With your life? Sure, you've
followed in dad's footsteps, but you've reaped the
profits! Do you really think you can replace Edmund
Webster? You must be crazy! You don't even come
close!'' Her voice rose and broke. ''Dad was right!
You got it all. . . the fame, the cove, everything!'' She
began to laugh as pent-up tears escaped and slid
down her flushed cheeks. Shannon could not stop.
''You filled all his engagements that year, didn't
you? That must have given you a nice start—with
enough left over to buy his house!''

''Stop it, Shannon. You don't know what you're
saying.'' The hoarse words seemed like a gasp, one in
which there was anger as well as pain. She brushed at
her eyes, wanting to see his face when he learned

what she really thought, but the tears and laughter continued to mount within her.

"Don't I? Even when I was ten and eleven, I read about you, Paul. And I heard my mother talk about you!"

"She couldn't have said that I kept that money!" His fingers gripped her shoulders.

"Y-you and your b-bitchy wife must have had a l-lovely time on dad's money. In dad's house!" She began to laugh at the incredible irony. "Now you have his treasure, too!"

"Shannon!" He gave her a shake, then let go. She would have fallen if he hadn't reached out again. He pulled her against him, smoothing her tangled damp hair away from her cheek.

She wept brokenly, quietly, without protest or struggle in his arms. She didn't object when Paul lay down beside her, cradling her body against his.

"I know. I know you hurt, Shanny. I know." Dully she noted the childhood nickname and took comfort from it. He held her quietly, knowing that she wasn't hearing him, wasn't feeling the soothing hands brushing back her hair, smoothing down the rumpled dress over her thigh, massaging the tense muscle knots in her shoulders and back.

When her sobs subsided, he spoke slowly, as though afraid that sudden sound or motion would return her to hysteria or flight. "I didn't keep the money from those concerts, Shannon. I gave it all to Bonita through my lawyer. She thought it was insurance money." She neither moved nor answered.

"There are records. I can give you proof if you want it." Still nothing. "Edmund didn't have much insurance. He had cashed in a lot of it, gambling on finding that treasure. When he found out about his throat, he was a poor risk, of course, even if he could have bought more."

Her breathing was more even now, and Paul looked at her flushed face on his shoulder. Shannon's eyes were closed, and he wondered whether she had fallen asleep. One closed fist was knotted against his chest, and he put his hand over it, opening it to lie relaxed between them. Yes, she must have dozed, exhausted.

Paul continued, almost as if to himself. "I borrowed to buy the cove, because I knew Bonita needed money more than she needed a house where she no longer wanted to live. I suggested that she keep the orange grove and your little valley, and then later I wished I had bought that, too, because the part of Edmund's dream that I want to fulfill most of all is the part about the school. I know now why Edmund was tired of concert life. It's grueling. It can hurt a person." He sighed tiredly, drawing her closer. "I don't want to be hurt anymore."

The hand that was caught between them stirred so that the palm crept up an inch toward Paul's scar. Shannon wasn't asleep. She had listened. Out of the depths of her own pain and doubt she wanted to reach out. She needed something—someone—to hang on to. A life raft. A lifeperson. Someone who needed her, too. Someone who would give strength and reassurance and comfort, all the things she couldn't resurrect for herself, but maybe for someone else. . . .

She couldn't speak, couldn't ask for help. All the words she knew had drowned in the tears she had shed. Yet her need was so great that she whimpered, feeling suffocated. Her fingertips touched the ridge of Paul's scar and moved restlessly over it, caressing the wound, wanting to heal it.

She felt his breathing stop, and then there was the pressure of his mouth against her hair, and he caught her tense fingers and brought them to his cheek. "It's all right. Sleep if you like," he murmured.

The cradlelike motion of the boat, the reassurance of Paul's words and his arms, gently wrapped around her, gradually soothed Shannon. Worn-out from the struggle with her resurrected trauma, she slept. Paul continued to hold her, moving only to brush his lips across her hair or to stroke her tender flesh gently in a touch meant to share the unbearable sorrow.

And after a while Paul, too, slept.

WHEN SHANNON AWOKE, she didn't know at first where she was. Too soon the memory flooded back as she felt the loose embrace of the sleeping man beside her, the rocking motion of *The Dream* and the tears and sorrow still fresh in her heart.

Scarcely moving, her head in the hollow of Paul's shoulder, she looked at him. He looked vulnerable, almost childlike. So much like Jason in sleep. Her love for Paul rose in a longing surge, and she laid her hand lightly on his chest. In the dim light from the bedside lamp, she watched the rise and fall of his deep breathing.

She watched him for some time, willing herself to turn away from her doubts and accusations of Paul forever. He could never have wanted Edmund's death, could never have been involved in it. She knew that now. Her fears had been a child's fears. They were gone now. Only her love remained. If only he loved her, too. . . .

She thought of his kindness. His patience. In spite of his admitted desire for her—and of his reputation with women—he lay beside her now, comforting, soothing, giving her what she needed. Her love for him surged deeper.

As lightly as butterfly wings her fingertips touched the scar at his throat once more. In his own way, did Paul need her as much as she had needed him tonight? *Why do I deny him—and myself—when we need each other so much?*

What did it matter if there was only tonight and no tomorrow for them? Paul was right, she told herself. It was wrong to deny one's needs. It was reasonless.

She thought of tomorrow and the desolation of not seeing Paul, of not feeling him beside her with his arms holding her. Of never having welcomed his body to be bound with hers. "No," she whispered against him. "Oh, Paul, I need you so."

She moved her head on his shoulder, tilting it upward so that her lips could find the scar she had learned to love. It was his mark of vulnerability, a wound that she had helped to heal.

She touched her tongue to the proud flesh and felt the change in Paul's breathing. She willed her kisses to heal the hurt as she pressed closer, and her long fingers found the U-shaped place on his collarbone as she began to murmur words of love.

"Shannon?" he asked huskily. He moved back on the pillow and took her face between his hands. "Wake up, Shanny."

"I'm awake," she whispered, threading her fingers into his hair.

"It's all right. We've both been asleep." He kissed her forehead and then swung his long legs off the berth, pushing her gently away from him. "Rest a bit more, Shannon." He stood up. "Try to rest." He pulled a blanket over her and turned toward the door.

She heard him open it and felt lonelier than she ever had in her life. She couldn't let him go. "Paul!"

When he turned, she was standing beside the bed, the blanket tumbled around her feet. Her eyes were wide, asking. She took a step toward him and fell, her feet tangled in the soft woolen fabric.

Paul picked her up, his strong sinewy arms surrounding her, plunging her into breathless desire. She clung to him. She tightened her arms around his powerful neck and buried her face in the hard contours of his shoulder. "Don't go," she whispered. She felt Paul's body tense with excitement, and her own heart sped in anticipation.

He set her gently on the bed and stood above her, hesitating, searching her face for a sign of doubt. His eyes wandered the length of her, pausing to note her breasts as they responded to his gaze. Shannon held out her arms and Paul eased himself onto the bed and gathered her close. He kissed her face tenderly, tracing the contours and angles of her forehead, her eyelids, her cheekbones, the tip of her nose.

She tugged at his hair, pulling his head down so that his mouth found her parted lips, moist and inviting. Shannon could feel the muscles along his body grow tense and hard as he instinctively tightened the reins of his desire. Shannon sought his eyes and beseeched them with her own. "Don't," she whispered. Once more she pulled his head down, and with her lips, her tongue, she made him understand her need. Paul's tongue savored the intimacy of her mouth and her body began to fill with sweet hot desire as she felt Paul press urgently upon her.

"Shannon." He took his lips away, and Shannon felt the loneliness that would always be there when she could no longer be close to Paul. His face, inches from her he searched her eyes, his own blazing with desire. He spoke softly, intensely. "Shannon. You have to tell me what you want, honey."

She didn't hesitate. "I want you." She heard her own whisper swell and fill the room with her need and knew it was true. "I want to make love to you."

She heard the groan that escaped Paul's lips, and she knew that for him it was also true.

"Don't leave me, Paul. I need you."

She guided his hand to her breast and gasped with pleasure when he kissed the cloth that her breast was straining against. "Paul," she moaned. "Oh, my darling, Paul." Shannon fumbled with Paul's shirt, and when she couldn't work it away from him, he helped her. She kissed and caressed the firm flesh.

Soon he had taken off all his clothing, dropping it in a heap. When he turned back to Shannon, she, too, was naked. Sweeping her into his powerful arms he looked deeply into her eyes. "You must be sure. Are you sure, Shannon?"

"Yes, oh, yes." She longed for the release, the deep sense of being a part of Paul, which she knew instinctively their lovemaking would bring. She wanted to be lost with him, healingly lost, taken to a place where only he and she existed and where there was no more confusion or pain or sorrow. "I want to be with you."

Slowly. . .slowly, Paul rained kisses over her face, her throat, her shoulders, her breasts. His tongue left traces where he had been, where he had tasted, tempted, probed and teased. His hands traversed her body and Shannon began to tremble, passion drowning her with waves of fire and ice.

Shannon's hands explored Paul's body. She needed to know every curve, every angle, every detail. Her hands grew bolder as her desire became more demanding. He guided her patiently and tenderly, whispering reassurance. Sensitively, Paul brought her to the threshold of her desire. She arched her glistening body in urgent readiness. When still he hesitated on the very brink of their union, she blindly touched his face and was astonished to find it wet. "Paul," she whispered, "don't you want me?"

"I don't want to hurt you, sweet Shannon. Never that. I don't want you to hate me."

"But do you want me?"

"Yes! More than anyone, ever!"

She didn't care about any other woman in his life. Tonight there was only her great need, her own claim. She took Paul's head in her trembling hands and guided his face to hers. Willingly she gave herself to Paul as she murmured again, "I want to be with you!"

Paul swept her passionately into his arms and soon they were lost together, guiding, exploring, demanding, accepting. Shannon pressed her body around him, her need greater than anything she had ever known. Her body was dancing to the rhythms of nature as she undulated and rotated, closer and closer, riding on the crest of a wave rushing toward the shore.

As she accepted Paul, Shannon cried out softly and then instinctively arched her body as tremors of pleasure began to overwhelm her, and together they began the quickening journey to the kingdom where the only law was feeling, and reason never interfered. Shannon's eyes and mind closed to everything but Paul. Yesterday was gone, and tomorrow had not yet been born. Life was the moment of living.

Shannon wound her fingers through his shining hair. Higher, higher they rose. "Yes!" she cried as she held him, as she became fully a part of him, and he of her. Moving together in perfect rhythm, they were one flesh, their hearts beating together like twin metronomes, weaving together the wonderful harmony of their union.

Together they soared beyond the moon and stars to the distant Eden, where they trembled at the apex of their flight, finally spiraling down, down in dizzy undulations until they found themselves at rest in each other's arms. Shannon released her breath in a long expressive sigh, holding Paul, loving him.

Once more Paul reached for her tenderly, to smooth her tousled hair. His fingers were gentle as they stroked stray strands away from her eyes. He leaned on his elbow and gently placed feather-light kisses on her eyelids, her cheeks, her lips. He languidly traced her parted lips with his fingertips, pausing only to hold her eyes with his penetrating gaze. "I didn't know you were a virgin," he whispered. "I didn't want to hurt you."

"It's all right." She cupped his chin before she slid her hand to the back of his head, pulling him close for a long, deep, lingering kiss.

He moved her effortlessly into the hollow of his shoulder, letting his hand rest on her hip. "Go to sleep, darling. Go back to sleep. We'll go back to the house in the morning."

Shannon wanted only to rest. She and Paul were back on earth, and their troubles were still here. But they didn't hurt as much anymore, because they had been shared. She would deal with them. Tomorrow.

CHAPTER THIRTEEN

WHEN SUFFUSED SUNLIGHT touched her eyes, Shannon awoke. She reached for her travel clock; not finding it, she closed her eyes once more with a sigh as she kicked aside the blanket, for the morning was already warm.

Saturday morning. The day she would leave Pirate's Cove. And Paul. As she thought of him, the memories that had been lost in sleep crowded back into her mind. She had slept with Paul and had not gone back to the house.

She remembered, too, the grief that had been renewed after ten years. Yes, and the insidious, corrosive doubts about Paul. She pulled the blanket over her nakedness; it was Paul who had brought her back to wholeness with his words of comfort and his shared body. She had needed him, and he had given himself to her.

She thought of the night without shame or regret. Last night it was she who had urged their lovemaking, and it had been sweet. Healing. And she knew that the hour she had asked for and so freely received had deepened her love and passion for Paul. That he was a vulnerable being, prone to mistakes and capable of anguished remorse and determined commitment, brought him closer to her heart than ever.

She touched the pillow where his head had lain and lived again the memory of his kisses, mounting in passion as they had journeyed over her body. Wishing that he had stayed until she awakened, she gave herself over to the cradling movement of *The Dream* as it rocked at its mooring. She must be delaying Paul and Jason's cruise by her presence. Yet she sat up with reluctance. If only Paul loved her... how many times had she said these same words?

Nothing had changed. He didn't love her. Oh, it would be so easy to become his mistress. To enjoy the part of his life that he would allot to her. But when it ended—and it would—she would suffer unbearably. She thought of the sweet soaring joy of the night and knew that Paul's fulfillment had been as great as hers. But there had been no words of love.

I should be grateful for his honesty, she thought. *Right now he needs me as an accompanist and surrogate mother for Jason. And as a lover. All those needs will pass, and then what will be left?*

She must still leave him. It was a matter of self-preservation.

She looked around for her dress. It wasn't on the shelf where she had tossed it or on the floor. She went to the hanging closet at the end of the berth. Maybe Paul had put it there. The door stuck, and when it opened suddenly, she staggered back just as Paul entered in time to steady her. "Good morning," he said, kissing her bare shoulder and turning her around to let his eyes caress the delectable curve of breast and hip. "Are you okay?"

"Yes," she said softly and shyly. She indicated the empty closet. "Why have you taken my clothes?"

She caught the glint of humor in the brown eyes. "It's a good way to keep you where I want you."

"Well, but I must be holding up your trip. And I ought to be starting north myself. I don't even know what time it is." The cabin was dim, the only daylight entering from the opaque skylight.

Paul sat down on one of the berths and pulled her onto his lap. He ran his hand playfully up her arm to let it settle along the side of her neck and jaw. He kissed her, and she felt a spreading thrill. Why did his every touch and glance ignite a yearning answer in her? Why couldn't she command a cool indifference? "Now then," Paul said when he felt her relax against him, "I don't believe I heard you right. What was that about going north?"

She pushed away from him, settling beside him and pulling the edge of the blanket over her. "Please give me my clothes, Paul. You heard me right. Nothing has changed." She spoke softly to take the sting from her words.

His eyes seemed to recede into darker shadows. "Last night, Shannon...didn't it mean anything to you?"

Impulsively she put her hand on his knee and felt the hard muscles contract. "Of course it did. But we can't go on. *I* can't. I thought you understood."

"I'll never understand you! We get close, and then

you run away! The closer the relationship, the more determined you are to break it off. How can any man be expected to understand that?''

"I've told you, Paul. I don't want an affair. I can't just... just live with you for the next six weeks and then go back to school and forget the whole thing. I'm not made that way. Things go too deep with me, I guess.'' She was trying to be patient.

"And they don't with me? Is that what you're saying?''

"I don't really know,'' she admitted with a trace of sadness. "You've had affairs before. You know what ending them means to you. I don't, but I think it would be... hard for me. I have to keep myself together for this final year at school. If I'm all torn up inside, I may not make it.''

"Why are you talking about six weeks? Didn't I suggest marriage? Did that slip your mind?''

"No, but you've forgotten that I won't marry without love,'' she said gently.

"And you've apparently forgotten that you asked me not to leave you last night,'' he retorted. "Why did you say you wanted to be with me if you didn't mean it?''

"I did mean it!'' But with dismay she understood that Paul had thought she meant for some time, longer than just the few hours when she thought she couldn't survive without him. "I wanted to be with you last night, even though it meant that it would be harder to leave today. I wanted everything that we had last night, Paul.''

"And it was sweet," he said huskily. "Don't put it all away, Shannon. Don't run away again."

She drew the blanket closer. "I must. Don't make it harder. Please give me my clothes so that I can go to the house, Paul."

With his foot Paul slid open the locker under the opposite berth. "Your things are here," he said gruffly.

Shannon gasped when she saw that her suitcase was aboard. "Paul, why is my luggage here?" Suddenly the slow and deep motion of *The Impossible Dream* registered in her consciousness. It was not the dip and bob of a boat moored at dockside. It was the rhythmic waltz glide of a vessel at sea anchor. "What have you done?"

"You asked me not to leave you."

She pressed one hand to her head. What exactly had she said? What had Paul inferred?

"It was you who asked me to stay with you," he said mercilessly. She rose, and as the blanket sagged he put it around her and drew her close. "You asked to be with me, and I want you with me. Don't retreat," he pleaded again.

But she did retreat. She wrenched away and stood at the closet corner of the tiny cabin. "You can't make me stay with you!" she cried. "I want to get off this boat. Now!"

"Please keep your voice down," he advised. "I'd rather Jason didn't know that you are aboard unwillingly." He nudged the door shut. "He's probably in the galley by this time, hungry for breakfast."

"What have you done?" she demanded again breathlessly. "Where are we?"

"Several knots out of St. Augustine," he said calmly. "After breakfast we'll weigh anchor and go on to Daytona Beach, where I've arranged to pick up a piano so we can go on with our work."

"This is kidnapping!"

"Piracy," he corrected, the dangerous glint back in his glance. "We've been practicing piracy for quite a while now, wouldn't you say?"

"How could you!" she stormed. "My mother is expecting me—"

"No, she isn't," he contradicted. "I called her to say that I had persuaded you to finish your work agreement. She seemed pleased that you were going to keep your word after all." He folded his arms over his chest. "Now come back and sit down. I have a few things to say to you."

His dominance made her bristle, and she didn't budge. "Well, I have things to say, too! Number one, you can take me back to shore at once!"

The dark eyes gleamed dangerously, but he spoke evenly. "There is a robe in the closet. Put it on."

Shivering as much from the chill that his hard tone gave her as from shock, she reached in and removed the only garment in the cabinet, a short white terry swim robe. Shrugging into it, she sat gingerly on the edge of the berth. "Well?"

"I had called Bonita earlier to invite her to Pirate's Cove for the Labor Day weekend as a surprise for you. I thought it would be pleasant for you to have her company on the long drive back to Illinois. That was some time ago, when I was still thinking in terms of your returning to the university.'' When she started to interrupt, he ordered, ''Sit still, Shannon, I'm not through.

''So you see, it was only common courtesy of me to call and discuss your change of plans with your mother.'' He stood up and began the restless pacing that she remembered from the night before. Three steps, turn, three steps, turn. ''A couple of days ago I decided that you had no valid reasons for running away.''

''*You* decided!''

He ignored her outburst. ''I decided that I would just bring you aboard and simply start the engines.''

''And I made it so easy when I fell right into the bed—''

''Berth.''

''And slept through the night!''

The quirk at the corners of his mouth pulled into a grimace. ''Don't spoil last night, Shannon.''

All the euphoric delight of the night was erased in disillusioned anger and embarrassment. He had used her. She had played right into his sensuous hands. She had never felt so manipulated.

''Oh!'' She crouched against the bulkhead, her legs tucked under her. ''I will not be shanghaied this way!''

''And I will not have Jason upset,'' he said harshly. ''He thinks you have changed your mind, that you want to stay with us as long as you can. It makes up for the loss of his mother, who, by the way, is aboard a plane for New York right now. She hired Jim to follow with her car.'' His lips twisted sardonically. ''I told Jim that you were going to work for me for quite a while. He was glad about that. He'll be working for me, too, so you'll be able to see each other.''

She glanced up sharply. Was the cruise to be short-lived, then? A matter of days instead of weeks? And damn that enigmatic look of his! What did he think was going on between her and Jim? Did he think she was just ''easy''?

She dropped her head in her hands to escape his probing eyes. ''You misunderstood, Paul. I wanted to be with you last night, but I don't want to stay with you.''

''The hell you don't! Everything about you last night told me that you do want to be with me.'' He leaned against the door, and she suddenly felt imprisoned by the harsh-voiced twin of the man who had held her so tenderly only hours earlier.

''I didn't mean what you think. You can't make me stay!''

''No? You think you can control what we think and feel? What we *need*? How did you feel last night? How do you feel now?'' He turned away from her. ''I'm not even sure about my own feelings. I just know that I need you. I want you. I don't want what there is between us to just. . .die.''

''Then take me back.''

''You're not going ashore,'' he said flatly. ''There's no reason for you to leave. You agreed to work till

September. We need that long to work this thing out.''

"We'll never work anything out if you insist on keeping me captive!''

"We will. We'll have to. We'll be together, and somehow we'll learn to understand each other. Now get dressed and come to breakfast.''

Her anger seethed hotly at his high-handedness. ''Pirate!''

"Listen to me, Shannon. This cruise is to acquaint my son with his people. It is to give Jason and me time to become close and to understand each other. We'll be separated when I begin my tour, but this space of time is to give Jason a firm foundation, a feeling of family and belonging that will sustain him. I won't allow you to jeopardize that, do you hear me? Your presence will give him even more strength and security.''

Shannon read implacable purpose in the black pupils so close to her own. Paul was demanding her cooperation for his son's sake; it was no longer an appeal, but an order.

"Now you listen to me, Paul Cypress!'' She was furious enough at his continued autocratic treatment not to care what he thought of her. "You can go straight to hell with your piracy and your stony commands! I never volunteered to help you with your family problems! And I will not have you ordering me about! I'm not your slave; I don't even work for you anymore! Now either you take me ashore or I will manage to get there myself!''

"I don't think so! You gave me no choice, you

know. I told you I wanted you to stay until September, and you agreed. Then you suddenly decided to go home, and I had no choice but to—as you so delicately put it—shanghai you.''

"Don't you believe in freedom of choice? *My* choice? I'm certainly mature enough to make my own decisions!''

"You haven't proved that. Decisions to run away are pretty childish, I'd say!''

"Oh! You...!'' She could think of nothing uncomplimentary enough. "You have no right to take control of my life this way! I won't have it!''

Their voices had been laced with anger, but they had been kept low, grim but staccato. Shannon glared, her jaws clamped shut now, determined to make good her threat to escape.

As soon as there's an opportunity to escape, I'll take it, she thought. And what about Jason? Paul would just have to make an explanation to his son for her disappearance. He was good at that. But would Jason understand that she did care for him? Would she ever see the boy again?

There was a tap at the door and Jason's voice said, "Shanny, are you awake?''

Paul straightened. "I've been honest with you.''

"But you're asking me to lie, to pretend for Jason,'' she retorted softly. "So you are, after all, deceiving your son. How ironic.''

"Can I come in, Shanny?'' The door opened a crack and Jason stuck his head in, curls mussed and eyes still heavy with sleep. "Oh, hi, dad.''

"Hi, son." Paul drew Jason against him affectionately. "Shall we start breakfast for Shannon?"

"Okay. Shanny, I'm glad you decided to come. Dad woke me up last night to tell me, and then Leo helped us come aboard so we could get an early start. We're going to have a super time. I brought all the stuff we found yesterday so we can clean it right here on the boat."

Shannon managed a stiff smile. "Good, Jason. We can go right on playing pirate on the cruise."

Paul's eyes warned her as he said, "Come on, son, let's give Shannon a chance to shower and dress while we get the pancakes going."

"Sure," Jason agreed with a grin at Shannon. "Isn't it fun sleeping on *The Dream*?"

Paul propelled him out the door so that she couldn't answer.

Shannon marched into the small head that separated the guest cabin from the galley lounge. Dropping the terry robe, she stepped into a cold shower that shocked away some of her angry resentment. There would be options. She would not submit to this high-handed piracy!

She wondered how he would have carried out his plans if she had not fallen asleep. Had the gift of the dress, the entire pleasant evening, especially the heady drinks, all been cunningly calculated to lull her? Did he plan on her being so relaxed that somehow he could get Jason and just take off? Unlikely! Or was Leo an unsuspecting accomplice? Was he to bring Jason aboard while Shannon was sleeping?

Probably the Pratts, like Jason, had been told that Shannon had changed her mind about the trip.

When she stepped out of the shower, she faced her reflection in a long mirror on the door. She had never thought of herself as beautiful. Beautiful was tall and stately, like Merlene; or maybe diminutive and exciting, like Jeanie. Shannon was somewhere in between. Smaller than average but well proportioned.

She studied herself, touching the small firm breasts that had learned to react so quickly to Paul's caress. Why couldn't he be content with her...and only her? Was it because beautiful women orbited around him for the choosing, as the media continually suggested? Could any woman love him more than she did?

Slowly a feeling of despair welled up inside her. Paul had been honest with her. He had told her plainly that he wanted her as a mother for Jason, young as she was. Jason liked her and had been good all summer, in spite of his recent rebellions at school. Shannon liked Jason, too; they had fun together. With her as a part of the Cypress household, the judge would have no qualms about giving Paul full custody of his son.

She had no doubt that she could and would function quite well as wife-lover for some time. Then when she returned to school and Paul went on tour, the idyll would be over. Oh, Paul might prefer that she remain as his wife in name for Jason's sake. He might even prefer it because their careers could eventually mesh. And perhaps because with a wife he could fend off undesirable liaisons.

"Why am I so sure it couldn't work?" she asked her reflection softly. "Didn't it work for my father and mother?" And for the first time she allowed herself to reexamine carefully the scene in the studio ten years ago. . . .

Merlene had come quietly when Edmund was alone. She had gone to Edmund and pressed her lithe body close. He had seemed surprised. Shannon had expected her father to be angry and to send the woman away; only her mother should speak to him with her body that way. But Edmund had appeared to joke, to dismiss Merlene's advances as playful banter.

Merlene had been persistent, murmuring soft words that Shannon had not been able to hear; she had smiled, turning up her pretty face and running her hands over Edmund's chest and face. He had moved away. She had followed.

At last he had looked at her as though seeing her for the first time. His arms had come around her slowly, and then he had bent her backward with the force of his kiss. Paul had interrupted.

Is it because I saw how easy it is for a handsome and popular man to be attracted to another woman, she asked herself sadly. She had never believed that there was anything significant between her father and Merlene, and she didn't now. But maybe in time there could have been. And she was positive that her parents had been in love with each other. Hadn't her mother given up her own career to travel with Edmund and make a home for him, no matter where he was?

Could I do that? Well, the question was academic. She would not marry Paul.

The insurmountable problem was that Paul did not love her. He had been hurt, his marriage had soured him and he refused to be vulnerable again.

Maybe the hurt went farther back than his marriage. What was it he had said? Edmund had been like a father to him until Paul thought that Edmund had hurt him, too. Too? Had his own father hurt him? Was that why he rarely spoke of his home and family?

Sighing, Shannon shrugged into the robe and returned to her cabin. The questions were endless, the answers elusive. The only solution was to leave as soon as she could. It would be hard, but not so hard as to try to put the pieces of her heart back together in six months or a year.

She dragged out her suitcase and opened it on the berth. With chagrin she saw that it contained all the things she hadn't thought immediately necessary: a bag of soiled clothing, a few shorts and tops. She dug out a pair of red shorts and a plaid shirt. Shoes? She wondered whether she had any but the burgundy sandals she had worn last night.

Shoes would weigh her down if she found that *The Dream* was close to shore and she decided to make a dive for it. She found her bundle of yarn hair ties; pulling her hair over one shoulder, she braided the heavy mass into a single plait and fastened the end, thankful that there had been a small comb in the pocket of yesterday's denim shorts.

Eyeing the open luggage, she wondered whether she would ever see it again if she managed to get away. Well, she would not be shanghaied, that was certain.

BAREFOOT, SHE PADDED into the galley, where Jason was setting the table and Paul was complacently frying bacon and pancakes.

"You slide in first, Shanny," Jason said, pointing to the wider end of the booth. "Dad's going to take the outside so he can get more pancakes for us."

"Okay," Shannon agreed, trying to sound casual. "I'll just take a quick hike up on deck to see what the day is like. Be right back."

She ran up the three steps to the salon and crossed the thick blue carpet to the companionway up to the aft deck. Dismayed, she noted the wide strip of water between *The Impossible Dream* and the unfamiliar shore. She could tell by the color and undulation of the sea that it was deep.

"Don't try it," Paul cautioned. She hadn't heard his quiet approach. "You wouldn't make it. Breakfast is ready."

Her purpose blocked, she followed him below.

Shannon hadn't thought she was hungry, but the food was delicious in spite of its ruthless cook. Jason's excited chatter about the cruise covered the tension between the other two.

Paul carried his and Jason's dishes to the sink. "Time to head for Daytona, son. Want to come to the helm for a navigation lesson?"

"Sure," the boy agreed enthusiastically.

Shannon let her fork clatter to her plate as they left. If Paul thought she was going to do KP, he was badly mistaken.

Returning to her cabin, she pushed open the hatch to let in the fragrant sea air. She glanced around the compactly neat cabin, reflecting that under other circumstances she would have enjoyed the beauty of the cruiser and the adventure down the coast of Florida.

Her room was done in cheerful yellow and orange, with the sloping bulkheads painted off-white to reflect the hatch light. The thick pads on the V-shaped berths were covered in yellow, gold and orange stripes. The cushions were yellow and gold, and the pie-shaped floor space was carpeted with a gold tweed shag. Shallow shelves were recessed into the bulkheads, and a closed locker overhung the narrow prow. At the foot of the port berth there was a hanging locker, and at starboard there was a small chest.

She stuffed the laundry in the locker under the berth and rummaged through the rest of the things in her luggage. There were no shoes. They were in a shopping bag in a corner of the closet at Pirate's Cove. Also in the closet were the dresses, coats, blouses and other things she had intended to hang on a bar across the back seat of the Chevette. There was no makeup. That was in her purse. No purse! She hadn't taken one with her last night.

Never one to brood over problems beyond her immediate control, Shannon looked around for something to do, something to take her mind off her dilemma until she could become more dispassionate about it. She wished she had packed a book.

A burst of laughter from Jason and Paul wafted through the open hatch, and Shannon listened with envy, sorry when it vanished. Once she had been a part of their fun. Now it was all spoiled.

To be honest, Shannon had to admit that she herself had a hand in the spoiling. Paul was right about some things. She *was* afraid of her reaction to him, just as he had once suggested. She was afraid that her love for him would draw her into an affair that would break her heart. She had tried to run away. But now she was a prisoner. And that was *his* fault!

She folded the blanket at the foot of the berth, straightened the pillows and closed the suitcase. That was all the housekeeping the cabin required. No sense putting the few things in her luggage in the closet and drawers when she had no intention of cruising much longer.

She passed through the still cluttered galley, avoiding looking at the congealing syrup and bacon grease. In the salon she peered out the wraparound windows and found that there were other yachts and small boats nearby. They must be approaching Daytona Beach. Good. Surely there would be a chance for her to slip ashore when Paul was busy with the piano purchase.

There were magazines in the rack and books on the shelf, but now Shannon was too restless to sit still. She eyed the galley reluctantly. Such a mess. But she was stubborn.

She flicked on the stereo, and a soft voice began to croon. The lyrics were those from last night, and her heart swelled with the memory. She brushed aside a tear, for last night had been beautiful, though fleeting. She shut off the record. Silence was better than empty dreams.

She needed time to think. She would have liked to stand on the foredeck, letting the wind blow away the turmoil in her mind, but she had no wish to be in Paul's line of vision. Instead she went out to the aft deck.

The white wake fascinated her; she felt a kinship with its turbulence. She climbed down the ladder to the transom platform. Linking her arm around the ladder rail, she dangled her feet above the water, reveling in the cool splash of the foam as it slid back from the hull. Between the twin wings of sudsy whiteness, the sea was an incredible blue. Opaque, it hid the teeming life it nurtured.

Suddenly Paul was beside her. With one hand he grasped the rail and with the other he reached for her arm and hauled her upright. "What now?" His lips were taut. "Get up on deck."

"Why?" There was no room to struggle on the small diving platform, so she preceded him.

When she would have stopped aft, he gave her a gentle push into the salon. "Did you think I wouldn't guess that you would try to escape as we neared Daytona?"

Shannon laughed and had the satisfaction of seeing Paul's puzzled frown. "What's so funny?" he demanded.

"*You* are, if you thought I was going to try swimming across a harbor full of propellers."

His eyes narrowed. "I don't think I believe you."

"Okay," she said with a shrug. "Suit yourself."

He let out an exasperated sigh and indicated an upholstered chair. "Shannon, I want you to understand why you had to come with me on this cruise."

"I have a pretty good idea," she said sarcastically.

"Damn it, why is it so hard for you to accept the idea of a place in our lives, Jason's and mine? I know you care for my son. I've seen that every day. And I know you're young; I wouldn't expect you to be his mother. And he adores you. Surely you know that."

That was one of the things that hurt. She did love Jason.

"We work well together, Shannon. I'll help you with your education and with your career, I swear I will. I've got the top agent in New York. He won't touch beginners, but he'll handle you if I ask him." He paused. "You know how much you've helped me. But since this insane bickering between us, I haven't sung...I haven't been able to sing. I'm all tightened up."

She glared at him. "If you ask me, you sound just fine today."

A mischievous grin softened his mouth. "Must be because of last night." Shannon turned her face away, but Paul went on, "Once you get over your pique, you'll enjoy the cruise, Shannon. I know you will. It can be a trial run. You, me, Jason. We'll see how it works."

"You mean a trial marriage? No thanks," she said flatly.

"We'll forget the marriage, since that doesn't seem to appeal to you."

"Oh, a trial affair then? Do you think that would help the judge decide in your favor?" she asked innocently.

His eyes were darkening dangerously. "If you want an affair, you've got it," he snapped. "If you don't, we'll try out the rest of the script and see how it develops."

"Are you saying that you'll keep your hands off me?" As soon as she had said it, she knew it was a leading question.

The gleam of humor returned to his eyes. "Can you keep yours off me?"

She felt the red heat climb past her neckline and suffuse her face. How crude of him to remind her that it was she who had reached out to him last night. "You bet," she snapped, "but we won't be together long enough to make it a problem for either of us."

"We'll see." She refused to look at Paul, but she

thought she detected amusement in his tone. "Incidentally, I don't expect to have to go beyond the pier in Daytona; if I do, you're in charge of Jason. Can I trust you not to desert him by jumping ship, or shall I lock you in your cabin? Accidentally, of course."

Shannon's look was scathing, but she refused to answer. She started for her room and Paul called after her. "Want to come up and learn navigation? We're approaching Daytona Beach, so I'll have to take the wheel from Jason now. No? Well, if you're bored, there are things that need doing. You're headed in the right direction."

She knew that he was referring to the messy galley she had to pass through. She didn't care if there were no clean dishes left at all.

"Hi," Jason said, coming up behind her. "Dad said maybe you'd help me shove things around so there'll be room for the piano."

"Sure." Physical activity was welcome as long as it didn't conflict with her principles. It was a simple matter to move the two chairs farther apart and put the low table in front of the lounge.

"Shanny, you ought to come up to the helm. It's neat, and dad lets me steer. Want me to ask him to give you a turn?"

"Not right now, Jason."

"Yeah. Better wait. We're almost at Daytona, and he'll want to dock *The Dream* himself, I guess. Come up and watch, Shanny."

"You go ahead. I'll watch from the afterdeck. I'm eager to see the new piano."

Jason scampered away, and Shannon followed as far as the deck. *The Impossible Dream* glided past an endless skyline of high rises and condos pushing into the bluest of skies. Broad beaches were dotted with color—brilliant bits of brief swim attire, rectangles of towels and blankets and circles of sun umbrellas. A constant parade of cars inched back and forth on the hard sand while orderly formations of sea gulls sailed gracefully overhead, riding air currents to the last hotel, circling and gliding quietly back.

Paul guided the cruiser into the Halifax River and nosed it against the dock in a commercial area south of the tourist area. He came down alone, pausing to say, "You're not to go ashore, Shannon. Do I trust you not to try, or do I lock you in?"

"Trust me or not, as you like," she said carelessly, "but you'll have a struggle getting me behind a locked door, so take your choice."

Paul threw the mooring lines to a dock attendant and leaped lightly ashore. She watched as two burly men jostled their way toward him. There was some conversation that she couldn't hear and some impatient gesturing. Paul was apparently dissatisfied. With a glance back in her direction, Paul went with them.

Quickly, Shannon jumped onto the pier. The dock area was crowded, and she angled carefully away from the place where she had last seen Paul. She was glad, for once, not to be tall. She would easily be able to lose herself in the maze of surging humanity. She looked back at the yacht, hoping to wave reassuringly at Jason, but he was not visible.

When her bare feet touched sand, Shannon was exultant. She was free! All she had to do was find a policeman.

CHAPTER FOURTEEN

"WHERE YOU GOIN'" in such a big hurry?" While Shannon had looked over her shoulder, she had bumped into a brawny fellow whose bulging muscles and stomach strained the fabric of his stained shirt and sagging jeans.

"Sorry," she apologized, and tried to push past him. His meaty hands stopped her flight.

"Hold on, baby. There's a nice bar over there." His head jerked toward a street back of the waterfront.

Shannon stared at the stubbled cheeks and chin, the small eyes and bulbous nose in the dirt-streaked face. She could smell stale sweat and tobacco as the man pulled her out of the traffic.

She tried to wrench away. "Let me go!"

Too strong for her, he laughed, showing yellowed teeth. He looked at her bare feet and legs, letting his eyes slide up her form suggestively. "Aw, c'mon. I'll buy you a drink." He began to propel Shannon across the sand, his arm pinning her against his fleshy side.

Terror gripped Shannon. Physically she was no match for him. *The Impossible Dream* was a haven compared to this. "Let me go!" she cried again. "I'll call the police!"

Again he laughed. "Ain't no police around. I saw you runnin' off the dock. Bet you're a runaway, ain't you? Lookin' for a place to stay? I can help you, baby."

"Paul!" she screamed. The man clapped a thick hand over her mouth. It smelled foul, and she felt sick. She tried to bite him, but again he laughed. His callused hand must scarcely have felt the imprint of her teeth.

"I'll let you breathe if you quit hollering," he said, taking his hand away. "Make a sound, an' you'll be sorry."

Shannon felt herself dragged to the door of a sleazy tavern. Fear seemed to smother her.

With his hand on the door, the burly giant suddenly slumped with a dull grunt to the sidewalk. Shannon gaped, first at him and then at the man who had just delivered the blow to the back of her captor's neck.

"Paul!" It was barely a whisper.

He caught her as her knees began to buckle. A few people paused to stare at the fallen ruffian. Paul took Shannon's hand and almost pulled her off her feet as he hurriedly led her away. When at last they reached the afterdeck of *The Dream*, Shannon was gasping for breath, able to say nothing in response to Paul's tirade. Jason stood wide-eyed in the companionway.

"Couldn't you see what kind of an area this is?"

Paul scolded. "I had to leave Jason alone while I chased after you. I shouldn't have trusted you. I should have locked you in your cabin."

Shannon saw Jason's shocked expression. Paul was not facing the boy and probably didn't realize that he was listening.

"You couldn't even make a phone call," Paul stormed. "You have no money. What did you think you were going to do?"

"Just...." Shannon glanced at Jason. He hated quarrels. Had witnessed so many. She struggled to get her breath. "Just explore a little. I should have gone up to the helm with you, Jason. I guess I could have seen enough from there."

Paul, too, took a deep breath; he understood Shannon's message. Turning to Jason, he said, "It's okay, son. Shannon didn't realize that she'd run into trouble, I guess."

"The piano's in," Jason said, jerking a thumb toward the salon. Obviously he was eager to change the subject. "They asked if they could bring it aboard, and I said yes."

Paul darted a stony look at Shannon, but his voice was no longer rasping. "We'll take a look." He held the door for Shannon and muttered, "It's not what I ordered."

A small spinet stood under the starboard windows. Shannon ran her fingers over the keys and was delighted with the sound. It wasn't a grand, of course, but the tone was good and the size perfect for *The Dream*.

"I ordered an upright. The longer strings would give better vibration. I wouldn't have let them bring this aboard if I'd been here."

"This is fine," she said.

"Do you mean I've finally managed to please you?"

Shannon pursed her lips, watching Jason go below to the stateroom. "Several times," she said provocatively, "but not lately."

It was some time before Shannon heard the engines roar into life to take *The Dream* out into the river. She lingered at the piano, touching the keys with delight. It would be a pleasure to learn the feel of the new instrument.

As she thought this, her eyes widened in surprise. She was reasoning as though she had no intention of slipping away as soon as she could. It would have been easy at the beach—a trip to the ladies' room, an appeal to someone for help...the police....

Earlier she had been angry enough not to care that her escape would hurt Paul. Without money or clothes, she would have had to explain her predicament in order to get help in returning to the cove. Paul was always good news copy. The media would have had a field day.

The brief and terrifying experience ashore had sobered her. Paul had saved her from...she didn't want to think about her probable fate. She was glad that he had come after her, whatever his reasons. She wanted to think that he cared what happened to her;

but it could just as well have been that he knew she would blurt out her story to anyone who helped her escape the intentions of the man she had met on the beach.

She thought of Jason's shocked face as he listened to their quarrel. Bad publicity could only hurt Paul's chances of gaining custody of his son. And Shannon was convinced that the two of them ought to be together.

I can't hurt them. I love them both. Yes, she had been angry—"furious" was a better word—but she knew that she could never want to do him serious injury.

What was the alternative? To submit to captivity? Well, she wouldn't be a captive if she played for Paul as she had agreed to do until Labor Day. Hadn't he said he would leave her alone? Would he keep his promise? Could anyone keep promises that they didn't truly believe in?

Maybe she could reason it out better after lunch. Hungry, she wandered into the galley, wondering what time they would eat. Perhaps on a cruise one ate whenever one pleased. She eyed the stack of dirty dishes. Maybe the sound of clattering china would remind Paul of food.

There was a jar of peanut butter on the counter. She looked for bread and butter but couldn't find them. There was milk and cold meat in the refrigerator. No fruit, no potato chips or snacks. With a sigh she poured a glass of milk and munched a slice of bologna. Then she washed the incredibly sticky dishes. What a long trip it would be, she thought ruefully, if she refused to do anything.

She climbed up to the helm. It was exhilarating to be high above the rippling water as *The Dream* sped between the banks of the Halifax and out into the Intracoastal Waterway.

"Where are we going?" Shannon asked, standing beside Paul and letting the wind tease the short hairs from her braid.

"We'll drop anchor at Titusville. I'd like to take Jason to the Space Center at the cape. And maybe the Museum of Sunken Treasure, but. . . ."

"I'd like to see them myself," she said slowly.

"I can't put you on a leash," he said testily.

She grinned mischievously. "What if I promise to be good?"

His eyes told her he didn't believe it possible.

Okay, be difficult, she thought. "Where is Jason?"

"In our stateroom, I guess. He was upset."

"I want him to have a happy cruise as much as you do, Paul."

"Then you'd better talk to him. Convince him that we're just one big happy family on a pleasure cruise," Paul suggested sarcastically.

Shannon went below. The stateroom was larger than the guest cabin, its port windows open to let in the sounds and smells and light of the seascape. Jason was curled up on the blue-checked spread of one of the twin berths, but he wasn't asleep. An unopened bag of potato chips was next to him.

"I finally cleared the galley," Shannon said. "Would you like some lunch?"

"I'm not hungry."

"I am," she admitted. "Any chance I can share your chips?"

He pushed them toward her. She sat on the opposite berth and tore open the package. When Jason continued his silence, she said, "Your dad and I are sorry we argued; we didn't mean to upset you."

"Why was he mad at you?" He sat up, dangling his legs over the side of the bed. "He said he ought to lock you up. And, Shanny, he told me not to bring your purse. I saw it on your dresser, and I asked him. Why didn't he want you to have any money?"

Paul was right; it was best to be honest. He himself was always a stickler for the truth. "I really thought I should go back to Chicago this weekend," she told him.

"Then you didn't want to come with us, huh?" he asked sadly.

Shannon got up to look out the window. She hadn't been on a cruise since she was ten. She had forgotten the soothing rhythm of the waves and the beauty of clear skies and deep seas. The sun and wind on her face had brought it all back with poignant clarity. "Jason, have you ever thought that something was wrong for you, and then after a little while you discovered that it was right after all?"

"I guess so," he said. "Like when dad and mom and me got split up. But I guess we have fun at the cove. Here, too." He came to stand beside Shannon. "Don't we?"

She put her arm around the thin shoulders. "You bet." Consciously or not, he was making a substitution. He was making Shannon a third of his personal trio. Exactly as his father had suggested. *Oh, Jason, it won't always be that way,* her heart warned.

For Jason's sake she would make the trip. Paul had said that its purpose was to introduce Jason to his family; for some reason Paul had not been close to them, it seemed. Once that was accomplished, Jason would have a feeling of belonging, even though there would be spaces of time when Paul couldn't be with him. That would be a better time for Shannon to leave him.

She gave him a little squeeze. "This is going to be the best cruise anyone ever had, right?"

"Right, Shanny! Guess I am hungry after all," he added. "I only had peanut butter a while ago."

"Just peanut butter?"

"Sure. On a spoon, like a sucker. Don't you eat it like that?" he asked, surprised.

She wrinkled her nose. "I like it on bread, but I couldn't find any."

They went to the galley, and Jason opened the oven door. "It's in here. I put the stuff away, and I couldn't find a bread box. Dad said we'd get more things in Titusville." His face became serious as he spread the peanut butter on slices of bread. "If you tell dad you won't run away, I know he won't lock you up, Shanny."

She laughed. "Okay, I'll tell him."

"What will you tell me?" Paul stood in the doorway.

The engines were quiet now. "Are we in Titusville, dad? Are we going to get groceries now?"

"No to both questions, son." Paul's eyes slid over the neat galley and then to Shannon. "We're idling off Merritt Island."

"That's where the Space Center is!" Jason exclaimed. "Can we see it, dad?" He took a bite of his sandwich before he remembered to add, "Shanny's not going to run away anymore, so it's okay."

Paul continued to consider Shannon, waiting for her to speak.

"We're going to enjoy every minute of this cruise," she said. "All three of us."

One shaggy eyebrow rose as he gave a short nod. Shannon knew that she would have to prove that she could be trusted. She sliced through her sandwich and handed half to Paul.

Jason went topside to see what the island in Mosquito Lagoon looked like. Paul's unwavering gaze still held Shannon. "What did you tell him?" he demanded.

"That we were sorry that we quarreled and hurt him. That I honestly had thought I should go home to Chicago but—" she paused teasingly "—that now that I'm here, I've changed my mind."

Paul's nod was slight, tentative. "You wouldn't lie to Jason." The slight inflection made it partly question, partly statement.

"No." She couldn't force his trust. "I'll change clothes," she said, "though I do wish you had thought to bring what was still in my closet. The only shoes I have are the heels I wore last night. They're not comfortable."

The hint of a smile tugged Paul's mouth. "Your sandals were under the bed. I threw them in with my gear. Your jacket, too. I'll get them. And there are a few things in the locker above the berth. They're yours."

Puzzled, Shannon went to her room. Standing on the berth she could just reach the sliding doors of the high shelf. Inside she found two boxes and beside them a pair of deck shoes, brand-new. On top of the boxes was the mauve dress. She pulled out the cartons and dropped them on the berth. Kneeling beside them, she flipped them open.

To her astonishment, the first one contained a colorful peasant skirt with circular bands of rainbow colors that would swirl around her legs. The sheer yellow blouse, like the skirt, was handmade and embroidered. Its drawstring neckline was adjustable for moods of shy modesty or of daring coquetry. The sleeves were long and full. She held the skirt up to her and then the blouse. "I can't let him do this," she said aloud. "He has already given me so much. I don't want to be indebted." Nevertheless she peered eagerly beneath the tissues of the other box.

Pale green slacks and a matching sleeveless blouse bore the name of a famous designer. She lifted them out almost reverently. Beneath them were shorts, a skirt of darker green and a shirt of every shade from deep emerald to palest chartreuse. She shook her head; there was no way she could accept all this, of course. But the green was such a lovely color that she just had to see how it looked on her. She stepped out of her red shorts and shirt and donned the slacks and blouse. The full-length mirror was in the head, and she would just take one quick look.

She gasped as she stumbled into Paul, bare to the waist. "Luckily, I'm just shaving," he said with a grin as he wiped off the last of the soap. "Jason had the other head."

"Sorry," she said, starting to back out. She had forgotten that this bath had two entrances, one from the galley.

Paul caught her arm. "Don't rush off. I'm through. Do you like it?"

Her eyes were even with his bare bronze chest with its broad V of crisp black curls, and she nodded. Yes, she did like what she saw. When she tipped her head back and saw him appraising every curve of her green-clad figure, she knew that he had been referring to his gift. "Oh, yes, but I can't possibly accept—"

"Why not?"

"There's no reason for you to do this," she told him firmly.

"Did you read the note?" When she looked mystified, he brushed past her into her cabin and retrieved a scrap of paper from the bottom of one of the boxes. "Read it. I'm not good at this sort of thing."

The note was brief: "Let these make up for the piracy."

Shannon stared at the message, remembering the note that had accompanied the corsage the night of the concert at Illinois. Each was short, each a kind of apology and each came with a peace offering. "But it's too much," she insisted.

"They suit you. I'd like you to wear them." When she shook her head, he added, "I can't take them back. I threw the tags away. Besides, you said most of your things are still at the cove."

"When did you get these?" she asked wonderingly. "How long have you planned this little adventure?"

"I did a lot of things yesterday. Buying the clothes was one of them. I've had the Indian outfit for a long time, though no one has ever worn it."

Shannon sighed resignedly. "It wasn't very nice of you not to bring my purse. I wish I could buy something for you and Jason. I can't just take all this. And the mauve dress, too."

"You don't owe me anything," he said gruffly. And then the curious tuck reappeared at the corner of his mouth. "Under the circumstances, your being here is something of a gift."

"But—"

His raised hand stopped her. "You certainly overwork that little word. I told you that weeks ago," he reminded her with a frown. "Don't worry, there are no strings attached."

Playfully he pulled her thick braid, turning her

profile toward him. "From this angle you look quite sophisticated with your hair as slick and smooth as a satin cap. And like this—" he tugged the braid the other way so that the heavy plait bordered her face "—you look like the little girl of ten I used to know. Confusing."

She pulled the braid away. "If you're through in the bathroom...."

One long step put him there before her, and he tossed her sandals through the door and then her jacket. "I'm gone," he said sounding more cheerful than he had for days. "Meet us on the aft deck. And wear what you have on. I like it."

Shannon washed her face and combed her hair. It fell in neat dark waves from having been braided all day. She looked forward to the Cape Canaveral visit. How could she possibly stay angry at Paul when he so obviously wanted her to enjoy the cruise?

When she joined Paul and Jason, Paul nodded his appreciation of the green slacks and blouse, and Jason whistled. "I hope you'll lend me enough to buy some lipstick and a brush," she said.

"I will," Jason volunteered. "I got money."

Paul rented a car, and they motored across the long NASA Causeway to the Visitors' Center on the island, where they joined a crowd of tourists who could hardly believe the miracles they saw in the great Space Museum and in the various science demonstrations.

On Merritt Island, not far from where the Spanish New World was born, they were told that the technology of the future was being fashioned. Thousands of scientists, technicians, engineers, repairmen and craftsmen would come from all over the world to be flown in spaceships launched and landed at Cape Canaveral; their projects would range from placing workshops into orbit to cleaning up space debris. It was an awesome thought.

It seemed strange that adjacent to the space-age complex was the Island National Wildlife Refuge, a 140,000-acre park in which alligators, bobcats, raccoons and hundreds of species of birds, including the rare bald eagle, were protected.

The three of them were especially interested in the Museum of Sunken Treasure at the cape. More than a million dollars' worth of treasure had been recovered from the sea and was on display. Jason quickly found coins similar to the ones he had found. The display of jewels and gems, precious metal cups and plates, military supplies, perfumes and wines in sealed containers and hundreds of priceless old cargo items was staggering.

They dined at The Surfside on a variety of seafood, salads and freshly baked breads. Afterward they stopped at a supermarket for fresh fruits and vegetables. Paul was about to pick up some frozen meals when Shannon stopped him.

"How about letting me cook?" Before he could tease about galley slavery, she hurried on. "I like to cook. You won't suffer."

"I'll help," Jason offered, "and you can do the dishes, dad."

"Who will pilot *The Dream*?" Paul wondered solemnly.

Jason's face fell. "I knew I'd get stuck with the dishes."

Paul grinned. "We'll work it out."

Shannon selected groceries, keeping in mind her meal plans and the limitation of storage space. Jason slyly added a candy bar as they checked out. When nobody objected, he laughed happily. "Gee, this is fun."

After lugging their supplies into the galley, Paul drove the rental back to the dealer. Shannon put the supplies away while Jason got ready for bed. She was on her knees, storing the last of the staples in the bottom cupboard when Jason came up behind her.

"Today was nice," he said. "Staying mad is a bummer. It's more fun like this."

She put her arms around him. "You make a lot of sense," she agreed.

When they stood in the doorway of his room, he pressed against her once more. "Wish you could stay with us forever, Shanny."

It was only recently that he had shown such open affection, and she dropped a quick kiss on his tousled black hair. "Let's not worry about forever," she said with a smile. "Let's just think about the fun we'll have on the cruise."

How could she ever have contemplated running away without even a goodbye? It would have been a grave mistake. She thought of Paul's mistake in letting Edmund take the boat out alone, something he would painfully regret for the rest of his life. She, too, had almost made a mistake that would have hurt others. She could almost thank the ruffian who had aborted her flight.

She found Paul lowering his long body tiredly into a deep chair in the salon. His discarded shirt was on the piano bench. "Would you like to practice?" she asked.

"Later, maybe." He ran his fingers through his hair while he hooked another chair with his foot and brought it close. "Sit down, Shannon."

"I'm rather tired," she began as she sat on the edge of the chair, "but I do want to thank you for the pretty clothes and for rescuing me at Daytona Beach, too."

He dismissed that with a wave of his hand. "I heard what Jason said just now," he said abruptly. "You could, you know."

"Could what?" She pressed her fingers to her lips, knowing as soon as she spoke what he meant.

"You could stay with us. As my wife."

Shannon leaned back, her wide amber gaze seemingly on Paul; but she was seeing Merlene, hearing her say, "Whichever one of us marries and provides a complete set of parents and a home for Jason will win custody." To Paul, marriage was custody insurance.

"You'll be making a big mistake if you marry Paul just to make a home for Jason," Merlene had said, and, "He'll ask you." Shannon shook her head to dispel the memory. "I thought we weren't going to talk about marriage anymore, Paul."

"Can't blame me for trying when it could be good, Shannon," he said.

"Merlene said you'd ask," she said quietly.

She heard the sharp rasp of Paul's breath. "Merlene! She has nothing to do with us."

"Don't say any more, Paul. Let's forget it."

He got to his feet and came toward her slowly. His eyes traveled over her face and the quickening pulse above her collarbone, slid over her shoulders and breasts and touched her slim waist and the tapered V where the green slacks divided. When they roamed back to her face, they were shadowed. "Don't pay more attention to Merlene's assumptions than to your own desires," he said thickly. "I tell you it could be good with us."

She knew that he was thinking about last night. Yes, it was good.

"I told you I'd help you, Shannon. You can be on my billing. Or we'll arrange for your concerts at parallel times and places. We'll take Jason with us. We'll find a good tutor."

Ah, there once more was the real reason for the proposal. Shannon shook her head, her eyes veiled. His need for her as a woman was secondary. "Please drop it, Paul. I don't want to marry you." She made a move to get up, but Paul leaned on the arms of her chair.

"How about a reason?" he said tersely. "I never thought I'd consider marriage again. Is it possible that you and Jim . . .?"

She knew now that he wasn't jealous. He was just

looking for reasons. "You really can't understand why a woman doesn't jump at the chance to be your wife, can you?"

"As I see it, we both have a great deal to gain through marriage."

His face was close to her own, and she begged silently, *don't kiss me. If you do, I'm lost.* "Let's not argue, Paul. We promised Jason, and he's just beyond that door."

Lazily he pushed himself upright as she watched the muscles ripple over his chest and arms. The aching desire to touch him and to be touched by him was beginning deep inside her, and it was with an effort that she denied the impulse to caress the bronze skin and the wiry V of curls.

"Just think about it," he said. "In the meantime, we'll go on as usual. You're still working for me, right?" She nodded. "So let's enjoy the cruise."

She waited till he had taken a step toward his stateroom before she rose. "I'm sure I will," she murmured.

But he came back to her. "I'm glad you're here, Shannon. You're being a good sport. I hope you'll enjoy the Everglades."

"The Everglades? Is that where we're going?" she asked in surprise.

"My people are Seminoles. I thought you knew that."

"Yes, but—" she saw his eyes narrow, measuring her reaction "—I've never been to the Everglades, and I guess you're the only Seminole I know, Paul."

She paused. "I guess the cruise won't be so... bad after all." Her eyes were bright with expectation and interest, and Paul smiled with satisfaction.

"Good." Idly he pushed a strand of hair behind her ear. Why did his mere touch fan the flame within her? "There's to be a big celebration, a welcome for Jason mainly. But my people often combine several rites, as you'll see." He stretched his long arms and yawned, letting them fall gently to her shoulders. "Do I rate a good-night kiss for good behavior today?" he asked with a grin.

"I don't think...."

But he bent his head to nuzzle her hair for a moment. "You always smell bewitching," he said as he let her go. "Good thing I'm dog tired. However...."

She knew he was teasing. How could he be so casual when she was not? Semiangrily she flung out, "Go to bed. Try dreaming of somebody else."

He followed her to the galley. "Who?" he demanded plaintively. "The reports of my conquests have always been exaggerated, you know."

"How about Jeanie?" What was the matter with her? How many times today had she said more than she intended?

"Jeanie!" He sounded incredulous. "What on earth made you think of her?"

She shrugged. "I don't know." She stole a glance at him as she edged toward her door, and she was astonished at his broad, amused smile. "I didn't introduce you two, did I?" he mused. "I was so surprised to see her; hadn't seen her for years. Lovely girl. She'll be at the Seminole celebration.''

''That's nice. Good night.''

''Wait a minute. Come here, Shannon,'' he coaxed.

But Shannon only smiled enigmatically as she shut her door.

CHAPTER FIFTEEN

SHANNON TOSSED RESTLESSLY, feeling small and lonely in the split berths. They merged at the head, completely filling the forespace. The truth was that she missed Paul's arms and body and felt lost without him. At the opposite end of *The Dream*, were his longings the same?

She thought about Jeanie. Why had her name popped so suddenly to mind? She berated herself for mentioning her; she knew she had sounded jealous, the last thing she wanted Paul to suspect!

So Jeanie would be in the Everglades, too. Shannon recalled the girl's dark high-cheekboned face and lustrous black hair, suspecting that she might have a Seminole background, too. An old sweetheart? Not very old, that was for darned sure! Suddenly Shannon sat up. Could Jeanie be a family member? Was that what caused Paul's amusement? The darkness hid the flush that spread over Shannon's cheeks; no wonder Paul had been laughing at her.

She tried to remember exactly how Paul had kissed Jeanie. Like a relative? Or like a lover? But she had turned away too quickly, unwilling to observe Paul's ardor for someone else.

Well, much as she would like to know exactly what Jeanie meant to Paul, she would not bring up her name again. Anyway, if she was a cousin, cousins did fall in love and marry. In some cultures it was usual, even customary. She had no idea what the Seminole customs were.

She wished she had thought to hunt up a book in the St. Augustine library about the Seminoles. Why hadn't she thought of it? Mostly because Paul rarely mentioned his family, she supposed. She sensed that there must be a deep-seated reason for this reticence. She was sure it had nothing to do with his being Indian; she recalled how proudly he had sung the Seminole lullaby in Illinois, and he had been constantly working at recording other tribal songs. In her spare time Shannon had worked out notations and accompaniments with him.

No, the problem must have something to do with the family. Whatever it was, perhaps it would be resolved on this trip. Already Paul seemed more relaxed than he had been at the cove...that is, once Shannon had agreed to stay until September. She was eager to hear him sing again and to try out the new piano. *He'll probably sound relaxed and just fine, now that everything is going his way,* she thought. Which was good.

But what about me, she wondered. Could she afford the luxury of this cruise, loving Paul as she did? Would it be harder to leave him in September than now? And would being with him day by day in such close quarters make it impossible for them to maintain a physical distance? There was no denying their strong sexual attraction for each other, and now that they had been together intimately, was it possible *not* to be lovers? *It has to be possible,* she told herself in the darkness. Eventually troubled slumber claimed her.

In the morning she wished ruefully that she had purchased some liquid makeup to daub on the shadows beneath her eyes to disguise her fatigue. After she put on the new green shorts and shirt, brushed her hair with her new supermarket brush and fastened a lock from each side with the gold clasp at the back of her head, she thought she looked considerably better.

She couldn't put off her lingerie laundry any longer. She washed her things in the basin, then scrubbed the coffee stain from the pretty mauve dress. The tiny bathroom was too small for a clothesline; besides, Paul or Jason might need to use it. So she strung the cord belt from the terry robe between the bulkheads just inside her door and hung her laundry there before she hurried to the galley to begin breakfast.

Paul and Jason came to the galley together, summoned by the aroma of waffles and sausages. Paul looked cheerful and rested in hip-hugging denim shorts and a navy T-shirt. Jason looked like a miniature carbon copy. Their shower-damp hair clung to their temples, and their eyes sparkled with fun.

"You're right," Paul said. "We won't suffer with you as our chef." He slid into the booth after Jason. "Make mine four deep."

"Me, too," Jason echoed. "Dad's been telling me about grandpa's farm, Shanny. I don't remember it. Is there a barn and kittens and chickens?" he asked hopefully.

"A barn, yes, but I don't know about the animals. Your grandparents and uncle are cattle farmers, Jason."

Jason sighed. "I don't know much about cows."

"We used to have horses," Paul said. "Maybe they still do. Anyway, your cousin Steve will keep you busy, I'm sure." Steve, Paul explained to Shannon, was Jason's age, but the boys hadn't seen each other since they were four.

"How come, dad?" Jason asked interestedly. "Did we have a fight or something?"

"Not you boys," Paul told him, spreading syrup on his waffles generously. "Why don't you and Shannon have a treasure day, and clean the coins and things we found in the cave?"

Shannon suspected that the change of subject was to divert questions away from family problems, but she readily agreed to the suggestion. Jason helped her make the galley shipshape, and then they carefully followed Paul's directions for preparing to clean the treasures. Jason measured a tablespoon of detergent into a pint of warm water in a plastic bowl. "Never use metal," Paul had warned. "The various metals could interact and ruin the coins."

Shannon suggested that they take turns reading Elizabeth's journal to Paul at the helm while they waited for the soaking process, for he hadn't had a chance to see it. Once more they relived the romantic and tragic story recorded in Elizabeth's notes. But before long Jason grew restless. "Can we check on the coins?" he asked.

"Go ahead," Paul told him. "Just leave the journal. Way out here, away from everything, I can manage to read a bit."

They carefully scrubbed the coins with an old toothbrush Jason had brought for the purpose. The silver ones were, according to the book Paul had packed along, pieces of eight, random shapes of approximately the same size. Obviously they had been cut from silver bars and then stamped. Gradually the markings began to stand out, and Jason compared them to the pictures in his coin book.

"The dates are 1787 and 1790," he reported, "and that's King Charles IV of Spain."

Shannon came to look over his shoulder. "Minted in Mexico and circulated in the United States." She added, "These coins are very old. Collectors will pay a lot for them if you decide to sell."

"Really? Gosh, I hope so!"

Shannon was curious. "Why, Jason? Your dad is not a poor man. You have everything you want, don't you?"

"Well, if we had lots of money, dad could build that school and stay at the cove with me most of the time. He said that's what he'd do if he could. And he said we'd see that coin collector on the cruise, you know. I brought that gold coin for him to look at. Maybe he'll buy it."

The gold coin was beautiful when cleaned. It, too, carried the face of Charles IV and the 1790 date. On the reverse was stamped the royal coat of arms of the king of Spain. Shannon read from the book that it was a gold doubloon, probably struck on this side of the Atlantic, a common practice in the late eighteenth century.

"What's it worth?" Jason wondered, rinsing his prize.

Shannon read on. "It was called a doubloon because it was worth four pistoles, or the equivalent of sixteen dollars. It was also called a doubloon of eight because it was worth eight gold escudos."

"Sixteen dollars!" Jason marveled. "I'm rich!"

"That was in 1790," Shannon reminded him. "Gold is very valuable now, and this coin is an antique. You know," she said worriedly, "we've got an awful lot of valuable stuff on board. Maybe your father ought to put it in a bank vault somewhere."

"We've got a safe in our stateroom," Jason told her. "That's where it's been all along."

"Good," she said, relieved.

The dagger blade was a perfect shaft of tempered steel, its point tapered to needle sharpness. The ridge centerline flared to a gracefully rounded guard from which the bare tang extended. The hilt was missing. "Maybe the hand was of wood or ivory," Shannon guessed. "Something that broke off." She balanced it on one finger and shuddered, wondering whether it had ever drawn blood. Could Juan, the tender lover, have been capable of plunder and murder?

Jason polished the half-inch cubes with their numbered indentations and tossed them on the counter. They rolled sluggishly, as they were heavier than modern dice. Big buccaneer hands must have found them challenging.

Shannon exclaimed in delight as the beauty of the jewelry became apparent. The earring was a droplet of gold in which was set a single large clear stone, no doubt a diamond. The gold ear wire was bent, but with pliers she carefully reshaped it.

The ring was a band of gold with eight perfect rubies. "Gee! That ought to be worth a lot," Jason said, more impressed with its cash than romantic value. Shannon couldn't resist the temptation to put it on her finger. As she suspected, it fit perfectly.

They lined a bowl with soft paper toweling and put the treasures in it. "Come on, Jason, let's take these up to show Paul."

Paul admired the results of their work, but he vetoed Jason's plans to sell everything to finance the music school. "This all belongs to Shannon," he said quietly.

He flatly refused to listen to her plans for sharing, and Shannon finally stamped her foot impatiently. "Paul Cypress, I want that school as much as you do. Have you forgotten that it was dad's dream in the first place? It's as though we found the treasure right under the very site for the school, right at the foundation. It was *meant* to finance the institute, can't you see that?"

Paul laughed. "You're almost as stubborn as I am.

You're generous and impulsive," he said more seriously, "and I won't take advantage of your nature."

"We don't even know for sure whose property these things were on," Shannon pointed out. "That chest could have been back to back with the wall of the storage room."

Paul changed the subject. "I wonder why Elizabeth's personal jewelry was in the chest; that is, if these pretty things were hers and not part of the treasure. Elizabeth never lived at the cove, did she?"

"I don't think so," Shannon said. "Dad said that his grandfather, Joseph Webster, came to St. Augustine from England. Elizabeth's journal says that she went to England before her baby was born. She never mentioned returning to America."

"Must be just forgotten loot," Paul mused. He pointed off to starboard. "Out there lies a Spanish galleon loaded with silver bullion worth about seven million. It's been there for four hundred years. Think we ought to take up diving?"

"Yeah!" Jason agreed enthusiastically. "Would that be enough? For the school, I mean?"

Paul tousled his son's head. "The tides have buried the wreck pretty deep. Lots of divers have tried to find the ship and failed. How about taking the bowl down to Shannon's room now so it doesn't accidentally get spilled overboard. I'll put it in the safe later."

Reluctantly Shannon took the ruby-and-gold ring off her finger. "We all worked hard to find the treasure,'' she said, dropping the ring into the bowl. ''It's only fair that all three of us share it.''

Paul leaned back in his pilot's seat and squinted toward the west. ''We'll drop anchor soon. We pushed hard yesterday. The rest of the trip will be leisurely.''

''Paul, didn't you hear me?''

For a time only the hum of the twin Crusader engines and the soft whistle of the wind against the plexiglass screen answered her. ''Edmund was so close to finding his treasure,'' he said. ''He had studied the chart in Elizabeth's book, and as soon as the storm was over, he said we'd go for the treasure. He was going to explain it all to me that afternoon, but the journal was missing. He thought he must have mislaid it.''

''Jimmy and I had it.'' Shannon wondered what Paul was leading up to.

The tuck in the corner of his mouth appeared briefly. Paul nodded. ''And then time ran out. If I had gone with him to the reef, I'm pretty sure we could have managed together in the storm.''

But Shannon had been thinking about his earlier words. ''Are you saying that dad knew the storm was coming?''

Paul hunched over the wheel. ''Sure. It was a two-day blow, remember? No, of course you don't. Divers and boatmen know these things. We both knew it was due. That's why Edmund wanted to go out and photograph the reef before it struck. It came hours before we expected it, though,'' he said sadly.

"And I was so angry about Merlene and him that I didn't think about the storm at all when Edmund went out alone."

"If you had gone with him, you might both have been killed!"

"I doubt it. The point is that in a matter of days Edmund would have had the treasure if it existed, and now we know that it did, at least partially."

"The point is that you would have found it together," she retorted, "and you would have shared it with dad."

"I was an employee, not a partner. The treasure was always for the school. For you and Bonita."

But Shannon's mind was already dealing with something else. "Paul, if dad thought right up to the time of the quarrel that you would be going out with him on *The Bonnyshan*, don't you see what that means? I'm right about dad and Merlene. He never expected her to be aboard. They weren't having an affair."

She heard the engines hum at a lower and slower tone as *The Impossible Dream* was allowed to idle. Paul turned around on the swivel seat. "I think you're right, Shannon. Now get into your bikini and bring Jason for a swim. It's time to cool off before we try out the new piano."

Obviously that was to be the end of the discussion.

"My bikini is hanging in the shower at Pirate's Cove," she said crossly.

"Hmm. I suppose you could do without. It doesn't cover much, anyway." The grin was back. "Find something else. And bring Jason," he shouted after her as she disappeared aft.

She ducked under her makeshift clothesline and peeled off the green shirt and shorts. She found some faded shorts that needed patching, but she put them on anyway and knotted the tails of an old shirt at her midriff. She was in the bathroom tying up her ponytail when she heard a strange, strangled sound from her cabin.

"I knocked, I swear I did," Paul grumbled, peeling lacy underthings from his bare shoulders. "I just wanted to tell you...what's so damn funny? Get me out of this mess!" But Shannon was helpless with laughter, doubled up on the berth. Paul had apparently walked right into the clothesline, which had collapsed around him.

The hilarity was contagious, and Paul began to chuckle, too. When he began plucking off the panties, bras and hose more deliberately, examining them appreciatively, Shannon scrambled to her feet and yanked them away from him, blushing as she did so. "Why didn't you tell me you needed a laundromat?" he asked.

"Why didn't you tell me you were going to shanghai me?" she countered. "I would have left out the suitcase with all the things I really wanted."

"You mean there was another suitcase?"

"Under the bed at the cove. And don't get any bright ideas about more new clothes," she warned. "The laundry bag is full of perfectly good ones. I just have to wash them, that's all."

"Well, then hang them on deck. The sun and wind will dry them in no time."

Shannon eyed the underthings she was still clutching. "I will not hang these things out for all the world to see!"

Paul refastened one corner of the rope sash to the bulkhead. "Then I'd better help you hang them up again in here," he offered guilessly, "since they're not dry yet."

"Forget it!" She ducked into the head to wrap them in a towel until she returned. "Time for a swim."

The Dream WAS ANCHORED in the lovely bay near Melbourne with other cruisers whose owners were splashing in the clear water. Shannon, Paul and Jason dived from the transom platform and capered in the sparkling blue. It was smooth and calm, and after a while Shannon turned over to drift on the gentle swells.

Her freedom was short-lived, for Jason grabbed her ankles and in a moment she was thoroughly dunked. Laughing and sputtering, she surfaced just in time to be carried below once more by Paul. When he brought her up again, he didn't let go. Jason was choking with glee and salt water. "We're pirates!" he shouted. "And you're our captive slave girl!"

"Yes," Paul hissed in her ear. "What's for lunch, slave?"

"Bacon-lettuce-and-tomato sandwiches with jellied salad and hot cake pudding—if I live long enough," Shannon said laughingly as she tried to free herself.

"Good. I'm starved. Relax, slave. I'll tow you back to the hideout."

Seeing a chance for retaliation, Shannon lay back beneath Paul's arm while he struck out for *The Dream*. Acutely aware of the muscular arm across her shoulders and breasts, she tightened her hold. Even in the cool water the familiar flames were ignited wherever he touched her. She couldn't allow herself to respond so quickly and completely; she had to break the spell.

When the next swell buoyed them up, it was easy to lift Paul's arm and slip beneath it. His exclamation of surprise was muffled as she made her body sink down along the pale line of Paul's legs. Grabbing his feet and pulling, she had the satisfaction of knowing that he was deluged.

Shooting to the surface, Shannon swam strongly toward the transom platform, where Jason was drying himself. Clambering out, she turned, expecting Paul to be ready to haul her back into the water. She scanned the water, but she couldn't find him. "Jason, where's Paul?"

"Gee, I don't know. I wasn't looking." He caught her note of concern. "He's a real good swimmer, Shanny."

The thought flashed across her mind: *Edmund was, too.*

She dived in, trying to see in the opaque light beneath the surface. They had been so close to the boat. How could he have disappeared so quickly? She broke water, dived again, staying down and searching frantically until she thought her lungs would burst.

When she surfaced, gasping, she heard Paul's laughter as his arms went around her. She held him with trembling arms for a moment. Then she pushed him to arm's length, as far as he would release her. His laughter stopped as he shook the wet strands of his hair back. "I didn't mean to frighten you, Shannon. Let me tow you in."

Still shaken, she didn't object. She felt an unreasonable anger at the way the games had ended. He had tricked her into showing that she cared.

Her teeth were chattering when Paul lifted her to the platform. Jason waved and disappeared up the ladder. "You scared me to death!" she scolded.

Paul climbed up behind her and quickly barred her way up to the deck. "Just a minute, Shannon." He reached for a towel and dried her face and shoulders.

"I can do that," she said as she tried to take the terry towel away from him. But he only reached over, loosened the soggy yarn holding her hair and freed it to be dried.

"Were you worried about me?" he asked interestedly.

"I'd even worry about a—a burglar if he were drowning," she snapped. "Now give me the towel."

Paul laughed softly as he slipped the towel around her neck and drew her close. "You're enjoying the cruise after all, aren't you, Shannon?"

She had to brace her hands against him if she didn't want to be pressed against the length of him. But even the feel of the patches of his skin under her hands made her heart begin to thunder. Even worse, she felt her nipples harden to yearning points, and she knew that he could see the proof of her desire through the clinging wetness of her shirt.

"I'm trying to make the best of it."

"It can be so good, Shannon."

"You're not playing fair, Paul. . . ."

"I'm not taking you to bed. I'm not even kissing you." But she could feel the surge of his desire and the answering pulsing of her own body.

"Jason. . .?"

"He's in the shower, washing off the salt," he said close to her mouth. He gave her a quick kiss. "Mmm, you taste good. I like salty women."

"Stop," she commanded. "You know I don't want—"

"Ah, but it's so nice."

"No!" She struggled in earnest, and Paul's arms slid away.

She must stay in control so that after the cruise she could go home with a reasonably whole heart. Home? Could Chicago—or any place—ever feel like home, now that she had lived at Pirate's Cove again? That was home. The cove and Paul. She knew how Elizabeth must have felt when she was separated from Juan and her island home. Shannon moved away and Paul did not reach for her again, but inwardly she could not help wishing that he had.

In MIDAFTERNOON PAUL SANG, and Shannon thought he sounded better than he had at any time during the summer, in spite of the fact that he had skipped rehearsing for some days. She liked the touch of the spinet and coaxed a full-bodied tone from it with her strong fingers.

Paul had brought the selections he had chosen for his autumn tour, and after the warm-up exercises, he sang "Di Provenza il mar" from Verdi's *La Traviata*. Shannon rose from the bench to applaud when he had finished. "Bravo, Paul! That's the best you've done! You're going to be fine!"

His hand went to his throat, but he was smiling. "Maybe," he said, obviously pleased. "It's easy to relax out here, away from everything. I'm glad I didn't have to break in a new accompanist."

She sat down again. That could have been a real chore, and she was glad now that she hadn't put him through that. The important thing was his voice. "You are going to be ready by mid-November," she said enthusiastically. "No problem."

"The end of August," he corrected. "I've promised a couple of numbers for the celebration marking the first sighting of the St. Augustine beach, you know. With your help, I'll make it."

"I hope they haven't requested 'The Impossible Dream.'" But by the lift of his brow, she knew that her hope was foolish. "Paul, you're the star. Tell them it's impossible." She smiled with him at the unintended double entendre. "Why not suggest a medley of the Seminole songs you've been working on? The range is less demanding, and they're at their loveliest when you sing them softly. I think the audience would like that, especially since the history of St. Augustine is Indian history, too.''

"Good idea," he agreed. "But I always finish with 'The Impossible Dream.' It's sort of a trademark of mine. I don't like to disappoint anyone."

"You will if you botch it," she said practically.

Paul chuckled. "You call 'em as you see 'em, don't you? Well, we don't have to decide today." He leaned forward lazily. "About my fall tour, I've had my agent move it up to the end of October. It means six weeks in Australia and New Zealand, but home for Christmas. How does that sound?"

"You can do it."

He nodded impatiently. "I mean how does Australia sound to you? Ever been there?"

"Paul, I've never been anywhere except in a line from Chicago to St. Augustine."

"Come with me."

It was Shannon's turn to laugh, though a bit breathlessly. "I don't graduate till next May, you know."

"Maybe I'll just kidnap you again."

"Let's get back to work. You're talking nonsense." She began to play "Bess, You Is My Woman Now" from Gershwin's folk opera, *Porgy and Bess*, but found it disconcerting when Paul leaned on the piano and sang the tender words so close to her.

She made no comment when he had finished. She could tell that his voice was beginning to tire, so she leafed through the hand-written Seminole songs, searching for one that would not be taxing, one that he might want to perfect for the August program. The last one in the notebook was one she hadn't seen before. Only the melody was there, quite different from the other Indian tunes. "Something new, Paul?"

He glanced over her shoulder. "Oh, that," he said carelessly. "Yes. It's not ready yet."

But Shannon was already fingering the notes. The melody was hauntingly sweet but not at all like the other folk tunes he had taught her. "I like it," she murmured, adding a harmony. "Am I getting it right?"

Paul took the book off the rack. "I said it's not ready. Maybe it never will be." He turned the page. "We'll finish up with this one instead."

SHANNON FORGOT ABOUT the little wordless song until after supper, when she was baking brownies. Paul and Jason were fishing off the bow. Paul's curt dismissal of the tune piqued her interest, and after she slid the brownies into the oven, she went to the piano in the salon. To her surprise, the loose-leaf booklet was no longer there. Returning to the galley, she passed the desk. On impulse she opened the drawer. The book of folk songs was there.

She opened it again to the last page, half-expecting that the song might have been taken out. But it was still there. She longed to play it, to work out an accompaniment, for it haunted her somehow. There

were only four bars and then a repeat. Whatever the
next phrase was, it was incomplete. Looking at it,
Shannon could imagine what would come next.

It suddenly dawned on her that it might be something that Paul was composing. It was in the range
that was most comfortable for him. And it was different from the minor-key Seminole songs. She remembered his saying that he enjoyed composing but
had little time for it.

Curiously she turned the last page. On the reverse
were words written in Paul's bold slanted writing.

> Woman of moonlight
> Woman of sunlight
> Singing
> Laughing
> Weeping
> Loving
> Woman of starlight

But it was the heading, two words at the top of the
page that stabbed into Shannon's heart. The embryo
song was dedicated, "To Yahala."

CHAPTER SIXTEEN

THE DAYS SLID PAST smoothly, pleasantly and un-
eventfully. The weather was ideal, sunny but with
just enough breeze to provide comfort and a gentle
rock and dip to their progress. Sometimes they went
ashore to laze on the sugar-white beaches or to explore quaint villages or smart resorts. Sometimes
they fished for their supper, and occasionally they
dined ashore.

Shannon thought she had come to terms with her
feelings and that she had accepted her place in Paul's
life...a temporary place. She didn't doubt that he
was sincere in expressing a need for her, a need that
he thought she might fill better than any other
woman he knew: musician, mother for Jason, mistress. But because he couldn't look into her heart, he
couldn't understand the magnitude of what he was
asking.

Many times she caught his intense dark gaze fastened upon her, but Paul had been a model of courte-
ous, friendly behavior. Sometimes his hand brushed
her shoulder, or he would absently tuck a strand of
hair behind her ear. Each time, it would seem that
smoldering embers somewhere below her heart would

flare into life, demanding more of the fuel that his touch had supplied; and she would turn away to let them die to ashes.

She was convinced that Paul didn't love her and never would. There were others, always others. She would not let herself become just one more, to be used and someday replaced.

If she didn't daily witness Paul's love for Jason, she might wonder whether he was capable of deep and lasting love. She had wondered this once before when Paul had forced his attentions on her. Now she wondered about his marriage to Merlene, whether he had ever cared deeply for her. And who was Sylvia, whom he had called "darling"? And Jeanie? And Yahala? Especially in the dark of night the names would jumble together in her thoughts, banishing sleep.

Although she yearned for his touch, she was grateful that Paul had been undemanding on the cruise. She could never quench those embers of love harbored in the center of her being, but she could resist them. She could play the part of being a happy companion and helper to Paul. And to Jason. That's what she told herself.

Every day Paul's voice gained in timbre and strength. Sometimes he sang as he stood at the helm to the delight of the passing boats whose pilots idled alongside for a while and saluted with horns and ship's bells. In the evenings Paul and Shannon worked out the notations for the lovely Seminole ballads and taped many of them.

Once when he had been singing behind her, she finished with a repetition of the chorus in the lower register of the piano that imitated the tone and rhythm of drumbeats.

"You have an instinct for our music," Paul said softly, and his hands suddenly pressed her shoulders.

Her hands fell to the keyboard in a discord, breaking the mood that the song had woven around them. "What do I know about Seminole music?" she said with a shrug that shook off his touch.

"You play from the heart. I told you that long ago," he said.

Shannon treasured the praise from the man whom she considered among the finest and most versatile musicians in the world. But all the discipline she thought she had mastered was in jeopardy from a simple caress.

She got up from the bench, murmuring that it was getting late and she wanted to write a letter to Bonita. Paul watched her narrowly but made no comment.

In her room she found it hard to concentrate on the letter. She needed to do something more physically demanding. The laundry. There was always the laundry. With a sigh she decided to tackle the dirt-crusted cutoffs she had worn the day they discovered the treasure. They were still rolled up in the plastic bag at the bottom of her suitcase. Probably torn, too. Once clean, they'd have to be mended.

She ran hot water in the miniature basin in the

head, then squirted in some soap. After she had the worst of the soil scrubbed out, it would be safe to toss them into a laundromat washer with the rest of their dark clothes.

She dumped the contents of the plastic bag on the floor and reached for her shirt first. Then the cut-offs. There were two pairs...of course, one pair was Jason's. She had forgotten that she had scooped his off the bathroom floor that night and stuffed them in the bag with her own. She didn't want Thelma to put them with a regular load. Shannon had planned at least to rinse them out that night and hang them on the towel bar, but she had never gone back to the house. And the plastic bag, carelessly tossed into the suitcase, had come aboard with her.

She wrung out the shirt and draped it over a hanger in the shower. When she picked up Jason's shorts, they crackled. Searching the pockets she discovered the wrinkled papers he had stuffed into one of them. Shannon frowned, wondering where he could have picked them up.

She spread them out on the floor and saw that they were brittle and fragile. Careful not to crack or smudge them, she examined the small sheets. The script was faded and shaky as though written by an old person. "This must go first," she murmured when she saw a date heading one page: 1888. She found a name at the bottom of another page, and then she knew. The spidery signature was "Beta Gómez."

She gathered up the pages and ran through the galley and the salon calling, "Paul! Jason!" Jason opened the door just as she was about to knock.

"'S'matter, Shanny?"

Paul was lounging on the berth in cutoffs, a book in his hand. He repeated his son's anxious question, "What's the matter?"

"Look at these! They were in Jason's old cutoffs! They were written by Juan's second wife!"

"Huh?" Jason stared blankly.

"In the pants you wore in the cave!" Shannon tried to curb her excitement to explain. "I put them with my dirty cutoffs that night, and I just now got around to trying to wash them. I found these in your pocket."

"Now I remember," he said, catching her excitement. "That's the junk that was in the hole we found, the one with the air coming through it. I thought it was just stuffing of some kind."

"Well, you were smart to hang on to it," Paul said. "Let's see it, Shannon." He moved over so that Shannon could sit next to him, and Jason crawled over him to the other side. "Eighteen eighty-eight... she must have been eighty-two. Captain Collier's book says she came as Juan's wife to Panther Key in 1884, and she was seventy-eight then."

"Juan must have been—" Shannon did some mental figuring "—a hundred and ten." She bent her head over the pages. "Both of Juan's wives wrote notes," she mused, "and both seem to have made short entries, just enough to give a bare outline of what was happening."

But Paul was staring at the signature. "Beta...
Elisabeta...and the handwriting...."

Astonished, Shannon stared at Paul. "Are you
saying that you think...?"

He began to read.

"Eighteen eighty-eight. Last voyage to St.
Augustine island. Put twelve silver bars with
notes in air shaft for Joseph or his descendants.
If strangers find nearly empty chest they may
not notice."

"Joseph? Who's he?" Jason wondered.

"Elizabeth's grandson. Beta...Elizabeth...
they're the same person, aren't they, Paul?"

"I believe so."

Gave Joseph and Lady Sally the land as wedding
gift. Traced deed, found Juan had registered it
1841, nineteen years after I thought he was killed.
Knew he could not be alive at one hundred and
five but advertised in American papers for information about him.

Juan came for me, May 1884. Joseph begged us
not to tell the Kent-Willertons, so I came away to
Panther Key with Juan.

Joseph does not know how close we are when we
come for coins and bars in the night. Miss him,
especially now. Know I won't be well enough to
go to S.A. again. But have my Juan. 'Tis enough.

Beta Gómez

"Was she going to die?" Jason asked, awed.

"She was probably sick, and we know she was old," Shannon told him. "How cruel of Joseph to lock her out of his life! And after she gave him Pirate's Cove, too."

She was surprised at Paul's quick defense. "We don't know the whole story."

"We can read between the lines. Joseph was embarrassed to have a pirate ancestor and afraid his in-laws would disapprove. So he pretended Juan didn't exist, and Elizabeth chose to go with her husband. I say good for her!"

"You forget that they were never legally married," Paul said. "In 1884 that would have made a whole lot of difference to English nobility."

"Well, I bet they got married the minute they could locate a preacher. What's the matter with you, Paul? Joseph isn't even your relative, but you're defending him as if he did the right thing!"

Paul obviously bit back a retort. "I'll tuck Jason in," he said shortly. "He's almost asleep as it is."

Shannon bounced off the bed, ready to go back to scrubbing soiled cutoffs, but Paul said, "How about fixing us some hot chocolate as a nightcap?"

She nodded, but he was with her in the galley so quickly that she couldn't carry out her plan to leave his drink on the counter while she retreated to her cabin. "Maybe the old girl had bossed Joseph around long enough and he thought it was best for her to go her way while he went his with Lady Sally," he suggested.

"Maybe," she said shortly, stirring the cocoa and sugar together.

"Strange story," Paul muttered. "Love that lasted so long...unbelievable."

"To a person who doesn't believe in love at all, I suppose it is," Shannon retorted. She didn't look at Paul but she could feel his eyes on her, and she wished she hadn't said that. Paul had worked hard at being easygoing and pleasant, even on the days when his voice had tired too easily. She knew she was being short-tempered. "I wonder how her ring got into the chest," she said, reaching for a safer topic. "Maybe she was so ill and thin that it dropped off her finger. Or maybe she left it for Joseph to find."

"Some of this will always be a mystery, Shannon."

She looked around quickly then, for Paul's voice had gone husky. Was he moved by the love story of Juan and Elizabeth? Or was he annoyed at her rejection of his theory? She poured the hot milk into the cups. *If I didn't love him so much, it wouldn't hurt to know that he doesn't believe in love.*

"Come up to the fly bridge with me, Shannon. It's nice at night."

They climbed the steps carefully with their full mugs. Shannon sat gingerly on the L-shaped lounge; in the darkness it was hard to see whether the liquid was spilling or not. "I've never been up here at night," she said.

They were anchored in a small bay, and although she could see other boat lights, none was close. The night was clear, and the stars seemed close enough to be plucked for souvenirs. The waning moon gave only modest light, and it seemed as though their world on *The Impossible Dream* was very small and private.

"Maybe it was possible in the 1800s, but not anymore," Paul said.

"What?"

"Love like that," Paul said. "A woman's main function was to love, honor and obey her man in those days, but now her choices are too great."

Shannon's eyes were becoming accustomed to the darkness. She set her mug in the cup holder in the arm of the lounge. "Too great for what?"

"To great for her to want to be saddled with love and marriage for very long." When she didn't say anything, he said, "What, no argument?"

"No."

He leaned forward to put his empty mug on the pilot's chair. When he returned, he was closer, his bare arm against hers. "Why not?" His tone was husky and teasing, coaxing a smile from her.

"I was bitchy a while ago, and I don't want to be, Paul. You've been...nice, and I've been enjoying the cruise."

She heard his exasperated exclamation. "'Nice'! I don't think any woman I've wanted has ever said I was 'nice.'"

She tried to read his face, but his eyes and mouth were shadowed. "We'd better talk about something else," she suggested warily.

"Something safer?"

"Elizabeth said they put twelve silver bars in the air shaft. I wonder what they're worth."

Paul's laugh was raspy. "I carefully put the three we brought up into the safe at the cove, and the dozen are unprotected. Maybe they won't be there when we get back." He put his arm across the back of the lounge and let his hand rest on her shoulder. As the little flames began to lick awake inside her, she drew away, but he pulled her back. "Don't be so damned fidgety," he said softly. "I won't hurt you, you know."

"I'm tired, Paul. I guess that's why I was short with you earlier. I'd better get to bed."

He paid no attention, nor did he release her shoulder, but when he spoke, it was almost absently. "I did love Merlene at first. Or I thought I did. I'd known her at school a little. We were both in music. She dropped out, though. And then I ran into her in New York when we both tried out for parts in *South Pacific*."

"Is that when you decided to work together?"

Again he laughed shortly. "We didn't get the parts. But we kept in touch. Both lonely, I suppose. I couldn't dance, and she offered to teach me. And I helped her develop her singing style. But we didn't find jobs, and finally we were almost flat broke. So we moved in together to save rent money."

"I see."

"I doubt it," he said frankly. "I don't suppose you've ever been that broke. By splitting the rent and utilities, I could hang on another two weeks. Then it was back to sorting oranges in Orlando."

"Orlando?"

He nodded. "I had a job there before I went to the university. The boss even loaned me the funds I needed." Paul's voice was getting harsher.

"The night air is bad for your voice, Paul. We should go in."

He rubbed her shoulder with the flat of his hand. "I haven't touched you for days, Shannon. I love the feel of your skin. And your hair." He tangled his fingers in it and turned her head so that they faced each other. "I'm hungry for you, and I think you're hungry for me. That's why you shy away, isn't it?"

He was so close that she could feel his warm breath against her mouth. She could smell the musk scent he used after showering, and she longed to lift her hands to the wiry chest hairs she couldn't see in the darkness. "Don't, Paul, please." But her heart beat out a different message.

He heard and understood it, for his arms came around her gently. "Let's just hold each other a little while, Shannon."

"It won't stop there," she protested. "Please don't spoil things for us."

"Did I spoil it for you the last time? The time you asked me to hold you?"

"No, but . . . ."

He sighed. "But what?"

"But no more. Please." And yet her lips were

quivering for his kiss. "I have to be . . . free." Free of the claim that he had on her.

"I see." His arms relaxed and he pulled her back so that only one arm rested loosely across the back of the lounge. "I was right, wasn't I? Women have too many absorbing interests to be concerned very deeply with a man." Although his tone was light, there was an undercurrent of bitterness in his voice.

"No, Paul, it's not like that."

"You have a great career ahead of you. And you're a rich woman with your silver bars and whatever else is left of Juan's treasure. You'll do very nicely without a man. That's the way it was with Merlene, too. Oh, she liked to be linked to my name and my reputation, but she had other more important interests. I thought my name and reputation might appeal to you, too. But you'll be rich and famous before you even begin your musical career."

"Are you comparing me to Merlene?" Shannon asked, sitting up straight.

His tone continued to be light. "Does the shoe fit?"

"Your name and reputation do not appeal to me a bit. I suggest you try Sylvia."

"Sylvia?" He said the name as though he had never before heard it. "Sylvia who?"

"Sylvia *darling*."

Paul's laugh began low and soft and then grew into a booming guffaw. "Sylvia Ellison?" Shannon didn't answer, annoyed at his laughter. She had never heard him laugh so heartily. She loved the sound of his merriment, though she was miffed that it was apparently at her expense.

"What's the matter? Is she already married?"

Paul sobered. "Not right now. But I don't think she'd have me."

"Not even with your name and reputation?"

"Well, she has a really fabulous job, but it keeps her in New York. I think her arthritis makes it difficult for her to travel anyway." Shannon eyed him suspiciously. "My agent is about sixty," he said solemnly. "She really is a *darling*."

Okay, I've already made an ass of myself, so I'll just blunder on. "How about Jeanie?"

Paul began to chuckle again. "I believe you're jealous."

"Jealous! It's not jealousy...it's curiosity. I'm just curious to know where I fit in!"

"Jeanie is my sister, Shannon. She's a nurse in Orlando. I hadn't seen her for a long time."

"Oh, no...." Shannon's voice faded.

"I told you long ago that the media made me out to be much more of a Don Juan than I am," he reminded her. "Good copy sells the printed word. Even you bought it." He was grinning mischievously. "But I'm glad it bothered you."

She ignored that. "Why hadn't you seen Jeanie for a long time? Orlando isn't far from St. Augustine."

He sobered at once. "It's a long story." He paused, running his fingers through his hair. It was a disturbing story, his gesture said. "She's a private nurse, you see, and...." He stopped. Began again.

"I once worked in Orlando. Henderson Orange Groves. Henderson loaned me money." Paul's voice became husky, his tone bitter. "He was a bastard. Before we were through I hated him. But I paid him back. Every penny!"

Shannon respected the intensity of the memory for a moment. Then, "Is he the reason you don't talk about your family? Including Jeanie?"

Paul returned his attention to her. "Yes. Because of him they lied to me. You see, in our culture, a lie is unthinkable among us. Unforgivable. I was brought up that way. And when my own family lived that lie. . . ." The pain was still there in his eyes. Shannon yearned to comfort and heal him, as he had healed her when she needed him. She touched his cheek.

"Jeanie knows this Henderson?"

Paul nodded. "He was ill. She nursed him. They're friends. But—"

"But now you and Jeanie have found that you and she can still be close in spite of your differences," Shannon said softly. "That's good. It's a step, Paul."

He looked at her with eyes that really saw her. "We do know about steps, don't we, Shannon?" His voice was deep, but the strain was gone. "Come here." He put his arms around her. His kiss was gentle, gradually moving against her lips to part them. She responded with her arms and lips.

Paul lifted his mouth to say, "You know I need you, don't you?"

"Yes, I know."

His eyes questioned her, and she pulled his head down for her kiss. Paul's hands spread across her back, his thumbs working circles to stir the sensitive skin to life. She pressed her breasts against his chest and knew that he felt their pressure. "Shannon, Shannon," he said as his lips moved over her face. "Don't ever leave me."

She felt a rush of joy. *Ever...forever!* Hope surged wildly within her. Her hands became more importunate. "I don't want to leave you," she whispered. "I want to be with you. Oh, I do!"

When his hand sought her breast, her joy increased, and she moved her own hands eagerly across his well-muscled back. "Oh, Shannon, we've got to be together," he said.

"Yes...."

He unbuttoned her shirt, caressed her breasts and kissed them, took her down upon the vinyl cushions so that his mouth could light the fires of her body. She held his head against her breast at last, her hands winding in his hair. The night air played over their bodies, fanning them into ecstasy.

The rising began again for Shannon, the lifting to the spangled horizon that she loved, the place where only Paul could ever lead her. Once more there was no tomorrow, only the beautiful night and Paul. She whispered, "I love you," into his hair, so softly that it was lost in the darkness.

They lay together, touching, stroking, kissing, arousing until there was no delaying the sweet joining that would carry them beyond the night and the stars to the epitome of indescribable pleasure and passion, where they became incredibly one and yet were joyously free.

Breathlessly they spiraled down, still undulating, holding, clinging to their togetherness as they found their rest. "Paul, my own love," she breathed.

Paul pressed her head closer into the hollow place she loved near his heart. After a time he said, "We belong together, my darling. You see that, don't you?"

She rested her hand against his scar as she tipped her head to look at Paul. "Nothing else matters when we love each other, does it?"

The hand that had been cupped against her cheek moved to her shoulder restlessly, and she saw the knob above the scar ride upward as Paul swallowed. "Are you saying that you will marry me?" The huskiness was in his voice again.

"If...if you love me." She spoke tremulously, already sensing that she might have concluded too much when he said, *don't ever leave me.*

His hand came back to her face gently. "You know we both want to be free." When he saw her eyes cloud, he hurried on, still gently. "Marriage is fine with me, darling. You know I care about you. More than I thought possible. But let's give each other room. We're career people, and we need—"

A sob almost blotted out her response. "You mean *you* need! Why can't you look at what *I* need?" She sat up and reached for her shirt.

"Shannon, we need to be honest with each other.

You yourself said you have to be free. It's what we both want." He reached for her, but she evaded him. "Let's just take some time to work this out."

"We just don't want the same things!"

"I guess not." They were both angry now, frustrated at the impasse in their relationship. "What you want doesn't have much to do with Jason and me, does it?" he demanded bitterly. "Except maybe for the duration of the summer."

"And you forced me to accept that," she cried defensively.

"After you said you wanted to be with me," he countered. "If it's the security of marriage—if that's what you think you'd get—I've offered it to you, even though—"

"Even though you didn't want to! Nice concession!" she flung out icily. "No thanks. That's not what I want in a marriage."

"I know, you want *love*, whatever that is. I tell you, Shannon, I feel a hell of a lot for you, and you're willing to throw that away because you don't have a bunch of words that mean...what? Who knows? I don't!"

"Okay, let's forget the whole thing!"

"Okay. You were probably right all along—we'd be better off apart. I'll make arrangements for you to fly back to the cove after we've been to Brighton." He paused. "I assume you will still meet my family. They're expecting you."

Shannon's stubborn anger would not let her soften. But she had to consider Jason. It would be easier to explain to him after their arrival at his grandparents' farm that it was time for her return home. "All right," she agreed.

The finality of the agreement seemed to ease some of the tension between them. Paul put on his shorts and looked down at Shannon.

"You're right," he said, his voice husky with the effort to control his seething emotions. "It's got to stop. We're tearing each other apart. It's crazy, having this much power over someone. It's...terrible."

He paced the bridge as though it were his cage. Shannon pressed the heels of her hands against her mouth, letting her eyes watch his steps through the bars of her fingers. If only one of them could think of healing words or touches to repair their lacerated spirits.... Shannon could only shake her head dumbly.

She saw the brownish columns of his legs move to the steps where they paused. "I'll arrange for you to fly back to Pirate's Cove with Jeanie and Ward."

CHAPTER SEVENTEEN

The Impossible Dream rounded Sewell's Point, turning inland at Stuart and gliding southwest along the St. Lucie Canal. "We're heading for Lake Okeechobee," Paul told Shannon and Jason, who were seated on the lounge on the fly bridge. "When we've crossed it, we'll be on Brighton Reservation."

Shannon had done the only thing she could do; she had tried to forget the episode that had occurred the night before. Impossible, of course. At breakfast she had not been able to look at Paul, and he left the table quickly to take the helm. But there was no escape, no way to avoid Paul in the confines of the yacht. No way to stop her turbulent thoughts.

The almost-affair was over. Paul had said so. Shannon was back at square one, loving him and despairing of his need for her. He had wanted her, but when he found her out of reach without his love, he had finally let her go. That was what she had wanted. But now that she had won, she felt totally bereft.

Paul didn't stop for lunch, but in midafternoon he sent Jason to the galley for a sandwich. Shannon had fixed the pimiento-and-cheese spread he liked and added stuffed olives and corn chips to the plate. "I'll bring up a thermos of lemonade for Paul in a minute," Shannon told Jason. She had to try to break the stony silence.

When she joined the two on the bridge, Paul scarcely glanced her way. She set her mouth in a determined line as she poured a cup for him and set it above the instrument panel. "Thanks," he said gruffly, not touching it.

How many times had she told herself, *we can't go on this way*? Their relationship had regressed last night to such an extent that now Paul, too, wanted separation. In the night, when Shannon had regained a measure of calm reasoning, she had wondered at the sudden awesome anger that had pried them apart so quickly...so soon after they had come together. He had made the break ruthless and complete. "You'll fly back with Jeanie and Ward." It was the break she had wanted. Why did it sound like a death knell?

At breakfast she had asked Jason about Jeanie. "Dad says I've got an Aunt Jeanie," he'd told her. "You mean her?" The boy knew very little about his aunt except that she was coming to the celebration. He knew nothing about Ward.

So Jeanie was part of an estranged family. And there was still the woman with the strange name. Yahala.

Paul's indifference was as chilling as his arrogant assumption that she would accept him totally and without reservation, though his need for her would be limited. She couldn't let things stand that way. She had to try to get through, try to take away some of the bitterness between them.

Jason fidgeted, sensitive to the strain that dampened the usual banter and fun the three of them had. "Will we be at grandpa's farm tonight?" he asked.

"No, son. The radio is predicting a storm, so we'll wait and cross Okeechobee tomorrow. It's a big lake. The second-largest freshwater lake in the U.S., next to Lake Michigan. I prefer to make the run in daylight, especially if it's going to be rough tonight."

Jason asked about the strange land bordering the canal, and Paul spoke directly to him, still ignoring Shannon's presence. He said that the inland plains and forests had once been marshland, but a whole network of canals had at least partly drained the land so that people could live there.

They passed low hills that Paul called hammocks. Some were covered with pine woods. Many trees were moss draped, some with clumps of air-fed orchids clinging to the branches.

It became increasingly hot and steamy, the slow progress of the cruiser providing only a stirring of the humid air on deck. Shannon and Jason stood at the rail and spotted a bald vulture brooding in a treetop and another soaring gracefully in wide circles against the pale hot sky. Once Paul pointed out a blue heron in the shoulder-high grass.

Gradually Paul shed his tenseness as Jason and

Shannon exclaimed in delight at the wild beauty of the strange new world. Occasionally they saw lazy-looking alligators basking in warm shallow pools.

They anchored that night at Port Mayaca on the eastern shore of the lake. As darkness brought a chill, the mist began to drift over the water and slither over the deck. "Spooky," Jason said. "Like there's nobody around but us." The night sounds seemed disembodied: the cry of the owl and the silly laugh of the loon and the slap of an alligator's tail. "I'm going below."

But Shannon stayed aft a while, grateful that the fog no longer frightened her. She understood it now. Because it had harbored mystery and death when she was a child, the fog had been a menace to the shrouded, forgotten part of her memory. "I've grown since I came to Florida," she said to the swirling mists. "You don't scare me anymore."

"Good." She hadn't heard Paul's approach.

"I'm ready to practice, if you like," she told him.

"No, not tonight."

"You should, Paul. You may not have much chance for a while."

"It doesn't matter." How harsh his tone was.

"This dampness is bad for your voice. You'd better—"

"Don't tell me what to do." It was like a slap. A rumble of thunder groaned over the water, as though some great ancient spirit expressed disapproval. She groped for words that might at least partially heal the rift. "We have to get past last night, Paul. It was crazy. But if we care at all, we can work past it."

"All right." That was all. Paul obviously wanted neither her company nor her conversation.

"Our time is short. Can't we be friends?" she pleaded. There had been good times and tenderness. Was it all gone? Was there no residue, no regret?

"I want you out of my life. You want that, too." The bald statement was her answer. She felt banished.

Pride made her leave him, her head high. It was too hot to go to her cabin, too early to go to bed. She wandered around the salon restlessly, wishing she hadn't dusted and swept in the morning. Everything was shipshape, leaving nothing for her hands to do.

She paused before the desk, tempted to see if the music book with the Seminole songs were there. She glanced aft and saw that Paul's long legs were still outlined in the misty pivot lights.

The notebook was not in the desk. Curiosity urged her to search for it. Had Paul been working on the song? Why hadn't she heard him experimenting with the notes? She found the book in the piano bench under a handful of sheet music.

Her heartbeat accelerated. Had he been working on the tune last night? Had he thought of Yahala even after their frustrating episode? *I don't want to know. I should put it back.* She turned to the last page, and her heart seemed to stop before it lunged on again. The notation was completely finished. A phrase, a repeat, a refrain, a repetition of the in-

troductory bars. There was no doubt. Paul had
worked out the melody last night.

Trembling, she turned the page over. Once more
her heart hesitated to go on. The words that had been
only vague descriptions had been worked into lyrics.
And the name was there.

> Yahala, lovely as moonlight,
> Woman of the sea!
> Yahala, radiant as sunlight
> Shining just for me!

Other words in trial lines were scribbled out, un-
satisfactory to the lyricist. But for Shannon, it was
enough. Perhaps Paul would have forgotten Yahala
if Shannon had given him what he wanted, but the
tenuous ties between her and Paul were broken.

In her heart she was certain that Yahala was waiting for Paul in Seminole country. She could feel it.
He was sure of this woman, and now he was ready to
return to her. It was almost as though Shannon knew
her; she could feel the tender adoration and the patience that the woman felt toward Paul.

She closed her eyes, thinking of Paul's passion being welcomed in someone else's arms. How could she
bear it? She must. She would. She replaced the notebook in the bench and sat down, her knees too life-
less to support her. She bowed her head against the
rack until she could control the nauseous finality of
loss. Though it was what she had wanted—freedom
from Paul's desire to use her—the reality of her vic-

tory was a shock. How was it possible to lose through winning?

Music, always a restorative for Shannon, would help. At first her listless fingers moved randomly over the ivory, creating strange, small, unconscious harmonies. At length they found the soothing melody of Chopin's "Nocturne" and then drifted into Debussy's "Clair de Lune" and the tone of imagined moonlight. But midway in the selection the notes accelerated into the beginnings of a passion that rippled like liquid and then carried Shannon to the height of the midnight moon itself, and she could not bear the remembered ecstasy. She broke off with a wild discord.

Behind her she heard a rasping breath, and without looking, she knew that Paul had come in and that he understood perfectly the emotions resurrected by the music. She got up quickly and escaped through the galley to her cabin. Exhausted, she forced her mind to blankness and eventually slept.

In the morning she awakened to feel *The Impossible Dream* cutting through deep rough waters. Rain spattered against the hatch while she dressed; but by the time she went topside, the sun was brightening the gray dripping clouds and mist.

She made no more attempts to mend the breach between herself and Paul. She would put her life back together, just as she had planned. She had tried to avoid such a violent rift by trying to leave the cove when Paul and Jason began their cruise.

Since that had failed, perhaps it was inevitable that in the close confines of *The Dream*, wanting each other as they did, the idyll could only come to a bitter end.

It would take a long time to get over the pain. Leaving Paul would have been a terrible wrench, no matter when it happened. At least now she was resigned, she told herself.

It was getting dark when they approached the lights of Lakeport on the western shore of the lake. *The Dream* nosed in among smaller boats and Paul tossed the bowline to the Indian on the dock, and she heard the engines die.

When Paul had leaped ashore, Shannon handed up the bags—all of her things, plus what he and Jason had packed for a week's stay.

"We need a rental car," Paul told the attendant.

"You can take my pickup."

"It'll be a week. Have you got another for your own use?"

The Indian's chuckle was dry. "Sure, two or three. You take it, though." He mentioned the rental price, and Paul paid him in advance. The man whistled. "Maybe I'll just buy another with this."

Paul tossed the luggage in the back and started the truck as Jason and Shannon climbed in. The clatter was so great that there was no point in trying to converse, and Shannon was glad of that. She and Paul had little left to say to each other, it seemed. Jason obviously enjoyed the bumpy ride in the noisy truck. He had never experienced anything like it.

"I hope you know the road," Shannon shouted once when Paul paused at a fork.

He leaned across Jason pointing to his throat. "Can't hear and can't talk," he said.

She sighed and leaned back. The wild ride stretched for miles, but finally they stopped before a neat two-story frame house that shone white in the moonlight. A porch light sprang to brilliance, and a tiny woman came from the doorway. She waited with dignity until Paul went to her and put his arms around her. Her great brown eyes, which softened the high bones of her face, were wet when Paul made the introductions. "Welcome," she said simply to Shannon, and to Jason, "Come in and meet your grandpa, dear."

Big Frank Cypress and his son, Ira, were just inside the screen door. A handsome dark-skinned boy came shyly toward Jason, saying, "Hi, I'm Steve." Ira's attractive wife, Wanda, came from the kitchen, where she had been making lemonade and setting out freshly baked cookies.

Frank's greeting was as reserved as his wife's was warm and spontaneous. Whatever illness had kept him in the hospital under Jeanie's care seemed to have been cured. He looked strong and in good health.

While the talk swirled around her, Shannon wondered whether the woman Yahala would come to the celebration. She felt she would recognize her instantly; she would feel the electricity emanating between the woman and the man who had written a song about her.

"PLEASE, have another?" Shannon looked up to find Lucy Cypress, Paul's mother, standing before her with the cookie tray. Guiltily she looked down and found that she had crumbled the one on her plate into fine bits. Lucy's eyes were like Paul's. Wide and dark, they seemed able to probe into her mind, to see what was there without having to hear words. "It was a long, hard journey," Lucy said softly. "You must rest with us."

Wanda came to sit with Shannon. "We're all so happy that Paul has come home," she said softly, "and that he has brought Jason. The boy was so young the last time. I'm sure he doesn't remember."

"Was Merlene here then?" Shannon asked.

Wanda laughed. "Not then. She came once before Jason was born, but never again. I don't think she liked it here. She was part of a different life. But we were glad that Paul came whenever he could with Jason."

What could have happened to make Paul forsake his family? Once he had said that they lied to him. What was the lie? What had brought about the reconciliation?

Wanda was tiny like her mother-in-law. Her thick black hair was straight, cascading down her back to below her waist. The Cypress men were big, strong looking; the women tiny and beautiful. Again she wondered about Yahala. And where was Jeanie, and who was "Ward," a name that had been mentioned along with Jeanie's? Would they be able to tell her anything about the mystery that seemed to surround this family?

SHANNON ADAPTED to farm life and enjoyed it. Rising early, she helped Lucy with the household chores and the meal making for the branding crew. She scarcely saw Paul; he helped his father and brother with the ranch work and was exhausted with the unaccustomed activity. Nevertheless, he looked stronger and more content than he had all summer. Often she heard his booming laugh from the porch **after** supper as the men swapped stories. But she was concerned about his voice; it was three days since he had sung.

Lucy set out two cups of coffee and motioned Shannon to a chair. "Time to rest," she said, pushing stray strands of hair into the clasp at the back of her neck. And abruptly, "I think we will have guests tonight. Has Paul told you about the trouble?"

Shannon shook her head. "I've wondered what kept him away. You Cypresses are so kind, and you obviously enjoy one another so much. . . ."

Lucy's smile was somewhat sad. "Not always. But maybe it will be so again. I hope we have done the right thing," she added. "Paul has a bad temper." She looked up mischievously. "I suppose you know that."

Shannon blushed. How much did Lucy Cypress know? Or guess?

"My son tells me that you wish to return with Jeanie and Ward?" Lucy made it a question. "I wish you would stay."

"Thank you," Shannon said gratefully. "I . . . can't."

Lucy looked at her sharply. "If I am wrong, I am sorry. I think you and Paul are having trouble?" When Shannon clasped her cup in her long fingers and said nothing, Lucy went on hesitantly. "My son closes himself up sometimes, and then it is hard to find him. Someone has to come from outside and unlock the door."

"I'm not the one," Shannon murmured.

"You are sure?"

"Yes."

Lucy sipped her coffee thoughtfully. "I was too proud to speak to Paul's father, and we lost each other." She spoke absently, as though she had just recalled a wayward memory. "The pain of not speaking couldn't have been any worse than the pain of being turned away."

Shannon frowned. What did she mean? Had Lucy and Frank been separated in the past? And was she suggesting that Shannon speak to Paul? Hadn't she already tried?

Lucy began to talk about the celebration. It was a festival for many things—the fall harvest, the homecoming time of those who lived and worked in the cities, the time to be happy together. Some young couples chose this time to marry in the Seminole way. There would be music and dancing and feasting and games of skill. "And we will hear Paul sing," she said.

"How many will come?" Shannon wondered.

Lucy told her that there were about two hundred and fifty Creek Seminoles on the Brighton reserva-

tion, but some would be too busy or too old to
come. Shannon set down the cup so suddenly that
coffee spilled on the table. "How can we feed so
many?"

Lucy's eyes sparkled with fun. Everyone would
bring something, and there would be plenty. Big
Frank would butcher a steer and roast it in the stone
pit in the yard. Even after breakfast there would be
food left over.

"Breakfast?"

No one went home till at least Saturday midday.
Some would sleep in the house and barn, some in
their cars and trucks, and some would camp. And
there were the "chickees," thatched open shelters
that some of the Seminoles used as homes or shops.
Lucy and Frank had lived in one on the stream a
quarter mile away; their children had been born in
it.

"Now I like my nice house better, but Frank still
keeps the thatch fresh and the floor swept smooth
and clean in the old place," Lucy said.

There were two other small chickees across the
clearing in front of the house. In one Lucy and
Wanda often worked, and Paul and Ira had built the
other long ago as a place where they could play in the
shade.

Shannon still thought about the festival. "Will I be
the only. . .?"

"The only white woman?" Lucy finished with a
chuckle. "Shannon, the Seminoles have never been a
single tribe, and now we are not even a single race.

Three hundred years ago several tribes came here from the north. My people were Muskogee Creeks, and my ancestor was one of the great chiefs in the Seminole Wars. 'Seminole' means 'wild and free' in the Muskogee tongue. It was the name given to all those who came here to form a new nation. Those of us who stubbornly stayed after the removal have the blood of our red fathers and of the black slaves who joined them and of the Spaniards and other white men, too. You must not feel strange with us.''

Under Lucy's direction Shannon made an Indian-corn pudding; the delicious spicy odor escaped from the oven and pervaded the house and the clearing. "It's my favorite, isn't it, mom?" Paul lounged against the doorway, sniffing.

"Shannon made it," Lucy told him. "In a few minutes you will see whether she pleases you with it."

Shannon saw the surprise in his eyes as he glanced her way. He stepped over the threshold and went to Lucy. "I didn't know you were ill last winter, mother. I would have come—"

Lucy put her fingertips over his lips. "You were traveling, son. I didn't want you to know. It was nothing, and I'm all right now. It is your father who needs you."

SHANNON SLIPPED AWAY, believing that she had been forgotten. She crossed the clearing, drawn to the smaller chickee where the Cypress boys had played. She tried to imagine how they had looked as small boys. Much like Jason and Steve, she was sure.

Jason and his cousin had become great friends. They rode the big farm horses, played pirates and explored the rolling fields all day long. Shannon felt the urge to explore, too. She stepped into the woods in the direction Lucy had pointed when she told of the chickee where Paul had been born.

Within a few yards Shannon was surrounded by a dim world that seemed never to have known a human step. Lizards eyed her before darting away like small dull lightning bolts. Ferns and vines and mosses and air plants and owls' nests clung to the trees, filtering the sunlight into a pale green veil. There must be a path. Shannon stood still until she saw it, a thin thread of trampled undergrowth. She followed it warily.

Suddenly she heard something crashing along the trail behind her. Instinctively she plunged forward, frantic to get away. She ran blindly, vines and thorns tearing her hair and clothes. Which way? She had lost her sense of direction. She couldn't go back. Something was following her. The old chickee must be to the left. She would find it and follow the stream back to the barn and the house.

She paused, breathing raggedly. The pursuit had stopped. Where was the path? How could she have become lost so quickly? She struck out to the left and was about to brush aside a hanging vine when two beady eyes riveted her attention and a split tongue flicked at her.

Shannon heard a scream of terror and knew that it had been torn from her own lips. She pressed her hands to her mouth to suppress hysteria. She turned back, knowing that she would never be able to retrace her steps.

In a small clearing, she paused. A swarm of mosquitoes circled and dived for her bare legs and arms. "Paul!"

At once the crashing began again, and fear invaded every inch of Shannon once more. "Paul!"

"Shannon! Stay where you are!"

"Paul!" Sobbing with relief, she turned toward the beautiful sound of his voice and ran to him as he plunged through the mass of foliage. She clung to him, drawing strength from the beat of his heart beneath her ear and from the protection of his arms.

"What are you doing out here?" He was angry, but she didn't care. He was there. That was all that mattered.

"Look at you! Your arms and legs bare...it's a wonder you aren't snake bitten or chewed up by insects. Why do you think we cover ourselves from head to toe?"

"I was j-just walking," she babbled.

"Off the path? That's crazy!" He swung her easily into his arms and started to walk, elbowing aside the vines with his sleeved arm. "Nobody walks here half-naked. Quit wiggling."

"Put me down. I walked in, and I can walk out."

He paid no attention until they had emerged into the clearing. "What did you think you were doing?" he demanded as he set her on her feet. "Running away again?"

"I wanted to see the chickee where you were born."

For a moment his eyes were bright with surprise. Then the mask slid back into place. "Why?"

She had no chance to answer, for the screen door opened and Jeanie raced down the steps and ran to them, brown eyes shining and coal-black hair gleaming in the sun. "Paul, I love you for coming!" She raised her face for a kiss. "Come and meet Ward."

Paul shepherded Shannon and Jeanie toward the house, making introductions on the way. A tall man in well-cut blue slacks and shirt came out to meet them. "Paul, Shannon," Jeanie said proudly, "this is my fiancé, Dr. Ward Poole." She turned her expressive eyes on him adoringly. "Ward's people are Mikasukis at Dania. We're going to stop there on the way home so that I can meet them."

Paul and Ward shook hands. "I landed the Cessna back of the barn in the pasture. I hope that's all right," Ward said.

"Fine. So my future brother-in-law is a pilot as well as a doctor?"

"I do volunteer work in the Everglades, and the Cessna cuts down on the hours and the miles," Ward explained.

"Right now Ward is the specialist working with Adam. That's how we met," Jeanie said.

"How is Adam?" Renewed huskiness showed in Paul's voice.

Ward spoke quietly. "He is in remission now. He is tired but feels quite well. He insisted upon coming with us. With Jeanie and me to take care of him, I thought the trip couldn't hurt him.''

"He's here?'' Paul's face registered shock as he turned to Jeanie. "I told you I would stop in Orlando on the way home.''

"Paul,'' Jeanie said, "when he knew that you would see him, he didn't want to wait. He knows his time is short.''

Shannon's thoughts were spinning as they entered the kitchen. Was Adam the coin collector Paul had spoken of, the one they were to visit in Orlando? But if he was ill...the one Jeanie had been nursing....

The old man sat stiffly upright, his veined hands clutching the rounded ends of the chair arms. His hair and mustache were thin and white, and the pallor of his skin hinted at serious sickness. Only his intensely blue eyes were compellingly vital in contrast to the frail body.

Lucy spoke. "Adam is welcome in our home.''

Jason came to clasp Paul's hand. "Mr. Henderson has a big coin collection, dad. I'm going to show him my gold doubloon and those silver pieces of eight. He's the one we were going to visit in Orlando, isn't he?'' he queried, pleased with his deduction.

Henderson...the orange grower for whom Paul had worked years ago. "Yes, son,'' Paul said woodenly, "he is.''

Lucy said softly, "Supper will wait while you talk.'' Shannon was about to follow the others into the living room, but Paul took her arm.

"Please stay, Shannon."

Why? This is between the two of them. She sat down in the simple kitchen chair Paul pulled up for her. He introduced her as his pianist-secretary, and Adam's smile was warm.

"I thought you might not have time to stop in Orlando, Paul." Adam Henderson's voice, though ravaged with illness and years, was deep and rich. "I know how busy your schedule is, and I did want to see you."

"I would have stopped."

"Knowing that does me good," Adam said humbly.

"I was sorry to learn of your illness," Paul said stiffly.

The older man's face relaxed in a smile. "It has brought us together, so I don't mind in the least."

"Father—"

Shannon drew in her breath. She had only suspected. Now she knew. Adam Henderson was Paul's father.

Adam raised his hand. "I have very little pain now. If I have some time to become a friend to you once more, and to my grandson and to this lovely young lady, I am content."

"You shouldn't have taxed your strength with this trip," Paul said. "I would have come to you."

"It is better this way, son," Adam said gently. "Now I can see your beautiful mother, talk to her, touch her hand. Your stepfather is very good to me, Paul. He deserves the love and respect of all his children. All three of you." He coughed, and Shannon got him a drink of water. He nodded gratefully.

"Jeanie tells me that your mother never discussed me with the family. That's why I wanted to see you, Paul. I'm sure you must have misconceptions. I want you to know the truth."

"It doesn't matter," Paul said quietly. "I know now how consuming a passion a man can have."

"Truth always matters, son. Your faith in your mother, your love and forgiveness of her do matter. They matter to me."

He leaned back tiredly, his eyes closed. "Your mother worked in the Henderson groves when she was young. She worked in the sorting room, where I was learning that phase of the business, and I couldn't take my eyes off her."

Paul stirred, old resentments flaring in his eyes.

"We fell in love. For me, there has never been anyone but Lucy." He sighed, went on. "Then my parents died, and suddenly the responsibility of managing the entire business fell on me. I was swamped with work I knew too little about, but I was determined to master the job. I did—" his voice broke "—but I lost Lucy. I'm sure she thought there was no place in my life for her. I neglected her as I did everything except the business of growing and marketing oranges. Then suddenly she was gone."

"You could have looked for her." Paul was still judging.

"Do you think I didn't try? Lucy had never told

me where she came from. Have you ever tried to find a Seminole who doesn't want to be found? I combed the Everglades. I hired detectives who fanned out as far as Oklahoma.

"By the time I traced her to the Brighton reservation, she had married Frank Cypress and had a son. I didn't know that you, Paul, were *my* son."

"Nor did I." Bitterness was still there.

"Lucy kept it from you because she loved you, Paul. She believed that knowing would only complicate your life." He was earnestly pleading on behalf of the woman he had never stopped loving.

"So I went to work for you after high school, knowing only that mother had once worked for you. I suppose she told you I was coming."

Adam shook his head. "I hadn't seen or spoken to her after she left Orlando. My personnel man does the hiring. I didn't even know he had hired a Cypress."

"But you knew when you offered to lend me money to go to school," Paul accused. "My mother knew that I wanted to study music. She said there must be a way. Shortly after that, you offered to make the loan."

"Yes," Adam admitted. "Frank brought her to see me, and that's when I learned you were my son. I wept, Paul. She was still so beautifully proud. She hated asking, but she did it for you. I wanted to give more than she asked, but she refused, and so did Frank. I saw that he loved you as his own son, and I saw that it was best to leave it that way. So I made the money a loan."

"I repaid it," Paul said tersely.

"That was when I made my mistake," Adam said sadly. "I didn't want the money. I knew you were married and had a son. I knew that everything from your first year's tour had gone to Edmund Webster's widow and that you had borrowed heavily in order to take that Florida property off her hands."

Shannon was stunned. It was all true.

"It had taken you four years that I knew must have been grueling, but there you stood with the money, determined to pay me back."

"I always pay my debts in full, sir."

"I never meant to hurt you," Adam mused sadly. "I thought that if you understood how much—and why—I wanted to help you...if I told you who I was...who you were...."

"All I could think of was that everyone had lied to me," Paul muttered. "I wasn't Paul Cypress. I didn't know who or what I was. Everyone I had trusted had known all along. I decided to be my own person. I would never be dependent or trusting again."

"And that's where you made your mistake, son. It's no good going it alone." He smiled ruefully. "I ought to know. You live with shadows instead of splendor."

Paul got up and went to the window. When he spoke, the words were ragged. "I stood there with all that money. A fistful of bills. I thought you were trying to pay me to be your son...finally, after all those years, when I had a degree and was on my way in the music world. *Then* you wanted me." He went back to Adam. "I was wrong. It was too much to understand all at once. But I should have talked with you and mother. I'm sorry for the wasted years. Forgive me, father."

Adam struggled to rise, and Paul stooped to help him. Through tears, Shannon watched them embrace. It was a private moment for the two men, and she slipped quietly out of the room.

CHAPTER EIGHTEEN

AFTER SUPPER JASON showed the treasure coins to his grandfather. Obviously impressed, Adam murmured, "Beautiful! Excellent!" as he fingered the gold doubloon. "It could be another Brasher."

"What's a basher?" Jason wanted to know.

"Ephraim Brasher was a metal smith, a neighbor of George Washington. One of the doubloons that he struck was purchased recently for a record price of $430,000," Adam told him.

"Almost half a million!" Shannon exclaimed.

"Is that enough to build our school, dad?" Jason asked.

"School?" Adam repeated.

When Paul told his father about his dream of establishing a music school at Pirate's Cove, Adam's pale cheeks showed ruddy spots. "Let me help." When Paul shook his head, Adam added quickly, "Don't deny me this pleasure, Paul. Everything I have will, of course, be yours soon. Let me have the fun of watching you begin to use it. I'd like to see plans, equipment lists, maybe even a ground breaking."

Adam's excitement touched Shannon. "Paul, who

knows more about restoring the old orange grove than Adam? You do want to put the institute up there among the trees, don't you?"

"Are you ready to sell me that part of the estate?"

Shannon stared. In spite of the estrangement, she had continued to think of the school on *her* land and of somehow sharing in the dream.

"Ah, well," Adam said, watching her keenly, "there will be many details to work out. I haven't dipped my hands—or my money—into anything new for a long time. Who knows what new life this will give me? You must let me help."

"It's my gold doubloon that is starting it all, isn't it?" Jason asked anxiously, not understanding the vast sums of money.

"Yes," Adam nodded, "and I'd like you to keep it. Suppose I buy it from you and then give it to you as a good luck present? A present marking the day we found each other?" He glanced at Paul. "It will partly make up for the nine years when I overlooked his birthdays and Christmases and all the special days." He turned back to Jason. "You can invest the price of your coin in your father's school...its first investor."

"You mean I get the doubloon and the money, too?" Jason asked.

"Why not?"

"Gee! What a good deal! I like doing business with you, grandpa!" He looked at Paul uncertainly. "Is it fair?"

Before Paul could reply, Adam said firmly, "Of course it is. No question about it."

After supper, before Jeanie led Adam to his room, his eyes rested on each one of them as he said good-night. They rested longest on Lucy. When he turned to Frank, his lips formed a silent, "Thanks." Frank nodded, their eyes holding.

Later Paul asked Ward whether Adam would be there when he came home for Christmas at the close of his tour.

"Possibly," Ward said. "Happiness and new interests have often worked miracles." He hesitated. "Paul, I'd like to tell you about the man that Adam Henderson is. He has helped many of us with loans. You were the first, and the money that you returned to him became the core of a trust from which Seminoles may borrow in order to go to school or start a business. I borrowed from it. So did Jeanie."

"Jeanie? But I—"

"I know, you sent her money for nursing school, but then there was Lucy's long illness, and the ranch had some bad years. Your mother is a proud woman, but she will not see her children in need, so she told Jeanie about Adam. Paul, he was pathetically glad to be able to help your sister. He has always loved your mother, and of course he adores Jeanie. Who doesn't?" he added with a grin. "He cares for you, too. You must know that."

Paul turned away, his eyes contacting Shannon's. "Yes, I know." His voice was harsh. Suddenly he stood up and went outdoors.

"My brother has been unhappy for a long time," Jeanie said, an appeal in her dark eyes. "I think you could make him happy again."

Shannon shook her head. "There is someone else in his life." When Jeanie looked surprised and skeptical, she went on with a sad smile, "I saw the song that he wrote for her."

"The way he looks at you...we both noticed." Jeanie put her hand in Ward's. "Are you sure?"

"Oh, yes." If he hadn't worked on the song within the last days on *The Dream*...if he hadn't told her that she must leave with Jeanie and Ward.... She got up. "Please excuse me. I do want to talk to Paul about my cove property." Tomorrow would be so busy with the celebration, and the next day she would leave.

She saw his dark shadow moving at the edge of the clearing. He halted as she approached. "Paul? Can we talk?"

Silently he led the way into the work chickee. There was a wooden bench on one side, but he settled cross-legged on the ground. "Have a chair," he said sardonically.

She, too, sat cross-legged opposite him. "About the orange groves—"

"I'll pay whatever you ask. Surely you don't want to keep them. You'll never come back while I'm there, I'm sure."

"Have you forgotten that the institute was Edmund's dream?" she cried. "And then mine?"

"Things have changed since the dream began," he said hoarsely.

"Dad's gone, but I'm here! I won't let you exclude me, Paul!"

"Ha!" One explosive bitter note of laughter escaped him. "Now that the treasure is yours—"

"And yours!"

"You don't need the price of the land, eh? You can make Edmund's dream come true without me; you can keep me out of it entirely, right? Do you know why I wanted you to stay in the kitchen when Adam and I began to talk?"

Shannon shook her head. What did that have to do with the institute and the orange grove?

"I'll tell you," he said grimly. "I knew that my father was ill, that he wanted a reconciliation, that I was to be his heir. I was going to ask him to buy your land. I was going to suggest that the school be named for both Edmund and Adam—one for having the dream and the other for financing its beginnings. I didn't even have to ask, though, did I? Adam came through. But we still have a site problem."

"You. . .you were going to use your father?" Her voice was an unbelieving whisper.

"Yes, because I wanted to be part of Edmund's institute. I wanted us to work on that dream together," Paul said. "You and me. I thought we could."

"We still can. Oh, Paul, we can still do that."

"It's too late." He said it gently, dispassionately but with finality. "We're getting out of each other's lives."

Shannon pushed herself to her knees and stared through the darkness at the man she thought she had known so well. "If that's what you want," she said, her voice and eyes as dry as the hard earth beneath her. Paul didn't answer her. She left him and went to the room she now shared with Jeanie.

Shannon sat in a rocker by the darkening window for a long time, trying to accept Paul's rejective hatred. How terrible that in one bad hour, all the good things that had existed between two people could be destroyed. She went over everything that had passed between her and Paul from their meeting in the studio in Illinois to the night on *The Dream* when their passion had become ugly. Somewhere in that time she had learned to love him. And her love went far deeper than the passions that had brought them together in sweet healing delight. Her love existed still, burning brighter and steadier. . .and more painfully than ever, though it was not fed by an answering flame.

When Jeanie came in, she talked about her coming marriage. "We'll observe our own Seminole customs first, and then we'll be married in the church." She showed Shannon her collection of beads. She had received her first strand when she was twelve and another on each birthday or special occasion. At the Green Corn Ceremony next spring she would wear all of them over a new colorful dress, and after the rites she would lead Ward into a specially cleaned chickee where they would kindle a fire and consummate their Seminole marriage.

"I hoped—we all did, Shannon—that you and Paul would find happiness together," Jeanie said. "I just can't believe that there is someone else. His eyes light up when you come into a room.'' Impulsively she went on. ''Already I feel as though you're my sister. Forgive me, Shannon, but do you love my brother?''

How could she possibly be angry with the lovely girl? So happy herself, Jeanie wanted everyone to be that way, too. ''Yes,'' Shannon said, ''but maybe you don't know him anymore. He can be ruthless.''

''He's been hurt,'' Jeanie defended gently. ''It takes time to erase that. Oh, Shannon, you'd be so good for him, and we're all crazy about you. Don't go back with Ward and Adam and me. We can say there is no room. I'll put a lot of boxes and stuff in the empty seat. . . .''

Shannon had to laugh. ''It wouldn't do any good. Paul wants me out of his life.''

''I don't believe it! I'll ask him.''

''Don't you dare. Please!''

And Jeanie promised, for she knew from experience that love had to find its own way.

ALL MORNING THE WOMEN wrapped sweet potatoes and corn to roast in hot ashes. The two boys swept the house and the chickee floors and forked more hay into the barn loft. The men lined the clearing with chairs and benches and made a long table from boards and sawhorses, which they set in the shade at the edge of the woods.

The huge beef, suspended over the fire pit, was turned from time to time; it would roast all day until it was brown and juicy, ready to be sliced and served on the hundreds of rolls that Frank had brought from town. Adam Henderson enjoyed every minute of the busy morning.

When the first trucks began to spill out scores of guests, Lucy set Shannon to stirring the *sofkee*, a thin corn porridge. Shannon turned when she heard a soft moccasin step behind her. "Lucy grandmother, Annie Tiger," the old woman said, pointing to herself.

Shannon gasped. Annie had to be close to a hundred. "Shannon Webster," she murmured.

The brown face was creased with wrinkles, though the eyes were bright as a robin's. Her gray black hair was smoothed over a frame that looped above one ear, and she wore the traditional long bright skirt and capelet trimmed with rickrack and ribbon.

Annie scanned Shannon from head to toe. "Skirt too short," she observed. "Pale skin, funny shoes. No beads. Maybe Paul make mistake again, eh?"

Shannon felt the blush rise. What made the old crone think Shannon was Paul's woman?

Jeanie stood in the doorway in a long Seminole dress, her feet bare, her fingers against her lips suppressing a giggle. Shannon bent to unbuckle her sandals and slipped them off. "Better, Annie Tiger?"

Grinning toothlessly, Annie nodded. She pointed to the one chair left in the kitchen. "Sit," she told Shannon, and jabbing a finger at Jeanie, "You stir *sofkee*." From somewhere in the folds of her clothing she brought out bone hairpins and quickly molded Shannon's long hair over her hand into loose graceful loops beside her face and pinned them in place. She stood back, nodding. "Better. Now Jeanie." Shannon went to put on the longer multi-colored skirt and embroidered blouse that Paul had given her.

THE MAKESHIFT TABLE was soon loaded with dishes of squash, pumpkin, bananas, guavas, melons, cabbage palm, oranges, grapefruit and chewy lengths of sugarcane. There were bowls of honey and wild-game stews as well as jugs of sweet drinks and cold tea. Guests ate whenever they were hungry.

Games were played all afternoon, but Shannon was surprised to see that they were noncompetitive. Stickball, checkers and other games of skill were played cooperatively, children and adults helping one another make the best possible plays. "That's our way," Jeanie told her. "Sometimes teachers think our kids are cheating when they're just helping one another. Indian children get along well together. They don't compete."

When the sun was a great crimson ball in the west, Frank called everyone to the *chipola*, the clearing. "Frank is the *micco*, the chief of the Town Clan," Jeanie whispered.

Frank's speech of welcome for his daughter, son and grandson and their guests was a moving piece of oratory, the musical cadences and dramatic pauses giving great dignity to his words. Even the smallest children listened quietly while he spoke. Shannon watched Paul across the compound, standing with somber brooding eyes.

Frank called Jason to stand with him as he formally initiated the boy into the Town Clan of the Creek Seminole tribe. He placed a thong from which hung a small doeskin bag around Jason's neck. "I give you the Seminole name of Narcoosee—Little Bear," his Indian grandfather told him, "and this is your *chattahoochee*, a carved black stone that my grandfather gave me when I was a boy. Let it remind you always of your people and your heritage, Narcoosee."

Shannon saw Jason's mouth form, "Thanks," as he covered the talisman with his hand, his eyes shining. He belonged.

Frank lit the ceremonial fire just as the sun set, and Paul moved into the firelight singing "The Song of the Little Coon." His mellow baritone was like his own hand, reaching out in renewed friendship to his people, and they smiled in acceptance. They called out old favorites, and he sang them all—"The Alligator Song," "Little Rabbit" and "The Hunting Song." Only a low drumbeat and the sound of clicking gourd rattles accompanied him at first, and then the high obbligato of a flute was added. Shannon thought he had never sounded so strong and sure.

At a touch on her shoulder, Shannon found that Jeanie was beckoning her into the shadows. She followed and found that Lucy was waiting for her. "We've talked," Jeanie said, "and mother wishes to talk with you."

"Yes?"

Lucy clasped her hands tightly together. "I am intruding where I have no right," she began. "It is just that long ago I needed advice, and there was no one. A misunderstanding can become so big." She took a deep breath and went on.

"Jeanie tells me that you love my son. We both believe that he also loves you."

Shannon shook her head. "There is someone else. And Paul and I think too differently about—" she paused "—important things."

Lucy's brown eyes were large and undaunted. "Once I thought that Adam didn't care for me, and I went away." She smiled. "Now I have no regrets, because I have Big Frank and these good children. But then, those years ago, I was wrong. I should have made Adam listen."

"You want me to tell Paul that I love him? When so much is wrong? I can't do that," Shannon said.

Lucy nodded. "All right," she said reluctantly. "I just wanted to talk with you. Only you can decide which is best for you: pride. . .or love."

Lucy went back to her guests, but Jeanie stayed with Shannon. Paul was still singing, his voice seeming to gain strength and timbre with each number. "I can't believe how perfect he sounds," Shannon murmured. "He hasn't been practicing."

"Ira says they sing all the time on the range," Jeanie said. "They always sing when they work."

When Shannon heard someone ask for "The Impossible Dream," she led Jeanie back to the edge of the fire-lit circle. If he could sing that without faltering on the high notes, he could sing anything anytime.

Shannon's eyes filled as he began his familiar finale yearningly, tenderly. She saw dreams in the eyes of his listeners, dreams that he kindled with purpose, as his golden voice insisted that they were reachable. Was this what Lucy had tried to tell her? That she, too, must believe that all things were possible? Even if she had to suffer the agony of possible defeat, it could be no worse than the sorrow in her heart now.

As she thought about Lucy's challenge, Paul began to speak. "One more," he told his friends, hand upraised to quell the applause. "A little song that I have just finished." His eyes searched the crowd, looking for someone. "I wrote it for a very special person. You'll recognize our Seminole marriage poem set to music."

Shannon's hand went to her throat, for it was suddenly hard to breathe. *She* must be here. He was singing to *her*. "I'm going in," she said to Jeanie.

Paul had begun the song, and Jeanie caught Shannon's hand. "Listen!" she commanded. "Is this the song you told me about?"

> Yahala, lovely as moonlight,
> Woman of the sea.
> Yahala, radiant as sunlight,
> Woman, come to me.
>
> Yahala, you are music,
> You are laughter,
> You are life.

Come now, let me hold you,
Fold you to my heart
Yahala, soft as starshine
You are mine, my wife.

"Yes!" Shannon managed, and tried again to pull away.

"Listen to me," Jeanie said. "I know everyone in the tribe. I've worked with my people, and there is no woman of that name. Shannon, there couldn't be... it's not a name!"

Shannon stared at Jeanie. "It must be. It must be someone he knows."

Jeanie's brows puckered. "*Yahala* isn't a name, Shannon. It's a color." A slow smile spread over her face. "I think I know what Paul was trying to do."

"I don't understand," Shannon said, bewildered by Jeanie's words. "What does *yahala* mean?"

"I'll let Paul tell you that. All I'm going to say is that I believe he couldn't let you go away tomorrow without telling you what is in his heart. You are Yahala."

"But he said, 'My wife.'"

"Did he ever ask you to marry him?"

"Yes. But just so he could get custody of Jason."

Jeanie laughed. "That's not what the song says. I'd sure use tonight to find out, if I loved a man and he sang that song for me."

"But it isn't... I don't think...."

"Come with me. I've got an idea." She led Shan-

non to the deserted house, where they could talk and
plan uninterruptedly.

TRADITIONAL DRUMS, gourds, tortoiseshell and coconut shells, the flute and a concertina set the rhythms
of the ancient ceremonial patterns of the Seminole
rites. After a while Jeanie found Paul and pulled him
into the circle of dancers. They matched steps for
several minutes, and then Shannon joined them, now
wearing a short cape that Jeanie had given her. The
fire's heat made Paul's face shine, but he didn't
glance at Shannon. Ward claimed Jeanie as his partner, and they dropped behind.

"Your singing was beautiful," Shannon murmured. Paul continued to dance silently for several
drumbeats. Then, "You can fly back with Ward in
the morning."

Dismay flooded over Shannon at the dismissal.
She swallowed her pride. "I want to talk with you
once more. Tonight. Please."

Suddenly Jeanie was beside Shannon, moving easily in harmony with the others. She was wearing all
the strands of beads she had showed Shannon. Without breaking her rhythm, she slipped them off and
put them around Shannon's neck. Then she slowed
her steps so that Shannon and Paul could move past
her.

Shannon looked questioningly at Paul, but his
dark eyes were unreadable. "Will you take me to the
old chickee on the stream bank? I told you I would
like to see it. We could talk there."

The tuck appeared at the corner of his mouth, giving him a derisive look. "Do you know what you are asking?"

Shannon watched as another couple left the dancing circle. "Yes," she said softly. "I know that when a girl dances with a man and asks him to go with her, he must go."

"To talk?"

When Shannon didn't answer, Paul stopped and led the way through the dancers to the edge of the clearing. Shannon followed, her eyes on the bright design of his Seminole shirt. Neither spoke, and their passage was almost soundless as Paul held back branches that would have brushed against her.

When they came to the moon-touched stream, they followed it across the meadow to the trail along the wooded waterway. Eventually the brook scrambled over smooth rocks and tumbled into a shallow pool before it meandered around a tree-darkened curve.

The chickee stood in the shadows above the little falls. Paul stood like a statue before the chickee, waiting. Shannon broke a branch from a low hanging willow and knelt to brush the hard earth in front of the door. There was a small pile of white sand by the entry post, and Shannon took a handful and sprinkled it over the chickee floor.

"What are you doing?"

Shannon's knees were weak, and she knew that her face was aflame in the dim interior of the hut. "Will you...come in?"

He took a step, and his big frame seemed to fill the chickee. "What is this, Shannon? A final torment?" he demanded harshly.

If you love me, you will come. She took off one of Jeanie's bead strings and held it out to Paul. He snatched it and flung it to the ground. "Do you know what you're doing?" he demanded hoarsely.

"Yes," she whispered. "You asked me to be your wife. This is my answer."

A rough sound came from his throat. She moved past him and quickly touched a match to the shavings in the bundle of sticks she and Jeanie had laid on the stream bank. She came back slowly and raised tear-bright eyes to Paul. She felt among the beads for the gold chain, removed it and held it out to Paul. "Please accept this from me."

"I've wanted you so long," he said between clenched teeth. "Why are you coming to me now?"

"Because I think you asked me, one last time, in your song." *And if I'm wrong, I hope I die right here,* she thought in the moment before he came to her. She felt his hands at her throat as he unfastened the single button of the marriage capelet Jeanie had loaned her. He let it drop.

"You understood," he said wonderingly.

Shannon held up the gold chain that he still had not taken. "Will you take it, Paul?"

For answer he lowered his head so that she could put it around his neck. When he straightened, he pulled her against him hungrily. "I thought you never wanted to see me again," he said brokenly.

"My dearest love!" He kissed her tenderly tasting and sealing her mouth. "How I love you!"

Shannon ran her hands under his loose shirt, feeling the warm quivering flesh, the beloved hard muscles and firm bones. When she could free her mouth, she whispered, "I love you, Paul. I always have."

"I've never told any woman that I love her. I thought I never could. And then these last days... I wanted to die because I thought you didn't want to hear those words. Never from me."

"Always from you, my darling." She reached up to kiss him.

He groaned, holding her close. "Oh, Shannon! With you everything is so right, so possible! And I thought I had lost you." He touched her as though to reassure himself that she was actually there in his arms. "I'm nothing without you."

"Nothing without each other," she amended softly.

Their passion mounted quickly, as for the first time each one was eager to give and to receive totally. They undressed each other, Shannon standing yellow gold in the firelight, adorned only with the ceremonial strands of beads. Paul took them from her one by one, dropping them at her feet. Then he touched the gold pirate chain he wore. "Tonight I've taken this from you. Tomorrow I will give it to you to keep."

"Yes." It was a sigh of acquiescence. Her wide tawny eyes caressed his muscular male body, reveling in the desire she saw that she had awakened. She remembered the delicious shock she had felt the first time she had seen him in swim trunks long ago in her little valley. It was nothing compared to the excited yearning she felt now. His body was ruddy in the firelight, his skin glowing, inviting her to touch. He held out his arms, and she went into them with a cry of joy as she molded her form to his, raising her face to receive his kiss.

She felt Paul's fingers at her hair, releasing the bone pins, letting the cloud cascade over his arms. He lifted her and laid her tenderly on the blanketed platform. He bent over her, his nostrils flaring as though to breathe in the sweet scent of her. She pulled his face against hers, her mouth welcoming his, her tongue mating with his.

For Shannon, it was as if the weight of Paul's body replaced the burden of all the doubts and unhappiness that had clung to her the last few days. Paul was real, her lover and her life.

Paul explored her mouth hungrily. He moved against her to let her feel his urgency and her arms tightened, her hands at his shoulders and back, asking for inseparableness.

The gold chain was warm but harsh between them, but Shannon cherished the hurt, for it meant that she and Paul were one, bonded by the symbolic links. Their pirate legacy. "Paul," Shannon whispered again, "I love you."

He kissed her throat and shoulders and slid downward to taste her breasts as the dark tips became invitingly tumid. She moaned with pleasure as his hands learned the shape of her, measured her waist and stroked the warm satin of her flesh.

The need that had lain sleeping within her awoke and demanded fulfillment. With passionate need, Shannon clutched Paul's shoulders, coaxing him to satisfy her. "Love me, Paul!"

"I do love you!" It was music, never sung to anyone else.

As Paul's body moved upon Shannon, the fires of intense craving licked at her every sense. Only Paul could ease the ache of her burning desire, and she whimpered in supplication. Her body welcomed his eager entry, and the exquisite pleasure of their union caused her heart to swell and soar. She cried out in delight. They were one flesh.

Shannon began the familiar ascent, leaving behind the whole world. There was only Paul, taking her to heights she had not reached before, thrust upward and upward on the crest of a wave that was more blue than sapphire, more fragrant than gardenias. Again she cried out when she felt herself carried to the tip of the curling wave in Paul's arms, felt herself held there against the length of his beautiful bronze body. Together they trembled at the top and then rode the peel of the wave into the quiet trough where they could rest.

They lay a long time, their breaths and heartbeats and bodies united. Paul finally raised his head to gaze at Shannon. He rested one hand along the side of her face, watching the firelight reflected in her eyes. "Yahala."

Her smile was tender. "What does it mean?"

"It is the color of your eyes with the flames in them. It is our word for a summer sunset."

She drew his head down for her kiss. They cradled each other in the warm darkness that pervaded the little chickee. There was no other world.

"That night on the boat when we quarreled—"

She put her fingers over his lips. "Forget that night."

"No," he said, kissing the tips and holding them against his chest. "That was the night I discovered I cared so much that I couldn't go on hurting you. We were hurting each other, and we had to stop. I was afraid to trust my love, and I thought the only thing to do was to tear myself away from you."

The same conclusion I came to earlier, and for the same reason, Shannon thought. "Let's promise that we'll always talk things out," Shannon said, "because we always seem to get things all wrong when we don't!"

"Better yet," he suggested, "let's not fight about anything, ever."

She nodded in the hollow of his arm. "Good. Because now that we're married, the treasure isn't mine or yours. It's ours."

"Shannon. . . ."

She twisted around to face him. "Jeanie says a Seminole marriage is recognized by Florida law. You do want to be married to me, don't you, Paul?"

"Oh, yes!" Paul said huskily. "Yahala, wife." He stroked her side and thigh, stirring again the embers of desire in her.

"Oh, Paul, I shall hate to be in school this fall while you're in Australia," she said as she threaded her fingers into the wiry black hairs that divided his chest.

"Do you think I can let you leave me now, Yahala?" He buried his face in her hair. "Darling, when I kidnapped you, I hoped that I could teach you to care enough to marry me on my own terms. I never dreamed that we could have a marriage on your terms."

He looked long at her, his love shining proudly in his eyes. "Before we left the cove, I called your dean at the university. You will be given credit for your experience as my pianist on tour. She has arranged for you to graduate with your class, providing that during the spring semester you finish the courses you expected to take at Illinois. You can take them anywhere...like at Flagler College in St. Augustine."

She blinked, not sure she comprehended. "Do you mean I can finish my studies without being there? I can go with you? We can be together?"

He looked at her soberly. "I don't see how I could manage without you. Darling, you can have solos on my tour program. And when you're ready after graduation, you can have your own tours and programs. Or, if you like, we'll share concert billing and arrange parallel tours. We'll work it out." He grinned mischievously. "Sylvia will do anything I ask her to if I treat her right."

Shannon laughed. "Let's get that school started so

that we can fire Sylvia." She wound herself close to Paul. "Jason will be all right at the cove with the Pratts until we come home at Christmas, won't he, Paul? And then I'll be there." She chuckled again. "Jim and I will be going to Flagler together."

"I'm not going on tour for the rest of the year," Paul said with mock solemnity. "I'll be starting the school. And keeping a jealous eye on you and Jim every minute."

"How nice," she said contentedly. She rested her hand against his scarred throat. "You know, I love this place. Everything has come so right."

"All our scars have healed," he said softly before he began to kiss her once more.

WHEN THE STARS SANK away into firstlight and the red edge of the sun silhouetted the tall palms against the sky, Shannon felt her head being gently raised as the gold chain was slipped over her head. She opened her eyes to find Paul leaning above her.

"Shall we go back to the farm and invite everyone to a wedding at Pirate's Cove?" he asked tenderly.

Shannon thought about it for a moment. It would be nice to have everyone they cared about share in the beauty of a ceremony and celebration. "Would you like that?" she asked. If Paul preferred to let the traditional rite of his people bind them together, that was right for her, too.

"Yes," he said. "I would like you to be a bride in white, married to me a second time. That ought to tie us together good and tight. Would you like that?''

Shannon grinned as she held out her arms. "What girl would turn down a chance at two lovely wedding nights? Not me!''

SUPERROMANCE

Longer, exciting, sensuous and dramatic!

Fascinating love stories that will hold
you in their magical spell till the last page
is turned!

Now's your chance to discover the earlier
books in this exciting series. Choose from
the great selection on the following page!

Now's your chance to discover the earlier
books in this exciting series.

Choose from this list of great

SUPERROMANCES!

SUPERROMANCE

mplete and mail this coupon today!

----

ridwide Reader Service

he U.S.A.	In Canada
0 South Priest Drive	649 Ontario Street
pe, AZ 85281	Stratford, Ontario N5A 6W2

se send me the following SUPERROMANCES. I am enclosing my
ck or money order for $2.50 for each copy ordered, plus 75¢ to
er postage and handling.

☐ #26	☐ #32	☐ #38
☐ #27	☐ #33	☐ #39
☐ #28	☐ #34	☐ #40
☐ #29	☐ #35	☐ #41
☐ #30	☐ #36	
☐ #31	☐ #37	

mber of copies checked @ $2.50 each = $_____

and Ariz. residents add appropriate sales tax $_____

tage and handling $_____.75

                TOTAL $_____

close _____

ase send check or money order. We cannot be responsible for cash
t through the mail.)
es subject to change without notice.   **Offer expires August 31, 1983**

                       30456000000

ME_____
             (Please Print)

DRESS_____APT. NO._____

Y_____

TE/PROV._____

/POSTAL CODE_____

Enter a uniquely exciting world of romance with the new

Harlequin American Romances.™

Harlequin American Romances are the first romances to explore today's new love relationships. These compelling romance novels reach into the hearts and minds of women across North America... probing the most intimate moments of romance, love and desire.

You'll follow romantic heroines and irresistible men as they boldly face confusing choices. Career first, love later? Love without marriage? Long-distance relationships? All the experiences that make love real are captured in the tender, loving pages of the new **Harlequin American Romances.**

What makes North American women so different when it comes to love? Find out in the new **Harlequin American Romances!**

Send for your introductory FREE book now!

Get this book FREE!

Mail to:
Harlequin Reader Service

In the U.S.
1440 South Priest Drive
Tempe, AZ 85281

In Canada
649 Ontario Street
Stratford, Ontario N5A 6W2

YES! I want to be one of the first to discover the new **Harlequin American Romances.** Send me FREE and without obligation *Twice in a Lifetime.* If you do not hear from me after I have examined my FREE book, please send me the 4 new **Harlequin American Romances** each month as soon as they come off the presses. I understand that I will be billed only $2.25 for each book (total $9.00). There are no shipping or handling charges. There is no minimum number of books that I have to purchase. In fact, I may cancel this arrangement at any time. *Twice in a Lifetime* is mine to keep as a FREE gift, even if I do not buy any additional books.

Name _____ (please print)

Address _____ Apt. no.

City _____ State/Prov. _____ Zip/Postal Code

Signature (If under 18, parent or guardian must sign.)